Ben Alderson

A KINGDOM OF LIES

REALM OF FEY BOOK TWO

ANGRY
ROBOT

ANGRY ROBOT
An imprint of Watkins Media Ltd

Unit 11, Shepperton House
89 Shepperton Road
London N1 3DF
UK

angryrobotbooks.com
twitter.com/angryrobotbooks
Find your family

An Angry Robot paperback original, 2024

Cover by Sarah O'Flaherty
Edited by Eleanor Teasdale and Shona Kinsella
Set in Meridien

ISBN 978 1 91599 869 9
Ebook ISBN 978 1 91599 878 1

Printed and bound in the United Kingdom by CPI Group (UK) Ltd, Croydon CR0 4YY.

9 8 7 6 5 4 3 2 1

Jasmine, for being a passionate supporter for this series and encouraging me to carry on.

CHAPTER 1

Blood dried between my fingers as I held a hand over the fresh wound. It was a strange feeling, to heal without medicine or prolonged time. The smaller the cut, the quicker the flesh knitted back together. Large wounds took longer to heal, but still faster than it would have been *before*.

Before I claimed the Icethorn Court and became its king.

"Careful, little bird," Erix said, bending his knees with his blade raised before him. The dawn light caught its tip with a wink.

There wasn't a cloud in the clear blue sky, but even with the rising sun, there was still the chill of new winter in the air.

"Are you distracted, or will you blame your clumsiness on your lack of sleep?"

Erix knew exactly what to say to get a reaction out of me. And his words created a burning warmth that flooded my cheeks and made them stand out like twin red cherries.

"If you're concerned with my missing hours of sleep, then perhaps *you* should find another bed to stay in," I replied, fighting the sly grin that wanted to spread across my face.

Erix pouted, straightening his posture until every one of his eight mounds of muscle across his abdomen flexed. Yes, eight. I counted a few times to make sure I wasn't wrong.

To answer his question, it was actually the rolling bead of sweat that ran a course down his chest and across his lower stomach until it was absorbed in the hem of his training trousers that distracted me.

"Now *why* would I do that?" he said, one dark brow raised above his silver stare which was full to the brim with mischief. *And danger*. "It is more… exciting sleeping beside you."

"Except we don't sleep," I replied. "That's the problem." I shrugged, twisting the golden dagger in my hand without thought. It'd become an extension of my body in the past weeks. Training daily on rotation with Erix, Althea and Gyah meant that the dagger never strayed far from my hand.

Erix's brow peaked, his lip caught between his teeth.

"Careful," I repeated his initial warning. "Or you might find *yourself* distracted."

It was a thrill to see his mind catch up with my own unseen action. I sprang forward, the cut on my upper arm now a faded scratch, and ran towards my guard. Erix shifted his footing, but failed to take a complete step before I was on him.

The grass at his feet mutated to blades of frozen glass. Erix hadn't spied the creeping ice that I forced across the ground towards him during our conversation. It encased his feet, all the way up to his ankle, preventing him from moving a step.

"You tricky little–"

I was behind him in moments, reaching up on tiptoes until I wrapped my forearm around his neck and squeezed. With my free hand I held the golden dagger, the very one he had given me as a gift, directly before his face.

We waited like that for moments of silence until the low rumble of his laugh interrupted the stillness. "Very good, little bird. I must say I am impressed."

"Ah, ah, stop right there. Can't you just leave me with praise and not have to point out a flaw? I mean, come on, Erix, admit that I bested you and be done with it."

"All I was going to say is you should never stop until your enemy has truly been dealt with. Have I not made that completely clear in all our training?"

There was something about his bossy nature that turned me on. I was sure he knew it too because it seemed to only intensify during our morning training sessions in the private gardens within Farrador Castle's grounds.

"Do you speak to all your initiates like this?" I squeezed tighter, flirting the edge of the blade across his throat. "Or am I just getting special treatment?"

"You, little bird, are the only one who I would let get close enough."

I felt the pinch of something sharp at the soft part of my inner thigh, through the form-fitting trousers Eroan had crafted for me. I looked down to see Erix's own weapon turned on me, all without me realising.

"Fuck's sake." My eyes rolled as I released my hold on Erix.

"You were close this time. Closer than you have been before."

"But…" I added for him.

"*But*, as I said before, never leave an enemy breathing long enough for them to take the precious moment they require to end you. End them first."

I sheathed the dagger into the strap at my hip, admiring the calluses across my palm. Proof I'd worked hard to train since the Passing. Not that I knew who I was trying to prove anything to. Was it myself, or those who still refused to acknowledge my status as an Icethorn? Many fey still looked at me as the very reason for failed plans of domination over Durmain, the realm of humans.

To many, that was *still* all they could see when they looked at me.

"Then I should get in my practice, since my list of enemies seems longer than it needs to be," I said, drawing a picture of a man in my mind's eye.

King Doran Oakstorm – the man who used my father like a pawn to keep me in line.

Erix had a way of seeing the inkling of emotions I fought hard to hide from him. A frown creased his sweat-glistened forehead as he closed the space between us. His frame was so broad that he blocked the sunlight out entirely, bathing me in cool shade.

He pressed his hand to my cheek, holding it carefully in a cupped palm. My skin was clammy and wet, but it did not matter; I enjoyed his touch in whatever variety it presented itself to me.

"Must I remind you, little bird, that you are one of the most powerful creatures on both this side of Wychwood and beyond? Do not worry yourself with the likes of scum who wish to cause you harm. Your enemies are my enemies, remember that."

Erix wasn't wrong. My enemies certainly were his. King Doran's petition for Erix's head had only intensified in the past weeks. It was part of the reason we'd not yet left the safety of Farrador's boundary walls. Doran's soldiers waited beyond for the moment Erix stepped free of his sanctuary of blessed protection by the Cedarfall Court.

I dropped Erix's stare, unable to hold it as flashes of my father cursed my mind. It had been weeks since I last saw him, suffering from a sickness brought on by poison, a stab wound that had been inflicted by one of the Children of the Asp as they had tried to take my life under Tarron's orders.

"Do you want to talk about it?" Erix asked quietly.

I shook my head as his finger found the base of my chin and held it softly.

"There is nothing to say," I replied. "No words that will get my father back. Only action."

Father's abduction by the Oakstorm Court was the sole reason why I filled my days with training and my nights with Erix.

Distraction.

Distraction was the only remedy to stop me thinking about him. Not the promises from Althea, who'd taken it upon herself to counterpetition for my father's return. Nor her mother,

Queen Lyra, who swore to see him back in her lands even with his past as a Hunter common knowledge across the Courts. Only a distraction, whether training in combat and magic, or spending those mindful moments before sleep, entangled in Erix's strong limbs.

"He *will* be okay," Erix said, his tone almost promising. "Doran would truly be a fool to kill someone important to you. Your father would have been dead long ago if that was the case. But he is not, and that will be for a reason. That has to stand for something."

I gripped Erix's hand and squeezed as my mind suddenly raced, making me dizzy. "Erix, please. I – I can't think about this right now."

He moved swiftly until the tips of his boots pressed into my own. Taking my face in both hands, Erix pressed a kiss to my lips.

Like butter over an open flame, I melted. Melted into him as his tongue parted my lips and enticed my own to join its dance. This was what I required, and he knew it. Part of me felt guilty for using him when I knew it clearly meant more to him, more than just a way of taking one's mind off another matter.

But I couldn't burden myself with such worries. I gave in to the tidal wave of calm that always greeted me when Erix and I became intimate. Like a leaf down a stream, I allowed his tidal force to draw me away from my thoughts.

I wrapped my arms around his back, feeling his muscles tense in reaction. He released a groan as I gently scraped my nails across his skin, something that had him purring with pleasure during our nightly entanglements.

"Keep that up" – Erix broke away breathless with lips tainted pink – "and I will take you right here and now."

"Here?" I giggled, pulling back to survey the castle's outer wall and the many arched windows across it. Even now someone could be looking, watching, and that was likely since there was always a host of guards shadowing me, even if Erix commanded them to give us space. "What do you take me for, Erix?"

"Do you truly wish for me to answer that?" His mischievous grin flashed for a moment before he dove into the crook of my neck. I leaned back as his teeth grazed my skin, kissing and sucking until I couldn't tell if it was pain or pleasure that I felt.

My fingers clawed across his head, holding him from escaping. His hair had grown slightly since I'd first seen him riding into the Hunters' camp encased in silver armour. It no longer scratched against my skin but felt smooth. And I'd discovered that his hair was a warm brown with the faintest hint of amber.

"You will get us in trouble with those sinister thoughts you harbour," I warned with a wink.

"Sinister?" Erix broke away, silver eyes glowing from within. "You do know that the fey are not bashful and shy when faced with the promise of sex. No one would care if I tore the clothes from your body and you sat atop me like I am your throne. In fact, they would celebrate it."

"Well, believe it or not, but the humans hold some dignity when it comes to sex. I would prefer not to have an audience." A tingling chill spread up my spine. My mouth grew wet and cheeks puckered as though he held a sour cherry before me, and I pouted.

"As you wish. Then, shall we retire to your chambers?"

Heat unspooled in my belly like unravelling thread. Knotted and tangled around Erix. "I am beginning to believe you don't ever tire or grow bored."

"Bored?" He scoffed, pressing his crotch into me until I felt the outline of his very hard, very interested cock. "I have a storm within me, little bird, and I am ready to unleash it."

My hand pressed between us and ran down the dampness of his stomach until it tickled across the bulge in his pants. I grabbed it, asserting my dominance for this moment before it truly got out of hand. "A storm? How poetic you are, Erix. But I think it's wise we calm you down. All good things come to those who wait, after all. Anyway, I'd rather have something entertaining to look forward to this evening."

A flickering of disappointment pinched his brow, but it was only fleeting. "What if I told you I could manage it twice?"

I released his cock and patted his hardened chest as though he was a puppy. "How very valiant of you, and how lucky I am to have you as my guard. Always looking out for my best interest... and your own." I said the last part through the corner of my mouth. "Then again... we *could* give them a show–"

"Robin!" My name echoed loudly across the grounds. We both looked towards the visitor to see the bobbing of poppy-red hair atop the tall frame of the Cedarfall princess. She was dressed in similar clothing to me, material which hugged her body and was perfect for training, except hers was crafted from an ivory material that had her red hair standing out starkly against it.

"Bit early, isn't it?" I raised a hand to shade my eyes as I called out to her. Mine and Althea's magic training never began until after lunch had been served. She was usually tied up with courtly matters in the morning whilst I fooled around with Erix.

I expected a sharp-witted response from her, but she remained silent. That was when I noticed her pace was frantic and her cheeks were flushed as red as her hair.

Something was wrong. Erix shifted beside me as though he recognised it too.

"You are required in the throne room, Robin." Althea reached us in seconds, her face pinched with turmoil. "Both of you."

"What has happened?" Erix said, asking the question before I had gathered the courage to.

"I think it is best you both come and see." She referred to both of us, but why did she not stop looking at me?

I stood my ground, fists clenching in trepidation. "Althea, tell me. Is it Doran?"

It was not a command, but more of a request. If she said nothing and expected me to follow her then she was truly deluded.

Althea nodded. Her curved brow pulled down into a frown as she nibbled on her lower lip. I waited, with bated breath, for her to say something to put my mind at ease. Yet I knew that my worst nightmare was a mere few words away from being revealed.

"We have received word from Oakstorm regarding your father," she began, words careful as though she didn't want to break me with them. "This morning another letter arrived, but this was not full of the usual demands others held. It had something… else alongside it. Something from Doran, for you."

In a single moment the sun was covered by dense, grey clouds. I didn't need to look skyward to know the storm brewed, conjured from nothing until hardly a spec of blue remained. Winds picked up around us, shifting the hairs around Althea's face and blocking her worried expression from view. Our breaths fogged past our lips in puffs of silver smoke, greeting the sudden drop in temperature that enveloped us.

"Is he…" I couldn't find the words to finish my question, nor did I need to. Althea read my silence and answered for me, although it didn't award me any calm.

"Alive, we believe."

Erix bristled at my side. "What do you mean you believe he is alive? The answer is rather simple to give, is it not?"

Pain echoed in my head as more of my magic spilled into the air, lowering the temperature to match that which ruled within me.

"Robin," Althea said, reaching for my hand and taking it. Her thumb traced circles on the back of my hand, trying to console me. *Why do I need consoling?* "You need to come and see for yourself."

I drew back, leaving her hand outstretched before me, pale skin glowing in the darkened light of the storm. I watched intently as flakes of snow fell upon her skin, hissing out of existence from the flame hidden in her blood. Cedarfall power.

"Please," she said, stealing my attention away from the falling snow. "I promise we will help."

"Help?" I managed to repeat, echoing the word in a tone that suggested I didn't recognise the definition of help. "Weeks have gone by already. I don't think your *help* is doing much to get my father back."

Althea refused to lower her hand as I snapped at her. Instead, she kept it raised, waiting for me to take it again. I might not have the ability to read minds, but I knew something had worried her. I read it in the lines across her face, in her hunched posture as if the pressure of secrets weighed heavy on her. "Together, Robin, we promised we would do this together. Now please... come. It is only right that you see this."

CHAPTER 2

Blood stained the round marble table before us, a puddle of dark gore that reflected the sconces' light. The copper tang was faint, but still toyed with my nose, lathering the back of my throat with its lingering taint.

And the red liquid seeped from a package, small enough to hold a ring, which waited on the table's centre for my arrival. And all I could do was look at it. I was vaguely aware of Erix's presence behind me. Althea waited patiently beside her parents, Queen Lyra and King Thallan Cedarfall, who had given me nothing but painful looks of sympathy since I arrived.

There were others in the council room, old and young. Some dressed in similarly decorated uniforms to Gyah whilst others wore the outfits that marked them as serving staff.

I had an audience, one who flinched as my wild, winter winds ripped at the outer walls of the castle and caused the glass windows to rattle in their frames, like bones in a casket.

"Read. It. Again," I demanded, although my words were broken as I forced them out. All the while, I didn't remove my eyes from the bloodied package.

Althea cleared her throat, the rustle of parchment audible over the deathly silent room, then proceeded to read the letter for the third time.

"King Robin Icethorn, if you so desire the return of your father, then, in good faith, I will ensure it happens. However, without the

exchange of my son's murderer, you can expect your father to be returned to you in pieces. Little by little, bit by bit—"

"That is quite enough," Queen Lyra snapped, slapping a jewelled hand upon the table. "We have heard the tyrant's threats multiple times. Hearing them aloud again will not change them."

I raised my storm-filled eyes and rested them upon the Cedarfall queen.

"Does it make you uncomfortable? Or perhaps it's the bloodied fingertip sitting within that package that's making you uneasy?" I swept my gaze across them all, fearful that if I moved a muscle I'd explode with power. "Can any of you imagine how *I* feel? Standing here alongside you all instead of leaving for Oakstorm to take my father from Doran myself. Weeks wasted, and for what?"

"I cannot allow a civil war to start over one man." Queen Lyra knew she had misspoken the moment the words left her mouth.

"Doran didn't seem concerned with such issues when he sent his hordes of gryvern into Icethorn land to slay my family. He wants war, let me give it to him," I snapped.

"May I be the one to remind you, Robin, that you have no numbers. No army who hold your banner," Queen Lyra replied coolly. "By all means act with haste and retrieve him yourself, but in the meantime, we will continue to petition for your father's release without the need for bloodshed."

I heard Lyra, but that didn't mean I agreed. There wasn't room for rational thought in my head, not as I looked back to the blood-soaked package Doran had sent.

"And how's that working for you so far?"

Erix's anchoring touch landed on my shoulder.

"I understand you are angry." She ignored my question.

"Angry?" The air of the room plummeted in temperature. I barely noticed the gasp of the serving staff as they dismissed themselves from the room, unable to stand the magic's unnatural cold. "I'm more than *angry*. What lingers inside of me is pure fury, Lyra. Perhaps I don't need an army, not with the Icethorn power."

"Perhaps not," Lyra added. "But destroying Doran will only lead you down a path of more problems. He has no children to take his mantle."

"Is this why you hesitate? Because Doran hasn't got an heir left alive to take over the Oakstorm power? My father is the only family I have left and I'm not going to let that monster take him from me. He has taken enough."

"You are right," Erix said, forcing me to look at him. "But so is Lyra. We must act with caution."

I pried my eyes off the bloodied gift that King Doran had sent alongside his letter; I could not fathom returning my attention to it. The idea made my stomach twist, the room shifting beneath my feet.

"There must be something else we can do," Althea said, mimicking her mother's regal voice. "Robin should not have to sit and wait for Doran to have an excuse to send yet another threat. This one is more than enough."

"We are exhausting as many political pathways as we can. What do you suggest we do, daughter?" Queen Lyra said, tone almost defeated.

Althea's stare flickered to the man standing behind me for a moment long enough to understand.

Defence rose up in me like the very flames Althea could control.

"No," I gasped, looking between Erix and Althea. "No, I refuse."

"Little bird, it is okay." Erix stepped forward, towering at my side as he said, "There is one more thing that we can do. I will go to Doran."

No one spoke. No one else refused him. I watched and waited for Althea or her parents to tell Erix that his idea was stupid and for him to stand back in line. But they didn't.

"I said no." My heart thundered in my chest, threatening to crack free of my ribs.

"Doran wants me. He has already promised Robin's father's return in exchange for my arrival. So, I will go. It was only ever a matter of time before he got his hands on me anyway."

"Erix." I grabbed him harshly, trying to spin him around to look at me, but he was as firm as a rock in the middle of a ravine. "You can't leave me. I... I need you – I forbid it."

All of a sudden, my hold on the icy magic slipped through my fingers. The sky beyond the arched windows lightened as the threatening clouds dispersed. The deathly chill faltered until I felt hot enough to claw the shirt from my back.

"No, you do not." Erix's reply was detached and cold. I could see his desire to look me in the eyes, but he fought to keep his stare anywhere else. "Doran is a deranged man. This is the only way for you to get your father back and I cannot continue to stand in the way of that."

"Shut up!" I screamed at him, looking around the room at the cowards who could hardly hold my eye contact. "One of you say something. Someone tell him that he is wrong. Command him to stay."

"Do you want your father back or not, Robin?" Queen Lyra's words lashed into me like a whip of boiling fire.

The room was silent as the shock settled like ash upon us all. No one was brave enough to be the first person to speak, until Althea broke their cowardly silence. "What my mother means is it's Erix's choice, not ours to make for him. *Stupid* as it may be."

I could've laughed, but not as a result of happiness. Delusion. "It's suicidal, not stupid."

"Erix knows the choices he must make, and the effects those choices will have." Queen Lyra looked almost sad as she settled her eyes on my guard. "It has been a long path keeping you from him thus far, Erix. This is your decision to make, and yours alone. You came to me for sanctuary from him all those years ago. I gave you my word. I will only break that word if you are the one to make this sacrifice."

I had to place my hands upon the table to stop myself from falling in disbelief. My knees buckled.

"It is the only way." Erix held his chin high, his chest jutted out. And yet, when I looked at him, I saw a man struggling. As though his demeanour was calm, but a different emotion inside of him wanted out. My worry was confirmed when the atmosphere shifted. One moment Erix was calm, subdued, and then his fists shook as he clenched them at his sides. "I have thought nonstop about this since I took Tarron's life. It was only a matter of time before Doran used his leverage over us. I cannot stand in the way and be the cause of Robin losing the last family he has."

"Don't speak on my behalf." I mirrored his tension, hissing through gritted teeth. Anxiety rocked through my body, making even the dull light through the windows too intense to see. I just needed a moment, to allow myself a second to truly work out the impossible puzzle that had been put in front of me. I pinched my eyes closed and focused on breathing.

Someone's hand found my shoulder and held it. I didn't need to open my eyes to know it was Erix, whose touch was almost etched into my being at this point. I would know his hand and its print for all of eternity.

Think Robin, think.

It was hard to do anything but picture the bloodied part of my father upon the table. This was only the beginning, that much was clear. If we didn't respond to Doran's letter with our own then he'd continue sending threats. And when would they stop coming? When my father was dead, when there were no more body parts left to cut and carve to send to me?

Time was not on our side, it never had been.

"I want to speak with him," I finally said, looking back over the crowd. "Let me negotiate my father's return. It is the last thing we've not tried. No matter what Tarron did to me, he was still Doran's last living relative. Just as my father is mine. I'm not saying what Doran is doing is right, but in a warped sense it is justified. I want to speak with him myself before I allow anyone to make a sacrifice on my behalf."

Erix flinched at my comment.

"He may not come peacefully," Althea warned, flexing her fingers at her sides as though she stretched, ready for a fight.

"I don't expect him to," I replied, jaw clenching. "I'll be ready to greet him no matter how he arrives."

Erix turned his back to the room, facing me with an expression of pure terror, eyes wide, the usual bright silver now a dark storm cloud that mirrored the one I harboured within. Both his hands gripped my arms as if I would simply slip away from him. "Please, Doran is dangerous. More than you could imagine. Allow me to do this for you. I will go and save any more unnecessary timewasting."

"Why?" I whispered. "Why would you throw away your life for the sake of my father?"

I waited for him to admit his feelings, as though I longed to hear them aloud. I wished to hear how he felt for me in the hope it would conjure the same reaction inside of me. For me to feel anything but the deep, terrifying numbness that had clawed into my soul the moment my father's life became threatened at the hands of the Oakstorm Court.

"Because I am dangerous too. You saw what I did to Tarron, what happens when I lose control."

"That isn't an excuse, Erix."

He took a deep breath in, steeling his silver eyes. "You deserve the chance of normality." His response caught me off guard. "Do not question me again. Please, just let me do this. I deserve what is to come."

There it was. The truth that glimmered in his eyes. Guilt had eaten away at Erix, a silent assassin, devouring him from within. I could see through his false confidence as though his mask had slipped.

I sighed, longing to reach for his face and pull it down upon mine. But I stayed rigid to the spot, unable to give Erix the solace he longed for.

"Queen Lyra," I said as the void opened within me, hungry and emotionless. Erix dropped his stare to the floor, released my arms and stepped aside, defeated. "I would like to invite Doran for a conversation between two kings. Let me speak with him before anyone makes choices they will regret." I spared Erix a glance, offering my next words to him. "My decision is final."

Althea smiled, pride glittering in her eyes. "Demanded like the king you are, Robin."

I expected someone, anything, to refuse me, to tell me that my hope for an audience with Doran was wasted effort. No one did.

He may be dangerous, but so was I.

Queen Lyra nodded, silently gesturing to the decorated, aged soldier at her side. "There is one place where Doran would be foolish to bring violence. If you are certain you want to meet him then we shall do so on neutral ground. We shall send our invitation to Doran, with my seal of approval."

"Where is this place?" I asked, body trembling with adrenaline.

"Welhaven," Queen Lyra said, gaze fixed to me, pride etched into her expression matching that of her daughter. "Altar's blessed resting grounds."

CHAPTER 3

Magic sparked across my hands. Rings of sharp, crackling ice turned my skin a violent white. I let it devour me, forging my fist into a weapon of jagged ice, only to melt and reform over and over.

The power didn't conform. It spread with wild intention, devouring the brick wall beneath my fingers and my boots. If I didn't focus, the magic would soon spread across the room entirely until it glittered in silver and white. Part of me wanted to let go of my control, to allow my emotions to storm outwards until I felt some space within me for more positive thoughts.

Instead, as I listened to Gyah and Althea discuss our pending journey, I held the magic at bay. My full energy would be required soon enough, even if Althea's warning still echoed through me. The day had melted into late afternoon, yet the hours between this morning's discussions had not dampened the threats that came with it.

Welhaven is recognised as the creation point of the fey at the beginning of time. The land is unclaimed by any of the four Courts, and thus may not be a place for war, hate, or the spilling of blood. It is sacred land and was historically used as a neutral ground for disagreements between the Courts to be discussed peacefully.

It made sense as to why Queen Lyra wanted my meeting with Doran to be there. A way of ensuring he didn't go against the law of the land and anger his God. Yet deep down I knew there was nothing stopping me from unleashing this storm, not if the moment required it. After all, I would petition Doran to give back my father peacefully, or I would pry him from Doran's cold, dead hands.

"… then our focus may return to our shared enemy, the Hand."

I looked back at Gyah who spoke, running the whetstone across her sword.

"We have not heard from him since the Passing." Althea shifted on her seat, visibly disturbed by the mention of the mysterious figure who hid within the human realm of Durmain. "Nor have our guards sent word of Hunters… or the warped, powered humans that we saw weeks ago."

"They haven't just disappeared," Gyah added, not taking her focus from the edge of her sword. She flicked her thumb across the metal, inspecting just how sharp it was. "They will return. My suggestion is, we don't wait for them to make the first move. Little is known about this Hand and his creations. It is pure luck he has stepped back from the forefront of our minds whilst we deal with the more… immediate threats this side of the border."

"I know what you are doing, Gyah," Althea said, one brow raised as she surveyed the Cedarfall soldier.

Gyah shrugged her broad shoulders as if she didn't know what Althea suggested. But even I knew. Gyah hadn't withdrawn her request to join the frontline and monitor the Wychwood border alongside the Cedarfall soldiers. Since the powered human had walked through the Mists of Deyalnar, Queen Lyra had sent countless numbers of her legion to prevent another from stepping through alive. Gyah wished to be there, doing her duty, not babysitting a capable princess.

But since Briar had disappeared, it was safer for Althea not to be alone. The assassin, like the Hand's powered humans, would also return.

We all knew that Gyah wanted to join the efforts with a burning desire. She'd made that very clear. And yet, whilst other enemies still lingered in the shadows, it was important we had an Eldrae close by. Her ability to shift into a wyvern was rare, which made her presence paramount.

"There will come a time when I am required to be there, Althea," Gyah said, looking up from her weapon for only a moment. "There are many others capable and skilled to protect you."

"And until that time I am going to need you by my side," Althea replied curtly. "Why settle for anything less than the best?"

Gyah blushed, turning her head to the side to hide the reaction. But what I noticed from Althea's words was there was something that troubled her deeply. It had her losing herself to dark thoughts which devoured her in quiet moments. Althea did it now, fixating her gaze on a spot on the floor. Gyah briefly looked to me, both of us sharing our concern with a single glance.

"Does *she* frighten you, Althea?" I asked, sitting with them in the small circle we created.

There wasn't a need to speak the name aloud for fear of triggering Althea.

"Nothing has the power to cause me fear, Robin." Althea snapped her gaze to mine. She almost spat flame with the sudden reaction. "I only hope Briar is foolish enough to come and see me. There is much I have to say to her when she finally decides to show her face again."

"And she will." Gyah narrowed her golden eyes, the skin around them pinched into the pattern of crow's feet.

"You said that no one disappears forever, but the Children of the Asp have never been found. I want to find their burrow and burn it from the inside." I winced as heat radiated from the princess's skin. Gyah noticed it too. I'd never thought it possible to see a person spit flame but could tell it was moments away from happening.

"You could encourage her out of the shadows, if you offered the right amount of coin then surely the assassins would show themselves again?" I said, clenching my hands into fists to call in the power that gloved them.

They both turned to face me at the same time.

"What are you suggesting?" Althea asked, curiosity dripping from her tone.

"The Asps kill because of coin; Briar made that clear. Would there not be a way of putting forward an abundance of money that would even entice an assassin out of retirement? It doesn't need to be Briar who presents herself, only another sloppy initiate. Then we can find the burrow. Follow the lone Asp until it returns to its nest."

"Just like that, aye?" Gyah scoffed.

There were other reasons I could want the help of an assassin. Perhaps, if Doran refused what I had to say to him, I would find a way to hire one myself.

I gritted my teeth, growing bored of my ideas being brushed aside. "Yes, just like that. Unless you have a better suggestion. I'm sure we would all love to hear it."

Gyah forced a smile before returning to the sword across her lap.

I watched Althea contemplate my words. Her stare was lost to a painting on the wall behind me.

"Anyway, how is it we went from having an Asp at every corner before the Passing, but now there has not even been a whisper of one?" I said.

"Their benefactor had his head caved in by…" Althea cut herself off as she glanced at me. The name was on the tip of her tongue.

Flashes of his bloodied fists and twisted face of anger filled my head. "Erix."

Althea swallowed her next words, changing the course of the conversation before I could dwell on his loss of control for another moment. "If I was to gather the funds to put forward then I would need Mother's involvement. I may be a Cedarfall, but I cannot simply walk into the royal bank and demand the papers required. Such decisions and commands are not as simple as that. I hardly imagine Mother would allow it; finding Briar is not exactly on her list of current importance."

Althea was right. Our conversations bounced between the Hand or King Doran. The guild of assassins was solely a topic of discussion that kept our small group distracted from those other matters. That and the fact that Althea felt scorned and used; I'd come to learn those two emotions didn't sit well with the Cedarfall Princess.

"Could I help fund it?" I asked. The idea of having access to money was strange and new. It was still incredibly hard to imagine.

Althea's gaze brightened for a moment. "Perhaps. The Icethorn court should have access to coin, however it has been many years since anyone occupied the capital of Icethorn. The Court's vault has likely been ransacked during your family's... absence. Without visiting it's impossible to know whether the funds survived the storm, or if they were stolen during it."

And for that, we had to leave Farrador. Except we couldn't, not with King Doran's desire to capture Erix, making visiting anywhere but this castle impossible.

There was much to being a king that I'd not had the luxury of uncovering yet. Queen Lyra encouraged the idea of creating a council who'd help with my future ruling, since I had close to no idea how to rule anything besides a ramshackle pub, and those days were long gone.

Surrounding myself with people who had knowledge on courtly affairs and what it meant to be a ruler was a good idea. But creating a council required finding people who wished to see me take my place within Icethorn. So far the Council consisted of myself and Eroan – the seamster who dressed me – and I couldn't imagine the gentle threadmaster had much experience in courtly matters beside what they would have worn during important meetings. However, Eroan had been the only fey from Icethorn who had shown interest in returning.

I was a king of one.

Erix's voice filled my head, echoing amongst my anxieties. *A king of one is still a king.*

"When this is all over with Doran and his attention is diverted from me, then I will leave for Icethorn. I cannot be expected to hide within Farrador's walls forever. I have a responsibility now, I just need the chance to locate it."

"Hear, hear," Gyah cheered. "If I cannot visit the Wychwood border, then I require an excuse to stretch my wings."

"A little trip may be exactly what is required," Althea agreed, a fleeting smile flittering across her face. "I was never one for sitting still. And castle life is rather dull. It was why I left and threw myself into the missions of infiltrating Hunter camps and taking back the stolen fey. Gives life more purpose, you know? Makes it less boring."

"Life is far from boring." The comment slipped out of me without much thought. Deep down a small part of me would have traded this all for the chance of being back in Grove, sleeping in bed after a long shift at the tavern. My shoulders were less heavy, the burden almost non-existent.

"Could be worse." Althea nudged my knee with her own. "You might never have met us."

That conjured a smile, a small but genuine one that warmed my chest. Althea was right. I had never had friends like them before.

"Or me." Our heads snapped towards the door to my chamber to see Erix leaning up against the frame. His arms were crossed, his chest standing out prominently through the formfitting black top he still wore from our morning training.

Althea rolled her eyes, gesturing with a nod towards Gyah. "And *that* is our cue to leave."

"Oh, do not rush out on my behalf," Erix purred, striding into the room with his chin held high. "I just got here."

"Exactly, Erix," Althea said, turning her focus to me. "Robin, I suggest you get some rest tonight. You are going to need a clear head for tomorrow."

"I will try."

Althea raised a brow, her expression smug and knowing. "Say the word and I will dismiss him for the evening. I don't imagine the nights are restful with your personal guard warming the bed."

"Or messing up the bedsheets," Gyah added.

I leaned into Althea, mischief twisting in my chest. "Believe me, I have always slept better in a warm bed. And even if you dismissed him, do you truly believe he would listen to your command?"

"Not at all." The corner of her lip tugged upwards as she exhaled a light chuckle. "Gyah, I am going to need a drink to remove a certain image from my brain."

Erix cleared his throat, a sly grin creeping up his cheeks. "Thinking about me, princess?"

Gyah's chortled laugh was a mix between a bark and a grunt. "Actually, I think we will need more than one drink."

I woke to darkness. It was not noise that roused me, but the shifting of Erix's hard body as he peeled himself away from me. For a moment it felt as though we'd only just fallen asleep, but a single glance towards the endless black beyond the window told me otherwise.

"Where are you going?" I asked, voice croaky. Rolling over, I was met with the outline of Erix's bare back. He sat on the edge of the bed, just out of reach.

"You should go back to sleep," he replied softly.

"Then join me," I said, reaching out, fingers grazing his back.

Erix shrugged me off, his head turning enough to the side that I could see his sharp jaw and taut expression. I pushed myself up and crawled over until I was behind him on my knees. Reaching out again, I let my fingers trace the curve of his shoulder. This time he let me touch him. His skin was cold and coated in gooseflesh. Erix shivered as I wrapped my arms around his shoulders and brought my lips towards his ear.

"What's wrong?" I asked, already knowing the answer but being unable to shy away from it.

"My mind is just… busy. That's all. Robin, please. Go back to sleep. I will be okay."

"Firstly, you're not permitted to tell me what to do. Secondly, are we back to using my name, because I was beginning to enjoy the nickname."

My attempt to lighten the tension worked, evident as Erix sighed slowly. Two strong arms snaked around me and in one great motion I was sitting upon his lap, nothing but his firm hands holding me in place. Erix had a tendency to sleep without the constraints of clothing, however I noticed he wore trousers.

"Are you planning on leaving me?"

"I could never leave you, little bird." His nose pressed against my own as two strong hands ran down my back and cupped my hips. "I just could not sleep and needed some fresh air. I thought a walk would help. I never meant to wake you."

So that was why he was so cold.

I looked beyond the window, the sky pure obsidian – not even the stars had come out, hiding behind the dense, winter clouds that drifted through the night.

"Well, I'm awake now. And I command that you take off your trousers and get back into bed."

Erix pouted, fingers slipping and gripping slightly harder upon my butt. "Then as your personal guard I would have to obey."

"Good. Then stay." I pressed a small kiss upon his face, inches beside his lips.

It should have alarmed me how quickly his demeaner changed. One moment his expression was distant, but the next it sparked with emotion as though there had never been a problem.

"Do you have any other requests for me? I am awake, after all… perhaps a walk is not the only activity that would clear my mind."

I didn't want to acknowledge what worried him, because the same thought also filled my mind. Morning was not far away and with it came the meeting with King Doran. Erix would stay behind, as agreed, and let me petition for the safety of everyone I cared about.

Clearly, he struggled with that idea. But he had to learn to trust me, just as I trusted him.

"Hmm," I replied, voice light and full of innocence. "Now, what else could we do? I can't think of anything else but sleep…"

That was, in fact, a lie. There was something else we could do – something that would distract us both.

"That is a shame." Erix stood from the bed, picking me up with him. My legs wrapped around his middle to keep myself aloft. His hold was unwavering, hands still splayed and firmly grasping my ass. He moved away from the bed, my stomach jolting with sudden excitement.

"Because my mind is full of ideas," he finished. "Would you like me to share them with you?"

Erix stopped only when my back was pressed up against the wall. There was something thrilling about sharing the night with him. It was as though the fear of darkness vanished when he touched me.

It was easy to keep a hold of his eye contact for the silver glint pierced through even the darkest of shadows. Although I enjoyed the moments in the dark, when only my sense of touch was useful.

"Erix?" I said.

"Yes, little bird," he replied, so close to me his breath tickled my cheek.

"Why did you offer yourself up so freely?" I asked, as though the volume of my question determined the mood of the room. I'd not braved the question yet. There was nothing good about this time to ask it, but then there never would be.

Erix didn't reply straight away. Instead, he leaned into me, nestling his face into my neck, pressing his lips to my skin. It was a good distraction technique, but I read his actions for what they were.

Erix was hiding from me.

"I know what you are doing, Erix," I said.

"Please." His voice was muffled as his mouth pressed into my neck. "Can we talk about something else?"

I gripped the back of his head and tried to pry him from me. "Only if you promise to never do it again. Never say you will leave me so easily. You are supposed to be my constant. I cannot imagine a time when you would not be."

Erix's lips stilled on my skin, teeth grazing slightly, enough to cause a shiver to race up my spine. He leaned back enough that his reply was clear when he spoke. I wished he hadn't, because his expression was twisted in turmoil. "How do you look at me and see someone who does not deserve pain for what I have done?"

The air stilled at the sudden depth of his voice.

"You did what you had to do."

You killed Tarron because of what he did to me.

"Did I?" Erix interjected so quickly it snatched my breath away. "It could have ended differently. Tarron deserved to suffer, but I took that possibility away during my mindless loss of control. Deciding who lives, and who dies, is not my decision to make. I... I lost control."

Erix dropped me slowly until I was standing on the ground,

no longer supported by his hungry hands. He stepped back from me, face obscured by the lack of moonlight. Part of me wanted to reach for him, to apologise for ruining the moment, to beg for him to return his lips to my skin.

I didn't. There was no hiding from this anymore.

"What can I do to help you ease this burden, Erix?"

Erix turned his back on me, stepping away. "You cannot offer me what I require. No one can."

"And what is that? If you know I can't give you reprieve, then you know what you are looking for," I said, voice breaking slightly. "Perhaps you should give me the chance to help you instead of turning your back on the possibility that someone else can help you carry your burden. Tell me, Erix, what can I give you that will help?"

"Forgiveness. Not from you. From the people who are no longer walking this realm to give it."

Silence thrummed painfully, the cord finally snapping after days of unspoken tension. "Then you will punish yourself until the end of days searching for such a thing."

"If that is my penance, then I must pay it. But there is something I can do that will lighten the burden. If I return myself to the Oakstorm Court and right my wrong by ensuring you have your father back, that will lighten the load."

"No, my answer stays the same." I raised a hand and placed it upon his upper arm, stopping him from moving any further away. It lasted all but a moment before he shrugged me off.

"You do not know me. Not entirely." It was impossible not to hear the undercurrents of deep sadness as he spoke. "You either do not wish to see what I am, or you are ignorant to it."

"I do know you," I snapped, unable to hold it in. "I have explored far more with you than I have with another before."

"What I am and who I am are two starkly different things. It was a mistake ever getting this close to you. I had to feel a connection that I had not in a long time. A silly dream. And it now ends the same way as it did before." Erix faced me slowly, his eyes glazed with tears, not a single one brave enough to take the first fall. "After tomorrow I retire as your personal guard. How can I keep you safe from others if I am not confident that I can keep you safe from me?"

I shook my head, confusion mixing with annoyance. "I have never heard something more ridiculous in my life. Stop speaking in riddles, Erix. It is late and you are clearly tired. Can we please just talk this through tomorrow morning? When our minds are clear and we are rested. It is always harder to face our anxieties in the dark of night. I promise, this will be easier come dawn."

Erix just stood there and stared at me, shadows creating shapes across his face. "Ask me what I am."

"No, it doesn't matter." I shouted. My breathing grew frantic, chest rising and falling in an awkward, unnatural rhythm. "I refuse to play this game, Erix. It's not what you are, but who you are that matters."

"Ask me," Erix snarled, his eyes darkening.

I didn't flinch away, but the urge was simmering.

I shook my head, unable to look into his wide, panicked eyes. "I said no."

"Robin." His voice deepened, his fists balled. "Ask me."

"No!" My shout was muffled by a rush of frozen air that exploded outwards. It silenced Erix, snatching away those same two words he was about to repeat. As he studied me and the curling of freezing mists that danced at my feet, it was not with fear… It was with something else entirely. "I do not care to know what it is you think is so deeply important. What you are, Erix, is the gentle soul who saved me from the Hunters and helped me through this unexpected and frankly unwanted transition in my life. You are not a result of your actions. Do you hear me?"

I waited for him to reply, to say something… anything that would take back this entire evening. There was a part of me that wished I had the capacity to sleep without him by my side.

"Then I ask that you promise me one thing," Erix began, his deep voice gruff with emotion. Even in the dim light I could see the sharp rise and fall of his shoulders as he also struggled to even out his breathing.

I had heard enough. "Erix, it's time we try and sleep."

"Robin, *please*." It was the use of my name that stilled my refusal to listen. "Tomorrow, no matter what happens, I want you to know that I will forever be sorry. Sorry for what I have done. Sorry for what I will no doubt do again. I hope you see me for the man you have come to know, and not the monster I have fought hard to hide."

I couldn't find the words to answer him.

Then, Erix left the room, leaving behind his shirt and boots in his desperation to flee. And worst of all, I didn't stop him. Not that I had the chance.

Bathed in darkness as my guard dismissed himself from my presence, I was numb to the core. I opened my mouth to call his name, to demand that he return to me at once. But no sound came out. I failed to even catch a confident breath. All I could do was listen to the slap of Erix's feet as he left me behind, until only silence and emptiness accompanied me within my chambers.

CHAPTER 4

A storm brewed across Wychwood's horizon, mirroring the one buried within me. From the moment our small party left Farrador's walls the sky was a deep grey and the visibility of our journey was close to non-existent. It was my doing, magic making my dark mood dance across the landscape. My power seeped out of my body and encouraged the gale to scream around us as we moved through Cedarfall's autumn-entrapped landscape.

I was thankful for Althea who rode upon a mount beside me, and Gyah who sat perched before us, steering our company through the sheet of snow. Their presence was calming, making it slightly easier to make sense of the meeting that was going to unfold when we arrived at our destination.

Focus was proving difficult when all I could think of was Erix and how he'd left me last night. Although I was glad because leaving Farrador this morning would've been difficult if I saw him. Especially after the news that had been brought to me this morning.

Althea had been the one to tell me that Erix had, in fact, retired as my personal guard. Just as he threatened last night. I had never seen someone so close to letting steam explode from their ears. Althea was seething at his resignation, and the lack of answers as to why he had done so.

"Whatever happened between you two I am sure it will blow over. In the meantime, let him fucking sulk," she'd told me as I attempted to move my aching, exhausted body and dress myself. "I have asked that he is kept guarded in case he changes his mind and comes after you."

. I found some peace that he was back in Farrador, even though his abandonment pained me deep in my core.

I clung to her words throughout the long morning of travel to Welhaven. There was a patient part of me that could understand that Erix was going through something he didn't wish to fully divulge. But the other part of me, the louder part, wished to have the luxury of simply walking away from him. And I was far from having that luxury because I'd grown attached; my walls had come down in the weeks we'd shared together and his closeness was both required and necessary to survive throughout the day and night.

"We are here," Gyah announced, drawing me from my thoughts of Erix.

I wouldn't have noticed that we'd arrived at our destination as tall oak and yew trees had grown so close together it was impossible to know where one began and the other ended, like a giant wall. But as our party slowed, and then fully stopped, I finally saw Welhaven; hints of aged stone peeking through blankets of wisteria and creeping vines.

Welhaven was a place of quiet. Even the air stilled around the ruins of what had looked to be a cathedral, an old forgotten place of worship and power. Time had devoured the light stone ruins, allowing vines and foliage to grow amongst them, as though nature had claimed the place as its own after years of being forgotten.

We traversed the consuming foliage, under an archway of budding violet-coloured flowers. They shifted in the light breeze, dancing as though celebrating our visit. That was when I sensed something lurking beneath the silence of this place. An ancient power. Archaic and wise.

. Like called to like as the power inside of me seemed to wake, lifting its head as though searching for a missing part of itself.

I wasn't a religious person; I never had been. Stories of the Creator, as the humans had named him, filled homes through teachings passed down from parents to children. Tales of how He crafted the world with His bare hands, plucking His own strands of imbued hair to create humans, designed in His image, yet powerless compared to the fey.

But then there was the God named Altar, whom the fey believed to have created them, giving life to the four Courts and gifting them with the magic that now pulsed through my blood.

I hadn't spared much thought as to whose belief was more justified, because I hardly cared. But now, standing among the ruins of Welhaven, I could not ignore the aura of pure power that radiated within this place; it was as true as my own.

"We are alone," Gyah said as she joined Althea and the small circle of guards who surrounded me. "The scouts have returned and confirmed that there is no sign of Doran, nor a track to suggest he has been here yet."

I could not discern the wary nature of the fey guard as her golden eyes continued to survey the overwhelming forest.

"I thought he accepted the invitation?" I said, feeling a lump of worry budding in my throat, one that I could not swallow away.

"He did." Althea scanned the ruins, stopping to admire the circular glass window which still hung unbroken above the remnants of a dais ahead of us. It spread vibrant colours of blue, red and green across the overgrown ground. It was near impossible to see if the floor was once made from the same stone as the ruin's walls since grass and other thick foliage now created a soft bed beneath our feet. "I have no doubt he will soon show himself when he is ready. You have to be ready, Robin. For anything."

I didn't need to ponder the statement to provide a sharp, curt reply. "I know."

"Take solace that this is a safe place. Doran would not disrespect Altar and defile his sacred land with aggression. However, if you leave the boundaries, you are free to an attack in his eyes," Althea warned, echoing the same words she had shared before we left Farrador. "If you require it, we can stay with you."

"We informed Doran it would just be me and him during this meeting. Doran needs to trust me, and for that you need to let me do this alone," I said. "If I need you, you'll know."

It pained me to say it. I wanted nothing more than to have Althea and Gyah by my side as I petitioned for my father's release with nothing to offer in return. But this was my fight. One I would win alone, no matter the means.

Althea nodded, offering me a weak smile that didn't reach her eyes. "Let me be the first to admire your bravery. But the moment I sense something is wrong, we will come and break up your meeting. That is final."

"I have no doubt," I replied.

The anxiety storming within me was like a siren call to my magic. It took most of my concentration to keep it smoothed, controlled.

"We *will* be listening," Gyah confirmed through a light snarl. "I do not trust Doran and nor should you. No matter where he finds himself standing. It is clear he sees himself as more than his title for he has already broken Altar's balance once before."

When he ordered his gryvern pets to kill my mother.

"I will be fine." I hardly believed myself as I said those words. Would I be? I had nothing to bargain with. Nothing to offer Doran in trade for my father. But I had to try.

"Good luck." Althea rested a strong hand upon my shoulder and squeezed.

"And what if he doesn't show?" I asked as Gyah began to guide the princess away. They both paused, shared a strange look and then glanced at me.

"He will come," Althea confirmed, stoic. "Doran is many things, but reckless is far from one of them."

With that, they left me alone, bathed in this silent and powerful place. I hugged my arms to my chest as our small party walked out through a curtain of hanging vines held up by broken pillars on either side. All I could do was wait and hope that Doran would come before my worry consumed me entirely.

There were pews buried beneath green foliage to my left. Whatever this place had been used for before likely involved a crowd. I recognised the shapes of more stone and wooden benches on either side of the room, mirror images of each other, and a relatively clear pathway down the ruin's middle.

I decided to sit and wait, unsure if my legs would have given out with the heavy weight of anxiety that had rested upon my shoulders.

Time was an unclear concept here. I focused on the branches of pink blossom that protruded through a half-crumbled wall before me, unsure how much more of this deathly quiet I could stand before I gave up and walked away.

Welhaven warned me of the change before I noticed it myself. A prickling sensation spread up my spine so fast it had me gasping out as I instinctively looked towards the dais. I watched as the air above the podium split as though sliced with a knife. It parted in two spindles of light, and from it stepped a man with heavy feet and laboured breaths.

King Doran Oakstorm had arrived.

I stood abruptly, hand resting on the dagger sheathed at my waist, magic rising to the surface just in case. But Doran didn't pose a threat as he stood with limp arms at the sides of his bulging, swollen belly. He was simply a man, one full of greed. Even his hands looked bloated, his fingers a deep scarlet as the rings adorning them constricted the blood flow.

"I am pleased to have received your invitation," Doran rasped, voice echoing across the ruins. "Robin Icethorn. I was beginning to think that you would never reach out personally. The Cedarfalls have inserted themselves in your business for far too long."

I had to stop myself from thanking him, as though relief that he had actually turned up flooded through me.

"Did only half of my invitation arrive?" I replied, keeping my voice as calm as possible. "Because, from what I remember writing, it was for both you and my father. Yet you have come alone."

"I thought it best to let kings discuss matters without distractions."

The man made me sick to my stomach. He spoke with clarity, although he was utterly dishevelled. As he got closer, carefully plodding down the steps from the dais to greet me on an equal level, I could see the dark stains across his dirtied tunic. How his golden-thread jacket was frayed at the edges with seams that were unrepairable. Even his face shone with grease, prevalent around the plump chin and cheeks that looked hard to the touch.

"So, I am here. What is it you have to say to me."

"I want you to return my father," I demanded before Doran stopped walking. "Not in pieces."

"Well, of course you do," Doran replied slowly. The way his voice scratched up his throat made me want to demand he coughed; it irked me, itching at my skin. "Alas, it would seem that *want* is something shared between us. Because I also want my Tarron returned to me. My *son*. Do you see how we do not get everything we wish for in this world?"

"My father wasn't involved in Tarron's death. This has nothing to do with him."

"Except your father is a Hunter, is he not?" Doran asked, tilting his head to the side. "And it was Hunters who took my dearest wife from me. So, you see, I do have a quarrel with him."

Doran continued walking towards me, but I refused to step back. I didn't want him to see that his presence caused me discomfort. I simply kept repeating Althea's confirmation of my safety. Doran's touch might not cause me pain, but I still didn't want it. "I understand the grief you—"

"Ah, now I see it. You wish to relate to my pain so we can work through it together. Manipulate me just as you did my son."

"Excuse me?" His words stung as though he'd slapped me across my cheek. "I did no such thing."

"Tarron Oakstorm was a strong man. Smart and focused. My prized boy. Until you came along and ruined it for him. Although I understand it was not your hand that took his life, your presence certainly caused it. You poisoned his mind with ideas of a future that Tarron would never have dreamed to discuss with me. He knew what was required, and you distracted him from it."

I spluttered a laugh, feeling heat rise up into my cheeks. "You cannot seriously look at me and point the blame. Your son died because he tried to kill me. How is one life more important than another?"

"Because Tarron was *mine*."

Silence grew taut between us. Not even the winds dared make a sound. Doran's face turned scarlet, his eyes bulging as spit dribbled down his chin. For a moment, through his cracks, I saw a man gripped with desperation and madness. It soon faded as he recollected himself, rubbing the back of his hand across his lips to clear them of spittle.

"Just as my mother, Julianna, was mine?" I asked, voice cold as the magic that lurked within my skin. "That didn't stop you from killing her though, did it? You have spent days demanding Erix's return for whatever sick actions you believe will bring you peace. However, I haven't once petitioned for you to be brought to me. I'm beginning to think that's what I now want... The same revenge you sought with Erix? I wish to have with you."

"You are a pathetic excuse for a king," Doran hissed, the whites of his eyes bloodshot. "I will not be threatened by someone whose balls are no more impressive than hairless plums."

"And yet I'm an Icethorn. And the last one, thanks to you."
I hardly cared for the spittle that'd shot towards me as Doran
spoke, not as I focused on keeping the wave of rage within
me.

"Meaningless blood," Doran shouted. "A waste of power
and potential."

I waved him off, ready to test Altar's boundaries and destroy
Doran where he stood. "Calm down, you old fool, before you
tire yourself out."

Doran could hardly keep a breath in. His large, protruding
chest rose and fell, tugging at the worn buttons across his
jacket. "You want to bargain for your father? Then bargain."

I turned around the space, arms wide. "I have nothing but
a promise."

"And pray tell, what is this promise? More concealed
threats?"

"That depends on your answer, Doran," I said, shrugging.
"If you don't return my father, then I *will* hunt you down. In
this realm, or the next. Do not be the hand that causes me to
lose the final thing I have left. Do not be the reason I break.
There is nothing…" I spat this time, hissing through clenched
teeth. "*Nothing* more frightening than a man with nothing left
to lose."

Doran narrowed his eyes, the corner of his lip twisting in a
sadistic smile. "Ah, a matter we both agree on."

If it was not for the ominous power that hummed through
Welhaven, I would've unleashed my ice upon him. But Welhaven
whispered its warning, cautioning me to keep it in with nothing
but a feeling.

Was Altar watching? Waiting for me to step out of line and
unleash his wrath upon me in return?

Even with that thought niggling in the back of my mind, I
knew I'd still make the first move against Doran if I had to. No
matter the consequence. If my father's life required my action,
I would do it.

"You must wish to see your father terribly," Doran sang, expression melting from one of fury to serenity in a moment. "I cannot disagree with you, Robin. It does not feel right to be the one to keep you from someone you love. Perhaps I will give him to you after all."

"More tricks?" I asked.

"No," Doran said. "I have not the time for tricks."

I flinched back as Doran raised a hand before him, splitting the air in half until the spindle of light allowed for a hunched body to be pushed through. My breath caught in my throat, my world falling away from me as I lost myself to the visitor.

I watched, frozen to the spot, as my father was deposited on the ground at my feet. In that moment I cared little for what Doran saw me as. The walls of confidence I had built crumbled as I threw myself to the ground, cradling my father with gentle hands.

"An Oakstorm is loyal to their word," Doran mumbled, watching as I searched my father's pale face. His skin was cold, yet slick to the touch, so terribly pale that I could see hints of his veins beneath.

"Why?" I looked up through blurry eyes as tears of anger threatened to escape with a single blink. "All of this, all of your requests and demands, and you give him to me so willingly. I don't believe it could be that easy. I *don't* trust you."

"Then you are smarter than I gave you credit for." Doran chewed on his lower lip, flashing yellow-stained teeth. He raised a hand and weakly flicked two fingers in signal for the masked guard to stand by his side

"What do you want, Doran?"

"I have everything I require."

"Ro… Robin," Father croaked, distracting me. "L–leave."

I looked down to him, relaxing my features, as I cupped his bearded cheek. "I'm here. I've got you."

"My Robin…" Father gargled on his words. Before my eyes he was slipping in and out of consciousness. I was no empath, but I sensed his pain and suffering as if it was my own.

"Touching, truly," Doran cooed, his face pinched in disgust as he watched us. "Seeing father and son reunited. Something I never believed possible after Tarron's life was taken from me."

Should I have shouted for Althea? All I could think about was getting my father as far away from here as possible. Away from Doran. And I was prepared to fight my way out if the moment required, even with the low hum of warning as the ancient presence lingered through the atmosphere of Welhaven.

"I will not forgive you for what you have done," I spat at the deranged king. I briefly caught a glance of my Father's hand, which was wrapped in dirtied, brown-stained bandages. I could hardly look at it without the rage erupting inside of me. I knew what waited beneath the wrappings just as I knew what didn't.

A finger. A finger that resided in Farrador.

Was that Doran's plan? Goading me into attacking first?

"Believe, my boy, I do not require forgiveness. There is nothing I want from you anymore. As I have told you, I have everything I need."

I smiled, knowing the man he had spent weeks petitioning for was still miles away, in the safety of Farrador's walls. "Well, that is just not true, is it, Doran?"

"Is it not?" Doran returned my smile, one that seemed to glow from within his mischievous gaze. "You are not the only one who has had a reunion with someone of their blood today. You took something from me, but in return have given something as well. And for that I must thank you."

I watched as the mad king raised a hand and placed it on the shoulder of the statuesque guard. The steel-wrought mask obscured their features, a monstrous face carved into the metal, one that would inspire fear in those unfortunate enough to be close to them. "I do not need to hear any more from you. We are done here."

"Stay," Doran purred, pouting slightly as though I had offended him with my wish for haste. "I have something I would like to show you before we part ways again."

He leaned into the fey guard's shoulder, hand covering his mouth, as he whispered into their ear. I couldn't hear what Doran said, nor did I care. My focus was on my father. I wrapped my father's arm around my shoulder and hoisted him from the floor. For a man of his age and size, it should've been impossible to carry him alone. But the weeks had been unkind to him. I could feel his bones beneath the thin, tattered layering of his clothes.

"Tarron was my prized possession. His mind sharp, his spirit unbroken. He was whole. Special, one would say. Besides his younger brother Lovis, who was stolen with my wife, all my other... offspring never seemed to be entirely... right. They were given a name in my Court, one that no one dared speak before me, but I heard whispers anyway. A title given to them from infancy for the demonic outbursts of aggression and anger. Some had even killed my Mounts... *their mothers* for the smallest of matters that other infants would have simply cried out for: hunger, tiredness. Do you know what that title is, Robin Icethorn?"

"He did not want to know," came the voice of the guard. A familiar voice that had me looking up at the guard, Doran never removing his unrelenting grip from their shoulder as he continued to gloat aloud.

"Then I will tell him. Robin, I had spent many years making sure my twisted children were killed. Even being the one to draw the knife across their little soft necks. I could not trust others to do what was required to younglings. Then I had a change of heart, when I understood their potential–"

"Get to the point." I took cautious steps backwards, slowly moving through the overgrown foliage towards the concaved entrance and those who waited beyond it. Althea, Gyah. I needed them.

"Show him," Doran commanded, but not to me. He spoke to the guard in his grasp.

The guard's finger lifted, grazing the metal mask, hesitating as though he fought internally to stop himself from lifting it. And it was that hesitation that entrapped my attention upon him.

"My creations, the warped and monstrous ones, were called Berserkers." Doran tilted his head downwards, grin extending from ear to ear. His lips split slowly, linked by lines of spit which he spoke through. "Do you understand now?"

The world fell away from beneath my feet. Time stilled as I settled my eyes on the guard again, recognising their outline, their posture. My focus had been so completely on my father that I hadn't even contemplated the impossibility stood beside Doran until they removed their mask.

I spluttered a gasp as it fell freely to the floor.

"Hello, little bird."

CHAPTER 5

The vision of Erix didn't waver. I rubbed my eyes hard once, twice, and still he stood before me.

It *was* him. Not a trick of the light, an illusion crafted by Doran's power over the light. The shine of his silver gaze confirmed that. But something was different. Dark shadows that hung beneath his eyes; the hollows of his cheeks deeper against the dulled tone of his usually sun-kissed skin.

"This isn't real," I muttered, body numb as Erix walked towards me. "Erix is… he is in Farrador." My royal guard took a step forward, his footsteps crunching over broken stone. "Keep away from me. Stop! Whatever this is… end it."

"I am flattered that you believe me to be powerful enough to conjure the unreal, but I am no god," Doran said. "At least not yet. What you see before you is very much real. Touch him, see for yourself."

A faint breeze picked up Erix's scent the closer he came, warm cinnamon and crisp fallen leaves on a mid-autumn's morning. Still, I refused to believe it.

"This was your plan," I said, voice a pathetic whisper. My hold on Father grew tighter as Erix loomed above us. "You left me and gave yourself up."

"I did, and now you have what you want." Erix's reply was as cold as the power that longed to escape my body. One single thought and I could devour this entire place in ice and wind.

"And I too have what I desired," Doran gloated from behind Erix.

I stared at nothing but my guard, unable to formulate a word. Father groaned as I still fought to hold him up, and all Erix would do was look down at me with his empty, uncaring eyes.

"What has he done to you?" I sobbed.

Erix's lip curled, flashing teeth. "Forgiven me."

"Of course I did," Doran said, clapping meaty hands together. "He is my son, after all. My last hope."

"Lies," I screamed, spittle flying beyond my lips. "All lies–"

"No, Robin. It is true. Doran is my father, I am his son. His berserker."

Questions thundered through my mind; it was near impossible to only pick one and not spill them all out at once.

"Have you known all this time?"

"Yes. As did Althea, Queen Lyra. I came to King Doran expecting to be killed for my crime. Instead, I have been given another choice. Another chance."

"Forgiveness!" Doran shouted from behind Erix, interrupting the moment. "I gave him what he sought. Do you see now? I am not the heartless monster you think me to be. You have what you desire, and I have what I desire."

Something was still missing, a move on the game board that Doran had set up. I just couldn't work it out yet.

"His forgiveness doesn't matter," I seethed, tears spilling freely down my cheeks. It was easier to ignore Doran as I focused on my former guard. My Erix. "What was all this for if you leave me?"

"I did it for you." Erix's lips twitched.

"That's not good enough."

"Robin, I told you to ask me about what I am. I gave you the chance. But you were stubborn and refused to."

Everything was falling into place. How Tarron and Erix's relationship was so taut yet so intertwined with secrecy. And Tarron knew, he had to have. He'd called Erix *berserker* before,

I just didn't place my questioning in the right place. I would never have guessed it was a nickname shared between siblings. Half siblings, but family all the same...

Erix was Tarron's brother. His blood.

Half Oakstorm. Half monster.

"You see now, Robin? I was within my rights to demand Erix's return. He is my property. He, like your father to you, belongs to me."

I could hardly hold a breath. My chest shuddered in rhythm with my heart that hammered within it. Physically, Erix and Tarron shared no similarities, however, as my eyes darted between Erix and the mad king behind him, I could see subtle hints. In the colouring of his hair which had begun to grow over the past weeks and the light tint of King Doran's eyes.

"What now?" I spoke the haunting thought aloud. "If you're an Oakstorm by blood, where is your magic?"

"Powerless in the sense you are imagining," Doran confirmed. I hadn't seen Erix with an ounce of magic. During all the fights and training, I'd never seen a slip of Oakstorm power. It had only been his controlled, yet buried aggression which kept him swinging a sword.

"Berserkers are nothing but mutts. We qualify for magic different to what you have come to know," Erix said, his voice a low growl, as though gravel and stone filled his throat. For a moment I was certain the shadows that hung beneath his eyes moved. "I am danger incarnate, as I warned you."

"You are Erix. *My* Erix, duty and pleasure, remember! You don't need to stay with him," I pleaded to him, praying he felt my desperation and heeded it. My speech was frantic, my eyes flicking back and forth between the two men. "We can leave. Together. *He* will not fight us here."

Erix turned away from me in silent refusal. Doran laughed softly as though my begging entertained him greatly. Dread sliced its hateful claws through my soul as I looked upon the man I had known. Who I *believed* I had known. *I was wrong.*

"Berserkers are interesting creatures. I admit I regret killing the majority off. I could have had a legion of chaos and destruction at my fingertips much earlier if only I had given them a chance. Or at least more than I do now." Doran strode towards Erix with pride. "Tarron was *almost* perfect, in all ways. However, he had one flaw that resulted in his downfall. The inability to listen to commands and follow through as I so wished. I blamed his mother for that. Yes, Tarron should have killed you, however, you burrowed yourself into a pocket of his weakness and, ultimately, it resulted in his demise. Berserkers, well, they are different."

I could no longer ignore the way Erix flinched as Doran returned a bulging hand to his shoulder. Even his lip lifted into a snarl of refusal, but his body didn't move an inch. It was as though his mind and body warred with one another. But Erix didn't fight him off. He complied, allowing the man to touch him as though he didn't have a say in the matter.

Like he, as Doran said, was being controlled.

"I've had enough of this," I said, my arm going dead beneath the weight of my unconscious father. "Our meeting has finished."

I looked to Erix, pleading with wide eyes for him to come with me. But with each step I took backwards, my heart broke into one more piece, for Erix didn't follow.

"Wait, Robin. What is the rush? I have more to share with you. Did your dear father not teach you manners when addressed by your elders?"

"Fuck you," I snarled. "That's what my father taught me."

Doran's face elongated into a gasp of horror. "Terrible choice of words. How unbecoming of a king."

I felt nothing like a king. I could pretend all I wanted, but deep down I knew.

"Please, Erix," I begged a final time. "Come with me."

"He stays because I command it." Doran laughed as though he was proud of himself. "He will do everything and anything I so desire. It is the curse of his kind. Once they give in to the darkness, there is no clawing their way back to the light."

The atmosphere shifted quickly. A sense of danger itched at the insides of my ears and scraped along the bottom of my spine up to the base of my skull.

"Speak," Doran commanded, fingers digging into Erix's shoulder. "Tell your precious little bird just how correct I am."

Erix screwed his eyes closed, taking in a deep breath, preparing himself. Then, when his eyes opened, they were slightly lighter than before. That was when he shouted at me. "Run, Robin. Now!"

Erix's outburst had my blood turning to ice.

"Silence," Doran bellowed, and Erix's mouth sealed shut before another word could be uttered. His eyes shifted back to the empty dull sheen that I'd seen this entire time. For that single moment, it was as though a mask cracked and I saw the true Erix behind it.

Fear bridled within me, knowing the pure control Doran had over him.

"Can you just imagine the possibilities?" Doran's free hand reached down to the bulge in his worn trousers. "Now I have what I require I can lose myself for days with the Mounts who wait for me back at Court. I have many years ahead of me. All it takes is minutes to secure more of Erix's kind."

My stomach twisted, bile rising in the back of my throat. "You sicken me." It was a natural reaction to spit on the floor before Doran. The taste in my mouth was too unbearable to swallow at the thought of the disgusting creature bedding those he spoke of. Doran's red, swollen hand gripped the space in his crotch and squeezed, gargling a laugh as he revelled in my reaction.

"Surely you are not rushing off, Robin," Doran replied, frowning. "Not without bidding your lover goodbye?"

I shook my head, unable to look at the empty shell of the man who held the name Erix. A man who I'd spent nights with, lost in his touch and taste. A man whose warm hands had left imprints on my body.

Doran ran his yellowed tongue across his equally yellowed teeth, making a sucking noise that made my skin crawl. "Erix, kiss him goodbye."

"No," I spluttered as Erix began stepping towards me. "Stop, Erix, don't do this. Fight his control."

I cared little for the warning of Altar as my magic seeped from my body. I would not, *could* not, let Erix near me, even if a part of me longed for his touch a final time. Because that was what this was, a final time, I knew that truth deep down.

Erix was lost to me.

The greenery around me crystallised as a cool breeze of ice spread. It didn't deter Erix, who kept coming, even though his boots crunched the blades of iced grass and stone with each step.

Father was growing too heavy to hold as I stepped backwards towards the exit. I couldn't risk seeing where I walked.

"Robin, do not regret missing the opportunity to say farewell to your love." Doran's voice deepened as though he concealed something beneath it. "I admit I never had a taste for boys. Not when the Mounts within my Court present themselves like honey to the tongue. But in this light, I can see what entrapped Tarron. What piqued the interest of my berserker."

"I don't want to hurt you, Erix," I snapped, defeated as my back pressed against something hard. I turned to see the vine-wrapped pillar I had walked into. Father slipped from my arm and crumpled to the floor, wheezing upon impact, but I could do nothing to help him now. Not as I held both hands out, pressing them into Erix's chest with as much might as I could muster. My back arched against the stone as Erix still forced forward, my arms shaking with the effort of keeping his unwanted mouth from leaning towards me.

Ice spread across the leather of his breastplate, devouring the dark material until it glittered beneath my hands. I turned my head to the side, trying everything to stop his mouth from coming closer. "No."

"No?" Doran called from somewhere behind Erix. "Say it louder. Scream it."

"Get off me!"

"Louder," Doran commanded.

"Please…" My voice was broken, shattered like my soul. "Erix, stop!"

Doran spoke to Erix as though he was a dog upon the end of a leash. "Hold."

And Erix did, frozen in place, his lips inches from my face. I was crying, tears turning to beads of ice as they crusted upon my cheeks. I closed my eyes, turning my head to the side to stop myself from seeing Erix's shadowed face so close to mine.

"Release him."

I spluttered as the hold on my upper arms released. My legs gave out, my back slipping down the vine-covered pillar until I was in a ball at his feet.

It took everything in my power not to look back up at him. To my relief, Erix stepped back, stare locked to a spot on the pillar behind me. He moved as though he was soulless, empty and void of who he truly was. It was hard to hate him for his actions, that fact shattering my soul more than I believed possible.

He *was* mine, but now Erix belonged to another.

"Help the *Hunter* from the floor, my berserker."

Erix followed Doran's command, gripping my father's frail shoulders and hoisting him from the heap he lay in at our feet. I tried to stop him, reaching out for my father, but Erix battered my attempt away. The back of his hand cracked into the side of my face, sending me sprawling back to the ground. Teeth cut into my lips, filling my mouth with blood, stifling my frustrated cry.

"Now…" Doran purred, dragging out the word until it was unbearable to listen. "Shall we end this?"

"Give him back to me… Erix…" I stared deeply into his unseeing eyes, pleading.

I reached out again, winds howling around us like screams that mimicked my inner turmoil. But before I could so much as get off the floor, Doran gave a final command.

"Kill the Hunter."

"Father!" I screamed as winds ripped up throughout the ruins. The ominous presence no longer warned me to stop. Magic thrust outwards, but a moment too late.

There was no stopping the crack of bone. It sang above my winds, the clearest noise I had ever listened to. I was powerless to stop Erix as he twisted my father's neck. For a brief moment, I watched as my father's eyes exploded open, full of knowing before the life drained instantly from them.

All I could do was watch, disbelief storming through me.

This can't be happening.

This isn't real.

Dark, scarlet blood oozed from the jagged wound on the side of Father's neck where bone protruded through skin. It spread down his neck, covering Erix's hands. Helpless, I watched as it splashed to our feet. And there it melted the ice-covered ground until the foliage drank it.

I blinked once, twice, only to see the greenery turn black. It rotted before my eyes, spreading quicker than my ice until the ground was covered in dead grass and vines.

"Oh dear," Doran sang, his voice muffled as though he spoke beneath a body of water. It was near impossible to hear through the ringing in my ears. "It would seem I have angered a god and a king all within the same moment. How *terribly* inconvenient."

A growl built in my chest and exploded outwards. I first believed the shaking that gripped the world was a result of my fury, but it was the ruins themselves that trembled, caused by an unseen hand.

Erix lost his footing and dropped the lifeless body of my father to the ground. Doran's pleased face cracked with concern as he watched Welhaven tremble.

"I'll kill you!" I screamed, black rot devouring the ruins around me. It drained the colour from the beautiful flowers that draped from beams and filled trees. Where my father's blood spread, so did the decay, until plants shrivelled and the sweet smell of death filled the air.

"Best we be off. Erix, come."

I jolted forward, nails reaching for flesh, only for the ground to shake so violently I lost my footing. Stone fell down around the scene, cracking against the earth, all whilst Erix walked calmly through the ruin towards Doran, who waited by the dais. There was a hint of fear in the king's eyes as he looked around the ruins. Dust showered us as the deathly cracks of stone began to explode, no longer held up by the strong foliage as it perished.

Welhaven was dying. Altar's sacred land had been defiled by my father's blood and His anger echoed through the air of this place.

But my fury was nothing compared to that of Altar. It boiled inside of me, bubbling like Althea's flame, so inconsolable the temple could've fallen on me and I would've welcomed it.

The air grew thick with cold mist as I allowed the magic to be free. In the place where my heart had been was now a storm of ice.

I thrust a desperate hand outwards, battering a wall of frozen wind towards the bloated king. But he cast it away with a gesture of his jewelled hand. "You may have power, but you still do not know it. You do not have the power to kill me, Robin Icethorn. I am your equal in magic. And I shall sleep well knowing I took everything from you." Doran grinned, lifting a hand before him until the air began to peel in two, revealing his portal of light.

My mind was hardly allowing me a moment to make sense of what had happened. All I knew was fury and a thirst for death.

"You run like the coward you are." I seethed until the magic in my body ached against the skin, begging for release. "Wherever you go, I will follow."

"And I will be ready to greet you with my army, whereas you will be alone. No army, no one to fight for you."

"No, not yet," I growled, pushing my hands forward as spears of dark ice exploded across the ground. By the time my power ripped towards Doran, he disappeared through his spindle of light which blinked closed behind him.

Ice cracked into the wall beyond the dais, devouring stone and mortar in a second.

I sagged forward as Welhaven crumbled around me. I encouraged my ferocious winds to keep rubble and stone from falling upon me. And then I screamed, unleashing every ounce of pain and anguish as I looked down on the lifeless face of my father's dead body.

CHAPTER 6

I stood deathly still as Queen Lyra Cedarfall's words rested upon me. They echoed within my head so violently that if I closed my eyes, I'd be confident she spoke them repeatedly just to taunt me.

It would've been easier to look away rather than see the burning sorrow that lingered within the queen's tear-filled eyes. The way she looked at me, as though I was the most precious thing in the world, caused my skin to itch with discomfort. Because if she truly cared, she would have given me what I had requested.

"Mother," Althea snapped, putting her body between me and the throne upon which Queen Lyra sat. "Find some heart!"

"I cannot allow it, Althea. My decision does not negate the grief I feel for Robin. Regardless, it is the right one to make." Her response was final, even I knew that. "One day you will be in my position and understand that difficult judgements are required to be made by someone whose shoulders are already heavily weighed down from the responsibility of ruling. But I cannot grant Robin our army."

Althea's grunt of disapproval sounded through the throne room as she turned her back on her mother and faced me. "I am sorry, Robin."

Four short words and she dismissed herself. Did I expect her to fight harder for my cause? Or did I expect her not to? I couldn't see the difference as the twisting of anger only gripped its claws deeper into my soul.

"I need your army." My voice trembled, but not from sadness. I didn't feel sad. It was strange, as I expected that to be the emotion that came naturally with losing a loved one. All I felt was unbridled vehemence. As if that anger kept the grief at bay. And it came in waves. The moments of emptiness felt as though time itself didn't exist. It was the same feeling I experienced when Althea found me within the centre of the rubble where Welhaven had been, sheltering my father's broken body with my own. The journey back from Welhaven to Farrador had been a blur. I couldn't remember a single detail. Only the silence. And *him*. Father's body, draped over Althea's mount and covered in Gyah's burgundy-fringed cloak. How it moved with the rhythm of the stag's trotting, tricking me into believing that he was waking beneath it, ready to tell me this was all some twisted trick.

He never did.

Father was dead and there was nothing in this realm, or the next, that would bring him back to me.

I was thankful for my wrath. The moments of anger sharpened my mind, giving me a sense of refreshing clarity. I saw every expression of those who filled the throne room. The flick of an eye or the turn of a lip, I noticed. Even the tones in which Queen Lyra and her consort, King Thallan, spoke to me when we had arrived carting the dead and broken body of my father back to Court.

Pity oozed from everyone around me, and I despised it. Because if they truly pitied me, they would give me what I want. But alas, they refused my request for an army over and over.

I'd gone from stopping a war to desperately wanting one.

"Our numbers are stretched thin across the border of Wychwood. It would not be a wise choice to send the little we have to Oakstorm's gates to demand revenge. Robin, I understand you have lost more than many of us will ever experience. However, I cannot fulfil your request."

"You don't understand," I muttered, body rigid as my nails dug crescent moons into my palms. "He killed my father. There was no reason, yet Doran commanded Erix to do it anyway. If you think that I will stand here and do nothing…" I choked on my next words, taking a moment to breathe and calm myself. "Lyra, if you will not stand beside me as the ally I had come to believe you were, then I will find another."

Another ally who'd hate the king as much as I did – someone who would enjoy the chance to kill a fey.

King Thallan leaned forward in his throne, elbows resting upon his knees. "You are a king now, Robin. You have the Icethorn Court ready and habitable. In time you will grow an army, although I hope you see that war is not the answer. Focus this emotion into rebuilding the Court and the support will come in an abundance of numbers."

"Time is not a luxury I have," I replied through gritted teeth. "Doran's life is mine. I will destroy him before he takes another life. He had my mother, now my father. Erix is gone. You may be happy waiting for him to shift his gaze to…"

Who? Who did I have left?

"Doran has angered a god, leave his fate in Altar's hands."

"No," I snapped with great urgency. "Altar will not take this from me. Doran. Is. Mine."

My words silenced the room entirely.

Lyra shared a look with her husband. She nibbled on her lower lip, eyes flashing wide for a moment. "Something has changed, Robin. News from Wychwood and Durmain's border reached us alongside your arrival back at Farrador, reporting of strange happenings. Altar is angry about what occurred in Welhaven, that much was clear when the ruins crumbled after your father's murder. A storm is coming, one conjured by the Hand. We must focus our efforts on them before we see any more fey under threat."

Plans formed in my mind. I couldn't focus on anything but the fact that Lyra was right.

This mysterious figure hated the fey, I wondered how they'd react if I gave them the chance to destroy one of the fey leaders.

"You're right. A storm is most certainly coming." I turned from the ruling monarchs of the Cedarfall Court until my back was to them. Althea and Gyah waited before the closed doors, expressions pinched from inner turmoil. "My desire to see Doran dead is far more than a threat. It's a promise. Your god did little to stop my father's neck from being snapped. His rules warned us against spilling blood, yet for such a powerful being he just simply watched without intervening."

"Careful," Lyra warned. I glanced over my shoulder to see her stand from the throne, flames dancing between her clenched fingers as she called back at me. "I would choose your words wisely, Robin. You are in my Court and I do not care to listen to your disregard and blasphemy."

My jaw tensed as I carefully picked my next words. "I thank you for your *strained* hospitality, but my stay here has come to an end."

I raised a hand, willing a gust of frozen wind to screech through the throne room. Gyah and Althea moved in time before my power slammed into them. Instead, it crashed into the doors, throwing them wide until they slammed against the walls beyond.

Someone was shouting after me, but I no longer cared. For I had nothing left to care about. My father was gone. Erix was gone. And I was alone.

And as I warned Doran, there was nothing more terrifying than someone with nothing to lose.

No one had stopped me from leaving Farrador with my father's corpse resting across the stag I'd claimed. When I reached the outer walls of the city and the grand gates, I almost expected resistance. But what I found was them already open for me.

If anything, it proved that I truly was alone.

For hours I rode without stopping, until the air thinned and snow began to settle over my shoulders, coating the lump of my father's corpse in white. I didn't have a destination, but I felt the overwhelming desire to go home. To take my father back to Grove, to our house, and shut myself away from the world.

But I couldn't bring myself to get that far. I felt the draw of Icethorn land and followed it, passing the marker stones until I was in a different home – one which I'd never known existed months ago.

Only then did I stop. My body moved on instinct. It was better to do something than sit around, staring at the corpse, waiting for my dark thoughts to consume me. So I built a pyre from wood and set my dead father upon it. As wild winds ripped around me, it took countless strikes of the flint and steel from my pack to get the single spark. But that spark was all I needed for the fire to burn. And as it caught and built into an inferno, I laid myself upon the floor, curled into a ball and closed my eyes.

That was when the tears began. Once the flood gates opened, it was as if the anger stepped aside and finally let the grief rear its ugly head. And ugly it was. Painful and sharp, all-consuming and devouring. My broken-hearted sobs that shattered out from my chest and filled the night, blending in sympathy with the crackling pops that were my father's bones and flesh charring to ash.

I closed my wet eyes as the warmth of my father's burning body embraced me. I pretended he was here, arms wrapped around me, offering me comfort in the moment I needed him most. There was another I longed to be here. Erix. The man who once offered me everything, but aided in breaking my world apart. I don't know when sleep finally claimed me, but I was glad for the darkness. For the first time, I wished it took me and never spat me out again.

* * *

The leather of the reins rubbed my palms raw. I refused to let go. The pain helped keep me from slipping into my dark thoughts. The little sleep I had next to my father was interrupted as distant howls woke me. I thought it was wolves, but anything could've been possible. I almost lay there and waited for them to come and get me. But something told me to keep moving, a focus that I now had and which was all I could contemplate.

An army. I needed an army. But for that, I had to focus on the path ahead instead of looking back at the smouldering pyre that glowed proudly against the night. It was hard not to turn and watch as the glow of orange shrunk in the distance the further the mount clopped away.

I left my father's body to burn beyond the border of Icethorn land. I didn't know exactly where I was, but the feeling of being home had told me I was within my Court. But where I needed to go was South, towards the border of Durmain and beyond. And that was where I guided my stag, using the compass I took from Farrador to aid me in the right direction.

I rode for hours, the dark grey cloak tugged tightly around my shoulders to keep out the night. Most of the journey was exposed as I clambered over steep hills laced with snow or passed through empty, forgotten hamlets and villages that reminded me of Berrow.

Icethorn was a quiet place, which was both a blessing and a curse.

Eventually, I gave up fighting the heavy droop of my eyes. Sleep came in brief waves. Not even the horror of what waited for me during sleep could keep me from finally giving in, aided by the steady rhythm of the stag, who showed no signs of slowing.

I woke again only when I nearly slipped from the stag's side. Time passed in a haze of exhaustion.

Eventually my in-and-out rest broke as I was greeted by clear blue skies and the end of Wychwood forest. Once I passed into Durmain, leaving the snow-dusted ground behind, my focus was sharp as a blade.

It didn't take long for me to find a human village. My plan was simple. Locate someone who could give me clearer directions back to Grove. But the welcome I received, as the stag trotted into the first village I found, was not what I expected.

Faces looked up at me, all with wide eyes and expressions of disbelief. From both sides of the street, people watched as I rode upon my mount before them. It took me a moment to register that the people were humans, evident from the rounded ears and now more noticeable lack of grace that the fey held.

I turned around, no longer caring for the gasps of those who watched, likely expecting I would lash out. A slow smile spread across my face but it only lasted a moment. I could've lifted my hood and hid my ears, but I needed word that a fey had entered human land to spread. It had to reach the right people.

My pocket of happiness for my success was ruined by the realisation that my father was dead. For a brief moment I had forgotten.

All at once, grief rushed over me, intensified by guilt as a result of my forgetfulness. The rage followed swiftly.

But I had to focus.

"Where am I?" I called out, pulling on the reins until the stag stopped in its tracks. I was almost certain I felt the wobble of the mount as though its legs were seconds from giving out.

There was a long pause before someone brave enough to shout at me broke the silence. "Go back to where you came from."

"No one wants you here."

"Yes!" Another voice chimed in. "Fuck off."

All around me humans, young and old, hurled abuse towards me. They, as I would have been before my life turned down its chaotic path, would've been shocked to see a fey beyond the Wychwood border. Perhaps that was because they never made it far enough before the Hunters found them. But I'd grown up around humans, and never experienced such a reaction.

How far had the Hand's poison spread. Most importantly, how quickly?

All around me the humans reacted with both shock and anger, encouraged more by each other. Even the small voices of children cried out.

I gritted my teeth, glowering through the shadow of the cloak's hood as I studied the faces to see if there was anyone or anything I recognised. Besides the black-beamed and white-panelled buildings, the town around me looked no different to any other settlement that peppered Durmain's expansive lands. And from the carts and stalls that the people stood amongst it was clear the town relied heavily on street trade rather than the traditional experience of shops in the bigger cities.

I was close to Grove. Home. But how close still remained a secret.

The stag huffed in discomfort as the crowd grew in confidence and stepped closer to me.

"Keep your distance." My warning was wasted, drowned out by the cries of the crowd gathering around me. I yanked my arm towards me as a man with dirtied hands and a mouth full of missing teeth reached for me. "I said stay back."

"Lost, are you?"

"Looks like it. Took a wrong turn."

"Fucking fey scum."

"Someone call for the Hunters!"

Yes, I thought. *Let them know I am back.*

Something wet crashed into the side of my face. I whipped my head around, my fingers reaching up only to come back wet with a thick, white liquid that made my stomach heave.

I blinked once and saw red.

"Enough!" My cry tore through the crowds, sounding no different to a torrent of screaming winter winds. All around me the crowd tumbled backwards, forced by the hands of my storm. A chorus of their frightened shouts froze, immortalised in a cloud of breath that fogged beyond their mouths.

No one else spoke, not as they looked up at me with intense fear.

I didn't blame them for their reaction. Power radiated from my very skin. It spread across the cobbled street, lacing up the closest building's outer walls until everything was devoured in a glittering layer of ice.

My stag bucked, causing the humans closest to me to get out of the way. I would've kept spilling out the powerful magic to instil fear, but my eyes caught the terror-stricken face of a child, no more than five, gripping onto his mother's skirt where he hid. His wide, tear-filled eyes reminded me that this fury could be controlled. I reined in my power, calling it back within.

"I asked a question." I drew out my words, struggling to force some decorum. "And would very much appreciate an answer. Where am I?"

My heartbeat drummed in my ears as I waited for a response.

"You have no dealings here." A woman spoke, the very same who had her child tucked behind her in protection. "There's nothing for you."

"Answer the question and then I shall leave," I called out, allowing everyone to hear. "It's rather simple actually."

Her lip curled in disgust, then parted as the answer came out. "Ashbury."

The moment the woman confirmed our location my brain raced with pinpointing it upon the blurry map in my mind. Perhaps it was my sense of urgency to leave that made the destination familiar. Ashbury was half a day's ride to Grove, a trading town that sat in the heart of a collection of villages; many could get food and items they required without travelling miles to Lockinge. I hadn't been here for many years which was why I'd not recognised it.

Now I had my answer, there was no need to hesitate to leave. I was already clapping my heels into the stag's side and urging him forward with a click of my tongue when the shouting began again. Keeping my head down and body tight to the stag, I allowed the loud clatter of its hooves to signal the crowd ahead to move out of the way.

As I rode against the wind, cheeks stinging with cold, I wondered how long it would take for the Hunters to catch word of my appearance. I hoped my short stop in Ashbury had piqued the interest of those whom I wished to know I was here. Just not yet. There were some rather pressing matters I wanted to take care of before the Hunters caught up to me. Then they were welcome to find me.

Let them come. My dark thought encouraged a grin. *I have use for them.*

CHAPTER 7

The King's Head tavern was as busy as I last remembered it. Even as I trudged through the main street of Grove, I heard the noise of drunkards singing and ale-thick laughter spilling beyond the aged door and iron-framed windows.

I'd waited for night to fall before entering Grove. Unlike with Ashbury, it was best I didn't make a scene. I left my stag at the village's outer limits and as far from human eyes as possible. Then I slipped into town during the darkening of early evening; no one paid attention to another cloaked figure fighting their way through the cold breeze that ripped through the narrow street in search of a drink to warm themselves up.

The welcoming stench of stale ale enveloped me as I entered the tavern, bringing a sense of comfort. I'd almost forgotten how strong the scent was, stubborn enough to cling to clothes for days no matter how many times they were washed through with warm water. And the taste of ale... I longed for it.

Most notably, it reminded me of my father. Reminded me what I was here to do.

I kept my head down and hood up as I navigated my way through the wall of bodies before me. To my luck, it was rather dark in the tavern. Only the light of the hearth gave it a warm glow that barely covered the inside of the low-ceilinged building.

The seat I found was in the far corner of the main room, surrounded by shadows. It gave a perfect view to the bar and the countless familiar faces of the barmaids who rushed around pouring pints of amber ale and flutes of more piss-coloured liquids. I caught glimpses of people I recognised as I studied the crowds before me, people my father had worked beside, even those who had treated me with some respect as I'd spent evenings helping behind the bar or cleaning the dirtied mugs and glasses.

Being half-fey never bothered the people of Grove. And if it did, I wasn't aware. My father protected me from it. That was his legacy. I was under the impression my father's reputation kept the hate at bay, in this village at least.

Now only I was left to protect myself.

I gripped onto the table as the ghost of my father suddenly played out before me. I imagined him knocking back jugs of beer with friends as he did frequently during a shift. I blinked and saw another taunting memory, one of him carrying a fresh barrel full of drink across one shoulder, not a bead of sweat brave enough to soak his brow.

This had been a home away from home for him. A place, I could now imagine, that took his mind off my mother in the years after she'd walked away from him – from us.

A distraction.

There was no fighting the single tear which trickled down my cheek. Until a hard-edged voice called through the haze, snatching my attention. "If you don't want a bloody drink then shift yourself, boy. That seat can be for another who's willing to part with the coin." I didn't notice the person standing before me until their foot kicked into my boot, snapping me out of my thoughts.

"Sorry," I spluttered. "Yes, a drink. I'll have a drink."

At least it would dampen this pain.

"I'm not a mind reader. Ale, beer, spirits?" The barkeep leaned in, peaking beneath my hood. "Name your poison – Robin? Is that you under there?"

I pulled away as the woman's calloused fingers threw back my cloak. "Why didn't you say it was you?"

There was no point averting my eyes from the speaker anymore, not since my face was exposed, and the two points of my ears with it. Looking up I took in the entire vision of the rose-pinched cheeks and bundle of grey hair.

"Mable." I forced a smile in greeting, rubbing my cheek as though it had an itch, and not because I wanted to clear any evidence of the tear away. "How've you been?"

Mable had worked in King's Head for as long as Father had. She was a short, round and powerful woman, cheeks speckled with red veins and eyes heavy from age. Mable had a way of always fiddling with her apron, worn and stained from overuse; the stains across its material told stories of the pub's history far more than any book would have.

"Overworked and under-appreciated. The usual." She punched out a fist, knocking it into my shoulder. "Where's your bastard father? Henry hasn't come to work for weeks. Got the rest of us sorry lot covering his shifts whilst he is off galivanting around doing who knows what, with who knows who."

My fake and forced smile faltered. Now was the time for me to lie and pass off my father's absence with a made-up story. But I couldn't bring myself to.

"He's gone," I said through a lump in my throat.

I could see from Mable's expression that she didn't know what to make of my comment. Her lips twitched as though she was going to laugh, but then she caught the lack of emotion on my face and she stopped herself.

"Well, wherever he has gone to, tell him he'll be lucky to have his job back when he returns. Boss is fuming. Anyway, you didn't come here to listen to my gripes. What are you having?"

"Ale," I choked out as grief wrapped hands around my throat and squeezed. "Half-pint."

It was my father's favourite drink.

Mable nodded, looking everywhere but back at me. As she turned from the table I reached out and grabbed her wrist. "Aren't you going to ask where *I* have been?"

If she had noticed Father's disappearance, then surely she'd noticed mine.

"It's not my business worrying about what young lads get up to," Mable replied sharply, as though she rushed out her response because she simply did not want to answer it truthfully. "Two ticks of a lamb's tail, and I'll be back with that drink."

Mable tugged her wrist from my hand. I could've sworn she muttered something else beneath her breath as she waddled away from the table like a stiff goose.

Maybe I should've raised my hood, but there was no point since those near me had caught a glimpse. The patrons of the pub didn't look at me in the same way those in Ashbury had. This was different. They recognised me as I recognised the majority of them. Each stare was full of wonder and confusion, but mostly shock more than anything. They were surprised to see me. It shone across their wide, untrusting stares as clear as looking through polished glass. It had me sitting straight with my hand only a hairbreadth from the dagger at my waist, the very dagger Erix had given me.

Erix. I looked down at the table as my head spun for a moment. *Father.* My stomach jolted aggressively, the thought of them both making me want to vomit across the table. Pinching my eyes closed, I focused on breathing. If I didn't, I would've given in to the anger that itched to be released, but the time was not right.

Not yet.

I was three half-pints down when the door to the pub slammed open. In strode the very person I'd travelled all this way to see. A small twisting of disappointment flooded through me as the only man who'd entered was James Campbell. He wasn't followed by his reedy friend, the one who had taken my mother's bracelet the night they both sold me off to Hunters.

James took two steps into the pub, chest heaving as he searched the crowd. I knew who he was looking for long before his stare settled in my direction.

"I want no trouble tonight, James!" Mable shouted across the now deathly still crowd. "Best that you leave before you upset my patrons."

James was so angry he could hardly formulate a word. All he could do was raise a finger at me from across the room and shout one word. "Outside."

I raised my empty glass and tipped it from side to side, calling back. "Fancy something to drink? It's on me. Mable, another two perhaps?"

The gossip of my arrival had reached James, but I'd hoped it would've been sooner. A clearer head would be better for this encounter. But at least I was somewhat prepared, whereas James had woken up this morning believing he wouldn't see me ever again.

Yet here I was.

And there he stood.

He embodied the very reason I'd become what I was now, the reason why Father had to travel to Wychwood, putting him on the path to his death. In my eyes, James Campbell had caused this all to happen when he sold me out to the Hunters.

I couldn't punish Doran yet, so I needed someone else to face my wrath.

James was the perfect, and only, option.

It took a moment for James to utter something back to me. Perhaps it was his disbelief muting him, or the rage at seeing me in this place when he believed he had gotten rid of me. When he did speak he only managed one, sharp word. "How?"

I kicked out beneath the table, sending the wooden stool on the other side clattering to the ground. "Why don't you come and join me? And I will tell you everything. Unless you wish for everyone to listen?"

"You have a death wish coming back here, boy."

I was getting tired of old, hateful men calling me boy. Actually, thanks to him, I was a king.

"I'll take that as a no," I whispered to myself, standing from my seat and letting the dark cloak unravel to the ground. "There's much I wish for. Perhaps death is one of them. But I can promise you I won't be the one dying tonight."

"No, no, no," Mable said, cheeks redder than normal. "Both of you out. Now."

James grunted like a wild boar, snatching the dirtied blade from his belt and brandishing it before him. The patrons around him stumbled out of the way, some surging for the door, but the majority stayed for the entertainment. The King's Head was not impartial to a fight.

James paced towards me, looking down the edge of his blade as he spoke. "I could sell you again, you know. Probably would get more this time around."

I paid careful attention to the reaction of those around James. People I'd smiled alongside, grown up amongst, to see if they were shocked to hear James's revelation. People I saved by claiming the Icethorn court and preventing a war that they never expected. But there was not a single wince. Even Mable's expression stayed stoic.

They all knew. All of them.

They had known what James and his accomplice had done to me. Who they had sold me off to. Which made it easier for my conscience to deal with what was to come.

"Come closer and say that again," I spat, hands lifting at my sides. "You were lucky the last time, but I can promise you it will be different now. Go on, I *urge* you to try."

"Don't play games with me."

Pressing fingers to my lips, I stifled a dramatic gasp. "Trust me, James, I'm taking this very seriously. I'd go so far to say I've never felt more serious about anything in my life. Look…" I plucked the golden-hilted dagger and threw it with vigour, the blade's tip sinking into the wood flooring between James's boots. "No weapons besides the one you hold like a child. Come, let's dance this out like men."

"You are no man," he snarled, lip curling over stained teeth. "Fey–"

"Don't... excite me." My shout reverberated through the room in a cloud of rolling mist. Glass shattered as my frozen touch met with tankards upon tables, held in hands, and panes between window frames. The ground was littered with shards, crunched beneath the heavy boots of people who left the pub with haste. "Be careful what you call me, Mr. Campbell. A wrong slip of the tongue could cause you great harm."

James stood still, hair quivering by my conjured winds. I wondered if any of the other patrons watched with the same fearful gaze that spread across his face. The knife James held shook as his fingers gripped tighter. It was about all the movement he risked as I paced through the parted crowd towards him, my lingering freeze of magic still present in the air around us.

"Lost for words?" I asked quietly, as though he was the only one in the room. "Do you have nothing else to say to me now you see who I am? *What* I am!"

More people scurried from the pub, the door slamming wildly behind them. Those brave enough to watch placed themselves behind tables and black-painted pillars for protection.

"All I know," he began, lips curling into a cruel smile, "is I could've gotten far more coin for you in the first place. Whispers say that the Hunters favour those with magic. You are dangerous. I did the village a favour by trading you off the first time. It will be the same again."

I sighed, disappointed at his reply. In a different world, during another time, a kinder choice of words may have saved this man's life. Now, all it did was solidify the taste for blood that had settled within me since Father's death.

"Don't stop," I encouraged him, arms wide in welcome. "Tell me just how you feel. Come on, I can take it."

"If we had the chance, you would've been driven out of this place years ago, you and your scum-fucking father." James sucked in a disgusting gargle of snot and spit then gobbed it to the floor at my feet. I looked down, stomach churning, like the splatter of green and yellow liquid dribbling into the grooves of the slabbed floor. "Believe me, *boy*, you are nothing I have not seen before. Do not think you're special, for I've traded many of your kind for coin over my years. The only difference is you made it back. Your tricks do not scare me. Know that."

"I don't wish to scare you, James." Even with the knife now pointed inches from my chest I felt calm. Calm knowing that the blade would do little to stop me. It felt like I'd won before I'd even made my first move.

"Where's Henry?" The way James said Father's name made my skin shudder. "Sent his little creature to battle on his behalf, did he?"

My chin lowered to my chest as though a sudden weight on my shoulders was too heavy to bear. I looked up at James through narrowed eyes, fingers flexing at my sides.

"You have brought this on yourself," I said. "Sealed your fate the moment you picked me as your next trade. This is the path you choose to walk, I am simply ensuring you meet that path's end–"

"James, enough! Leave the boy and go."

I turned my head to look at Mable as she pleaded from across the bar a final time. Her voice was an unexpected anchor, dragging me out of my darkened thoughts. Her face, although stern, was soft and familiar, a face I had looked upon for years, one that had lined with compassion for me and my father during that time.

She was different to James Campbell. Mable was kind. The way she looked at me now with furrowed brows and lips pursed with concern reminded me that not everyone had the same thoughts as James.

But the moment shattered when James's sloppy shout revealed his next move.

I turned as he lunged the final inches towards me. It was selfish of me to pinch my eyes closed so I couldn't see what happened next. I exhaled a powerful breath; conjuring a wave of frozen air that spread out before me, ensnaring my attacker in thick mists.

The piercing of James's knife never made it past the charcoal grey tunic I wore.

It was the screams of those who watched that had me prying my eyes open. Before me, encased in jagged blades of ice, was James Campbell, frozen in place with his mouth captured in an eternal cry, the sound still echoing in my mind.

I stumbled back a step, a hand pressed to my chest.

Come on. My inner voice was a screaming storm. *Come on.*

Where was the feeling I had expected? The relief. I expected this revenge to piece my heart back together. Yet it still rattled in pieces within my chest. I waited and willed it to return to me. To make me feel something. Anything. It had been part of my plan from the moment I left Farrador.

If I couldn't avenge Father's death by ending Doran's life, then I wanted to go to the man who had started this all. But as I looked on upon him I still felt the same endless hollowness within me.

"You've killed him…" Mable's voice shook as she walked towards me. I barely heard her over the ringing in my ears. I watched as she reached out to James's body to touch the encasement around it. Could she see how James's skin had turned a dark, bruised blue beneath? How his final breath seemed to have caught in a pocket of ice beyond his frostbitten lips?

As her finger touched James, he broke apart.

It wasn't exactly Mable's touch that shattered the ice, but me.

My fist clenched and James Campbell broke apart. I almost felt bad. *Almost.* Mable's gasp of horror itched up my spine as the crack spread wildly across James's body.

I couldn't move as he crumbled at my feet. His limbs and body cracked as though his skin and bones were made from glass, spreading out in small pieces across the tavern's floor.

Someone gagged, followed by the splattering of vomit across the stone floor. Others cried out in revulsion. And all I could do was watch as the bloodied, shattered mess of a man smashed into countless pieces. I studied the smattering of ice, blood and flesh, finding it impossible to believe that a body had even stood before me.

"Get out, Robin." Mable smacked her fist into my arm, pounding over and over. "Get out! Get out!"

I didn't know it then, but her hearty sobs would haunt me for a lifetime.

"I'm not sorry." My lips hardly moved as I spoke. "He deserved this. He did."

I was trying to convince myself, repeating my words over and over as Mable continued slapping and hitting me. My feet began to move as my mind was completely numb. Even as my boots trampled over the crunching of ice and flesh, I couldn't truly register what was happening. What I'd done.

Where is the relief I desired?

Why am I not fixed?

Something heavy crashed into my back, sending me stumbling forward. A metal tankard clattered to the ground. Then another hit me, pain spreading across the side of my face. I raised a hand to my cheek and felt something warm. Blood coated my fingers as I pulled them away. The remaining patrons of the pub threw things at me, bellowing for me to get out, calling for guards to arrest me.

Murderer. Killer. Evil.

I allowed the words to settle in my soul. They were right after all. I was all of those things.

The door to the pub crashed open, cracking against the outer wall, as I was driven out into the night.

Blood trickled down my face from the cut across my cheekbone, mixing with the tears that had begun to fall freely. I couldn't clear them away as I still held my arms above my head to stop the objects from hitting me.

It was dark in the street outside of The King's Head. The world seemed to spin violently, as though the street shook beneath my feet. Night was endless, every single star a witness to my actions as I put distance between the pub and those who wished me pain for what I had done.

I stopped suddenly, eyes pinching shut as a flash of burning red fire exploded before me. The fiery snake spread in a wall, surrounding me on all sides. Panicked at the sudden, unnatural flame, I whipped my head back and forth, searching for the source, already knowing who had found me. My attention became fixated on a parting in the smouldering wall as two figures stepped through; like a curtain it separated, rushing back together once they both stood in the centre of the roaring fire.

Althea Cedarfall swept through flame without fear or hesitation. "Robin, what *have* you done?"

CHAPTER 8

I squinted, trying to focus through the tears and firelight, a new panic searing out of me as I took in the reality before me. "You can't be here," I shouted over the flames, voice hoarse. "I don't need you, Althea. Gyah. You need to leave. *Now*."

"You absolutely *do* need us. Look at what you have done, the mistakes you are making." Althea gestured to the tavern behind me. A smudge of ash marked her high cheekbone, her skin glowing against the fire, deep reds that matched the braid hanging over her shoulder. "This isn't going to bring your father back."

"I agree with the princess, Robin. This madness must stop. We understand what you've lost, but that doesn't justify losing yourself." The second figure shifted to her side. Gyah. Her golden eyes were bright, even from a distance, as though the creature within begged to be released. "It's easy to drown in grief. Trust me. We can help keep you afloat."

They both surveyed me with weapons in hands. Althea with her flame, Gyah with a tall blade.

Tears streamed down my face, threatening to blind me. "You can't possibly understand what I feel. Not you, not Althea."

"We can compare cock sizes another time, or perhaps save the conversation for somewhere less... public." Gyah looked around the circular space created within Althea's fire, beads of sweat dripping down her dark bronze skin. It was not the fire she studied, but the outline of silhouettes beyond it. Humans.

The moment the wall of fire was dropped I was confident that many would be standing watch around us.

"Isn't this what you want, Robin?" Althea called, lips pulled tight in a snarl. "To create a spectacle? We heard rumours about a fey, you haven't kept your appearance here very secret. Do you even understand what you have done. Whose gazes are turning towards you!"

Of course I did. It was the very reason I was here. But Althea and Gyah had to leave before those people came.

My tears dried upon my cheeks, hissing near the heat of Althea's fire. "Turn away whilst you can, Althea. If you know what is coming, you know to leave. I don't need you for what I have to do."

"Don't you?" She tilted her head to the side. "I understand you are hurting. I understand that you are acting out of pain. But it is my duty, as your friend, to stop you from making more bad decisions."

"Hurry," Gyah warned, knees bending as she lowered herself like a cat ready to pounce. She sensed something beyond the fire, something that set her on edge. "We do not have long."

Althea stepped forward, extending a hand out towards me. Ruby flames licked around her fingers like a glove. Although her expression burned with anger, her eyes softened with a sorrow that I recognised as a friend. "Come back with me, Robin. You will not find peace here. We will find another way."

"It's not peace I'm searching for."

Althea's hand trembled, but she refused to drop it back to her side. "Then what is this all for? You have come here and left a perfectly mapped trail behind you for anyone to follow. The Hunters are coming for you after your short stay in Ashbury; you have practically begged them to find you. And when they do, there is nothing I can do to stop them."

"Turn away." Even I could hear the dark edge in my voice. "Let them come for me."

I felt detached from the moment. Where Althea's warning of the Hunters should have brought on fear within me, it now conjured the opposite.

"Why?" Althea asked, voice no more than a whisper.

Because I have a plan. One that requires the attention of the very people I escaped Durmain from.

"Your family refused me an army, so I have gone searching for one elsewhere–"

"I strongly suggest we finish this conversation another time!" Gyah shouted.

I glanced just as she shifted forms, skin melting into shadow and retracting into the long, scaled body of the winged beast that lurked within her.

Gyah shouted again, a roar that hid the undertones of her warning to get down.

That was when the air whistled as a bolt struck through the wall of fire. Time seemed to slow as I watched the sharp edge of the projectile pass inches from Althea's body; only a whisper of hair moved. Althea gasped, turning back to look as another bolt hissed through the air.

This time, the projectile's aim was true and met its mark.

A scream of pain tore through the night as Althea fell to her knees. Her hands reached for the short splinter of wood that protruded from her thigh. My senses exploded to life in that moment, as though a bucket of iced water had been thrown upon my head.

I moved for Althea, who writhed on the ground. It became hard to see her as the wall of fire dropped, no longer fuelled by her magic. With the dispersion of the heat came the rushing of darkness again.

Gyah roared, wings flaring wide in warning, threatening the many who stood around us.

Hunters. They found me, just as I wanted. Except this wasn't my plan, not with Althea and Gyah. They should never have followed me.

Hunters greeted us down the scope of crossbows, each with readied bolts pointed towards us. A wall of shadows armed with weapons.

Althea grabbed my tunic and dragged me down towards her. "My magic. It – it is gone."

A loud pop sounded in the distance. I looked away from Althea's paled, pain-creased face to the sky. At first it looked as though the stars themselves were falling from the heavens. I blinked, unable to make sense of what I was watching.

Then the noise of clinking metal revealed the truth.

By the time I realised what was happening, I couldn't warn Gyah.

A web of chains fell from the sky, unravelling into a blanket as it cascaded over the hissing Eldrae. The moment the net touched Gyah, her scales melted away. Smoke curled from the creature's body, now held down by the heavy metal web, until she writhed in her fey form upon the cobbled street.

Iron. It had to be. The only element strong enough to subdue a fey's power. The same as the bolt protruding out of Althea's thigh.

Althea was still kneeling on the ground as she choked out, "Fight, Robin. They'll kill us."

"I would strongly suggest not resisting," a deep voice rumbled out from the wall of Hunters. "Surrender yourself peacefully, and no blood needs to be shed."

"Do something... Robin." Althea's grip on my tunic was failing. Her eyes fluttered as she struggled to keep them open.

I looked from the Cedarfall Princess, who wrestled with consciousness, to the powerless Eldrae, who didn't move beneath the web of chains, then to the Hunters; countless, narrowed eyes poised above weapons staring unflinchingly at me.

"I'm sorry, Althea..." I muttered, pulling myself from her weak grip as I stood. "I warned you. You should never have followed me."

"What have you done...?" Her whisper haunted me as I regarded the army of Hunters, turning my back on her.

I did what I thought was right, but now I had to pay the price and hope it was worth it.

"Steady!" That deep voice shouted again, followed by the shifting of bolts and the taut pulling of strings. "Ready yourselves in case our friend here has a valiant change of heart."

Slowly, I raised my hands at my sides. The last thing I needed was for them to see me more as a threat. I had an innate awareness of the many humans watching from the safety of the King's Head tavern and the surrounding buildings that lined Grove's streets.

This was a spectacle that couldn't be missed, one they would likely gloat about for generations.

I lifted my head, jutting out my chin and rounding my shoulders back. It was time to be the king I continued to convince everyone I was. The first set was letting the unnatural authority ooze into my voice.

"I request an audience with the Hand," I called out above the ruckus. Clearly my request was a surprise, because the Hunters calmed to an almost silence. Until the laughter began.

"Surely my ears deceive me. Have I just heard you correctly?"

Although I couldn't see the person speaking, that didn't take away from the intense gaze pinned to me, how it scorched my skin from head to foot.

My hands shook violently, my legs numb, but I fought to keep control over my voice. To keep it steady. "You heard me correctly. I wish for an audience with the Hand," I repeated, swallowing a lump that crept into my throat.

"Ah, I see. This was all some grand plan to get our attention, was it?"

I nodded, knowing the speaker could see me. "Yes."

I wasn't going to fight. It would have been pointless, and that was never part of my plan. Nor was Althea and Gyah being here when the inevitable happened.

The chains above Gyah and the bolt in Althea's thigh suppressed their powers. One wrong move from me and I would be in the same situation.

Iron. Each of the Hunters was armed with it. I would be next if I was not careful.

"As I am sure you are not surprised to hear, you are in no position to make demands." The speaker finally stepped forward, separating from the wall of Hunters.

A man, dressed in the same black tunic and trousers as those behind him. The only difference was the cloak he wore. Even in the dark street I could see the shimmer of red silk beneath the cloak and the small, white hand mark embroidered across his chest. "However, I'm intrigued to hear what you wish to say to the Hand. Usually the fey run from the mention of him, not towards him. Go on, spit it out before I bury a bolt in your head."

"I'm merely accepting his invitation–"

The Hunter snatched a crossbow from another near him and raised it towards me as he stalked forward, making me flinch. Physically angered by my comment, the Hunter didn't stop until he was a foot in front of me, our boots touching and the sharp tip of a bolt tickling the skin between my eyes.

"Cuff the others!"

Twin emerald eyes hardly blinked as he shouted the command to those behind him. Eyes I recognised, the bright green so poignant even in the dark. I could hardly risk a breath as I listened to the footfalls around us. If I dared look away from the Hunter, I was fearful the bolt would find itself buried within my head before I even had the chance to get what I required.

All I could do was look at him, wide-eyed, as he watched me.

"Hello, again," he said, confirming what my inner anxiety suggested. We had met one another. "It's not every day you get to capture the same fey, in the same place, again. What a pleasant surprise."

I took him in, his features caught in the glow of the tavern behind me.

The Hunter's dark brown hair hung above his shoulders. The lack of distance helped me discern the colour, hidden strands of honey among deep russet. He was tall – enough that I had to lift my chin to keep a hold of his stare – but not so tall that I'd get a crick in my neck after a while. Beside the snarl etched into his face, and the creasing crow's feet beside his hate-filled eyes, the main feature that stood out was carved beneath his eye, a scar that ran from its outer corner down to his cheek, as though a tear had left a mark that could never be removed.

"You," I said, knowing this was the same man that James Campbell had run me out my house to crash into.

His bright eyes narrowed. "You. How does it feel now that you have the attention you have clearly desired? Never have I met a fey with a death wish quite like you."

I wouldn't allow myself to blink. I wouldn't miss a sudden move from the stranger.

"There are not exactly clear instructions on finding your *kind*," I muttered, heart thundering in my chest. It was so loud I was certain the Hunter could hear it. "I figured you would find me. Save me a job."

"And find you we did," the Hunter whispered, eyes narrowed as he regarded me. "Why do you not fight?"

"What good would that do?" I replied, trying to keep myself still.

"For you," he breathed, a faint smile creasing his face. "No good at all. For me... it would make my evening one to remember. It's the excuse I need to see the life drain from your eyes when this iron pierces your skull."

He was telling the truth. I could almost sense his tension as his finger hovered above the crossbow's trigger.

"What's stopping you?" I asked quietly, breath fogging before me, magic begging to rise in protection.

I squashed it down, knowing every single move had to be careful.

The silence that followed allowed me to catch the string of pungent swears from Gyah as she tried to fight against those who must have rallied around her. What unnerved me most was the silence from Althea.

"I wouldn't be able to answer that," the Hunter snarled, pressing the sharp bolt into my forehead. I gritted my teeth against the prick of iron into my flesh. "If I had it my way, this conversation would not be happening. But alas, there is someone watching out for you."

I couldn't help the audible sigh of relief when the crossbow lowered. The bolt tip had cut my skin, deep enough to draw blood that dribbled into my line of sight, but shallow enough to begin knitting together.

"The Hand?" I asked, keeping my hands fisted at my sides.

"His hospitality might waver when he learns of the body you have left, shattered into bloodied pieces, in the tavern behind you."

My skin shivered, stomach twisting in disgust. "I'm not the only one with blood on my hands. I've witnessed your Hunters murder a fey, treat them like cattle for the slaughter. And the reasoning? Shall we compare and see whose conscience is less scarred by their actions?"

"General Rackley," another Hunter interrupted, snatching the attention of the scarred man before me. "Shall I cuff this one?"

"No." His deep voice rumbled with restrained fury. "This one is *mine*."

General Rackley. That too was a name I'd heard, spoken from the Hunters in the camp before Erix arrived.

It was clear the scarred man was in charge here, evident from the subtle glances and nervous auras of those near him. They, like me, feared him.

"Master... Rackley," I said, testing his name, trying to show a lick of respect in hopes it saved me.

"My name is Duncan," he added, sweeping his eyes over me a final time.

"What does it matter what I call you?"

His smile crept over his lips, twisting my insides into a maelstrom of fear. "Because when you die, and you will die eventually, I think it's important you take the name of your murderer to whatever realm you find yourself in next."

His words and his name rang in my head as loud as unwanted bells during early morning. He snatched the strange shaped object from the Hunter's hands and shoved the crossbow at him. Slowly, Duncan turned back to me, enigmatic smile plastered across his face, as he lifted the metal towards me. It took a moment to realise where I had last seen that iron collar, wrapped around the necks of the fey at the Hunter's camp, the fey who held magic that required iron to subdue.

"That isn't necessary. I won't fight you." I couldn't fight the desire to step back as Duncan moved the contraption towards my neck. But he lashed out, firm hands gripping me and keeping me in place. "It is unnecessary for me to wear that. I wanted you to come here. This was all to get your attention. If I wanted you dead," I snarled, "you already would be. I'm *not* your enemy."

"You. Are. My. Enemy," Duncan snarled, body stiff and lip curled. He struck forward, thrusting the cuff around my neck in an instant; it snapped shut with a click that set my nerves ablaze.

I reached up, fingers desperately pulling at the lip of the cuff that closed around my skin. The desperate need to get the cuff removed was so all-consuming that I hardly noticed the heavy and hollow cavern that my body had become – severed from my magic once again.

My mind caught up and I stopped my struggle. Duncan stepped backwards, a true and honest smile filling his devilish face.

"It suits you," Duncan said as he turned his back on me. I was left to watch the wall of Hunters race towards me with outstretched hands. True to my word, I didn't fight them as the Hunters grabbed and pulled at me. All I cared about was pleading for my friends, begging that they were spared, even though each word was wasted breath.

What have I done.

CHAPTER 9

I was pressed down on the floor of the cart, splinters of wood cutting deep into my palms. With each jolt of the screeching wheels, the cage rocked as we navigated over potholes in the road, forcing my back to slam into the iron bars.

There was nothing I could do to create comfort, not when a chain linked me to the iron bars from the cuff around my neck.

I was leashed like a dog. We all were.

If it wasn't for the chain that connected Althea to the cage, she would've slumped to the ground. I sat opposite her, unable to do anything but watch as her eyes would flutter open and closed. Even in the dark night I could see the thick sheen of sweat that clung across her forehead. The wound on her thigh still oozed blood; it was close to impossible to ignore the tang of copper as it spread in a dark puddle beneath her leg. The bolt had been ripped carelessly from her thigh before the cart had moved. Because of the iron cuff around her neck, she hadn't been able to heal. It was clear her body couldn't handle the lack of power; unlike mine, it was not used to being severed from her natural abilities.

Gyah was not unconscious like Althea. She sat in the corner of the cage, watching me like a starved hawk sizing up a fleshy meal. Disdain pulsated from her, silent, taut anger so palpable I gave in to my guilt and refused to look her way.

Around the cage the Hunters rode upon the back of obsidian-coated mares. The cage was being pulled by many as well, the backs of tall Hunters all I could see ahead of us. Duncan was among them, but where, I wasn't sure. There was something about him that conjured a kindling of fear in my gut. Every now and then I could feel the stinging of eyes across the back of my neck. I would turn to search for him, but never find him. I was still confident Duncan was among the throng, watching with the same hateful stare he'd given me as he held the crossbow between my eyes.

This wasn't how I saw this ending. Being locked in a cage of iron was far from a possibility. I was so blinded by my desire to cause Oakstorm's mad king pain that my mind had sugar-coated the idea of finding the Hunters and requesting them to take me to the Hand.

Becoming a prisoner was far from what I imagined, but it was now a painful reality. I put some hope in the knowledge that the Hand wanted an audience with me. But that hope came crashing down when my eyes settled back on Althea.

I dared to close my eyes for a moment of ignorant bliss. It was easier to give in to the darkness of my mind than fight to not look at Gyah, or ignore the army of Hunters and pretend that Althea was not suffering before of me.

Selfish little bird. A voice haunted my mind. *You search for reprieve in the dark, but you deserve nothing but the reminder of what you have caused.*

I couldn't discern the voice. Was it my own? Something else? It echoed across my skull, impossible to ignore.

"Something troubling you, princeling?" Gyah spat, her tongue as sharp as a knife.

Reluctantly, I opened my eyes to regard her. The moon above flickered beyond the bars. It was not full, but its silvered glow danced across Gyah's dark skin like dawn's light across a still lake's surface.

"Gyah, I didn't want this to happen. Believe me." I spoke in hushed tones, aware of the many Hunters around us.

Gyah didn't seem to care who heard. In fact, her voice rose in volume, alerting the few riding beside her to listen in. "I admit you never struck me as a pathetic, careless fool. I gave you the benefit of the doubt over and over. But now look at you. Tied up like cattle being taken to slaughter and still you do not see the reality of what is happening."

Her words felt like a punch in the stomach.

I rested my head upon the iron bar behind me, pleading for some support but finding it lacking. "I did what I had to."

"If that's what gives you peace to believe, then you are more the fool than I think."

She hated me. Not for any other reason than threatening Althea's life. I could read that in her silence.

"I am doing this for *him*," I replied through gritted teeth.

"He's dead, Robin." Gyah's features softened, her gaze dropping from mine for only a moment. "Do you truly believe your father would have wanted this? He kept you from the Hunters, turned his back on them himself, yet you have run straight into their arms. And for what?"

"An army," I admitted, to the amusement of the Hunters around me, who laughed. In a way, I hoped Duncan would listen in. Maybe it would stir something in him, something that would help me get what I needed. "I need an army and no one north of the Wychwood border is willing to aid me against Doran. This is not a path I wished to go down, but the lack of support has placed me here. I'm desperate, Gyah."

"That you are, Robin Icethorn. Desperate."

More laughter echoed around us, turning my gut in on itself.

"You truly believe the Hand will aid you?" Gyah asked, although I could tell she already knew the answer. I did too.

"He prepares an army of powered humans. His stance on the fey is clear. If I can give him a reason to attack Oakstorm then he may embrace me. May let me live."

Gyah stared at me with furrowed brows, judging me as clear as day. "You are forgetting something important. A piece of information that contradicts everything you have just explained to me."

"Enlighten me."

Gyah reached up to her ear and flickered it with a finger. "You are fey. We all are. If this Hand wants to go to war against us, that will include you."

"Maybe it isn't as simple as that. Erix would not have–" A lump formed suddenly in my throat. I covered my mouth, shocked at the response I had to saying his name.

"I understand it may be hard for you to see it, but Erix didn't have control over what he did. Even now he is not the same person we have come to know. Erix is nothing but a vessel for Doran now. A puppet with gold strings."

I'd not allowed myself more than a short moment to think of Erix. Even with my father's murder replaying in my mind, I always tried to ignore the hands that took his life. The vacant look in Erix's eyes as he followed the command his father had given him.

Turning my head, I gazed to a huddle of Hunters riding beside us. They could hear what we discussed, confirmed from their assumed laughter and chatter.

"Did you know what Erix was?"

Althea moaned, stealing my attention. Her eyes were cracked open, the whites bloodshot and skin pale around them. She struggled to push herself up to sitting, wincing with a hiss as she dragged her leg back towards her. "We did."

Those two words sent a sharp chill up my spine. It confirmed what I'd already thought.

"Althea," Gyah gasped, relief smoothing her features. "Are you alright?"

"I'll be fine." Althea brushed Gyah's concern away with a weak hand as she replied to me again. "Robin, I knew everything about Erix and his truth. What he was. What that meant. I should have told you, but it was not my story to tell. And for that, I'm sorry."

The wind was knocked from me. "He begged me to ask him. I refused. Maybe if I'd just allowed him to reveal his truth, he would never have…"

Left me. Turned himself over. Gave up.

Althea scoffed and smiled grimly. "The truth hurts, Robin. For both the person saying it, and the person hearing it." Her eyes rolled into the back of her head, losing her battle with consciousness. "I – I would know."

"Althea, you need to stay awake." Gyah spoke over me, stopping me from saying something I regretted. "Keep talking."

A string of inaudible sounds flooded from her paling mouth. Then the Cedarfall princess fell silent once again.

"Althea!" Gyah screamed, pulling against her restraints, trying to reach across the cage.

Nothing roused Althea, her body slumping back to the ground. Gyah continued to fight against her chains, to reach for Althea, but failed miserably each time. The roar she let out finally had Hunters' heads turning in our direction.

"If she dies," Gyah looked at me, through me, piercing me with her stare. "Her blood is on your hands."

Gyah was right. This was my doing. My fault, and there was nothing I could do or say to fix it.

It justified punishment to listen to Gyah's shouting as she commanded Althea to open her eyes. The iron bars groaned as Gyah tugged and yanked to get closer to the unconscious girl ahead of her. Her desperation was so raw that I was certain the bar would've snapped in two if the cuff was not suppressing her abilities.

The cart slowed suddenly, sending me jolting to the side. Around us the Hunters circled on horses, each looking in at the chaos before them. Heavy boots squelched across the sodden ground beyond the stationary cage. Darkness coated everything, making it impossible to see clearly. There were no lights of villages and towns, only the quiet, dark and barren landscape of Durmain with nothing but Hunters around us.

Gyah was too engrossed in her shouting for Althea, her panic hot like pure fire, that she didn't notice the Hunter come up behind her. But I did. I tried to warn her, but her focus was solely on Althea. Until the hands reached through the bars and latched onto her chain.

The Hunter pulled hard, yanking Gyah back against the bars of the cage. The crack of her skull against metal turned my stomach. It silenced her pleading, and a single gasp escaped her mouth as her expression pinched in pain.

"That's more than enough excitement for one night." A face peered through the bars. Deep, forest-green eyes narrowed as he looked across the cage at me.

Duncan Rackley. Finally, he'd shown himself again.

"Don't"– I pulled forward, straining against the chains – "fucking touch her."

"Believe me, I've no intention of soiling myself." Duncan released the chain, allowing Gyah's head to roll forward until her chin was pressed against her chest. I watched, seething, as Duncan stalked around the cage. Not once did he take his gaze off me, not once.

My chest rose and fell, all the while I didn't take my eyes off Duncan. I stalked him, as he did with me.

"Care to explain what all the fuss is about?" he asked.

It was as if we were the only people in the world, Duncan and I.

"Althea, she's bleeding out," I said, jaw taut and voice deep. "Unless you let her have access to her magic, she'll die."

"And that is my problem? What do I care if she dies in this very spot? One less fey in the world is exactly what I want."

"Oh, but you will care when you have to explain to your master why you have let a Cedarfall fey die. A princess!"

There, I saw it, a flicker of something across his dark expression that told me my words had settled into him. "She's the enemy. If she dies the Hand will hardly pay it any mind. Her body would only join the piles growing in honour of his name."

"You're wrong, and you're lying."

"Attentive little thing you are." Duncan smiled, flashing straight white teeth. "I'm impressed."

"From my understanding, the Hand likes to collect fey with raw power. If you let Althea die, you prevent him from obtaining a fey with the ability to burn this party of Hunters and the acres of land around us with a single thought. Would you truly keep someone with such abilities from him?"

Duncan stopped beside me. My neck ached as I kept my stare on him, not wanting to show defeat by looking away.

There was a weighty moment of silence between us, Duncan studying me through narrowed eyes just as I studied him.

Then he looked at someone behind me. "Change our course to Finstock."

"But General Rackley, it will add days onto our journey," the Hunter replied with a light voice overspilling with hesitation. Clearly he wanted to speak up against Duncan, and I could understand why.

Duncan's face pinched into a frown, his lips curling back from his teeth as though he was a beast that longed for flesh. "I didn't ask for your opinion, Novice. I gave you a command, follow it."

"Apologies, General Rackley."

Duncan turned his attention back to me. "I will see that she is cared for. I wouldn't want her bleeding out on the Hand's carpet, that's no way for a greeting now, is it?"

Shock vibrated through my bones, and all I could think to say back to him were two words that tasted wrong in my mouth. "Thank you."

Duncan winced as my thanks settled over him. The expression pulled at the scar beneath his eye, making it look hollow as it etched deeper into his skin. "Don't thank me yet. Where I'm about to take you, you will soon wish to be put back in this cage no matter who is dying within it."

With that, Duncan smacked a palm onto the cage. It jolted forward. And once again we were on the move. All the while I watched Duncan as he disappeared into the darkness, as if he belonged to it.

CHAPTER 10

Finstock was a fortress of grey stone nestled in the barren landscape of Durmain. I didn't know what to expect as we arrived, but this cluster of towering, aged buildings was far from what I imagined.

It had been a long night, one full of concern for Althea's wellbeing. I'd tried to distract myself with racking my brain for any mention of such a place as Finstock. There was nothing. Perhaps my anxiety made thinking about anything other than the leaking wound that still poured scarlet blood without sign of stopping impossible.

I had come up as clueless as I was when Finstock was first mentioned.

Early dawn was upon us and with it a brisker chill that had sunk into my bones. It was a battle to stop my teeth from chattering and my skin from feeling numb to the touch. All there had been, along the dirt path we rode, were rolling hills and glades so far away that my mind played tricks on me as if I could see the glittering surface of the ocean in the distance.

All of a sudden Finstock was before our party, jutting out amongst the calm of the landscape like an angry blade of stone that reached, unwantedly, into the cloud-filled sky. Torn, black banners hung from the stone face of the fortress. They danced in the wind, slow enough to see the recognisable handprint stained in white. The emblem was everywhere I looked. A mark of the Hunters. The very same that had been imprinted into my father's flesh.

I recognised the tug in my chest at the thought of *him* but felt it best to bury the feeling deep down. This was no time for grief, not as the Hunters carted us beneath a stone walkway into a courtyard in the belly of the stone fortress.

My focus was getting Althea healed, then as far away from here as possible. Even my plans for an army had dwindled as I faced the reality of my mistakes. I could not change them, but I could work to make up for them.

Starting with Althea and Gyah's safety.

All around the straw-covered courtyard Hunters of all ages stood watch as we were paraded within. I caught a glimpse of a few who spat at the wheels of the cart, and others who scowled with such burning intent that I could almost read their minds. They didn't have to speak aloud the thoughts at seeing fey in this place. It was abundantly clear. Hate, excitement, danger. Each glittering in every set of eyes I caught.

But the Hunters were not the only people to dwell within this place. Nimble, small frames adorned in deep, veiled maroon habits flittered across walkways and through the crowded space. I couldn't see their features as the heavy material obscured them from view. They paid us no more heed than the Hunters paid them.

Not a single one turned a head to look in our direction as they hurried past in small, quiet groups.

What is this place?

Gyah broke her hour-long silence, startling awake where she sat in the cage. "What is going on?"

Her voice was rough as cracked stone. I looked across the cage as she fought to keep her eyes open, reaching a hand to the back of her head and wincing as she touched it.

"We made it to our destination," I replied. "Are you alright?"

Gyah shrugged my question off, narrowing her gaze beyond the cage where she took her time to look at each and every

Hunter surrounding us. Her stare was fierce, one that I didn't want to be on the receiving end of, even with a cage of magic-nullifying iron around us. "No good is to come from this, Robin."

"I know," I hissed, sweeping my gaze around the courtyard. "They are all Hunters. All of them. Just don't fight them, let me solve this. For Althea–"

The cart had not even stopped for a moment before a flood of Hunters rushed towards it.

My warning clearly was missed. Gyah jeered, pushing herself into a crouching position as close to Althea's unconscious body as she could stretch. Even in the face of sudden danger, Gyah was a warrior without the need for steel or claw-tipped wings. Whereas I was a coward, powerless and pathetic, unable to even move a muscle as the threat of so many who hated us rushed forward.

My heart hammered in my chest as the heavy bolt clanged at the cage's exit. I pulled my legs into my chest, hugging them tight as the door was thrown open and greedy, gloved hands reached inside.

"Keep away from her!" Gyah roared, snapping teeth as she tugged on the chain at her neck. "Touch her and you die."

To taunt Gyah, one of the Hunters laid a finger on Althea's cheek. Gyah gnashed teeth together, but it didn't deter them.

No matter how hard Gyah tried, she had no power to stop the many hands from unlocking the chain at Althea's throat and then pulling her limp body from the cage until she was hidden in a swarm of leather-clad bodies.

In a matter of seconds, it was only the two of us left. The Cedarfall Princess was taken from view through an open, dark door in a building to the side of the fortress.

Gone, without question or comment.

Gyah was screaming bloody murder. The veins in her neck were straining as she pulled hard on the cuff and chain but to no avail. It was as though the creature within was battling against

the iron. And, for a moment, I believed the transformation
might have even happened.

Until the sound of someone clearing their throat snapped
my attention back to the cage's open door. In the place the
crowd had been now stood three men. Two unrecognisable
and the third… the third was Duncan.

"The Cedarfall will have her wounds seen to," he said, voice
dull as he studied his nails carelessly. "In the meantime, I'd
recommend calming yourself down before you force me to do
it for you."

"Can we follow her, please," I pleaded, glancing worriedly to
Gyah who silenced herself so quickly that the sudden change
frightened me.

Her golden stare was fixated on Duncan. It swirled with
hungry vengeance and something more terrifying – promise.

"No. That isn't how this is going to work."

"But," I began, only to be silenced as Duncan whipped his
hand up.

"I think you're forgetting your place, fey." Duncan simmered
with diluted hate, his eyes never leaving me for a second. "She
needs to be healed, that is what you wanted, is it not? Because
say the word and I will personally drag her back out by her
pretty red curls and start off on the long ride to Lockinge. We
could even place bets to see if she will survive the journey. Not
that you have much of worth to offer up."

I sat back, defeated and without argument.

Gyah had not given up so easily.

"Take *me* to her," Gyah demanded through gritted teeth.

"Why?" He scowled, long fingers flexing at his sides. "Don't
you trust my hospitality?"

"No. Surprisingly, we don't," I replied.

"Well, I don't particularly trust you either. So, I regret to
admit that we have something in common. Even if that
thought alone makes me wish to scrub boiling oil across my
body just to clean it."

That comment caused the two Hunters behind him to snigger, looking at each other like a pair of mischievous cats.

Duncan glanced between us both, grinning slightly when his eyes found Gyah. "You both are going to follow me. In a moment my good friends here are going to unchain you and I trust you will behave. This is no place to act the hero… do you understand? I may be able to control my desires, but I cannot say the same for some of these men and women."

It irked me that he didn't refer to me when he spoke. The threat was aimed at Gyah. Duncan knew I needed to get to Lockinge to have an audience with the Hand, although that desire was barely a simmer now. Whereas Gyah would fight tooth and nail to get to Althea and escape if she had the chance.

He saw her as a threat, he saw me as a fool.

"Give me the chance and I will tear your face off."

Duncan rolled his eyes. "I admire your conviction, but this is my domain, *Eldrae*, you would be a brave idiot to attack me here. Brave yes, but still an idiot. Do not give my Hunters a reason to cause you pain; it's taking me enough conviction not to grant it myself."

"We'll behave," I muttered beneath my breath. "As long as you stick to your end of the bargain."

"You have a lot to learn, boy. I don't deal in bargains. Why don't we show you to your accommodation first though, yes? We are going to have plenty of time to speak. By the time we reach Lockinge, I have a feeling we are all going to be very, very close."

Even with the countless burning hearths and wax-dripping candelabras, Finstock was a cold place. If the damned iron cuff was not on my neck, I might've even enjoyed the comfort of the winter, how it seeped into the stone walls and clung to the itchy sheets that were fitted onto the bed before me.

There was no reprieve from the cold here, no place to hide from it.

Gyah paced the flagstone ground before the door, arms crossed, as though she kept them from battering the very walls down. Trust me, she'd already tried. Furniture lay scattered and shattered around the door. "I can't just sit here and wait for news knowing Althea is left with those twisted bastards. They could be doing anything to her – anything!"

"There is nothing we can do but wait," I said, hating the truth of my words. "Duncan made it clear. The more we cause a scene, the longer we wait. He is toying with us."

Gyah sneered in my direction, setting my skin on fire. "Do you mean there is nothing you *want* to do? You are right where you wanted to be, aren't you, Robin? In the belly of the enemy all because you had a whimsical thought that they might help you in your quest for blood. Well, look! Blood is what you have got. Althea's blood."

"You're right," I said, edging back until I was pressed into the bed.

Gyah's shocked expression suggested she expected an argument from me on the matter. I had no fight left in me.

"Listen, if there is a chance to get to Althea, you must not take it. With or without me. At least, not yet. You saw where we are. How many Hunters are around us. One wrong move and we may jeopardise what little help they are reluctantly giving Althea. For the meantime, it's not a risk worth taking."

"I told her we should not have followed you." Gyah stopped dead in her tracks, hands reaching for a sword at her waist that was not there. "Althea was adamant, worried about you. See how she thinks of others but you barely spare a thought for anyone but your wants and needs? I told her you need space, but that was not something she was willing to grant you. I have never seen her so concerned. And there was nothing I could have done to convince her otherwise."

I couldn't hold Gyah's scrutinising gaze, opting to look at my scuffed boots instead. "I had no idea."

"You wouldn't have. For that you would have had to stop thinking about yourself for a moment to–"

"I get it, Gyah. And I'm sorry, okay? If I could change it, I would. But that isn't going to get us out of here." A string in me snapped, one that I had not realised was pulled too tight. "My father was killed before my very eyes by a man I was beginning to let myself love. In the space of weeks, I have gone from believing I had a family to learning that I have no one. You were right, you should not have followed me."

Hot, sticky tears sliced down my cheeks. They clung to my lashes, soaked my skin, made me reluctant to blink for fear of becoming blinded by sadness.

Gyah just stared at me, standing within the room of minimal comforts that I'd named our prison, a room that'd been bolted and locked from the outside with god knows how many Hunters listening in.

"Say something then!" I pleaded, unable to handle the harsh silence. "Scream at me, tell me what you really think. Go on, I'm all ears, Gyah. There is nothing you can say to me that I haven't already told myself."

I flinched as she strode towards me, preparing myself for a grounding slap or punch to the gut. It never came. Instead, arms wrapped around me, pulling me in tight. One long exhale and I practically melted into Gyah's embrace like ice above an open flame. Her hand found the back of my head where she supported me. Her chin rested upon my shoulder as she, too, exhaled a breath full of heavy emotion. "Robin, I have been unkind with my choice of words."

"They… they have been justified."

Gyah squeezed me tighter. "If I am being honest, I'm scared. It is a feeling I am not used to and one that I do not wish to continue experiencing. I fear for Althea, and I fear for you too."

"I get it."

I was scared too. Scared to death that my choices would lead to more death. Althea's life was in the hands of people who paid coin to hunt her kind and that made me feel as though I was stepping across a bed of knives.

Gyah pulled back, holding me at arm's length as her eyes studied me from top to bottom. "You really want to do this, don't you?"

She didn't need to elaborate. I shook my head in refusal. "I needed an army to face the Oakstorm court. But this isn't the way. I didn't think, I see that now. The only one I could think that would jump at the concept of killing a fey king was the Hunters."

"They're our enemies. King or not, Doran or you. We are all the same in the Hunters' eyes." Gyah chewed on her lip, gaze unfocused as she stared at nothing. Her words hurt, because they were true. "But I can see you have made up your mind. You do not want to be helped. So, once Althea is back to me, and the right moment presents itself, we will leave."

"I know." Defeat settled in my chest, making me hollow.

Doran had killed my family. I would repay that debt, but not this way.

"What do we do now?" I asked Gyah, feeling as though she was calm enough to think whereas my mind was a storm of guilt and grief.

"First, we get some answers. Anything we learn about this place and the people here may be useful information for when the chance to escape presents itself," Gyah whispered, eyes wide. "If there is one thing I have learned during my years of training, it is that the art of listening is one of the greatest passive weapons we all have access to."

"In a twisted way, I'm glad you are with me." I couldn't imagine being here alone, knowing Duncan and his Hunters filled the many rooms within the fortress. Part of me could not help but believe the locked door was not only to stop us from leaving, but to prevent unwanted guests from entering.

"As much as I enjoy your company, I admit there are other places I would wish to spend time with you than this." Gyah looked around the room with a distrusting stare. "We're not safe here."

"I was not safe back in Wychwood. Assassins. Monsters. Doran Oakstorm." Gyah didn't tell me I was wrong. "What is to say he will not send his pets after me again?"

"Perhaps Doran will, but you were also never alone in Wychwood. If you followed on this path, you would've been. It would've changed everything, not just with you and Doran, but you and the fey. The people who are going to expect you to be a king and lead. They'll never follow you if they know you wanted to side with the Hunters."

She was right. Just the thought of what I'd done twisted my gut into knots, making bile creep up the back of my throat.

I gritted my teeth together, refusing to make comment. Gyah noticed, her shoulders slumping forward as if the weight of disappointment in me was too much to handle.

"Get some rest, Robin," Gyah said, releasing me and gesturing to the bed with a flick of a finger. "You'll need it."

I grunted and smiled, clearing the tears away with the back of my grime-smeared hand. "I don't mind taking the first watch."

Gyah simply shook her head in refusal. "I would very much like to be the one to welcome any Hunter who dares visits this room first. So sleep. I promise to behave, for Althea's sake, not theirs."

CHAPTER 11

It was the unfamiliar presence that woke me. Not a sound or slight sudden movement, but the knowing burn of someone's unwanted, silent stare that dragged me from the pits of the deep sleep I'd found myself prisoner to.

Abruptly, I sat up tangled in the bedsheets, panic coursing through my veins.

"Was it something I did?" Duncan leaned against the wall opposite the end of the bed, one leg propped up behind him. His arms were folded across his broad chest as he surveyed me with eyes glittering with intrigue.

Perhaps it was the grogginess, but it took a moment to register what was happening. Instinct had my hand reaching for my waist, but the golden-handled dagger was nowhere to be found. In the back of my mind I conjured a picture of it, forgotten on the tavern's floor of King's Head.

As discarded as Erix had become in my life.

I scanned the room for Gyah, but the lack of her presence was abundantly clear even without the need to check. I was alone, with Duncan. There was a hideous quiet among the darkening room which only added to the fear I felt with the man looming over me.

"What have you done to her?" I accused, arms shaking as I held myself up.

"Which one?" he replied curtly, simple words that made my anxiety spike even further.

"Gyah."

"Ah, the one who looks as though she wants to pick the skin from my very bones." Duncan kicked off from the wall, taking confident steps towards me. "I gave her the opportunity to see your friend. At first I thought she'd refuse, leaving you and all. But she had no problems leaving you alone. Never seen someone move so quickly out of a place."

His words were meant to hurt me, but I already knew Gyah's displeasure in me. I smiled anyway, glad that she was with Althea, hoping they would find their chance and escape. With or without me, they had to leave.

"Is something amusing you?" Duncan tilted his head, narrowing his stare until his scar pulled into a deep crease beneath his eye.

"Just wondering what a man like you is doing stalking me like a creep whilst I slept?" I questioned, thrusting my jibe at him in response. "Do you like looking at helpless men in your free time?"

"Stalking? Ha, hardly. And I never once believed you to be helpless," Duncan replied, taking slow steps around the base of the bed to its side. I felt the need to draw in my legs, but didn't want to show signs that his presence caused me discomfort. "I was going to wake you *eventually*, I promise."

"What do you want, Hunter?"

"The question is, what do you want... Robin Icethorn?" Duncan's cherry-red lips pulled into a tight line, his scar tightening down his face. It wasn't an ugly mark, but one that gave his aura of danger more of an allure. "Would you care to indulge me?"

"Do I owe you a conversation?"

He shook his head. "Well no, but I just ensured your friend is going to survive. So, out of common curtesy, I think some answers would be justified."

I took a deep inhale, wanting nothing more than to escape his gaze, whilst being pinned beneath it like a butterfly to a corkboard. "Ask away then, as you said, it's the least I can do for your incredible hospitality."

"Mouthy little thing, aren't you?"

I smiled. "It's certainly not the first time I've heard that."

Duncan narrowed his eyes, taking his time to run them across every visible inch of me. "What makes a man beg for the attention of the very people who would wish to see his innards spilled freely across the ground? I've never known someone of your kind wishing for an audience with the Hand, a person who supplies coin to encourage your capture and, in most cases, eventual death."

"Are you the mysterious Hand I ask after, Duncan?"

Duncan released a noise somewhere between a laugh and a gasp. "Do you think I would be staying in the likes of this hovel if I was?"

"Then the reason I request an audience is not your concern."

Nor do I want it anymore, but I kept that to myself.

I was coming to realise that Duncan had the ability of switching from calm to feral in a blink of an eye. I had no time to gasp before his weight was on the bed and his hand was gripping my chin, stopping me from uttering a word.

"I think you've mistaken me for a person who enjoys a game. Let me be the first to tell you, Robin, I hate games. You'll learn, sooner rather than later, or not at all. But for now, if I ask a question, I damn well require an answer."

His grip on me relaxed and he rocked backwards. My jaw ached from his strength, the skin tender where his finger left an imprint. He must've marked me, because suddenly Duncan reacted with what I could only describe as regret. I was surprised when an apology didn't fall out of his slacked mouth.

"Touch me like that again," I warned, sheets balled in my fists, anger fuelled by the pain. "I'll make you regret ever laying your fucking eyes on me."

Silence thrummed between us, as taut as a rope. It was Duncan who broke it. Again, not with an apology, but his tone had softened, his fingers flexing at his sides.

"Let us try again, shall we?" he said. "What is it you require from the Hand?"

"An army," I seethed, teeth gritted so tight that my jaw ached.

Although my desires had shifted, there was no point making Duncan know that. If he got wind I didn't want his help anymore, it could affect our plans of escape.

Duncan's eyes widened for a moment, quiet whilst he allowed my truth to settle in. "What does an Icethorn fey require an army for?"

So, you do not know who I am. What I am. Good, I thought, imagining my power flowing from my hands and turning his flesh to deathly, hard ice. *When the time comes, I will show you.*

"To kill a king."

Duncan blanched, skin leeching of colour. "Treacherous words do not befit you–"

"Not the human king. A *fey* king," I quickly interrupted, revelling in the way his face melted to shock.

"So you come running to the people who'd love the chance to help, except you do realise what you are, don't you?"

I swallowed, my throat dry as stone. "I do. But I got the sense that I'd only be joining a plan that this *Hand* already has arranged. And if that's the case then I would gladly aid him in his attempts."

"You know nothing of the war he prepares for." Duncan turned from the bed, stalking towards the main door of the room. The dark clothing he wore enunciated the V-shaped sculpture of his back. Duncan was tall and reedy, however I knew that beneath his clothes he likely housed a multitude of muscle. He certainly moved as though he carried the weight of strength across his body.

"Then tell me," I called after him, swinging my legs over the bed and coming to a stand. "What does the Hand want? He wants fey blood, I know that. But why?"

Duncan looked over his shoulder, emerald eyes full of judgement. I'd never experienced the overwhelming urge to read the inner thoughts of a person until now. There was fear in his gaze, mixed with a disgust as his lip curled. I first blamed myself for his reaction, but I couldn't shake the feeling it was the topic of conversation that displeased him.

"Let us go for a walk, shall we?" Duncan pushed open the door, which had clearly been left unlocked since he had entered. It unsettled me that I still didn't know how long he had been watching me for. Either way, I was still alive. That had to count for something.

"Not really in the mood for a walk. I'm content staying here."

"Don't you trust me?" Duncan pouted, clearly amused by the idea.

"Are you taking the piss out of me?" I bristled, heckles raising down my back. "Of course I don't trust you, General Rackley."

"Good, you shouldn't. And I don't trust you either, so we are on common ground. However, know this, if I had wanted you dead I would've finished the job a hundred ways whilst you slept. Believe it or not, you are likely safer with me than any of my fellow Hunters."

"You sound sure?" I mused.

"Considering I've heard the things they would like to do with you, yes I am. Now, follow me and you shall find out exactly that the Hand prepares for. What you will be used for once we reach Lockinge, unless you're successful in your petition. Otherwise, you'll be headed down to the Below with the rest of them."

I straightened at that. "The Below?"

Duncan smiled from ear to ear. "I hear it's lovely. Big open space beneath Lockinge castle. I could send word ahead and make sure a nice corner of the prison is made comfortable for you."

"You're talking in riddles," I snapped, swinging my legs over the side of the bed. "What do you mean the rest of them?"

"Fey," Duncan said, beckoning me. "The Hand's favoured fey. Hundreds of them, I'd wager."

He must've read the shock on my face because he finished with a twisted comment. "Not the army you were expecting, was it?"

No, I thought. *It wasn't.*

Gyah had said to listen and get information, I just didn't expect I'd have found out what had become of all the missing fey taken by Hunters. In my mind, I imagined them harvested for blood and discarded. Turned out I was wrong. But until I got more information, I decided to keep it to myself. Knowledge was only powerful when it was true. For all I knew, Duncan could've been luring me because maybe he sensed my change of desires.

It certainly worked.

I would've expected Duncan to leash me with iron as we ventured through the endless corridors of Finstock. Instead, he allowed me to walk freely, likely because he knew I wouldn't try and escape, and also that I understood the threat of Hunters that filled the fortress like ants across rotting food.

"I'll permit you four questions," he said, words echoing up stone corridors, scaring bats out from the alcoves above us.

I skipped a step, not wanting to fall behind for fear a Hunter would snatch me from the shadows. Night had fallen on Finstock, which meant I had been asleep for a *long* time. Outside the narrow-slitted windows all I could see was the dark sky and the dancing tongues of mist which clung to the empty courtyard.

"What?"

"Three left," Duncan said, amusement dripping from his deep tone.

"Where is everyone?" I asked, mind racing. I silently scolded myself for wasting yet another question on something so pathetic, but it was a genuine thought. Unlike when we arrived, there wasn't a Hunter in sight.

"Evening worship. And if I don't show my face I may be disgraced by the Hand before we even have the chance of reaching Lockinge. It's unbecoming for a Hunter to miss prayer, no matter the reason."

His short reply only conjured more questions. I felt as though I was reaching in a river for gold, unsure which lump to pick out of the bunch.

"I didn't realise the Hand was such a devoted follower of the Creator."

"He isn't." Duncan's jaw tensed, muscles feathering. Whereas I studied his face to see if it provided me any information beyond words, he only looked forward. His stare fixated ahead as though I was not by his side at all.

I was not a religious person, nor had Father been. Growing up in a household where Father scorned the Creator, rather than praised Him, it had made me look at the stories as no more than what they were.

Fiction.

The teachings of the Creator, the humans' god, were preached within schools and whispered about during holy sabbats that I never found myself joining. The humans and the fey didn't worship the same god; the Creator and Altar were different beings. Altar... the very god who'd graced me with his presence within Welhaven, tearing down his place of worship as my own father's blood spoiled his holy place.

"So you're cultists," I said. "Crazed people who worship a god who would smite them down with sickness and plague if given the choice. A cult of blood-thirsty humans, who follow the Creator in a twisted way that the teachings never suggest."

"As I just said, we don't put our belief in the Creator." Duncan paused in his walking, stopping suddenly.

"Well I don't imagine you worship Altar, considering you hunt his children for sport. Or am I wrong, and this is all some big twisted game?"

"Ah, fourth and final question." Duncan began walking again, his pace quickened this time as we split from the corridor and began our descent down a twisting staircase. The walls were narrow, so much so that I felt as though they pushed in from either side, restricting my breathing. I had to hold my hands out at my sides, steadying myself against the rough stone wall to prevent me from falling down. One wrong step and I hardly believed Duncan would break a sweat trying to stop me from tumbling down to the bottom.

"Then who do you worship?" I asked, chasing Duncan around the twisting steps until we finally reached flat ground.

"You will see."

A shiver ran across my skin at his words. "When?"

"Tonight. I would like you to join me for this evening's worship." Duncan shot a look back at me, gesturing to an arched, doorless frame in our direction. Beyond was the courtyard and a dazzling glow of warm, orange light through yet another archway further away. "Once we are finished you will be taken to see your friends. Then, as soon as Althea is in a position to travel, it's back on the road for us."

I thought the heavy thumping was coming from my chest as I stared, in wonder, towards to the glow. But it was not my chest. It came from the ground, a thundering of feet as Hunters stomped in unison.

"Quick," Duncan said, grin long and sly. He reached for me, fingers grasping my bare wrist. It was his touch that shocked me more than anything he'd said. The mention of prisons beneath castles and hundreds of captured fey. Gods and worship. It was the gentle grasp of his hand as he wrapped fingers around my wrist like a bracelet, a completely contrasting touch from that which bruised my jaw when he held me in the chamber room. "Tonight is a special mass, for we have a blood rite to witness."

I couldn't have refused even if I wished to.

Duncan guided me into the chilly courtyard, towards the glow of the door on the other side of it. I almost choked on the thick, incense-filled air; it climbed up my nose and dug deep into my throat, making every inhale feel like breathing underwater, and the exhale no better.

We waded through the short hallway that soon opened up into a room no bigger than the chamber we had left. Except this room was full of bodies. Hunters filled every possible space, each fixated on the podium raised at the far end. Without the countless candles that dripped wax down the walls and from the ceiling, it would've been impossible to see what happened inside. But the horror was illuminated in a red glow that danced off the dark, maroon habits worn by the people lined up like cattle upon the podium.

"–Duwar has been kept, starved, and broken, in a prison its own kin had forged. Tricked, it was discarded into hell with no hope to escape. Alone for no one to hear its crying pleas for forgiveness to the very ones who banished it into the dark place. Until Duwar was heard again, a small whimper in the shadows that the Hand had listened to, whispers full of promise–"

An old man spoke amidst the line of cloaked figures. His back was bent at an odd angle, as though he carried the weight of the world atop him. White hair fell in clumps from his head, knotting with the beard that hung down to the swollen belly within his plain brown habit held together with a frayed piece of cord. He swung a brass chalice on the end of a chain that spat out streams of smoke that coiled around his stout frame as he called across the crowd.

"Keep quiet and listen," Duncan murmured into my ear, sending a shiver down my spine. "This wouldn't be the place to draw attention to yourself."

I forced down the bile that crept up my throat, wondering why Duncan would even care to give me such a warning. But that thought didn't last long as I focused back on the words the old man continued to recite.

"You know what must be done for Duwar's sustenance," he wailed, bloodshot eyes scanning for a crowd as though he could hardly see an inch before him. "We must keep Duwar fed whilst we wait for its return as ordered by its voice. All hail Duwar, and the blessed mouthpiece they chose for a vessel."

"Duwar," everyone but Duncan and I repeated, as though entranced by the old man. "Duwar."

"Let the rite begin."

He stepped back, gesturing for the line of veiled beings, the same I'd seen walking within Finstock upon our arrival. There were five of them, each a different height than the one next to them.

"Kneel," the old man demanded, voice cracking against incense-spoiled air.

And they did, maroon habits kicked out around their feet as they got down onto both knees.

"What's going on?" I asked.

"Just watch," Duncan said, gaze fixed on the podium. A worried line formed between his brows which drew down into a frown. It was then I noticed that everyone else around us was muttering prayers beneath breaths. Everyone but Duncan.

"Oh, forgotten Duwar," the priest began again as the veiled figures reached for something on the ground before them. I couldn't see over their heads what it was they grabbed for until they each raised their arms up, hands held high to the sky. Across both palms they balanced a knife, one crafted from a dark dull metal that I'd not seen before. It seemed to swallow the light from the room, not even reflecting the glittering candlelight that haloed around them.

"Long have you been kept from this realm, from the hearts and minds of those who care for you. Patience is a gift only for a god, and a gift that you hold far greater than your kin. For a time is coming, and you will be brought redemption by your own hand, a second chance against those who scorned you; who locked you away; who kept your potential from us."

The five figures twisted the daggers until the sharp edges were pointed down from the sky. They each held a hilt in both hands with a sure, strong grip.

"There will be a time when you will be free again, but until we are graced with your presence…" The crowd seemed to inhale at once, everyone waiting on the old man's words with bated breath. "… *feed*."

The figures brought the daggers down simultaneously, slamming blades into their chests without word or sound. Where screams should've sounded, only silence replied. One by one they slumped forward – *dead* – as the crowd of Hunters watched, continuing their prayers. Then the room exploded in bloodthirsty chants of a name over and over.

"Duwar, Duwar, Duwar."

The brush of cold lips tickled my ear. I couldn't even flinch. My body was frozen in shock, my mind wondering if this was what my father had once done. The thought sickened me. The old man writhed before the blood-leaking bodies, arms held high, as he muttered strange words to himself. Every now and then he scooped up blood with trembling hands and doused his body in it.

"This is disgusting," I said, finding only that word coming to mind.

"Those with a belief are known to do desperate things," Duncan whispered in return. "Have you seen enough?"

I nodded, unable to blink or make a sound. All I wanted to do was leave, to rid my nose of the smell of blood by inhaling deeply out in the fresh air.

"Good," Duncan said, hand pushing at my back as he urged me out of the room, all without a single Hunter looking our way. "Now, are you certain you still wish to meet with the Hand?"

There was a warning hidden beneath his words, a double-edged threat that would have sliced deep no matter how he said it. It was as if he dove into my mind and retrieved thoughts I believed I hid from him.

Duncan didn't wait for my reply. He guided me away from the ominous chanting, back out into the fresh air. As I inhaled lungs full of air, riding the stench of incense and the taste of blood from the back of my throat, I couldn't help but cling to one important fact.

Duncan hadn't joined in with the prayers. He hadn't uttered a single word.

It was as if he was warning me of the nest of vipers before I stuck my hand in. But why?

CHAPTER 12

"If I had known we were surrounded by cultists I would have preferred to be left at death's door."

Althea looked terrible. Her skin was as pale as the sheets she lay on, although I couldn't discern if that was from the iron poisoning flooding through her blood or the information I'd unloaded after Duncan had brought me to her. Strands of poppy red hair spread across the pillow beneath her, loose curls stuck to her damp, glistening neck.

She'd already been awake when Duncan had practically pushed me within the chamber room, locking the door behind me. Gyah had looked up with golden eyes brimming with concern, fingers gripped on Althea's shoulder as though I'd interrupted a moment of privacy. She removed her hand quickly, but not before I noticed.

I'd proceeded into a breakdown of everything that'd happened. Their expressions were stoic until I finally drew a breath at the end of my tale. Not once did they interrupt me, not until I was completely empty of news.

"And you've never heard of the god Duwar before?" I asked, watching as both Althea and Gyah shared a look of confusion.

"I was hoping you would have had the answer for us, Robin," Althea said, wincing as she pushed herself into a sitting position despite Gyah quietly insisting she stayed lying down. "Humans are known for their strange beliefs and idolism of the Creator. But no, I have never heard of this Duwar before."

"Well, it must mean something to them." Gyah gestured to the door and the many Hunters beyond. "To take your own life in the name of belief shows that this Duwar is important. More than just a name and story."

"Or they are just the crazed fuckers we have always seen them as," Althea added, brows furrowing as she tried to shift her body to get comfortable.

"Except they helped you," I reminded, taking me back to another point of the conversation. I thought that admitting it aloud would help make some sense as to why Duncan would willingly heal a fey when he was personally funded to see them captured, slaughtered and stolen. "Now we know what happens to the fey who the Hunters capture. This Below, or whatever Duncan referred to the prison as, it sounds like there are hundreds of fey stuck there."

Althea chewed her cracked lip, contemplating the news. "I think we need to take caution with everything Duncan says. He is our enemy, he could be playing a game–"

"Duncan doesn't play games," I said, almost too quickly. Both women shot me a look, making me glance down to my fidgeting hands. "I just think there is some weight to what he said. If there are fey in Lockinge, it's about time someone does something to save them."

Althea narrowed her hazel eyes at me, studying every subtle detail of my face. "What point are you trying to make, Robin?"

"I don't know what I am trying to say. I think there is a lot we don't know here," I said, picking at the frayed hem of my shirt. "I am merely trying to make sense of this."

Yet in the back of my mind I knew what I was thinking. If there were fey imprisoned in the human capital, could I free them? Maybe my hysteria led me into this path for a reason – saving the fey.

"Aren't we all." Gyah pressed a hand to her head as though in pain. "All I care about is getting as far away from here as possible. Whatever they believe, I say let them, as long as we are at a distance."

"Robin," Althea said, snatching my attention away from a point on the wall which I had become entranced by. "If there is a chance to leave, we do so together. You understand that, right?"

"I think you're wasting your breath, Althea," Gyah interjected. "Robin had made his mind up long before this moment. Hadn't you?"

I would only admit to myself that, for the first time since this plan had somewhat formed in my head, I was ready to turn my back on the idea and return to Wychwood. But for Father's sake, for the vengeance he deserved, I would not.

"I need to go."

"What did I say!" Gyah said, laughing, but not from humour.

"Not for the Hand. I understand that idea was stupid," I said, staring them both down, refusing to look away. I needed them to see just how serious I was. "But what if I could find a way to free the fey?"

"We can't be sure if Duncan is lying or not, not without seeing it for ourselves," Althea said, brows lifting as she figured out she'd walked into my web.

"Exactly why I should still go," I said.

"Then we will come too," Althea confirmed, matter-of-factly, sitting up in the bed but wincing as pain coursed through her.

"You are in no position to go anywhere right now," Gyah groaned, lifting the bedsheet to look at the wound upon Althea's thigh. "Will you ever listen to me, Althea? For your own sake, if Robin wants to stay then so be it. But I cannot allow you to be here a moment longer than necessary. It is not safe. That is what I was hired for. What I was born for, to protect your family."

Althea rolled her bloodshot eyes, patting Gyah's hand where it rested on the bed beside her. "If the tables were turned,

I would only hope Robin would be saying the same, Gyah. I cannot just forget about him, especially now the Hunters' reckless and homicidal actions have only been confirmed as truth. Not to mention these imprisoned fey."

I shuffled forward, taking her hand in mine. "Althea, Gyah is right. We don't have enough information to rely on Duncan's word."

"At last, some sense," Gyah barked.

I shot her a wary glance, knowing she spoke too soon. "You both need to leave for Wychwood. Gather the numbers and prepare to help with freeing the fey."

"What about your army?" Gyah asked. "And Doran?"

A creeping chill passed down my neck, turning my skin to layers of gooseflesh. "What good is an army if I have no one to fight for."

Neither spoke back to that, only shot one another a look that suggested I was right. After a pause, Althea cleared her throat and spoke.

"Robin, see if you can get more confirmation about what waits in Lockinge. No decision will be made yet, and Altar knows I'm in no position to run either," Althea said, gesturing to her leg, lip curling over teeth at the smallest of movements. "Next issue is how we are going to escape here in the first place. We can't just run away with these cuffs on. The fact I'm powerless, and currently riddled with pain. I wouldn't make it far. Even if I wanted to go I couldn't. It is not a choice."

"And what about your family?" I asked; the question had been haunting my mind since we were in that rocking cage. "Surely they'll know you are missing and send aid for you."

Althea nodded. "If we stay here long enough it will only be a matter of time before they find us. But the Hunters know that. They are far from stupid, and I know that they will already be planning their next move. We will be long gone by the time my family can help, unless–"

"Unless we can stall." Gyah leaned forward, a smile lifting the corners of her full lips, eyes glittering with mischief. "I can certainly come up with a few ideas that would push back our departure from Finstock!" She laughed with pure joy, latching onto the first true potential of getting free. "The Hunters will not stand a chance if Queen Lyra sends a party after you. After your brother's passing, she will not risk the death of another child."

"How long until they realise you are missing?" I asked Althea, unsure what answer I wanted to hear.

She shrugged, the simple movement taking a lot of effort. "Days, two at most. Less most likely. Knowing her lack of trust and our failure to return after we told her we were trailing you to Icethorn, she would have had her own scouts following us. Her soldiers likely walk on Durmain ground as we speak."

A strange and sickly mix of relief and disappointment twisted in my gut. On one hand, for their sake, I desired for aid; no matter how their company eased the situation at hand, I would've preferred both to be far away from this twisted hell. But I also needed Duncan's answers.

Doran Oakstorm had to pay for what he did, but my plans were shifting with the tide. If the Hand didn't offer me an army, I'd take one for myself. That only worked if Duncan had told the truth about the fey in Lockinge.

"Then that's what we do," I agreed. "Wait until the rescue party comes and you – *we* get away."

There was no ignoring the way Althea's shoulders relaxed as relief settled over her. Forcing a smile, I fought hard to make sure my eyes screamed with sincerity, but one glance at Gyah and I could see that she didn't believe the mask I put on. She kept silent though, which I was thankful for. Gyah knew I would not go. Althea, perhaps, wished to believe I would give up on this path so easily.

You would be wrong, friend.

"I feel like death chewed me up, spat me out and then came back for seconds." Althea lay back, closing her eyes with a slight hiss through her teeth. "Allow me to be the bossy princess I was destined to be and let me sleep. This salve is wearing off as quickly as my nerves and I admit I cannot cope with the pain."

"Let me help you," Gyah said before Althea finished her next breath, reaching for the brown-glass pot of lumpy cream liquid that rested upon the oaken drawers at the bedside. And Althea did not refuse. "It would be wrong to allow such a *bossy princess* to apply her own medicine. How very beneath you."

"Gyah, never in all the years I have known you, have you harboured such sarcasm," Althea retorted. "It suits you."

"Robin is rubbing off on me," Gyah said with a smile, throwing back the sheets to reveal an angry, yellow, wet wound across Althea's thigh. Her grin faltered the moment her golden eyes laid upon Althea's wound. Even now, remnants of the Hunter's salve were dried across her skin. The sheets were stained green with pus that seeped slowly from the dark wound, but it was the smell that had my empty stomach nearly spilling what little was left across the floor.

"It doesn't feel right not knowing what is in this." Gyah dug her fingers into the pot and pulled out a glob. Carefully she slopped it atop of the wound, whispering an apology as Althea released a long curse.

"Not like there is much chance for me to be concerned." It was clear Althea was in more agony than I first imagined. Red-hot veins spread from the wound, the skin around it inflamed and leaking. "The relief it gives me is far stronger than the pain that iron bolt offered."

I moved to the side of her bed, carefully brushing red strands of hair from her forehead as Gyah worked at covering every ugly inch of the wound with cream. "I may not trust a single person outside that door, but I *do* believe they won't let you die on their watch. You, Althea Cedarfall, are far too valuable."

"My blood is valuable," Althea corrected.

"You are valuable," Gyah looked up, mouth drawn with tension.

Althea let the words settle over her, more so the emotion behind them. If I noticed, so did she.

"I need more time to speak with Duncan, one-to-one," I said, feigning confidence when the idea of being in a room with him again displeased me. "He has answers, and seems to be willing to share them."

"He shouldn't be trusted," Gyah said, as if that was a fact I hadn't already worked out.

"Is that why you left me with him this morning?" I replied, watching heat flood Gyah's cheeks. "If Duncan wanted me dead, or any of us, it would have been done. That must stand for something."

"Be wary," Gyah murmured, focusing back on the task at hand. "I believe Duncan has a lick of restraint, but that doesn't negate from the fact that he is the most dangerous of them all."

"Is that why you left me with him?" I asked, eyes narrowed. "Because you sense he has control over his desire to harm me?"

"No. I didn't realise he would stay behind. He took me to Althea, we left you in the room. If I'd known he was going to come straight back to you, I would never have left." Gyah stiffened. "He offered to take me to Althea, and as much as I care about you, she is my duty…"

My duty and my pleasure. The words, Erix's words, rocked through my core. They pierced my heart, reminding me just how shattered and broken it was.

I lowered my head, not wanting them to see the shift in my mood. "I understand. But I also think Duncan is different from the other Hunters." I blinked, visions of the hungry expressions that stained the many faces of the Hunters as they watched the five figures take their own lives filled my head.

"Regardless if he prays to Duwar or not, he *is* still one of them," Althea hissed, followed by another breathy apology from Gyah.

There was nothing likable about Duncan, but I still found myself hoping that his control over the Hunters in Finstock remained long enough for us to survive whatever was to come. Whatever this Duwar stood for, I was willing to bet that the hate for our kind was mixed within the faith. It was an unconfirmed hunch, one I couldn't put aside. There would come a time when answers would be required. We needed to know more about the Hunters and Duwar before breaking bread with the mouthpiece of the so-called god that drove people to end their lives in his name.

Perhaps Duncan had those answers. He wanted to show me the blood rite for a reason. Maybe as a warning, or maybe something more. There was only one way to find out.

"Can I sleep now?" Althea asked, voice a murmur, her eyes already closed. "You both should rest too. We need as much strength as possible."

Without opening her eyes, Althea patted her hand across the bed until her fingers slipped over Gyah's arm. She grasped her, brows furrowing and pale lips parting. "Just… do not leave my side, Gyah."

Gyah took a sharp inhale of breath, sucking air through her teeth before replying. "I wouldn't dare."

"Then I do not need to order it?"

"No, it would be a wasted one," Gyah replied. "I will not be going anywhere. I said it is my duty."

"Duty…" Althea huffed, a weak smile presenting itself across her beautiful face. "You make it sound like I am forcing you."

I turned my head, unable to watch the moment. It was too familiar, the tension raw and tender, reminding me of the man I left behind – the one who left me.

It didn't take long for Althea to find sleep. She slept before she would've heard Gyah's reply. But I did. It settled over me, words which were not meant for me still made me feel as though I was enveloped in a warm embrace, whilst taunting me and my past.

"It is both my duty" – Gyah lifted Althea's knuckles against her lips – "and my pleasure."

CHAPTER 13

Finstock, among many things, was a silent place. Even with the stone-cold rooms full of humans there wasn't a sound. It made falling asleep surrounded by enemies an easy feat. Althea, Gyah and I had managed to sleep in the same room as it became apparent that no one was coming to separate us.

At the arrival of dawn the next day, the serenity ended.

When the screams began, it shattered the illusion of being alone. The sound clawed into my consciousness and dragged me, unwillingly, from the dreamless state I'd found myself in.

It was Gyah who woke first, urging us all awake with her sudden shout of dismay. "Do you hear that?"

I rubbed sleep from my eyes, glancing at Althea who did the same. Colour had returned to her skin, the apples of her cheeks flushed red once again.

"I thought I was dreaming it." Althea pushed herself to a sitting position with less effort than the night before.

Gyah raced to the glassless window and was about to speak until her eyes settled upon something that caused her distress. She clapped a hand over her mouth, stifling the swear that clawed out of her.

I joined her side in an instant, shoulder to shoulder, as my eyes fixed upon the cause of commotion.

Fey. There were three of them, carted within a wheeled cage, surrounded by the stern-faced cultists. And they were screaming, begging to be freed.

Gyah slammed a palm into the wall, almost cracking stone. "This cannot be happening."

"What?" Althea called over, voice strained and pleading. She couldn't stand from the bed to see what was happening outside. If she had, iron cuff or not, I imagined an inferno would've devoured the world.

"They have fey captives outside," I explained, unable to take my eyes off the three horror-stricken, tear-streaked faces of the prisoners. The fey wailed like cats, each clinging onto one another as though they tried to keep afloat within stormy seas.

But that wasn't what sickened me to the core.

"They are…" My voice broke, unable to finish as bile raced up the back of my throat. I had to swallow it down, otherwise the little food we'd been given would've been wasted.

"Robin." Althea's tone was commanding. "They are what?"

It was Gyah who answered, her voice a simmering growl.

"Children." Gyah's palm became a fist as she punched the wall. Bone cracked against stone and her knuckles came back torn and bloodied. "They have children."

I'd been unable to put it into words, as though the cuff around my neck had tightened to a point that speaking was impossible. I was choking on the reality of what I witnessed. Three children, no more than seven years of age, were being carted towards a camp of crazed, hateful cultists.

"We have to do something," Althea growled, half from anger and the rest from pain as she swung her legs over the side of the bed. She sat on the edge, wild red hair hanging on either side of her shoulders as she fought to calm her breathing. "I refuse to sit in this room and listen to whatever end awaits them within this hellscape. Robin, help me up."

I didn't need to be told twice. Moving to Althea's side, I allowed her arm to wrap around my shoulders so I could hoist her up. She trembled at my side yet held firm. Her strength was fuelled by the growing volume of the young feys' haunting cries as their cart grew closer. "Let me see them."

"I don't know what we can do, Althea," I petitioned, voice shaking as violently as my body.

"Take me to the window, Robin." Althea glowered.

Gyah was practically leaning out of it when we got to her side, face pressed between the narrow slit as she began screaming. "Touch them and I will bathe in your blood, you pathetic bastards."

Not a single Hunter turned to look at Gyah as they ran through the courtyard towards Finstock's entrance.

Althea's hand rested upon Gyah's shoulder. Her touch seemed to snap Gyah back out of the throes of anger that'd overwhelmed her. As if shocked, she turned to face Althea, eyes red and cheeks wet from the flow of persistent tears. "Children, Althea. They are going to hurt them."

"Not if they have magic." Althea closed her eyes, lips pulling into a thin line. Gyah hung her head, chin to chest, as her own quiet cries became sobs.

"If they did," I said, speaking the obvious, "they'd already be on route to Lockinge."

There was no arguing my point. If the fey had been brought here, unharmed, it was because they didn't have magic. That's when I saw the bulking shape of a man walking across the courtyard with slow steps. Across his shoulder was an axe, almost the same size as him.

These children would never make it out of Finstock, not with breath in their lungs.

"We need distract them," Althea said, conviction dripping from her tongue. "There is no other option."

Gyah began thrashing against the window, slamming fists into the crumbling brink wall beside it. Althea was screaming, waving desperate hands outside. I got to collecting empty bowls of gruel we'd been given to eat yesterday. I hoisted them over my shoulder, throwing them out and upon the Hunters below.

It was working – somewhat.

All I could think about was how I'd devour the entire castle in an ice-born storm if I had my magic.

Another figure caught my attention beyond the window, just as I was about to throw the last plate down on the Hunters. I recognised him instantly. Duncan. He ran, legs pounding across the ground as he moved past the excited Hunters who had gathered for the arrival; even from our view I could see that something was wrong. Then his own shouts drowned out that of the children.

"Calm yourself down, the lot of you!" Duncan's deep voice thundered through the courtyard, echoing up the grey, stone walls towards our perch in the chamber room. With long strides he was out onto the worn path that led to the fortress. As he passed the large Hunter with the axe, he barrelled through him, pushing him to the side and knocking the weapon onto the floor.

"Is that?" Althea muttered.

"Duncan," I confirmed, narrowing my gaze to watch as he unsheathed his sword, the black metal glinting as he raised it towards the Hunter who led the fey into Finstock's courtyard. We could no longer hear him from the distance, but his movements were dramatic and frantic. He swung his sword wide, pointing it at each and every Hunter as he berated them.

"They are all distracted," Gyah said, eyes widening as the desperate idea came to mind. "Now is the time to get out whilst we can."

Althea's weight was taken from my side as Gyah took over, half dragging her towards the locked door.

"We need to think about this. If we get out this door, there is a wall of Hunters to get through before we get to the children. Althea can hardly stand, and we have no weapons or power."

"It is worth a try," Gyah countered. "It *has* to be."

I carried on watching the scene unfold beyond the window as Gyah and Althea smashed the few pieces of aged furniture into the door. Perhaps I should've helped, but there was something about Duncan and his reaction that captured my interest.

A horror that mirrored my own.

Duncan then cocked back a fist and cracked it into the face of the Hunter he was shouting at.

"They're fighting," I snapped, fingers gripping the stone ledge as I watched Duncan take another Hunter by the scruff of the neck. In a single breath, Duncan had snapped his arm back and smashed the hilt of his sword into the side of his skull. The Hunter went down, falling to the ground like a sack of useless shit. Blood leaked from a wound, bone gleaming beneath the crimson stream as he cried in pain.

"We do not need a running commentary, Robin," Gyah snapped, smashing the splintered leg of a chair into the door. "Get over here now and help us break this door down."

"No... I – I don't think they need our help." I couldn't explain it, but Duncan was violently displeased with whatever was happening outside. If only I could hear him. "Duncan is doing something."

What was he doing? Fighting his own people. Waving his sword around, the point aimed at each Hunter who'd just been celebrating the arrival of the three fey children.

"Althea. Gyah," I shouted, finally drawing their full attention. "Duncan... he is fighting the Hunter. His own..." I could hardly make sense of what I saw, let alone put it into words. "Just come and see."

Perhaps it was realisation that they weren't going to break free from the room, or the fact that a Hunter was fighting against his own people, that had them clambering back to my side.

The atmosphere of the fortress had changed. The giddy, hungry excitement of the Hunters who watched the arrival of the fey became a sombre mood as Duncan stormed back towards the fortress. He held his sword at his side, face pinched with pure fury. Then, for a moment, he looked up to our window and caught my stare. I stepped back, stopped by Gyah, who watched over my shoulder.

Duncan turned back to his Hunters again, this time close enough that we could hear him.

"Have I not warned you simple fuckers enough? Children! No children are to be brought to my camp. Not now. Not *ever*." Hunters parted out of Duncan's way as though he was a wave of boiling water ready to devour anything in his path. "Look at you all. Salivating like desperate dogs. Don't give me a reason to put each and every one of you down."

"It's sustenance for Duwar!" I couldn't see who had shouted, but the comment drained the blood from my face, and Duncan's.

He stopped dead in his tracks, fists clenched at his sides as he pondered the words that had silenced the entire crowd. Behind him the caged fey had already begun to move towards the fortress, guided by two large horses. But the children no longer cried; from fear, or confusion, I wasn't sure.

"Sustenance?" If it was not for the silent, tense gathering who watched for Duncan's reaction, I may have missed his reply. "If that is what you wish to provide our God then offer yourself up. In fact, allow me to spill your life in his name. Bitter as your blood may be, Duwar would find your sacrifice most satisfying... as would I."

A deep growl vibrated beneath Duncan's threat. I half expected him to snap his teeth. Perhaps even grow horns or fangs as he clearly caged a beast within him.

"Are you lost for words now?" Duncan turned to the crowd. He waited, as we all did, for someone brave enough to shout or comment. But the fortress and the bastards it housed were deathly quiet. "That is what I thought, you *fucking* cowards. Prepare me a horse. Now. I'll return these children back to Wychwood, since I can hardly trust a single one of you to scrub your own teeth let alone follow a simple command."

His voice dropped, and what I noticed was his whisper was far more threatening than his shout. "The next time you bring a bounty here, make sure it has age on its bones. Or face the consequences."

I couldn't formulate a single sound as I watched Duncan clamber onto the back of a midnight horse that was efficiently provided to him with haste. Nor could Althea or Gyah. Duncan dug heels into the horse's side and galloped to meet the cage which had already begun pivoting back in the direction it had come.

"I can't believe what I am watching," Althea finally shattered the surreal atmosphere as the party rode off into the distance. "Too many times I have heard stories of Hunters maiming children. Never have I heard – let alone seen – this. Duncan just saved them."

"Blood stains Duncan's hands, no matter his views on the age of his victims," Gyah said, simmering as she watched Duncan fade into the distance.

"I know, but he is different. I don't trust him for that very reason, but I recognise his contrast to the other Hunters." Althea gestured to the bed with her spare arm, the other wrapped around Gyah's shoulders for support. "Before I fall, I suggest you get me back to that bed."

"But we were going to get out."

Althea silenced Gyah with a smile. "Until *that* Hunter returns, I don't wish to leave this room. He, as reluctant as I am to admit it, is the only thing keeping us safe. I suggest we keep rather quiet until he arrives back. Now is not the time to draw attention. Especially not with a fortress full of very pissed off, disappointed Hunters."

I nodded, fighting the urge to look back out in the distance to see where Duncan had gotten to. There was something different about him. And like Althea suggested, I should *not* trust him.

But why did I feel as though I could?

* * *

"You saved them."

The door hadn't even shut behind Duncan before the words tumbled out of my mouth. It was late into the night when the bobbing flame signalled his arrival in the distance. Althea and Gyah, in their attempts to ignore the sickening hunger that had settled over us, slept. Whereas I couldn't. So, I busied myself looking out of the window and felt the spark of sudden thrill as I watched Duncan return.

I had a feeling he'd come for us the moment he returned. I couldn't explain it, but I knew it long before the lock clicked, and the brass knob of the door turned to reveal him on the other side.

Perhaps Duncan didn't trust his own people not to take his absence as an opportunity to attack, to treat us cruelly, especially since we'd heard them sporadically throughout the day whispering hateful ideas on the other side of the door. Although, despite the terrible things they'd uttered, the door was untouched.

Gyah woke abruptly, eyes wide and frantic as she watched the Hunter enter without invitation. I raised a hand at her, standing between Duncan and the bed in which Gyah had been awkwardly sleeping over with her head in her arms as I said, "It is fine, Gyah."

"I didn't save them," Duncan replied matter-of-factly, dark forest eyes looking me up and down with distaste. "I simply postponed the inevitable. Gave them a few more years until the Hunters are welcome to chase them down like wolves. I don't allow youth into these walls."

"For a moment, I thought you might have morals."

Duncan smiled from ear to ear. "Believe me, Eldrae. Give it a few more years and I'd enjoy hunting those fey down."

"Monster."

"Says the one who can shift their form into a beast."

Gyah smiled back at him, more threatening than even Duncan could muster. "You speak such things to me as though I will not sip the blood from your veins and use your frayed skin to wipe my mouth clean."

"Now, now, Gyah." Althea blinked sleep from her eyes, wincing as she woke. "That is no way to thank our host."

Duncan ignored the comments and slander, looking bored and tired. He clearly didn't view us as a threat, entering the room alone with not a single weapon visible on his person. "Talking about being a host, I thought you would like something to eat."

"What we would like is to be let free," Gyah muttered.

"That's not a want you all share though, is it?" Duncan replied blandly, looking at me as though to prove a point. "Since your freedom is not on the table, food will be brought to you shortly."

"How generous." Gyah rolled her eyes, teeth still gritted together. "You came all this way to say that?"

"I came all this way to make sure you all still lived," Duncan said. "You know nothing of the limits of my generosity. Don't give me an excuse to make those limits clear. In all of Finstock's history you're the most comfortable prisoners who've ever stayed here. But if you'd prefer different treatment than these comforts and offerings of food, then please say the word. I'll hand over your care to any other Hunters beyond this room. Believe me, many would be honoured."

"The food," I added quickly, preventing Althea or Gyah from speaking first. "We happily accept your offer. Thank you."

My thanks were strained, and Duncan noticed.

"*You*," he spat, "will eat with me."

His words snatched the breath from my lungs. "Pardon?"

Duncan ignored me and my confusion, hardly even paying me any attention as he spoke to Althea and Gyah again. "I thought you'd like to know that we leave tomorrow. Finstock and its occupants are unhappy with my actions today and those loyal to me and my views are few and far between. Healed or not, we move on."

With that Duncan turned on his heel, stomping back towards the door without another word.

I looked to Gyah whose expression was thunderous, and then Althea whose face was unreadable, the visage of a future Queen able to hide her true feelings behind a mask, a mask I had not yet perfected.

"But Althea is not ready to leave," Gyah snapped as Duncan reached for the door. There was no denying the pleading in her tone.

Gyah didn't notice it, but Althea spared her a stare with wide, glistening eyes. She then squeezed Gyah's hand with lips pursed in silent thought.

"It was not an opportunity to argue," Duncan replied, not bothering to turn and face Gyah, who clearly was irked by his lack of respect or care. "Rest and enjoy the food that will come to you. I cannot promise another stop before we reach Lockinge. And where we are going, the concept of a meal for your kind is a rarity. Now you, Robin, follow me. I have more questions about why a fey would want to turn against his own."

My reply came thundering out of me. "I do not wish for that–"

"No?" Duncan huffed a forced laugh, turning the side of his face to flash the grin upon it. "Have you changed your mind, because if you have it's a little too late."

There was nothing I could say back to that. I caught Gyah's line of sight, her teeth gritted as she subtly nodded at me. Although she didn't speak, I knew the message she was trying to convey.

I needed to distract Duncan. If he wanted us to leave tomorrow, we needed to hold off in hopes that Queen Lyra had sent people after us. It was the only way of getting them away from here – getting us away from here.

"What's on the menu?" I asked, chin lifted as I took careful steps to follow Duncan.

"Something delicious no doubt."

My stomach rumbled at the comment, noticed by Duncan, who smirked to himself.

"You must be really pressed for company if you'd rather break bread with the very kind you hate?"

Duncan paused, so suddenly I almost crashed into his back. "Hate, yes. But I admit, Robin. The idea of your motivations is as intriguing as I find you."

CHAPTER 14

Duncan Rackley's skin was no stranger to scars.

His back was facing me as he tugged the dark tunic over his head, flexing the muscles across his shoulders and the constellation of marks upon them. He was covered in them from the base of his neck to the narrowed pinching of his waist.

I couldn't do anything but watch as he undressed before the rising wall of steam that danced from the tub's hot belly of water. I waited for him to say something. Anything. Instead, he treated me as though I was a ghost, stripping the items of clothing from his body until only the undershorts were left. Then he turned, looking over his broad shoulder at me as though he suddenly remembered my existence.

"Are you waiting for permission to sit?" His tone was dull and unbothered.

"I thought I'd been invited here for something to eat?" I retorted, trying to keep my gaze upon his instead of glancing down at his exposed skin.

"Help yourself, my leftovers are on the side board."

He gestured pathetically to the side of the room where, in fact, a plate of cheese, meats and half-eaten bread lay waiting.

"I think I will pass," I said, not wanting to move a muscle as Duncan continued to undress himself.

"Then the company will do," Duncan said, kicking the pile of his clothing out of the way before reaching a hand for the brass tub's edge. "And conversation. It's not every day I get the chance to speak with a fey so freely. Usually, the circumstances of their stay here are… less fitting for idle chatter. So, sit, eat if you want, and let's talk."

I didn't have to be told twice. Water sloshed as Duncan climbed into the tub, but I kept my focus on perching myself on the edge of the bed that waited on the other side of the room. Although I'd disregarded the offer of food, I took it anyway, inhaling the few bits left just to stifle the discomfort in my gut.

With each inhale I could taste the strong scents oozing from the bath, sweet lavender with a faint hint of something sharper. Sandalwood. I recognised the smell from an oil Father had used to tame his beard.

Duncan sighed slowly, lowering himself further into the brass tub, water sloshing over the lip until he was submerged up to his chin. His eyes were closed, the furrowed brow I'd grown used to seeing him with relaxed. The lack of him viewing me as a threat irked me more than it should, so did the concept I was only good enough for left overs. Once again, I waited for him to speak, to shatter this silence. It was clear that the quiet was something Duncan was used to, his own company enough to keep himself amused.

"You're different to them," I said with a mouth full of hard cheese. I was unable to sit in this awkward silence a moment longer. It was clear that Duncan wasn't going to break first as he relaxed in the warmed waters.

"Oh, do tell me more."

"I don't think I need to."

Duncan peered at me through one eye. "Is this because I don't permit the murder of children?"

So the children would've died here, if he didn't intervene.

I nodded, eyes falling upon Duncan's undershorts that now rested upon the stone-slabbed flooring. "I would've thought you'd send them to the… Below, or whatever you called it."

"The Below is a place for Fey with magic." Heat flooded my cheeks as I quickly looked away. "Trust me when I say death would be a better outcome then ever reaching the Hand's prison."

I couldn't imagine just how terrible of a place that was, if death was a kinder option.

"You didn't join in with prayer during the rite last night either," I said.

"So it's my lack of outwards belief which causes distress, Robin?" Duncan asked, wet arms holding on to the tub's edges as fat droplets of water fell from him. "The way I practice my faith does not make me any less of a believer than those who would wish to see blood spilled from innocents."

"You see fey children as innocent? Even if they are the kind your fellow cultists have spent years hunting?"

"I see them as children, nothing more. When I spoke of innocents, I was referring to those who sacrificed their lives in the name of our God with the belief of providing that god sustenance in return for a blessing." Duncan reached a hand towards a wooden stool that held jars filled with creamy liquids and bars of chopped soaps. "Now, if you wouldn't mind passing me the soap."

I almost choked on the picking of stale bread. "You're joking."

"Not at all," Duncan replied, smirking. "Unless you are going to insist I climb back out of this tub and get it myself."

I couldn't believe what I was doing as I stood from the bed and moved towards the stool where the bar of soap rested. But the concept of seeing Duncan without an inch of clothing on him had me doing exactly as he requested.

"Careful you don't drop it, Robin."

My mouth dried as I swallowed, thrusting the square soap above the tub where I let it fall from my hand with a splash.

"Oops," I muttered through a sickly sweet smile, returning to the seat at the end of the bed. My eyes fell on Duncan with distaste for a moment as he fished the bar out of the murky waters.

"If that's all you require of me, then I ask to be returned to my friends," I said. "The promise of dinner was rather disappointing."

"I'm far from done with you. My journey today has given me a chance to form a rather impressive list of questions I have for you. When I am done, only then will you be permitted to leave."

I leaned back on my hands, fingers clawing the material of the bed, as I regarded Duncan. "Then ask away."

"You have pointed out my differences, but I must say yours are also rather alarming." Duncan's arms moved beneath the water. I dared imagine what he was doing but I hoped it was something innocent. "You are not a full-blooded fey, are you?"

I shrugged. "Disappointed? Does it lower my value with the Hand?"

"Yes," Duncan replied. "And no."

There was no time to work out what he was agreeing or disagreeing with.

"The differences are subtle. At first, I could hardly tell. But you move like a human. Speak like one. I would sit next to you in a tavern and hardly notice if your hood was drawn over your ears."

His comment shouldn't have felt like an insult, but it did.

I tugged at the cuff around my neck. "Take this off and I will show you just how *fey* I can be."

"I don't doubt that for a second. So how did a man, torn between two realms, choose which side he wanted to be on?"

A scowl pinched across my forehead, my jaw clenching until my teeth felt as though they would be stuck together for an eternity. "I've chosen no sides."

"Well, you had me fooled. I thought you wanted to join us, work alongside the Hand in hopes he assists you with killing that fey king you've mentioned. Forgive me, but that seems to me as though you truly have picked a side. Unless your motivation suggests otherwise. So, are you ready to tell me why it is you wish to kill one of your own?"

"He is *nothing* like me." A shuddering growl emanated from deep within me. If the iron cuff was not around my neck I would've devoured this entire room in cold winds with a mere thought.

Duncan waved a hand, flicking water onto the floor. "There's a story there and I want to know it from beginning, middle, to end."

We studied each other. Duncan the Hunter, and me his prey. I toyed with the idea of lying, telling him a tale that didn't do justice to the truth. But what would have been the point? Although his company caused my skin to itch, I still needed him to trust me. For answers about the Below and the imprisoned fey, for one thing.

Duncan, in many ways, felt like the gatekeeper guarding what I desired most. If I wanted to make it to the Hand in one piece, with a lick of comfort for myself, Gyah and Althea, then I felt the truth was the best place to build foundations of trust. Or something close to it.

Duncan combed his fingers backwards through his length of dark hair until not a single strand covered his devilish face. "I am waiting…"

"The man I wish to see dead took the one important part of my life away from me. Stole it right in front of me." A sudden, harsh sadness made my throat thick and shoulders heavy. I felt Duncan's stare on me, but felt too cowardly to hold it now, as though the truth made me more vulnerable than the naked, unarmed Hunter before me. "He killed my father."

Duncan visibly paled, the corners of his lips turning down.

"Then we share something in common," Duncan said, voice quieter than it had been before. "The fey are also the reason behind my parents' death. Seems we share similarities after all."

Should I have apologised? It felt as though that was the right thing to say in that moment. But I swallowed that word down and kept it buried.

"So that is your motivation, the reason behind what you do?"

"Are my motivations not justified in comparison to yours?" Duncan sat up in the tub, the curves of his muscles etched into his frame like lines within stone. "Murder is murder, Robin. Your desire for it makes you a monster, just like me."

"And have all the fey you've hurt had a hand in your parents' death? Or do you just tell yourself that as you wash their blood from your hands?"

"I will give you some advice when speaking with me, Robin. Don't ask questions you will not like the answers to."

I scoffed. "That's a cowardly response."

"Says the man who cannot face a single person alone, who needs the support and aid of those he'd deem as enemies, just to complete a task that is seemingly impossible to do." Duncan suddenly stood from the tub, not bothering to cover the swing of flesh between his legs. I hardly had the chance to snap my gaze upwards. I fixed my eyes to his, not wishing to see his vulnerability. It gave him a sense of power between us, one I didn't like.

Duncan dripped a puddle of water onto the floor as he wrapped a towel around his waist. "Am I wrong, or right?"

"Doran is powerful."

"Are you not powerful?" Duncan questioned, fingers resting upon his muscular hips. "Robin, let me tell you something. Be grateful you have his name to remember. To focus on. Knowing the names of my parents' killers is not a luxury I've had. And a name is a powerful thing. I would give anything to know it. Instead, I'm left with nothing but choices, an unlimited list of potential names which I mark off with a bloody sword with each and every fey I kill."

I watched, speechless, as Duncan stood before me, exposed from the waist up.

"I can see that you have been hurt in the process," I said, eyes trailing the multitude of scars across his torso.

"Believe it or not, Robin, but the deepest scars are the ones you cannot see. And no, these are unrelated to what happened to my parents." His long fingers traced a jagged mark beneath his strong chest. "A story, perhaps, for another day."

A knock sounded at the door, snatching both our attentions. From the look on Duncan's face, it was unexpected. Holding the towel in a fisted hand, Duncan moved for the door and opened it to reveal a veiled figure carrying a tray of food. More cheese and breads, meats and fruit, a medley of delicious items that had my mouth watering and my mind distracted from the conversation we were just having.

"Ah, look at that. More food for you, Robin. You can save some leftovers for me this time." Duncan pushed the door wide, allowing the figure in. "Set it down upon the table, sister."

The hooded figure nodded, entering in a long dress that swished outwards with each footfall. She didn't jump, as I did, when the door slammed shut behind her. Even with her face covered in the light lace of the veil, I still felt her cold stare on me. Was she frightened, or did she hate me like the rest of the people in this fortress?

Duncan seemed unbothered by her presence as he wandered back towards the tub, pulling a new set of clothing from a pile as he began to dress himself.

"Thank you," I muttered, trying to see past the veil. I kept thinking about the five veiled figures who had driven knives into their own chests. Was she destined to do the same? Take her life in the name of a god that was unheard of by most?

Her reply came as a tip of her head, before leaving the tray beside me and backing away.

I focused back on Duncan who ran a large hand through his dark, wet hair until it no longer obscured his face. His skin glistened from the remaining beads of water. He ran the towel up and down his arms, the sleeveless shirt he wore exposing the strength beneath his carved muscles.

For a monster, he's undeniably beautiful.

The thought was only brief, lasting no more than a second before guilt sunk talons into my chest. A vision of Erix filled my mind, and by the time I looked back to Duncan it was with a gaze of dull and muted tones.

"Eat and bathe if you desire. Tomorrow will be our final day in Finstock before a long journey to Lockinge. I cannot promise comfort outside of these walls so enjoy it while it lasts."

The veiled woman lingered at the door as if waiting for Duncan's confirmation to leave.

"Is this not your room?" I asked.

"It is, on other nights, but tonight I have no use for it."

"I cannot work you out, Duncan," I said, feeling a swell within my chest.

Perhaps my honesty was paying off, making him trust me. If this was what was required of me, to get close to the Hand, then I would keep up this illusion for as long as required.

Duncan moved towards the woman by the door, replying proudly as though his words were meant for all to hear, "I'm not a puzzle to be pieced together."

I went to reply when I caught a flash of silver and the scratch of metal against flesh. The woman, shadowed behind Duncan's back, shifted her weight before he had the chance to act.

"I always thought you were fickle, but moving on so quickly, and with a Hunter no less, how *scandalous*," the veiled woman hissed.

The knife was held to Duncan's throat, edge pressed into skin, leaving a trail of red. The veiled figure didn't shake as she gripped the man, relying on the knife to keep him still and in place.

"Sister, is there a problem?" Duncan asked, far too calm for someone who had a knife held to his throat.

He could've broken free from her grasp with ease, until I realised that her other hand, hidden behind his back, also held a knife. Its sharp tip pressed against his spine. One wrong move and he would be left for dead, or immobilised.

"Not at all, sweetie," she replied.

What caused me fear was not seeing him die before me. I was used to seeing death up close and personal. But it was the voice, the familiar tone that had haunted the dark shadows of night for days after my abduction from Farrador.

"Briar?"

I prayed to whatever god would listen that I'd be proven wrong. But gods cared little about me.

The voice I had wished to never hear again replied. "Hello, Robin. Did you miss me?"

CHAPTER 15

Duncan was control, his face void of emotion as though two knives were not pressed into his skin. He regarded me from the door, forest-green stare intense and unblinking. I wished to share his calmness. My heart thundered in my chest, each beat threatening to snap my ribs in half.

"Is the cutlery truly necessary?" Duncan asked, peering down his sharp nose at the blade.

"You tell me, Hunter. Are you going to behave whilst I complete my hit?"

I almost expected Duncan to refuse her, to fight on my behalf. But it never came. Instead, he retreated into silence as he studied my entire body. "Ah, so you've come for the fey. How exciting."

It was far from exciting, if Duncan actually knew what Briar was and what she'd done.

"How did you find me?" I asked her, watching for any slight movement, my anxiety screaming a symphony within me. I was powerless and clumsy compared to Briar, who was a trained assassin initiated into the guild known as the Children of the Asp. I'd hoped that I had seen the last of her, since her benefactor was dead. Turns out I wasn't that lucky.

"I have always been watching you, Robin," Briar replied, veil fluttering with each breathy word she spoke. "It's what I do. Wait and watch until the time is right. I had a hunch I would be called to this task again. Call it… intuition."

"Doran sent you, didn't he?"

Duncan laughed, breaking the tension with his misplaced chortle. "The king sends a single person after you, Robin? Clearly, he doesn't see you as the same threat you see *him* as."

I scowled, stomach churning as I finally realised I was alone in this room. It was my own form of intuition, but I trusted that Duncan would do little to help me if – *when* – Briar was ready to strike.

"You laugh freely as though I do not hold a blade at your back and throat," Briar hissed at Duncan. "I would happily break my code and kill someone separate to my hit, payment or not. Someone would want your head, General Rackley. There would be coin to collect for your life, in fact, I have been hearing some rather disgruntled whispers about you today, Duncan."

"You don't scare me," Duncan said, leaning into the blade.

You should be scared. When Erix once asked me what my greatest fear was, I told him it was the dark, as if I were a child holding onto a pathetic horror. Now my answer was different. I feared the assassin who stood before me. Briar was horror in the flesh, a real-life monster with unlimited potential to kill.

Duncan was a fool to ignore that.

I blinked and saw a vision of Duncan's naked body and the scars scattered across his skin. It was no wonder he didn't flinch at the presence of her blades; he had clearly experienced many before.

"I don't care for fear, Hunter. I care for coin. And this time" – her head turned back in my direction; face still covered by the veil – "I will finish the task."

I stepped forward, bravery burning in my heart. The feeling was sudden, perhaps conjured by the feeling of having my back pressed up against a wall with no possibility to get away. If Duncan was not prepared to aid me, then I would have to do it myself.

"What have I ever done to you, Briar?"

The question hung in the air between us.

Briar slowly lifted the knife from Duncan's back and used the sharp tip to remove the veil from her face. That opened up the opportunity for Duncan to make his move, but he didn't. He kept still and comfortable, as though he enjoyed witnessing what was occurring, even with a blade to his throat.

Finally, I could see her. Dark, jade eyes brimming with arrogance. Her hair, still short and cut close to her head, had been slicked back from the veil she had worn. Her soft pixie-like features had not changed, still the same trusting face that had fooled us all, Althea more so than anyone.

"Nothing," Briar answered, grin lifting her pretty lips at both sides. "Don't let your ego run away with you. This is purely business."

She returned the second blade to Duncan's back without glancing away from me. "Except, between the three of us, I made a rather large discount this time round. King Doran believed the death of his son was fair trade for a discounted price. Of course, I was happy to oblige, just for the chance to *personally* watch the life drain from your face. It is frowned upon for an Asp to let a hit slip from the net, so to speak, and you certainly are one slippery fucker, Robin."

"And what would Althea say if she heard you speaking in such a way?" I questioned, hoping to see some sort of reaction. And there it was. The slight flinch of her stare and faltering smile. "I trust you already know she's here," I said, taking the moment of her distraction to look for something, *anything*, to use as a weapon against her. "It must've taken true restraint to come for me before visiting her... although I can confirm she doesn't share the same eagerness to see you."

Duncan's eyes widened as he filed that piece of information away, silently connecting the dots.

"When I am finished with you, I will visit her. Consider it my reward," Briar replied, gaze unseeing as she slipped into a daydream. It only lasted a moment before she shook herself out of her thoughts and regarded me with a snarl once again.

"Your quarrel is with him, and I see no need for spilling unrequired blood. I just had the floor cleaned." Duncan murmured.

I expected Briar to refuse him, but she didn't. "You can go then."

She lowered the blades, one by one, and Duncan stepped aside. "Not worried I'll come back with a league of Hunters?"

"Even if you did, I will not be long."

Duncan tipped his head in a strange bow. "If there is room for requests, I ask that you try to keep his death as... tidy as possible. Not that it matters, but it would save the clean-up."

"Go," Briar growled. "Now."

He didn't wait around.

"Duncan," I spluttered as his hand reached for the doorknob. I had become invaluable to him so quickly. When he looked up at me as though he had completely forgotten my existence. Until he winked, mouthing *good luck* before slipping out the door and closing it behind him.

Then it was the two of us, just like it had been in my room before she drugged me, and in the dark pit that I had become prisoner in. Briar and I were alone, but this time felt different.

I was confident it would be the last time.

My lack of hope dropped in my stomach like a rock. If this was the end, I would drag it out for all its worth.

"Since we last saw each other it has become painfully obvious that you have a way with losing the men you spend time with. Tarron, well, we both know how that turned out. That Hunter left the room without much effort. And Erix, oh yes, I heard all about him. What a terrible thing to lose your last living relative to the same hands which had been all over you. There is something both tragic and poetic about it."

Bile crept up my throat, burning with every inch. "If you are here to point out my terrible taste in men then I fear you are not getting paid enough."

"Oh, believe me, the price offered for you is handsome. Doran is keen to see you dead."

"A sentiment we share," I said. Then I ran. Not to Briar, but away from her, towards a side door around the edge of the bed. She sprung after me, leaping over furniture, fingers grappling air to get a hold of my shirt.

I made it to the door, barrelled through it, then wedged my body against the other side. A few times Briar tried to knock through, but I held firm, legs straining against the force.

"I expected a little fight from you, Robin. But not for you to run away," Briar sang, her voice slightly muffled by the wood between us.

I scanned what was a closet. There was no other way in or out. Which meant I'd literally run myself into a corner.

All I could think to do was stall, in hopes Duncan did return with Hunters. "Go on, tell me how much I am worth to him." I shouted as the tell-tale scratch of a blade worked grooves into the door. "I admit I'm flattered to know it is enough for you to give this your best go again. Did you know I am a king myself now? I could rustle up some coin, perhaps even best his price, and turn the hit back on Doran."

Briar laughed, her cackle raising the hairs on the back of my sweat-damp neck.

"No one in Wychwood doubts your status, but you are a king of barren lands and empty homes. Imeria castle sits vacant even after all this time since your claiming the Icethorn power. You are wealthy in loneliness, that is all. You turned your back on your destiny and wandered into the hands of Hunters. There is nothing you could offer me to stop the inevitable from happening."

She barged into the door again. I pushed my hands on either side of the wall, trying to add more pressure to stop her.

But guilt tried to rear its ugly head within the storm of emotions riling through me. However, it was the easiest of my feelings to handle. How could I feel guilty for turning my back on a place that I had no personal ties to? No family or connections beside the whisper of my mother and her rule.

"Briar the snake, queen of giving up on all who love her," I called back. "What is it you rule over beside the hunger for coin?"

I couldn't see her smile, but heard it in the lightening of her tone. "Pity, you have *such* a way with words. Shame you will not be speaking them much longer. In fact, any last words whilst the opportunity presents itself?"

"Fuck you," I screamed.

A sudden, grounding calm rushed over me, dousing the flames of my anxiety with a blanket of cold ice. If this was the end, I was that much closer to seeing my father again. Would he be waiting for me in the realm of peace I longed for him to be in? Standing beside my mother as though they had never parted sides.

"It is almost a shame that I will not get the credit for killing you. An army races towards this place, and when they come, they will blame the Hunters for your death. But I suppose I can live with that, knowing my pockets are full and you are no longer a thorn in my side. Then they will kill everyone here and return Althea and her guard back to their home. And in time you will be forgotten. Doran may fill my pockets, but I owe him nothing. I'm simply saving him time, and resources." Her voice dropped to a whisper. Briar's mouth must've been so close to the door as she spoke her next words. "Erix is on his way to see you, I wonder how he'll react when he finds you dead. Will he be pleased I saved him a job, or angry that he didn't get the chance to destroy you himself."

"Erix." The blood rushed down from my head to my feet, making my body feel like it was sinking into the stone floor. "He is coming here?"

"He is. Followed me from Doran's door all the way to this one. Clearly, I was not trusted for the task entirely. I even contemplated letting Erix reach you first, letting him finish the deed but still taking the credit for it. Yet I could not give him such pleasure. He has a strong will even against the pressing force of his sire. Even I would not get in the way of a berserker, especially one like him. Sad you are going to miss him?"

I shook my head, fighting the urge to release the tears that clung to my lashes. Erix had been the one to murder my father. I should've hated him for it. But he was a puppet at the end of gold strings held by his father, warped and controlled. His will was not his own no matter how I longed for it to be different.

"When he finds your body, drained and empty, he will likely destroy this entire fortress before the Cedarfall soldiers arrive. I may even stay and watch. Nothing like some entertainment after a kill—"

I threw open the door, silencing Briar, whose wide eyes proved she didn't expect it. I reared my fist back, and sent it careening into her face. Once the crack sang, beautiful between us, knocking her back a step.

"Get on with it," I screamed, hands flexing at my sides, wondering if Erix was close enough to hear. Close enough to save me when no one else would. I may not have had magic to call upon, but my desperation crackled colder than any storm I could control.

Briar licked at her cracked lips, smearing blood across them.

A shiver raced up my spine and down my arms. I stayed looking at the door, gaze unflinching, ready to do anything to escape. That was when I felt it. The strange heat of the air, as if it had thickened in the time I'd been inside the closet.

It could only mean one thing.

"Briar," I said, a faint smile creasing my face. "I hope it hurts."

"Killing you?" she said, preparing her blades, her legs bending at the knees like a cat to pounce.

"No. I hope it hurts when you burn."

The door exploded inwards in a cloud of splintering wood, stone and *fire*.

In a single moment the world rocked beneath my feet. I felt the slice of a blade but had no time to worry if it was fatal as I tumbled to the ground, covering my head with my hands. Shards of rubble rained down upon me; it was all I could feel. That and the tongues of vicious flames that lapped at the room, coming from the fey who controlled them.

My ears were ringing, screaming, as I tried to shield my head from the debris of the explosion. I risked a glance upwards. Standing in the torn hole that had once been the door, amongst rubble and stone that burned with red-hot fire, was Althea. Her face was contorted by the shadows cast upon her by the flames, a goddess of destruction and hell, eyes pinned to the cowering body of the girl on the floor between us.

"And burn you shall," Althea Cedarfall spat, fire dancing around her feet like loyal serpents of ruby and gold. "*Bitch*."

CHAPTER 16

Fire hissed over Althea's cuffless skin. It wrapped around her neck like jewellery of amber and ruby, dripping from her, leaving her clothes unmarked. Although the floor beneath her charred and cracked as though not worthy of her protection, flames destroying everything she desired.

"Ever the goddess I have known," Briar strained, pushing herself from the ground to look at Althea. Her skin was stained with ash, her face red and blistered from the heat.

"Robin," Althea commanded, not once taking her eyes from Briar where she cowered on the floor. "Come."

I didn't waste a moment for questions or thought. With haste I moved towards her, careful to dance around the fire and rubble which seemed to litter the room entirely. As I reached the broken entryway, I glanced back at Briar, and a smile of pure relief lifted my lips.

"Seems you have failed again," I said, breathless from relief. "You should have given up the first time."

Briar jeered, spit flying from her paled lips. But there was nothing for her to say. No words that could harm me now. Not with Althea between us, no longer weakened by iron.

But how?

Gyah was waiting in the corridor, eyes narrowed with intent. She spared me a sour glance, both hands curled into fists, then flicked her gaze to the third person. Duncan, leaning against the wall upon one bent knee as though a powerful fey didn't ravage his fortress before him.

"You set her free," I said, moving beside him; my legs felt shaky and weak. I leaned against the wall and coughed, trying to clear the smoke from my lungs, my eyes burning.

"I did. Only for a moment though," Duncan said, revealing Althea's cuff in his hand and spinning it with his fingers. "Once the threat is dealt with, her cuff will be returned. For now, do not distract me from the show."

I looked back to the room, where Althea stalked forward, a figure bathed in flames. Her hands were contorted into claws at her sides, encouraging a line of fire to snake towards the outmatched assassin.

Briar choked on the smoke, tears streaming down the soot that covered her face in clear lines. Determination did not wither from her stare as she watched Althea, princess of flame and fury, walk towards her.

"I am glad you were foolish enough to come," Althea began, head tilting to the side ever so slightly. "I have wasted many moments thinking of ways to reach you, but here you are. So effortless, so easy."

"You hate me," Briar groaned, conviction creasing her once trusting face. "And I do not blame you, though I hoped you would see that this is purely business, my darling. Nothing more."

"I am not your *anything*."

"You were once." Briar was clawing into Althea's emotions. "How have your feelings changed so quickly? Or perhaps they have not, deep down you must still love me."

Gyah growled at my side, deep and guttural, with teeth bared in Briar's direction. While Althea was free, Gyah still wore the iron cuff; it was the only thing stopping her from shifting into her beast and devouring Briar.

Down the corridor chaos distracted me as a wave of Hunters with drawn weapons ran into view.

Duncan sighed, pushed himself from his position, and raised a hand towards them. "Stop."

They did, reluctantly, slowing their pace with confusion shared between them. A few carried on, looking between Duncan and us with disgust. "You let one of 'em go free! She'll burn this entire place down before we get some control on them."

"Do you second guess my intelligence, Stamon?" Duncan snarled, lip curling.

The man who had spoken stepped back, head down but eyes looking upwards. "No, General."

"Search this fortress for any other intruders before I decide to point the blame on one of you for this cock up. Turn it upside down if you must." Duncan looked back to us. "Leave these fey to me."

The Hunters jumped at the scream that tore from the room. We all did. The Hunters turned on their heels and ran, a luxury I did not have.

Althea glowed a bright amber, skin molten fire and ruby hair shimmering. Her hand was outstretched, holding Briar by the throat where she dangled two feet from the ground, with eyes bulging and lips quivering.

The smell of burnt flesh thickened in my nose; there was no escaping the scent as it crawled down my throat and threatened to turn my stomach inside out.

Briar slapped and clawed at Althea as she pleaded for her life. But there was no stopping the princess, nor the flame that devoured Briar.

Briar's hair singed, skin peeling back, blood boiling. Ash fell from her like darkened snow, fluttering gently to the ground below her dangling feet. The sounds of crackling flesh and the cries of terror would haunt me for a lifetime. Even after Briar became still and soundless, it still echoed within my mind.

It didn't take long for Briar to die. Althea released her grip and the body crumpled to the ground in a heap of charred flesh and bone. She stood still, watching, as the fire died around her until not a lick of flame was left, extinguished with only the memory of smoke curling from the destruction within the room.

Gyah was the first to enter, wrapping her arms around Althea's back like a shield. I tried to follow, but Duncan stopped me by putting his arm in my way.

"Do you see the destruction of your kind now?"

I couldn't form an answer, not as Althea's silence turned into sobs that shook her entire body. Without Gyah to hold her, she would have fallen to her knees; I was sure of it.

"Is that why you let her go free?" I asked. "To prove a point?"

"No," Duncan said, slowly lowering his arm. "I didn't know the limits of this Briar and her powers. For all I knew she could've caused a real headache for my men, and I would like to keep as many of them alive as I can. I think the saying is 'fight fire with fire'? However, if anyone else asks, you can use your excuse if you prefer."

With that, Duncan moved away from me, leaving me to my own confusion, as he wandered into the room with an iron cuff still held in his hands.

It pained me to watch Gyah quietly console Althea who trembled within her hold. The burned remains of Briar still hissed with smoke like the forgotten cinders in a hearth during a winter's morning.

"Impressive," Duncan said, standing before them both. "The Hand truly will be pleased to meet someone with power such as yours. Now, time to put this back on before my men return."

Gyah glared at him, snarling protectively like a cat over a bowl of fresh cream. Her reaction was wasted, for Duncan didn't flinch. Instead, he held the collar out with confidence and patience.

Althea looked over her shoulder at him, eyes red-rimmed and cheeks wet. "Do it before I have the chance to change my mind."

Duncan smiled. "Your cooperation is gallant."

"Now is our chance to go, Althea," Gyah said, pleading with wide eyes. "We can leave."

"Actually, *now* is not the time to be brave," Duncan said slowly, reminding Gyah of who stood before her.

"I don't have the energy," Althea murmured, face pale and limbs shaking. She shifted out of Gyah's hold and extended her neck for Duncan. I imagined her short time without the iron cuff would've helped her heal, that had to count for something.

I watched from the shadows of the broken doorway as Duncan clipped the iron cuff back in its place. From within his pocket he withdrew a key. He slipped it into a hole so small that if you didn't know its location, it would have been impossible to find. Then, with one gentle turn, it was locked.

"Are you okay?" I joined Althea's side, watching as the iron drained the colour from her skin. Even her eyes dulled as though the flame within was snuffed out, leaving her hollow.

"It had to be done. An Asp never gives up on a target and she would have continued looking for you."

"Althea, she would not have needed another opportunity. If you had not come for me, she would have completed her task." It was true. We all knew it. Even Duncan, who took the biggest gamble letting Althea free. A risk worth taking in my eyes, considering I had truly believed he had left me to meet my end. There would be a time for my thanks but now was not it.

"King Doran sent her for me, but she is not the only one on her way," I told them, trying to stop myself from looking at the smouldering remains.

"Who else?" Gyah asked, voice deep and terrifying.

"Erix."

The silence between the three of us piqued the interest of our captor.

"And who might be the man that can silence the three of you with only a name?"

Gyah straightened to match Duncan in height. "A berserker, a being capable of destroying this entire place without the requirement of magic and power."

Duncan's brow dipped and his jaw clenched as he regarded her. "And this makes you grin from ear-to-ear because?"

Gyah shrugged, focusing her attention on Althea as she wrapped an arm around her for support. "Can you take us back to our room now, Hunter? I think we should sit this visit out."

Annoyed, Duncan waved his hand towards the corridor in guidance. "After you. Your *room* awaits."

"How the tides have turned," Duncan said after I told him the rest of my tragic tale, pressing his fingers to his head as he pinched his eyes closed. "If Erix was the one who killed your father, why would you go through all of this to petition for the king's death?"

"I don't expect you to understand."

"And I don't." Duncan studied the view from Finstock, its surroundings cloaked in night and flaming sconces. "So, you loved this... man?"

The question made warmth flood my cheeks. "I cared for him enough to know that his actions were not actually his own."

"Because he is a berserker?"

I nodded, focusing on pressing down the sickening worry that had embedded itself in my stomach. Briar was a person I had not wanted to see, for many reasons. But Erix... I would have rather taken Briar's blade than see him again. "He is being controlled, body, soul and mind. Forced by a power I don't quite understand due to his blood tie to King Doran. If he comes here, it will not be as simple as unleashing one of our powers to stop him. He is... a monster. We should leave before he finds us."

"I am afraid that is not a possibility. I do not run from *your* kind. We will wait and greet him upon his arrival. No point leaving all this protection if he is just going to follow. Unless he's already here…"

My skin crawled at the thought. "Do you wish to cause me discomfort?"

"Is it that obvious?" he replied with a grin.

It was hard to discern what smile of his was genuine or forced. My mind screamed that Duncan was not to be trusted, but without him, I would have already been dead. I got the impression, to a point, he needed me alive. "Stay and wait to greet Erix, and those men you wish to keep alive will not survive long. Trust me, he is dangerous. More than I could explain."

"I'll think about it."

"There isn't time–"

"Patience, Robin." Duncan turned to face me, back haloed by the silver glow of the moon that dominated the sky behind him. He toyed with the loose strings of his navy tunic which still hadn't been pulled tight during the rush of the assassination attempt. His stare was heavy, I felt it on every inch of me, as though he studied the tones of my hair, the depth of my eyes. "You underestimate me. I've personally delivered many of your kind to the Hand, but never one as intriguing as you," he purred, eyes racing up and down me. "You have kings, assassins and now a berserker following where you go."

"Is that supposed to make me feel special?" I asked, frowning. "Because all it does is remind me that you are as much as a monster as I first believed you to be."

"Then I'm not the only one with conflicting views. Do not get me wrong, I do not like you. Far from it, in fact, but being in your company is a thrill and one I have not had in a while. Your conversation is far more interesting than the Hunters who still search Finstock for another *Asp* or whatever that little stalker referred to herself as. Perhaps my interest has something to do with the fact that you can hold my stare, an equal match. I have been so used to having those around me do as I say all without catching my stare for longer than required. Whereas you… you demand it."

I wanted nothing more than to look away. But instead, I fought to hold his gaze, not wanting to prove him wrong.

"I want you to know that I don't care what you think of me," I spat. "Your thoughts don't affect me, nor do they change what I need from this agreement."

"Agreement?" Duncan laughed. "Don't get comfortable. You are still my prisoner, and we have no agreement. I am delivering you to the Hand because that is what I do. It is my job to send magic-blessed fey to the Below. It just so happens that our motives align with one another, that is all."

No longer caring to be in his presence, I turned to the darkened corridor, facing the door which my friends dwelled behind. "Erix is not the only one coming for me. If you refuse to leave because of one man, perhaps you would heed my warning and leave before the Cedarfall army arrives. Otherwise, neither of us will be reaching the Hand, not alive anyhow."

"You could be lying," Duncan said.

I lifted my chin. "I'm not. Like you, I don't play games."

Duncan relaxed, leaning against the wall with a posture that irked me. "And what would you have me do? One man I can handle, but the idea of a fey army. I don't think Finstock will survive it."

I took a deep inhale. "Let Althea and Gyah go. Send them back towards Wychwood, prevent the army from reaching Finstock."

"What about you?" Duncan asked, head tilting to the side. "Do you not wish to go with them?"

I shook my head, looking down at the floor. "As you said, Erix would just follow. It would threaten all of their lives if he did."

There was another reason I couldn't leave with Althea and Gyah. One more pressing. It was Duncan's comment about the Below that reminded me. The fey who were left, with no army to come and save them.

They, like me, were alone. And I had to do something to help.

"So our lives don't matter to you, but those of your friends do."

"Well exactly," I said, sarcasm dripping from my tone. "I don't like you, Duncan. Did you think I do?"

I peered back at him, watching his lips purse in contemplation. The scar that ran down from his eye only enhanced his expression of deep wonder. The winter winds beyond the fortress walls ripped into the corridor, bringing with it the scent of Duncan. It was welcome, his smell, covering that of Briar's burned flesh and my own stench from days without a wash.

It was pleasant.

"I will think on the matter of releasing your friends," Duncan said, looking away from me for a brief moment. "No promises. As you can imagine, it will upset someone very important if I let a Cedarfall royal slip through my fingers... again."

"There will come a time you will learn to trust me," I said. "I only hope it is before everything burns around us because I am going to need you alive to get what I want. I've warned you, it's up to you if you fail or not."

Duncan watched as I reached for the door of our prison of comforts. Then he replied, voice echoing down the hallway and leaving its cold kiss upon the back of my neck. "I get the impression you are simply using me, Robin."

"Then we do share something in common," I replied slyly. "I just have not worked out what it is you want from me yet."

"*If* we make it to Lockinge you will find out."

CHAPTER 17

There was no room for complaints as I lowered myself into the muddied bath. By the time it was my turn to bathe, the water was almost black with grime, a concoction of blood and ash swirling in the lukewarm liquid. It was a relief, nonetheless, lowering my aching limbs into the belly of water. It was no wonder Althea had taken so long when she'd gone first. Gyah had to go in and check on her, only to find her curled in a ball crying over her actions that day.

Whilst it was Gyah's turn to wash her despair away, it left me to console Althea, whose silence spoke volumes of her desire to be left alone. Thankfully, the time Althea had without the iron cuff allowed her healing to accelerate. She no longer looked to be in pain, besides the mental war she currently fought.

I slipped beneath the water, still catching the faint scent of lavender blended within the less pleasant smells that left my body to join the gore of my friends. Only when my head was submerged and the sounds of Finstock were muted did I truly feel relaxed, even with the constricting iron cuff still locked around my neck.

I lay like that for as long as my lungs allowed, entirely submerged, as I willed the lapping of water to soak off the blood, ash and unpleasant grime that had clung to me since leaving Wychwood, convincing myself that if I stayed here then the worries of the world beyond would not matter. But then I remembered Briar's threat of Erix, which urged me back out.

It was stone cold by the time I was finished. The iron kept me separated from my power, returning my body to human state. Only the heat from the many melted candles provided me comfort in the empty room, and even their effort was pathetic. With winter devouring Durmain beyond Finstock's walls, everything was tirelessly cold.

I dressed quickly, back into the dark clothes that I had worn upon my arrival. We had comforts as Duncan's prisoners, but not luxuries, and a set of clean clothing was not an option.

As I entered back into the adjoining room Althea and Gyah immediately stopped whispering.

"Have I interrupted something?" I asked, too exhausted to care for niceties.

Althea looked to Gyah and shook her head slightly, stifling whatever comment was about to come out.

"You can tell him," Gyah encouraged, lips pulled thin.

Althea stood, hands folded before her. The skin around her eyes was red and swollen, pale lashes clumped together from all her crying, yet she still presented herself with the air of command, back straight and red eyes full of authority. "There is no saying what Erix will do when he reaches us, and I cannot afford the risk of waiting and finding out. It will be the perfect distraction for us to escape, and we did not discuss it with you because we know your stance. That is if Duncan doesn't agree to your petition for us to leave before."

"He will," I said, almost confident of the fact.

"You seem sure," Gyah muttered quietly. "Then again you do seem to be fraternising with the enemy."

"That," Althea said quickly, flashing Gyah a telling look, "has nothing to do with it. Robin was right, Duncan is different. We need the Hunter to trust him, and that goes for what me and Gyah were discussing. It would not be a wise decision to be involving you if it could affect your treatment once we are gone."

It was a lonely feeling, knowing your only friends had plans to leave you. Even though the plan had never involved them in the first place, I had grown accustomed to their closeness.

"If I can help, I will."

"Next time he comes to visit I recommend you're not here." Gyah's knuckles clicked as she stretched them out before her.

"There are not exactly many options for me to go," I replied. "Doors are locked unless he opens them. Finstock is crawling with Hunters who would stop you even if you made it past him. I've tried to convince Duncan to leave, but he is a fool thinking he can stand against Erix."

"Everything will be fine." Althea paced towards me, resting a hand upon my shoulder and squeezing. "The moment we reach my mother's army, I will tell them about the Below. We will follow you."

"And if Duncan doesn't agree to free you?"

"Well, Briar seemed to make it within this place without another even sparing much of a glance – that or the Hunters didn't care. If there is a way in, there is a way out."

I looked down to my feet, an unwanted sadness twisting in my gut.

"The easy way out is never the smartest." Althea's smile didn't quite reach her eyes. "There is no telling what will happen when Erix reveals himself. There is a chance he would arrive late and my people have already been and gone. But I doubt that. I know his determination, even when not fuelled by his controlled state. If Doran gets word that Briar failed, he will pull all the stops to make sure Erix finishes the job."

"You must not focus on that," I insisted. "Only getting out of here, one way or the other. Tell me what I need to do, and I will try."

This was my fault. Althea being forced to kill Briar, for both of their captures. It was all my fault. There must be a chance for me to put it right. Althea looked to Gyah, sharing a moment of tense silence as though they spoke through their minds.

"Just stay out of the way," Gyah finally said, taking over from Althea who seemed to shrink back into the shadows of the darkened room. "And stay alive. Play innocent. Because when we leave, and you are left to face Erix alone, you will need Duncan on your side. He has proven his desire to keep you breathing. Let us not ruin what already balances on a taut, frayed piece of string."

As we expected, chaos arrived to Finstock. We'd been taking turns sleeping, when the only sound was the gentle whistle of wind that caressed the fortress walls. I would've even described it as peaceful, until that all shattered.

The door slammed open, wood crashing into the stone wall.

Heavy footsteps followed.

Before I could sit up, uncaring hands snatched me from bed and dragged me to the floor. In the noise of rushed, urgent shouts, I could hear Gyah's angered cries. But I couldn't hear Althea, although I imagined she'd never show her panic with screams and shouts.

Hunters surrounded us, sharing commands which I couldn't make out.

"What are you doing?" I said, heart a lump in my throat, trying to elbow my way free. But the more I struggled, the more hands took hold of me.

And no one replied. I was helpless to do anything but let them take me, my feet dragging across the floor.

Focus. I remembered the night I had first been taken by Hunters. Pressing my panic down, I tried to study the details of what was happening. If no one would tell me, then I would have to piece the puzzle together myself.

It was dawn outside the window, another day lost. I looked down the corridor beyond the room, the sky beyond a pale plum colour with wisps of thin clouds. I was tired, but nothing was new there; the sleep I had been snatched from must have only been a couple of hours at most.

What was different to my first abduction was these Hunters were not calm or smug. Something panicked them. Their hold on me was harsh and rushed, their movements quickened by something that I had not yet figured out.

We were out in the open, the courtyard a mess of Hunters running across the straw-covered ground towards the rising stone platforms around the fortress's edge. They held large hunting bows almost the same height as them. Swords dangled from hips. Cloaks billowed out behind them.

I looked up at the shrill cry that split the sky. Large, fearless creatures cut through the sky, dancing through the air with precision. For a moment I thought the gryvern had found us, but it was birds that I saw. Hawks – large bodied and sharp-beaked. There was a storm cloud of them, circling Finstock from above.

We were dragged towards a familiar wheeled cage. Its iron bars caught the morning rays as it waited in the heart of the courtyard for us. Duncan stood beside it, his voice booming over the crowd as he shouted commands with haste. The expression on his face, grooved lines across his forehead and neck tense, encouraged my panic to take hold again.

He noticed our arrival, waving us forward as though the Hunters didn't pull us along fast enough. Another Hunter I didn't recognise stood close beside him.

This one was tall, but not as towering as Duncan. Pale, ginger curls cut close around a youthful but handsome face. Bright azure eyes were framed by his serious expression. But it was the hawk resting upon his shoulder that entranced me, how it chirped in his ear, whispering secrets of the skies.

Duncan knew this man in a different way to the Hunters who dragged and manhandled us now. I hadn't seen Duncan having conversations with anyone, usually barking commands or asserting his dominance as their general. But with this amber-haired man, they spoke as equals, Duncan even going so far as to listen intently before formulating a response.

"What's happening?" I called, trying to pull out of the many hands that held me. It was wasted effort.

Duncan spared me a glance, flicking his stare between the man he spoke with and me. "It would seem we have a *few* unannounced guests on their way."

Was it Erix, or the Cedarfall army? Whatever the answer, Duncan seemed spooked.

"Get them in the cage," he shouted at the men and woman holding us. "We leave Finstock immediately."

Gyah continuously shouted about the horrors she would unleash upon the men and women who touched her. It was a surprise they did not let her go just from the pure, haunting terror she promised them.

"Erix?" I said the name in question to Duncan as I passed him.

He ignored me, as if answers were not something I deserved.

Perhaps it was the company, or the person who stood as his shadow, but the usual smile was not upon his face. This version of Duncan was serious and stoic. "It would seem your Berserker has given up on you and instead marches with a horde of fey warriors. One man we could take, but an army, my Hunters are not prepared for that. It takes a clever man to know when to run and when to fight."

"And run we shall," the ginger-haired boy spoke, his hawk screeching in agreement.

I blanched, skin paling, the blood rushing to my feet. "Duncan. Althea and Gyah, let them go. They can stop them–"

"No, Robin. I cannot do that." Duncan turned to the red-haired Hunter. "Kayne, help secure them into the cage."

I latched onto the stranger's name as the Hunters hoisted me past him, pushing me up into the cage which rocked with my added weight, and I took note of our surroundings. There were clearly more Hunters around Finstock than before; they must have arrived with Kayne, bringing warning of the pending fey army's arrival.

"Has our time apart from one another made you forget, Duncan?" Kayne asked, long fingers gripped around the wolf-shaped hilt of the sword at his waist. "We're equals, mate. It has been many years since you commanded me."

Duncan huffed, rolling his dark-forest eyes as though he spoke with a sibling, one who both impressed him and equally annoyed him. "Then get *your* Hunters prepared. We will get a head start and wait for you at our chosen checkpoint."

Both men clasped hands, holding each other away by the width of an arm as they embraced. "It was always me who stayed back to fight whilst you looked for shelter," Kayne observed.

"That is because my name is far more important than yours, *brother*."

"Now that depends on who you ask, General," Kayne said with a wink, enjoying the drama around him.

Gyah tumbled into the cage beside me, a mess of reaching hands and screams. Those who had a hold of her were more than ready to release her, likely afraid of what her nails and teeth could do, even in this form. One of them had already figured that out as they stepped back from the cage with a hand pressed over a cheek; beneath their fingers I could see four fresh scratch marks.

By the time I looked back, Kayne was already racing off, pointing towards the armed Hunters who stationed themselves upon the fortress's outer walls.

Duncan offered a hand for Althea who now walked towards the cage unaided. She was calm but her expression was thunderous. "After you, *Princess*."

"You can try, but you will never outrun my people," Althea warned, ignoring the hand Duncan offered. He refused to lower it as he regarded her. "They will follow, and your soldiers will fail. Robin was right, it would be best to leave us here. Give us up now and they will stop following you."

Duncan responded, but not in the manner I expected. "It is rather a stretch to call this rabble soldiers."

Althea gripped Duncan's hand now, squeezing tight. "Heed my warning, Hunter. If they have found us, you will not stand a chance."

"I like a challenge," Duncan replied, putting strength behind his arm and urging Althea to step into the cage. "Shall I tell you why they will not be following? Because they don't have the numbers for what waits at Lockinge. Our trackers have confirmed as much. Finstock, maybe."

With that he closed the cage door right in Althea's face. She stood, hardly flinching as metal slammed into metal and the click of a lock finalised our imprisonment.

"Do not do this, Hunter."

His smile returned now as he gazed at Althea, subdued by the cuff, without any trace of fear. I hardly imagined he would hold such confidence if iron didn't stand between them. "How about we discuss this further a bit later?" he mocked. "There will be plenty of time for conversation between you and I."

Duncan left swiftly, moving into the fringes of his Hunters as they clambered onto the prison cart's horses.

Althea slumped to her knees, gripping onto the bars as she stared out at the Hunters.

Gyah was beside her in moments, hand on her shoulder. "Another chance will come. It has to."

"I would not rule this one out yet." Althea turned towards us, determination ablaze within her. "Many times I have led a party towards Hunters' camps and strongholds. I know the plans. They would not come in at one side, but many. It is time we put some faith in them. If not, we rely on our other plan, Gyah."

They both shot me a look. "Wait for Erix to find me?"

Althea nodded. "It would seem so."

The cart moved, jolting forward as we lost our footing. It was guided out of Finstock from a narrow path at the back of the towering building. Duncan waved a hand towards Kayne who returned his gesture with a nod. There was no sign of a

Cedarfall army arriving, at least nothing we could see. Now with the fortress between us, blocking the view of what we left behind, I could only imagine what had caused our sudden departure. For Althea and Gyah's sake, I hoped her comments of the soldiers' plans were right and we would be intercepted. But regardless, if the opportunity presented itself, I could not go with them.

I had a new purpose, a new motivation. And it was hidden beneath Lockinge castle. If I turned my back on the imprisoned fey, there would be no knowing how long it would take for us to ever return and free them.

Our party moved with haste, the cage violently rocking as the horses cantered forward. We had to grip onto the bars to stop ourselves being thrown like children's unwanted toys.

This part of Durmain was endless, fields and valleys stretching as far as the eye could see. We only slowed when the terrain changed and the horses struggled to tug us uphill. The dirt path had been worn in from years of travel, feet, hooves and wheels etching veins into the earth.

It did not take long for Finstock to become no more than a smudge of dark stone behind us.

Unlike the party of Hunters who'd taken us from Grove, this one was small. Around ten Hunters on horseback followed in a halo around us, Duncan at the lead alongside the two who pulled the cart forward.

By midday the weather changed. Cold sheets of rain fell upon us, drenching our clothes and soaking into our bones. It made the landscape almost impossible to see.

It was almost a shock when the cage began to slow. Duncan shouted a sharp, barked command and the Hunters each withdrew weapons in a song of steel against leather.

"Something is happening," I said, pushing myself to the front of the cage to try and get a better look.

"My people," Althea gasped, pure glee radiating in her voice. "I told you they would come. Gyah, get ready."

"No," I breathed, squinting through the sheets of rain and the frantic moving bodies of Duncan and his Hunters as they positioned themselves ahead of us.

I caught a glance of the figure's darkened outline standing before our party, motionless in the middle of the dirt path, cloaked and head bowed, twin swords in their hands that dug into the ground.

This was not Cedarfall soldiers, but a single person.

"What do you mean 'no'?" Gyah said, pushing beside me with a hand raised to shield her eyes from the rain. *"Fuck."*

I caught movement from the Hunters. It was Duncan, turning over his shoulder as he looked directly at me. His face dripped with rain, hair sodden and plastered to the sides of his head.

"He found me," I breathed, reading the warning in Duncan's eyes.

"This isn't good," Gyah growled, slamming a palm onto the cage bars.

I knew it was *him* before the cloak's hood was lowered from his head. It was his outline, one I had studied with my eyes, my hands; I would have recognised it no matter the conditions, time, or place.

Erix was here.

CHAPTER 18

Sheets of cold rain slapped down across the world around me. I was soaked to the bone, gripping onto the cage bars as though they'd break beneath my hold. My grip intensified with the horror of seeing Erix, knuckles white, mind screaming a maelstrom.

Gyah and Althea were huddled close to my side. It was clear that we all shared in the panic conjured by Erix's presence.

What it meant, how it would end.

An intense shiver had begun, one I could do little to prevent. It prickled across my skin, chattering my teeth as it sent my jaw into a never-ending spasm, encouraged by the anxiety that had seemed to replace the blood in my veins. It pumped around me with vigour, causing a shooting pain to caress my heart as though a hand gripped and squeezed it relentlessly.

"Both of you," Duncan shouted above the pounding of hooves in muddy ground. "Deal with this straggler."

The two Hunters Duncan spoke to jumped from their horses. Feet squelching in the muddy ground, they pulled swords from their scabbards and approached Erix with confident strides. I winced as one almost slipped on their arse; lack of coordination wouldn't help them when they reached Erix.

"Duncan," I shouted, pressing my face between the bars. "Duncan, look at me!"

Reluctantly he turned, squinting through the rain with a displeased snarl. With my eyes alone I tried to display my honest concern. It was not that I cared if the Hunters were slain, but I needed Duncan to escape the impending slaughter and help me make it to Lockinge.

"I've told you, one man is no threat. We will be moving shortly," Duncan shouted through the sleet, tipping his head in salute. "Sit back and relax."

My hair was plastered to my face and head, encouraging a constant stream of water to fall into my line of sight. Blinking it away I shouted, unable to hide the frustration within my tone.

"You don't understand! Your Hunters will not stand a chance, Duncan. Erix will kill us all, believe me, I have witnessed the twisted determination of his will."

My mind replayed visions of Erix caving Tarron Oakstorm's head in with his bare fists. What could he achieve with the weapon beside him?

"Then this will be fun," Duncan replied, dropping my stare and turning back to face the doom before him. "Allow me to do you the favour of dealing with him. It would be my pleasure."

"Fucking listen to me!"

Gyah gripped my shoulder, strong fingers anchoring me and chasing away the panic. "Let them face their end, Robin. Let us only hope Doran's control on Erix spares us."

It was not a risk I was willing to take. "Free us, Duncan," I pleaded a final time. "You are going to need us."

Duncan didn't look back, but his deep laugh reached me.

I couldn't catch my breath. My chest heaved and my hands grew numb. My legs would've given out beneath me if I hadn't been strangling the cage's bars.

The two foolish men that Duncan had commanded were close to Erix now. Erix had hardly moved a muscle since we'd first seen him. His swords still at his sides, stabbing into the muddy ground as he waited patiently.

All I could do was watch the final moments of their lives unfold before me. Perhaps they followed blindly because no matter if they died, they would have the promise of meeting their god, Duwar. Did they believe the entity was watching even now – judging their loyalty?

They reached Erix and stood before him with blades raised. I couldn't hear what they said, but it was clear they spoke with him, the conversation one way. Erix simply looked past them as though they didn't exist. His attention was entrapped elsewhere.

On another.

On *me*.

Frustrated, the Hunters released a battle cry and lunged forward. Erix joined their dance gladly. He moved forward, slipping between the Hunters before their blades had a chance to arch down towards him. His footing was confident, sliding across the wet, muddy bed and turning his body back to face them. As he did, his own swords followed. In a clean slice, one that severed through the rain itself, his blades passed through flesh and bone with ease.

Duncan hardly reacted as he watched his two Hunters die, their heads tumbling from their necks and splatting onto the ground. Their bodies followed, as though pushed by an unseen force. Blood sprayed out of the severed necks, a fountain of gore. He just stood there and watched, calculating how two lives had been taken so quickly, all in a moment.

Whilst Duncan was a prisoner to his thoughts, Erix kept moving, leaving the dead behind him as he began his approach towards his true goal. The blood-soaked metal of his sword made it appear as though they were forged by death.

"All of you. Go. Stop him." Duncan pulled forth his own sword, using the flat side of it to hit the backs of the remaining Hunters. "In Duwar's name, kill this man. His blood will be sustenance this night."

"Sustenance," the Hunters cried in return. There was nothing confident about their cries. They were timid. Pathetic.

I knew we were doomed as the remaining Hunters rushed forward to meet the Berserker. I watched, helpless behind cage bars, as Erix cut his way through the men and women; it was rare to see another's blade intercept his.

The closer he got the clearer I could see him. Shadows hung beneath his lightning-silver eyes. His black leathers were drenched in mud and gore, the white edges of his tunic and sleeves as sharp as the two swords he swung. He was striking, in both horror and power. And he was looking right at me, hardly paying any attention to the humans he cut down. They stood no chance against him, nor did they slow him down.

"This is it," I said quietly, voice buried beneath the cries of dying Hunters. "All this for nothing. Doran has won *again*."

Althea was at my right, Gyah to my left. Caged like animals, we were as useless as the humans whose blood now fed the earth.

"Do not give up yet," Althea said, "We are safe within the cage. When Erix is finished with the Hunters; he will have to take us out. In here, surrounded by the iron, it will nullify his natural abilities. We can take him."

"Althea, I could kiss you!" Gyah barked a laugh, one that sang of relief. "Your mind is truly brilliant, do you know that?"

Althea blushed, rain darkening the reds of her hair as it hung in wet strands across her shoulders.

"Then we know what to do."

"Get Erix in the cage, then fight him. It will be hard, but remember it isn't the Erix we knew anymore. At least in here it will be an even playing field. Let him come, for I have something I would like to say to him." Althea watched, unblinking and fearless, as Erix faced the remaining Hunters.

I heard Althea, but somehow my mind refused her words.

He looked like Erix. He walked like Erix. He was the man I knew, the man I loved and the one who killed my father.

"Robin, can you do this?" Gyah asked, noticing my distant stare. "Can you face the man who killed your father and provide him the relief from Doran that he requires?"

I couldn't answer. Seeing Erix had taken me back to the helpless feeling I'd experienced when my father had been killed before me. Even then I had refused to believe he was the one responsible, even though it was his hands that stole my father from me.

In my mind I'd worked hard to convince myself that it was Doran who was to blame. He'd ripped Erix's will from him and replaced it with his own. The Erix I'd come to know would never have hurt me.

But seeing him now, without his puppet master, I couldn't help but wish to take all my pain out on him.

"Yes," I replied through gritted teeth, jaw aching beneath the pressure. "I'm ready. I can do this."

"Sorry to interrupt," Duncan said, snatching our attention to the back of the cage. None of us had noticed him, our focus demanded by Erix and the death he left in his wake. "I think I'll take you up on your offer after all."

"I am afraid that offer has been retracted," Gyah said through a grin. Her dark skin was slick with rain, her golden eyes narrowed as she glared at Duncan. "Good luck out there, Hunter."

Duncan peered around the cage, wincing as the final Hunter died at the end of Erix's blade. His stare was calculating; I could almost hear the wheels turning in his mind.

"Run, Duncan," I said suddenly. "Get out of here and go whilst you can. He will not follow you. It is me he wants."

Duncan sighed, reaching into the inner pocket of his jacket and pulling out a closed fist. "Unfortunately, no can do. I'm going to need you alive, Robin. You're my bounty."

He thrust that fist through the bars and dropped something into my waiting palm. I knew what it was the moment the cold metal touched my skin.

It was a key. It was a chance.

"Free yourself and fight. Or are you going to let this Berserker ruin your only chance of avenging your father?"

His words hit a chord inside of me, the note beautiful and deadly.

Duncan tore the cloak from his shoulders, leaving it in the mud at his feet. He spared me a final glance, lips pulled tight, and shoulders squared, his question hanging between us. Then he left, stalking around the cage to greet Erix.

I wasted no time.

Althea gasped as I took her by the shoulder and turned her away from me. "The second you are out of this cage, you run. Both of you. This is the chance you have waited for. Get to the army, tell them about the fey in Lockinge. Perhaps numbers to help."

"No, Robin. We fight with you–"

I cut Althea off, panic surging up my throat and out in a wild scream. "Erix will kill anyone to get to me. You included. I can't lose either of you. Please. You need to run. If we beat him, I get answers from Lockinge. If we lose, then at least he will not kill me."

I hoped that was the case anyway. I was sure Doran had grand plans for me, death not being one of them. At least not swiftly.

The key slipped into the cuff around Althea's neck with ease. Even with the violent shaking of my hands I managed to turn it and the cuff snapped open. It fell to the ground; the echo of metal against wood was beautiful, the sound of freedom.

"I'm sorry, but I can't leave you," Althea said, wet hair stuck to the curves of her face. "There are other ways of getting what you desire than going with the Hunter. Let Erix deal with him. I promise we will find another option."

I saw it then, in Althea's defiant amber eyes. The look of a woman who, like me, had made their mind up.

But Gyah was different. She wouldn't risk Althea. Duty and pleasure, that's what she said.

I couldn't hold Althea's gaze, instead turning to Gyah who was ready to be freed. "Gyah, you know what you need to do."

"I do indeed," Gyah replied, practically ripping the iron cuff from her neck, and throwing it to the ground just as I pulled the key free again. Her hand wrapped around mine and squeezed, golden eyes brimming with her power. "Good luck."

I smiled, letting her take the key from my fingers and turn me around.

"Do what?" Althea studied us with wide, unblinking eyes. It was hard to tell if she cried, or if it was droplets of rain rather than tears that cascaded down her cheeks.

I couldn't answer her. I'd let Gyah carry out the necessary.

The key also worked for the cage's gate, unlocking it with ease. Old hinges groaned as I threw it open. One by one we clambered out of the iron prison and the feeling of power returned within a single breath. I almost lost my footing at the rush. My magic had returned, no longer imprisoned by the iron cage, or the cuff around my neck.

Magic flooded through my body, filling veins with ice and my soul with a storm. A pressure built in my bones, so intense it was a miracle my skin didn't flay apart. It was wild, strong like the force of a wild boar, but I focused on it and kept it close. It certainly felt good to have my magic back. I'd need it against Erix – every last ounce.

It was clear Althea and Gyah felt the same, but there was no time to enjoy the feeling.

"You've come all this way for him," Duncan's demanding shout reached us. I looked in his direction, Gyah shifting forms in a twisting of flesh, wings and talons. "Not that my opinion matters of course, but do you not think that behaviour is rather… creepy?"

"Ready to fight," Althea shouted, eyes ablaze with the fire that had been smothered until now; rain hissed upon impact with her boiling aura. "Follow me–"

Althea didn't get very far.

Gyah snatched Althea from the ground, making her gargle on a surprised scream. Winds billowed as Gyah extended her wings and pounded them furiously. Her urgency was to get Althea away from here. That was our plan – removing her from harm's way. I heard my name screamed from far away, but it faded as my friends flew away.

Slowly, I turned to Duncan who continued goading Erix.

I'm not ready.

But I didn't have the luxury to turn away from this. I had to face Erix. The time would have always come around; I'd only hoped it would not have been this soon.

I walked around the perimeter of the cage to greet him.

"Nothing to say?" Duncan shouted. Bodies of the Hunters littered the ground, the horses they had ridden no longer in sight, fled from fear, most likely. "All this way, all this effort and you cannot even spare me a word. Come on – give me something big boy."

Duncan held a sword, broad shoulders blocking out Erix who stood before him. His confidence was palpable, almost foolish and misplaced. Mud was splattered across his boots, his clothes drenched through. He must have sensed my presence for he stopped bouncing from foot to foot and spared a quick glance over his shoulder, not an ounce of worry creasing his focused, stoic face.

But Duncan was not the only one to see me.

The sting of Erix's eyes itched across my skin. I stilled, unable to take another step, feeling like I had only moments before, locked within the cage – absolutely powerless.

"Hello," Erix growled, lifting one of his swords and pointing it towards me, "little bird."

CHAPTER 19

"I was just beginning to like that nickname," I snarled, heart thudding in my ears. "Now not so much."

It wasn't exactly red I saw, but my vision tinted, hyper focusing on the man before me.

Duncan stepped aside as I strode past him. My legs seemed to move without command, fuelled by the sudden urge to close in on Erix and cause him pain. However, even with the pounding fury that overwhelmed me, I could still recognise a sliver of sadness coiled beneath it; it was nothing more than an ember, fighting to keep warm during a wild storm, never having a chance to catch.

"It is one of the reasons I used it," Erix replied, lowering his weapon slightly. It sounded nothing like him. "When I call you little bird, your eyes narrow and lines wrinkle beside your nose. Your discomfort made me feel a sense of... excitement."

His voice had warped, deepening in pitch and catching as if a snake was twisted in his throat. Doran Oakstorm – that was what I heard.

"You should have never come here."

Erix lifted his arms, raising both swords with them. His posture was that of an offered embrace, all whilst blood dripped from the steel's points. "I could not leave you."

"Why don't we cut the shit and get to the point where you tell me what it is you want?"

There was something forced about his posture, the way his shoulders were pulled back as though held up by a string. It wasn't the only disturbing feature. Besides the splattering of human blood washing from his face in the rain, it was the faint dark lines surrounding his unblinking eyes that caught my attention. Veins full of ink, spewing and spreading across his once beautiful face.

"Is it not obvious?" Erix cocked his head, silver eyes now a dark storm cloud. "I want *you*, Robin."

"Do you want me, or does Doran?"

A sadistic smile spread across Erix's face, confirming my suspicions.

"Unfortunately," Duncan interrupted, his narrowed stare not once leaving Erix as though he would pounce at any given moment, "Robin is going nowhere tonight. At least, nowhere with you."

"You allow this" – Erix spared Duncan a glance, one riddled with disgust – "scum to speak on your behalf? Does it not feel like yesterday that I came in and saved you from a party of Hunters, and here you are putting yourself before one."

"Look around you, Erix. Look what Doran has made you do." It was impossible to know if I stood in a puddle of blood or rain. One of the Hunters groaned, skin pale and eyes closed, grasping onto the slippery edge of life and death.

"This is all me." Erix swept his eyes across the pile of bodies before settling them back on Duncan. "What I am to do with that one... well, that is a command too sweet to refuse."

I stepped in Duncan's way, not thinking about the consequences. Magic crackled around my splayed fingers, the wind picking up, casting the rain in directions like a barrage of cold needles. "Leave, Erix. Scurry back to your master, and I'll let you live."

"No." Erix's sword lifted.

"Growing fond of me, are you?" Duncan whispered from behind me.

I refused to answer, refused to do anything but look at Erix and watch his every move. We'd trained together enough for me to know his movements. In a sense, I was ready. However, I wouldn't be the first person to attack.

I would finish it though.

Erix snapped his attention to Duncan, spinning the twin blades without much thought. "Little bird, step away from the Hunter so we can go home–"

I snapped, breaking at the use of the nickname. "You don't get to call me that anymore, Erix."

My fury was no longer contained, as though the nickname alone encouraged it to claim its freedom. I didn't flinch as the rain turned to hail. The frozen beads slammed into my head, my shoulders, stinging across my exposed skin, but the pain was hardly an echo in comparison to what stormed within me.

"I know that you are not in control of yourself," I shouted over the gale, sharpening the rain into arrows of ice with my will. "Doran has you under his control and you are simply following his command. You're as much a victim as everyone else he has hurt, killed. But I'm not leaving with you. Nor are you going to hurt anyone else."

Erix sighed, lips tugging down into a frown. "Do you not miss my company?"

"I miss the Erix I knew, but he died alongside my father."

Duncan stepped close to me. I could sense his presence like a shadow at my side. Erix noticed too, erupting with a guttural growl as though I was a bone, and he was the mutt who claimed it.

"Keep your distance, Hunter. He is not yours."

It was on the tip of my tongue to tell Erix I wasn't his either, but Duncan spoke up for me.

"Actually, he *is* mine. Now, are you going to make your next move, or do you expect me to begin the dance?" I heard the smile in Duncan's voice, let alone caught it out of the corner of my eye. "I'm more than happy to start if you have performance issues."

He was enjoying this.

A deep scarlet crept into Erix's handsome but tormented face. His eyes widened, the deep, dark veins beneath them more prominent than they'd been before. He looked back to me, spitting his next words as anger took over. For a brief moment, I thought he was struggling against something we couldn't see, fighting as he twitched and jerked his limbs. "You truly are the vision of your mother, Robin. And just like her, you will die for being an Icethorn."

Those where not Erix's words, but Doran's, spoken as though the man before me was a puppet. There wasn't a chance to react before Erix jolted forward, swords raised. Duncan followed, putting his body before mine. Metal clashed with metal as Duncan intercepted the attack. I felt the vibration, the swords' edges painfully close to my face. I would've thrown myself back, but the idea of dying was not as frightening as it had been before. Instead, I reached out for Erix, wishing to touch him; to let my magic turn his skin to glass just to watch him shatter.

Except I couldn't. Because I knew that this wasn't Erix, not really. My hesitation allowed Erix to move out of my way.

"Get behind me, Robin!" Duncan shouted, pushing me with such force it threw me off balance. I splashed in puddles of rain and gore, soaking my dirtied clothes with the stench of copper. Power poured from my hands, turning the ground where I lay to ice.

Duncan and Erix were locked in battle, grunts breaking past snarled teeth as they clashed sword into sword. Erix had met his match, at least for now.

I got the impression that he toyed with Duncan, leading him into a state of false confidence. But it was clear that Erix underestimated Duncan's skill. As had I. They moved with precision, jabbing and moving as though it was rehearsed. Where Erix swung his arms in circular, slicing motions, Duncan seemed to hack back at him, both hands wrapped tightly around his broad sword.

Two deadly soldiers, each cut from different cloth.

Kings would pay good coin to watch them duel. Shame my pockets were as empty as my patience.

Duncan was tiring quickly, his movements growing sluggish. If Erix wasn't controlled by a mad king's will, then perhaps he would've been tired as well. But in his state, there was nothing that could stop him.

I withdrew my power, worried the frozen mist and rain would blind Duncan. That worry didn't matter in the end. I saw Duncan's mistake a moment before Erix caught eye of it, a slip of a footing as he glided into bloodied mud.

My instincts took over. I threw out my hands, focusing on the moisture that wet Erix's boots and the ground beneath them. One simple thought and it hardened to ice as a gust of frozen wind washed over it. Erix's foot froze to the ground, giving Duncan the time he needed to regain his composure and arc his sword upwards – straight towards Erix's torso. The blade sliced through his clothing, cutting deep into skin. Erix threw back his head with a roar so mighty I was almost certain Gyah had returned to feast on the bones of the dead Hunters around us.

"Give up," I shouted to Erix, hoping the slither of old him would hear the desperation in my voice. "Walk away. This doesn't need to end in death."

I kept him immobile, encouraging the ice to spread to his other boot before he was able to take a step forward. Even with the scarlet gore dripping down his chest and the cry of pain, Erix didn't let up, swinging his arms with such vigorous power he hammered his blades down upon Duncan one by one.

"Finish this," Duncan called, straining through gritted teeth. It was close to impossible to hear him over Erix's angered shouts and the clang of swords as Duncan held his sword steady. Even in the dark I could see Duncan's hands shake, his gloved hands sliding over the wet edge of his blade.

All it took was a thought, a single command to urge the ice to creep up from Erix's boots across his legs. He hardly noticed, too enraged as he swung his swords. Sparks flew as the blades clashed. Even with my power keeping Erix in place, his strength only intensified as the fury took over.

This was the Berserker he warned me about. This was the monster he wanted to hide from me.

Duncan was forced to his knee, arms shaking with the broadsword held above his head. "I can't – hold him – forever."

My ice feasted upon Erix's body. Even with the hardening ice spreading across his chest, down his arms until his swords slowed their attack, Erix did everything in his power to fight against me. Until I stole his control completely – encasing it in a prison of winter.

Duncan dropped to his arse, sword clattering to the ground. His chest heaved with each breath as though he could not quite hold onto one. Sweat joined the droplets of rain running down his chiselled face.

"How long... how long will he hold?" Duncan asked above the screams and cries of Erix's anguish. I had retreated my magic before it spread above his neck; it was the only body part still able to thrash back and forth.

I reached for the bloodied blade of a murdered Hunter. My fingers were numb as I gripped its hilt and raised it before me. "As long as I allow."

Erix spat with each snarl, snapping teeth as though he was more beast than fey. Veins exposed themselves across his neck and forehead, deep and red, as though they promised to break at any moment.

"Are you watching, Doran?" I asked, stepping closer to Erix without flinching as he flashed teeth at me. "Is that how your connection with him works?"

I was inches before him, my closeness seeming to calm Erix down. It felt wrong, looking upon someone I'd believed I knew, only to find a stranger staring back at me. A face covered with fury, instead of my hands, my lips.

Erix was lost to me now.

"You are wasting time, Robin," Duncan bellowed, breathless from the excursion of his strength. "Kill the bastard, or I will."

"Shut up," I snapped, raising a cautious hand towards Erix's cheek. He snarled, teeth snapping at my hand, but I didn't stop reaching. Not until my cold, wet fingers brushed the stubble that I'd grown all too familiar with. "I don't want to hurt you, Erix. Even after what you have done. I know that it was out of your hands. Just like this is not you now."

Duncan groaned as he stood, picking his sword up with him. "You are wasting your time."

"His life is not yours to take," I warned as a freezing cold gale of wind begun to rip at the ground around me. "It is for me to decide what his fate is."

"Then make the decision before I help it along."

I pushed Duncan's threat to the bottom of my mind and faced Erix once again. With my hand pressed to his cheek, Erix seemed to calm. His curled lip softened, the darks of his eyes calming to the silver I had grown to love. "Give me a sign you are in there. Please, I'm not ready to give up on you yet."

It could have been mindless and easy to let my ice devour him only to shatter his body apart. But I couldn't bring myself to do it, not even now. Instead, I'd encased his limbs, keeping him safe from himself and me.

"Robin." A firm hand fell upon my shoulder. "If you can't do it, allow me. His death will not haunt my conscience as it would yours."

The sudden touch shocked me. Erix's moment of calm broke like glass to stone. He reacted to Duncan's hand like a feral creature, hissing and growling as though words weren't possible within his animalistic state.

I pulled my hand away from Erix's face, letting it drop back to my side as the other gripped tighter to the hilt of the stolen sword. "Do not underestimate me. Doing so has not ended well for others, the same will go for you."

My head was pounding as viciously as my heart. Deciding who lived and died was not an easy decision to make. Especially when it related to someone I thought I could love – someone I *did* love.

Duncan's breath tickled my neck as he whispered into my ear. "Then do it. Prove to yourself that this is what you've wanted. It begins with *him* and ends with Doran."

I couldn't raise the sword, not as I looked at the shell of the man before me. There were many possibilities of how this would end, but they were all just out of reach.

The hilt slipped from my hand, sword splashing into the muddied ground. "I won't do it."

"Won't or can't?" Duncan asked, voice as harsh as the blistering winds that danced around us.

"Both," I admitted. "If there's a chance Erix could be freed from this... this curse when Doran is dead, then I must hold out hope. He'd do it for me, I must do it for him."

Duncan squeezed my shoulder, rain falling upon us with vigour, then let go of me. "He killed your father; Duwar knows if I had the chance to face my parents' killers then I'd sell my soul just for a chance to show them my lack of mercy."

I looked back to Erix, a stabbing pain gripping at my gut. "To you, he is one more fey to kill in the name of that god you preach of. Just as I would not stand in the way of your revenge, you are not permitted to stand in mine."

I turned my back on Erix as he struggled in my conjured prison. "So, we walk away? Just like that? He will follow you to the ends of the earth, that much is clear."

"Yes, let's go."

Duncan didn't move. He stared at Erix, then to the bodies scattered on the floor around him. "Unfortunately, this fey has killed my soldiers. Men and women who have given their lives for a greater cause than your chase for closure. In their memory alone I cannot leave this fey alive."

I spun around, already reading what was to follow.

Duncan drew up his broadsword, ready to carve it down through Erix's neck. Time seemed to slow as the blade closed in towards the helpless and trapped Berserker. Even Erix stopped fighting, closing his darkened eyes, a soft look of peace smoothing his face.

There was no time to shout my refusal, only a brief second to act.

Nothing could stop the blast of uncontrolled, raw power as it ripped across the bloodied ground towards Duncan and Erix. It was my own inner Berserker, released into the wild without much of a thought, a beast of wind and ice. Ready to hunt its target, devour and *destroy*.

CHAPTER 20

Duncan and Erix were laid out before me, eyes closed and bodies buried by a torrent of snow. The force had appeared from nothingness, exploding out from my body as though I was nothing but a vessel for the frozen storm. Ice and snow slashed outwards, leaving a scar across the bloodied, wet earth until everything around me was stained white.

Then everything was quiet.

I tried to steady my breathing, focusing through the throbbing pain that careened across my skull. It was a struggle to pull back the power, for my emotions were wild.

Both men were unmoving, hardly visible beneath the snow covering them. Erix was closer to me. The encasing of ice shattered around him, splayed out like wings of glass beneath his unmoving body. Duncan was further away; I could only just see the glint of his body, cheeks red and skin so pale it was almost blue beneath the cold.

My legs moved without much thought, closing in on the unconscious body of my former guard. My Erix. The bedding of soft, fresh snow cushioned the blow as my knees hit the ground. With rushed hands I pushed the slush from his neck, pressing my fingers into his skin in search of a pulse. A pool of ruby gore spread beneath his head. My hands were shaking viciously as I pressed fingers into his neck, against his limp wrist before tearing back his shirt and pressing my palm against his chest.

I felt nothing. At first I thought there was a faint beat, the fluttering of tired butterfly wings. But it was brief, and the more I searched, the more my panic built.

"Wake up," I demanded, "Erix, wake up!"

I lowered my ear to his parted mouth, hoping to feel the brush of breath against my skin. But between the wind, the rain and snow, I didn't feel anything to suggest he was breathing.

There was nothing monstrous about Erix's expression. Calm, no different from being asleep. I could have laid my head down upon his chest and it would have been a mirror to the many nights we had spent together.

That would never happen again. Erix was gone.

I rocked back on my haunches, tilting my face to the dark sky. A keening scream tore out of my throat, ripping my soul apart as I unleashed my grief upon the world. I'd hoped the noise would wake him, but when I looked back down, his face was emotionless. Perhaps I should've checked the damage to his head, but I couldn't bring myself to reach behind his skull in search of the wound. Not that I'd find it. There was too much blood – it coated everything.

Small cuts kissed across Erix's face, marks left as a gift from the ice that had exploded around him. Ribbons of scarlet melted the snow plastered to his cheeks as it dribbled and spread beneath him.

"If you can hear me," I began, lower lip trembling as I held his cheek. "Know that I forgive you. Your will was not your own, I know that. Deep down I do. But please survive. Please…" I choked on the grief, on the hollow sense of loss. "You're free now."

With tears slicing lines down my face, I left Erix where he lay. Each step was torture, each second a chance for him to call after me and tell me he lived. But there was no such reaction. I had to focus on putting one foot in front of the other, carrying the hope that the deep, velvet voice I had grown all too familiar with would call my name.

By the time I reached Duncan, my world was in pieces behind me.

Duncan's eyes were wide open, flickering frantically around. He was alive at least. I'd killed one person today, Hunter or not, I couldn't cope with knowing I'd killed him too.

But Duncan didn't move. Besides laying his frightened eyes upon me, mouth parting and closing like a fish out of water.

"Get up," I commanded, standing over him. "We need to leave."

He didn't respond. Whereas Erix's expression was placid, Duncan's face was pinched in a scowl, agony etched into every line.

"Duncan," I snapped, trying to conceal the shake in my voice. Lowering myself down, I dug a hand beneath his back, trying to help him to standing, when my fingers felt something wet. "Our opportunity will–"

I pulled my hand back, Duncan hissing as if I'd just hurt him. Red dripped from my fingers, fresh gore lathered across my palm; it spread down my palm into the sleeve of my drenched shirt.

My heart could've stopped in that moment. Pulling him gently up into my lap, I could see the dark stain of blood across the ground and the mess of dark, matted hair upon the back of his head. Duncan groaned as I held him, a sound that was more beautiful than I could've ever imagined.

"Fuck, Duncan, I'm so sorry. I didn't mean to, I lost control. I–"

His hand weakly reached up and gripped my arm, eyes flickering open for a moment, revealing the whites now bloodshot. "I'll survive."

I wasn't convinced.

Holding Duncan in my arms I looked around, unable to swallow the panic. Not a single horse was left, only the cage remained, and it was impossible to even consider putting Duncan in it and pulling him to the nearest town for aid.

I had no idea where I was, not recognising any landmarks. The overwhelming urge to scream again almost took over. My magic had retreated, like a scorned dog punished for misbehaving. There was nothing to help me.

My mind, in its panicked and horrified state, focused on Duncan and keeping him alive. Perhaps it was a way to protect myself from what I'd done, but I knew in that moment, there was no way I was going to let him die.

"I need to get you help," I said, flirting with the idea of leaving him to find someone, *anyone*. How far was Althea's army? Could we wait here for them to turn up? But I knew the moment they saw Duncan they'd finish the job. He was the enemy, and I wanted to save him.

A weak hand lay upon my arm and squeezed, snatching my attention back down to him.

"Don't… don't you dare leave me, Robin Icethorn," Duncan warned, hardly able to keep his eyes open. He winced, trying to sit up but groaning as though his entire body ached.

"Then tell me what to do," I said, urgent and panicked.

Duncan took a rasped breath in, filling lungs with frozen air. "There is a village not far from here. Look for the church. *He* will help." His voice weakened, words broken by rhythmless breaths. "He will…"

Duncan's eyes fluttered closed and didn't open again.

"I can't do this alone," I shouted, shaking his shoulders and regretting it instantly. "You're going to have to help me. Stay awake, damn you, Duncan!"

I knew I had to act. Sitting around in the blood-soaked snow wouldn't achieve anything. Soon enough wolves and other creatures would catch the scent of death and come looking.

Latching onto the promise of a nearby town, I got to work.

It took a lot to pull him from the ground. Duncan was stubborn enough to keep himself on his feet even as he fought to keep consciousness. I tried not to think about the blood pouring from his head as we began to navigate ourselves away from the macabre scene.

I gritted my teeth, forcing my spine to keep as steady as possible whilst I hobbled forward with Duncan's arm wrapped around my shoulders. All I could do was focus on the darkening road ahead, hoping the promise of a village was true. My legs burned and my body ached, but on I pushed, putting as much space between us and Erix as I could whilst studying the distance for signs of life.

Ayvbury. The name of the village was carved into a wooden sign that swung in the nightly winds. It was the squeak of the sign's aged hinges that tore me from the strange trance. I'd been walking for what felt like an age, half dragging Duncan, whose arm clung to my shoulders and his awkward feet dragged across the ground.

All I thought about was moving my feet, one after the other. If it wasn't for the sound of the old hinges, I would never have looked up.

It took a lot of inner strength not to fall to my knees and shout for help when I realised I had made it. Before me stood darkened buildings, neatly stacked beside one another, on either side of a narrow street. Surely someone would hear me and come to help if I shouted? But there was no telling who dwelled here. A fey and a Hunter, which one would they welcome. I knew it wouldn't be both. So, onwards I pushed, knees shaking, as I carried on walking.

If I looked back it would've been to search for Erix, but deep down I knew he'd never follow. Never again.

The dirt path changed. Suddenly the soft ground became hard as cobbled stones spread out beneath me. Stubborn weeds wrapped around each cobble as though the earth tried to claim them back.

Keep going, I told myself.

Even my internal encouragement sounded tired. But at least it was something to keep me company. Duncan had not made a sound for a long while now. The wound on the back of his head covered his neck in dried streaks of blood.

Guilt kept me walking as much as my desire to put distance between Erix and us. If I had kept some lick of control, then Duncan would not have been in this state. It was my duty to get him the help he needed.

To reach my destination I needed Duncan alive. He was my focus now. If I didn't have one, I would perish too.

At first, it was hard to work out which building was a church. I'd never been inside of one, nor had I cared to pay them much mind. Father was not a religious man, perhaps due to his history with the Hunters, whom I know knew to be a group of cultists with their own faith. But there was *one* detail that caught my attention as I navigated through the empty streets of Ayvbury. There was a towering wooden building, the only one with a candle flame glowing in the uppermost window. Most of the other buildings we passed were darkened within, but this showed some sign of life.

It was the glow of candlelight that drew me towards the building but the symbol hanging above the arched, black-painted door had me slowing my step. A wheel, spoked by two crossing lines, pointing south, east and west, with the northern line passing over the boundary of the circle in an arrow-shaped edge. I didn't need to be a man of faith to recognise it as the symbol of the Creator. A circle that represented life, the lines pointing in all directions to show that the Creator's love always covered the people no matter where they dwelled.

But that northern arrow facing skyward represented the Creator's realm, a kingdom that was believed to exist in a world above the clouds.

I kept moving, changing direction as I passed through the gateless fence towards the main entrance. This had to be it.

Why did a Hunter care to be taken to such a place?

The wooden stairs leading up to the door groaned as I took my first step upon them. There was nothing steep about them, but it felt as though I climbed the face of a mountain with a boulder attached to my side, ready to pull me backwards without warning.

I could never have expected to enter a church like this; a fey, unwanted by their religion, alongside a Hunter who worshipped a different god. As I lifted a shaking arm, rapping my knuckles against the door, I couldn't help but recognise just how much my life had changed in a short time.

Time stretched out. I was confident no one would answer. I knocked again; this time harder, with desperation. I'd almost given up hope when I heard shuffling of heavy feet on the other side.

The door was thrown open, the warm glow of orange flame washing across us. "The Creator never rests, but his servants do. Could this not wait for dawn or do your sins require immediate repentance?"

Haloed in the light stood an ancient, stout man. He was short, belly pressing outwards in the cream, dress-like shawl he wore. His hair was clumped in white billowy tufts at the side of his head, leaving the top hairless and shiny. He carried a candle within a brass cup, lifting it out towards us as though his eyesight was poor.

I could only imagine what went through the old man's mind, looking out upon a grime-covered fey and a limp, unconscious man who bore the white hand mark of his faith upon a blood-covered jacket.

"My, my." He clutched at his chest, scrunching the material of his shawl into a ball as though his heart hurt. Amber eyes flickered from me to Duncan and back again, wiry, long-haired brows pinching into a scowl. "What a sorry sight this is."

Should I have said something? I couldn't find the words, except one that came out of me with ease.

"Help."

After a tense moment of silence, the man shuffled to the side, moving away from the entrance. "I think it's best you both come inside."

I hesitated, looking into the narrow corridor before me. There was nothing more than candles dripping down the walls and a long, red carpet runner. Most of the doors I could see were closed, all besides the one at the far end which was left open at an angle.

"*He* told me to come here," I finally said, feeling the heat of the ancient man's gaze as it skimmed across the points of my ears.

"Then in you come." He bowed his head, gesturing with the candle for us to enter. "Quickly, please, before you're seen."

I took a step, neck straining as I hoisted Duncan's limp body over the threshold.

"It would seem you have both had an eventful evening," the man began, the tone of his voice soft and welcoming. He ushered me out of the way, peeping out into the dark to see if anyone had watched us before shutting the door.

"He's badly hurt," I muttered, cringing as the door snapped against its frame. "There was a lot of blood."

Hunter's blood. Erix's blood.

My fault.

"Duncan Rackley always had a way of getting himself in trouble. Come, follow me. I will not profess that I'm a man of healing, but I will do what I can to help."

A chill coursed through my body, numbing my arms and legs. I couldn't move. I stood frozen as the man began to waddle down the corridor. He must have sensed my hesitation, for he turned and glowered at me.

"What is the matter?"

"I didn't tell you his name," I said through a lump in my throat.

The man smiled, shoulders relaxing as though he was a friend feeling comfortable in another's company. "No, I suppose you didn't. If there is one thing I remember better than my prayers, it is a name. Now, let us hurry before he bleeds out upon the floor, shall we? It would be hard to explain to the morning clergy why there's blood staining the carpets."

I kept still, arm tightening around Duncan's side, unable to take a step to follow him. The old man noticed, offering me what felt like a pitiful smile.

"You are welcome within my walls, young man," he said. "Pointed ears or not, the Creator's home is a place for all. However, the breeze you're letting in isn't. Inside, now. I have some reacquainting to do with General Rackley."

CHAPTER 21

I hoisted the heavy body of the Hunter up the winding staircase. My legs screamed with pain and my back was crying out with just as much agony. There was no denying my body needed rest. Whereas my mind was another story. By the time I had reached the final step I hardly cared for the man I trailed behind. I was more concerned with not giving up and dropping Duncan.

Just when I believed the stairs would never end, the floor levelled out into a narrow room with a low ceiling. Each inhale was filled with the thick scent of incense, spicy and strong, though there were no signs of smoke. It seemed the smell was absorbed in the walls of the church itself.

"Forgive my choice of room for you," the man said, huffing from the climb. He was doubled over, cheeks flushed with red veins. "It would be best that your stay here is kept between us. If the people of Ayvbury find out their trusted priest is harbouring the likes of *your* kind within these walls, I would be driven out."

"I thought you said the fey were welcome here," I said.

"I wasn't talking about you, dearest boy."

I looked around the attic space of the church, absorbing the details. I almost collapsed at the sight. A room much like the one I had left behind in Grove waited before me. There was a single bed with sun-stained sheets in a bundle upon the mattress. Around it, piles of books and scrolls littered the floor, some in boxes, others in wonky stacks beside them.

197

A single round window stained with blues, reds and yellows gave view to the dark night beyond. The man hobbled around the room, lighting many candles with the one he'd carried with him. Once the glow spread my eyes were able to make out more details, the most obvious being the large brass bell which took up the middle of the room with greedy pride. Its presence surprised me. It hung from a rusted chain, a frayed cord waiting at its side. Pulling it would be one way of waking the entire town.

"Put Duncan down on the bed," the man commanded through shaky breaths. "Then you will find some white cloths within the trunk over there. Get some out and bring them to me."

Hesitation thrummed through me at entrusting Duncan's care to a stranger, but I was tired and desperate to remove the added weight. Exhausted, the final steps towards the bed were the hardest. I had to peel Duncan from my side, our clothes stuck together with blood, dirt and melted snow. Duncan flopped down onto the bed, the glow of the candles highlighting just how pale his skin had become.

"Will he be okay?" I murmured, finally seeing just how terrible he looked.

"Just get the cloths, and we shall find out."

I did as he commanded without further hesitation, obtaining the folded material from the trunk as requested, a layer of dust around my fingers; this room was covered in it.

As I got back to Duncan's side, the old man was already waiting, perched on a short stool. He held the back of his swollen hand to Duncan's head, expression pinched in concentration. "His temperature is rather high, although that would be no corelation to an infection since the wound is fresh. It's too early to confirm if that would cause an issue. Likely a concussion, since the wound is superficial and the bleeding has already stopped. Praise the Creator that he still has a pulse. If you had arrived any later, he may have been far past the point of healing. It's the frostbite I'm concerned about."

The old man took a cloth from my shaking hands without thanks and pulled out an intricate glass jar from the folds of his robes, uncorking it with his teeth. I watched, helpless, as he poured the liquid onto the square of material until it was drenched through.

"Hold him up," he demanded. "Slow and careful."

I nodded, thankful to have something to do. It was impossible just sitting and watching as this stranger helped. Doing as he asked, I tugged at Duncan's arms until he was sitting up, shoulders slumped as he leaned forward on himself.

His body was dense with muscle and stiff from cold. I wished I had the power over fire to warm him, so instead I opened myself up to my magic and encouraged the chill to leave his body and enter mine.

It was the least I could do.

The sting of strong spirits tickled my nose as the old man raised the cloth upwards and pressed it to the back of Duncan's head. He held it there, mixing the strong concoction with the blood which had already dried within the strands of Duncan's hair.

The old man sniffed, blinking back tears. "I am glad this wine has found its use. Never did like it, too strong and offensive. The sting alone should wake up dear Duncan here. It will help clean the area and fight off any infection. There is nothing stronger than the Creator's blessed wine. Now, shall we discuss how this happened, my boy?" He spoke as though we were old friends, discussing mundane matters beside a fire with an ale in hand. "Starting with your name."

Names where a powerful thing, I wasn't about to go giving mine up until I knew his. "You first." My voice was sharp – distrusting. The old man noticed, his smile an attempt to prove me wrong.

As if shaking himself from deep thoughts, he came to. "Abbot Nathanial, but you may call me by the latter as I trust you're not a man of faith."

"Nathanial," I repeated carefully, as though his suggestion was a trick, and I was showing him great disrespect by ignoring his title. "How do you know Duncan?"

He looked back, a fatherly hand sweeping the strands of dark, blood-matted hair from Duncan's face. A wave of what could have only been sadness creased his brows, making the lines of age more prominent around his eyes. "Many years ago, Duncan Rackley was a young boy who stayed here when he had nowhere else to go. Believe it or not, when I was younger and time was less painful, this church doubled as a housing facility for children without homes of their own. He was one of many who passed through these doors, and one I would never forget. And just as I had told him when he left, he would always find his way back. The most troubled ones always do."

I looked back to the Hunter, body slumped over my hands as I held him from folding over. "He was an orphan?"

That was why Duncan knew this place existed.

"Indeed, he was. That very fact is the opening the cultists used to get their claws into him. And into him they did, deeper than his faith to the Creator ever reached."

The Hand and his followers, that was who Nathanial spoke of when he mentioned cultists. I knew it without the need for further confirmation.

"Which leads me to a question for you. I have always hoped that Duncan would see the truth in their warped beliefs and return to me. But never did I imagine it would be in the arms of the very *thing* that he holds such distaste for."

"Do you mean hate?" I asked, arms as numb as my mind. "Believe me, I never saw myself in this situation either."

"The world works in mysterious ways," Nathanial said. "Moved by the will of the Creator. Whereas you would see this moment as the outcome of an incident, I like to believe it is merely the Creator walking you down a path without you even realising He holds your hand."

A sour taste filled my mouth, making my jaw tighten. Now was not the time to say the wrong thing, but I was tired and my patience thin. "Apologies if this comes across as rude, but you are truly barking up the wrong tree."

That made the abbot laugh aloud, the sudden sound surprising me. "You *are* a peculiar one. How could I bark if I'm not a dog? If it is my chatter of the Creator that offends you, please do accept my sincerest apologies. I understand your kind hold belief for another but from years of my teachings and preachings, I say my god is truly ingrained within my daily language as though it's no different from pleases and thank-yous."

"I don't follow a faith," I whispered. *But I do believe.* In something at least. That much had been clear when Altar's temple had crumbled around me when Erix had slain my father.

"How interesting," he mused, smiling to himself. "You can lay him back down now. After morning mass, I shall venture into town in search of some better remedies. There will be all manner of herbs from apothecaries that will help aid Duncan in his healing, most of which I have not cared to house within my church since I do not get visitors for such physical ailments. Those who come knocking are usually in need of more spiritual healing, one that herbs and weeds are useless for. Now, until then, I shall keep our dear Duncan in my prayers tonight as I have since he left this place all those years ago."

Before Duncan's head had even hit the pillow, the abbot was standing.

"You are just going to leave?" I asked, paling at the idea of being left alone with no clue how to help him.

"What's the matter? Duncan is sleeping, as you should be too. If there are any problems before dawn, you can simply call down for me."

The abbot gave a final look down upon Duncan where he lay, his face softening as a thought overcame him. Then he walked towards me, waddling from side to side as his legs provided him discomfort with each step.

"House rules," he said, voice deepening into a scorning, serious tone. "You do not leave this room unless permission is granted by me. Not everyone in Ayvbury will be happy knowing both a Hunter and a fey dwell beneath this roof."

"I understand." I nodded, swallowing what I truly wanted to say and replacing it with something gentler. "Thank you for your help."

He waved off my thanks, large eyebrows wiggling in jest. "Just as the Creator's arms are always open, so is my church, no matter the vagrant who comes knocking. Wait for me to return tomorrow, then we will organise for you both to get washed down and dressed before you offend the noses of the woodlice and mice who frequent this attic."

I flinched as his hand found my head, resting it there so gently that it felt more like a whispered breeze. His touch was tender. If I had closed my eyes, it would have been no different to that of a father caressing his son; it instantly calmed me. "Bless you for seeing past his blackened heart to help him. I'm sure there is a story of how you have both found your way to my door and I look forward to hearing it." He looked back to Duncan. "From both of you."

I called after him as he took a step to leave. "My name," I said. "Is Robin."

Abbot Nathanial smiled, flashing neatly lined teeth, his face rounded and welcoming. "It is a pleasure to meet you, Robin. Even under such circumstances."

I woke suddenly to a room bathed with bright light. It took me a moment and a handful of blinks to see more than just the blur of white. Finally, details came into view alongside the realisation of where I was, and more horrifically, why I was here.

Expecting to find Duncan unconscious, I snapped my head around. But what I found was a complete contrast. Duncan was sitting up in bed, glass bottle of wine to his lips as he tipped it backwards. That was the sound that woke me; rasping, glutinous chugs as he downed the wine. I stood from the dusty, ancient seat that I had curled up on, my body aching more than the night before.

"You're awake." My voice cracked, thick with sleep. He didn't even look up from the wine as he carried on draining the bottle.

"I am."

My back ached from the awkward position I'd fallen asleep in, muscles complaining as I stretched the pins and needles out. "You should have woken me."

He tore the bottle from his lips, chin wet with liquid that had also spilt onto the thin sheet I'd covered him with. "If I am not mistaken, you are awake."

If I thought saving him would've helped our relationship, I was wrong. Then again, I only saved him from a fate that I caused.

"Good morning to you too," I groaned, annoyance curling in my stomach. Perhaps I should have asked how he was, but his thinned, wine-glistening lips and his pinched brows reminded me that he was far from helpless.

He winced, raising a hand to block the sunlight that cut through the dancing clouds of dust that filled the air. "I can't tell what is worse, my head or my back thanks to this bed. Couldn't be more different to the bed that I would have been waking in if your deranged ex-lover had not killed all my men. And an empty bed at that, how disappointing."

"Well, he's dead," I snapped, hating the reality of the words.

Duncan silenced at that, casting narrowed eyes over me.

There was so much I could say back to him, but it would've been pointless. Arguing wouldn't make being stuck in this room with him any better.

I could have sworn I heard the bones in my knees creak louder than the floorboards as I crossed the room to him. The only thing I wanted to do was steer the conversation away from Erix. I wasn't strong enough to face it yet.

"How's your head?" I asked offhandedly, pulling up the short stool that the abbot had sat on last night.

"If you care, it feels like it's been kicked in by twenty scorned lovers who have hunted me down to wreak hell upon me," Duncan said with one eye pinched closed and his forehead etched with lines. One hand still grasped the almost empty bottle of holy wine whilst the other reached for the back of his head. He hissed as his fingers came into contact with the mess of blood and hair. "But instead, it was all you. Powerful little creature you are."

"I preferred you when you were unconscious," I snapped, swiping the bottle from his hands, then taking a long swig. The moment the liquid cascaded down my throat, burning every inch of it on the way down, I realised why the abbot had chosen to use it on Duncan's head instead.

It was hard to tell if the desire to vomit was from the sharp taste or the slosh of it in my very empty stomach.

"Pass it back here if you are not going to appreciate it," Duncan said, flexing his fingers in request. "Strong as I remember. It will rid me of this bastard head pain whilst putting hairs on my chest."

"Surely it will make the headache worse?" I cleared the dribbles from the corner of my mouth as Duncan snatched the bottle.

He lifted it to his lips, stopping only to answer me. "I suppose we will test that theory."

"Has anyone ever told you that you have terrible taste?" I said, watching the dribbles of liquid run down his chin, his neck and over his rather sculptured chest.

"Eyes up, Robin." Duncan said, his own eyes were bloodshot but brighter than they'd been the night prior. "And to answer your question, too many to remember."

Embarrassment shifted to confusion as I heard the faint, monotone chant of a deep voice somewhere in the church beneath us. Until now I had been too occupied with Duncan to notice. "What was that?"

"Morning mass," Duncan explained as though reading my thoughts. "The longest ceremony of the day. I used to dread it. Tried anything to get myself out of joining, whether that was pretending to have come down with sickness or simply ignoring the abbot when he came calling for us at dawn. Never could worm my way out of listening to his drawl."

"He told me you used to live here."

"Live?" Duncan laughed, pulling a face at the now empty bottle as though he could not understand where the wine had gone. "I wouldn't call my stay here *living*. There was no choice in the matter. I was a child, left orphaned due to – may I remind you – your fellow kind's actions. I existed, not lived. Go on, tell me what his reaction was to finding me on his doorstep once again. Was it as smug as I could imagine?"

I shook my head, witnessing as the alcohol seeped its claws into Duncan, turning his words sluggish and emotions slippery. How much had he drunk whilst I slept?

"You speak of the abbot as though he harbours no care for you," I said. "The man I'd met clearly held a warmer emotion for you than you do him. He was concerned, slightly confused, but he looked at you as though you meant more to him than you make out."

"Ha, don't let the old man fool you!"

"You're drunk," I replied.

"Among other things."

The sound of muffled speaking became the lull of singing far beneath us. From the sheer sound of the voices, I could only imagine how full the mass was.

Duncan swung his legs over the edge of the bed, wincing as he did so.

"What *are* you doing?"

He swatted away my hand. "Getting up and getting out of here."

Duncan swayed as he stood, arse thumping back down upon the flattened mattress as though his legs knew better than to allow him to move.

"You are in no fit state to be going anywhere, Duncan. Look at you. What do you think will happen when the people of this village see a Hunter and a fey walking through the streets? Need I remind you that we are both covered in blood and smell like warmed horse shit?"

His dark, full brow raised inquisitively. "It would seem we have both bumped our heads. Need I remind *you* that you are my prisoner still, certainly not in a position to be commanding me as though our roles have reversed."

I raised my wrists, both held together as though an invisible cord of iron bound them. "Would you like me to pretend I'm bound to please you?"

Duncan could hardly fight the urge to turn up the corner of his lip. "That does not sound like a terrible idea."

Slapping my hands back down onto my thighs, I sucked my teeth in frustration. "Drunk and infuriating. A terrible mix. Perhaps you should sleep off the wine and concussion and we can discuss our next play when you are of sounder mind."

"Are you sour with me because I didn't leave you more wine?" He shook the empty bottle before me which I snatched from him in a blink.

I held the bottle by its neck, brandishing it like a weapon. "Do not give me a reason to put you back to sleep myself, Duncan. If we're going to be stuck here for a while you need to either drop your sarcastic and – may I add – repulsive attitude. Or, easier than that, learn to keep quiet around me."

"You find me repulsive?" he asked, leaning forward until his face was close to mine. His jade-green stare flickered between mine and my pursed lips which made holding my expression of concentration rather difficult.

The question hung between us.

I broke eye contact first, knowing that if I carried on my cheeks would have turned scarlet. "How about we discuss what happens next for us, rather than listening to my list of reasons as to why you are, in fact, repulsive."

"It will not be long before the Hunters expecting our arrival in Lockinge realise that we have been *unexpectedly* delayed. I give it a few days before a search party is sent out, finds the bodies and notes that mine is missing among the dead, then they will come looking for me."

"Us?" I asked, hesitantly correcting him.

"Oh, Robin, they wouldn't care for your life as they would a general. Finding you alive, with me, would simply be a bonus."

I scowled, unsure why I expected him to speak of me differently. "Then we are taken to Lockinge, and I get my audience with the Hand?"

I get my answers about the imprisoned fey and use everything in me to free them.

"If I was you, I'd be more concerned knowing the Berserker is still out there. What is to say he will not find us before the Hunters do?"

I paused, swallowing audibly. "I told you, he's dead."

"You could just be saying that."

My eyes burned with tears, but I refused to let them fall. "Shut up."

"Ah yes," Duncan slurred. "You stopped me killing him, why should I believe you finished the job? Instead, you gave him another chance to hunt you down. And I was beginning to think you were stronger. I suppose my view of you was misplaced."

"Because I did it," I snapped, voice raising, no longer caring who heard. "I killed Erix."

Intentionally or by mistake, it didn't matter. Not anymore.

The wooden stool clattered to the ground as I stood abruptly. "I don't care what you think of me, Duncan."

"Do you not?" he asked, verdant eyes drinking me in. "Because your reaction suggests otherwise."

It was easy to let my magic spill out of me, just a little, but enough to serve as a warning. An unseen breeze melted from my skin, tousling my hair as well as catching the loose papers and parchments along with it. Immediately, Duncan's wine-sharp breath thickened in a cloud beyond his lips which stole the smug grin that had been creeping across his face.

"Don't push your luck with me, Hunter," I warned, standing firm before him. "Don't make me regret saving your life, or I will correct that mistake and find my own way to Lockinge."

Duncan tensed his jaw, trying everything to stop his teeth from chattering as the cold breeze left ice spreading across the floor and walls of the attic.

"How peculiar," he mused, lip turned up at the corner.

I called the cold back, returning the magic into my bones. "What?"

"I *almost* believed you." He kicked his legs back over the bed until he was lying down, arms behind his head. He attempted to act as though he was carefree, but I noticed the wince as his hands brushed the wound at the back of his head.

"Not quite, but almost," Duncan continued, eyes closed as though he sleep-talked. "Keep it up and you may even make me fear you one day."

"Do you have any coin?" I spat, unable to bite my tongue.

"Never had much care for it, nor need."

"That's a shame. How else am I going to buy the fucks to give you?"

Duncan barked a laugh. "Excellent, truly excellent. Who'd have thought that your kind could be such stimulating company? I've a feeling these next few days are going to pass by in a blur. Don't you?"

Biting down on my bottom lip until copper filled my mouth, I stifled a response. I felt more like a prisoner, stuck in this attic with him, than I had during my time in Finstock.

The silence that followed allowed me to register my own feeling of drunkenness from the short swig I had taken of the holy wine. I would've preferred another mouthful – another ten mouthfuls – if it meant drowning out Duncan and what he had to say. But before long, the Hunter was snoring, mouth agape whilst the wine dragged him into sleep, leaving me to the chorus of his breathing and the people singing in the church below for company.

I contemplated smothering him with a pillow, but I knew now that death never brought peace.

CHAPTER 22

Abbot Nathanial had followed through on his vow and then some, returning when the sun was at its highest peak above Ayvbury with the beautiful offer of a bath, clean clothes and a good meal. It was incredible just how different my perspective on life was after my skin had been scrubbed and my belly was full of food.

We'd taken turns to wash, creeping through the empty church towards the abbot's private rooms where the tub of lukewarm water waited.

Duncan had either pretended to be asleep when the abbot had returned for us, or really was enthralled in his drunken haze, because he didn't stir. But by the time I'd returned to the attic, the bed was empty, and the abbot was waiting beside it, sitting upon the stool once again.

Hair still damp, my eyes flicked around the room as though he hid between towering stacks of books. "Where's Duncan?"

The abbot looked up, eyes fogged with glistening sadness. "It would seem he has been harbouring some negative emotions towards me."

"Perhaps I should go and find him," I said, paranoid that his dirt-covered uniform and blood-soaked hair would only draw unwanted attention to us. "I did try and warn him not to leave, not with…"

"Duncan was never one to discuss the thoughts that clouded his mind," the abbot said, shoulders hunching with one great exhale. "Even as a child he preferred the solace of his silence to conversation. He never saw the benefit of having the Creator to discuss his mind's demons with either. Even as a young lad he believed prayer to be nothing more than wasted breath. It's what surprised me most that he was drafted into the rabble of Hunters. What was so different from our god, to theirs, that made them so desirable?"

The answer was simple; the promise of vengeance.

"Do you know of their god?" I asked. "Because I've never heard of Duwar before. Not in any of the teachings when I grew up, or in mention from the fey."

"Because history has a habit of forgetting itself, then wonders why we repeat mistakes." The abbot's expression changed as quick as a summer storm, downturned expression lifting into a furious snarl. "I do, indeed, know about Duwar. But only in part. Only what… the angels sing to me."

Angels? Now this man was senile, for sure. "And what did those *angels* say about Duwar?"

"That Duwar *is* no god. Duwar is chaos incarnate. A monster. A lie for lost souls to follow."

"What about Altar?" I asked, watching the abbot's expression soften once again. "Do you view the fey god in the same light?"

"Not at all." Nathanial gasped, clutching his chest as though an arrow struck him. "I gave my soul to the Creator long before I even knew of gods. Then, by the time the first hairs grew on my chest, I knew my life's purpose as well as my own name. To spread the Creator's teachings to those who listen, and encourage belief in those with space for it. Angels visited me – great winged warriors brandishing gold weapons."

"Is the mention of angels just a figment of speech?" I asked, unable to hide my smirk.

"No, Robin. Angels. One day, you will see."

I nodded, hyper aware that I'd offended him. "And these angels, what did they say?"

"Well, they gave me purpose. Now, Altar is no different, Father of the fey and recognised deity of your people. But Duwar, that creature has no standing to be titled as a god."

A shadow passed over the old man, hardening his features as though Duwar's name had the power to turn him to stone with hate.

I should've left to search for Duncan already, but the truth the abbot was revealing kept me rooted to the spot. "I don't understand how Duwar's name has never been brought up before. How a…" I refrained from using the title god. Instead, I opted to use the same title the abbot had used. "How a creature has captured enough people's belief to encourage an entire faith yet is not mentioned before… besides your angels that is. Even in Wychwood the Hunters and their actions have been a mystery, believed to be tied with fey-blood and the desire for power. How does that tie to Duwar?"

"Sadly, I don't have the answers you seek. However, Duncan will. Have you asked my dear boy?"

I shook my head. "I wouldn't refer to Duncan as dear, and no. I witnessed what the Hunters do in the name of their… Duwar and it is frightening. But it is the Hand they talk about. I fear that's who Duncan really worships."

"There have been whispers of what the Hand desires for many moons. In recent years, those whispers have become more like muffled shouts. More and more of their kind sweep across the land in the name of this Hand, taking your kind for blood, knowing that the King's seal of approval will stop anyone from interfering. Yet the question I keep asking myself, one that even Duncan has refused to answer, is why? What is it they believe will happen? There was an age of Gods, written about in testaments old. However, that time has long passed and for most is nothing but stories you tell at night to keep naughty children from misbehaving."

"Why now?" I asked.

"That is correct," he said, eyes widening in curiosity. "Why now indeed?"

My mind was whirling with questions. It was hard to know which one to pick out first. Perhaps my silence was the abbot's signal that I was finished with our conversation, when in fact, I was never more ready to find out more.

"Before you go to look for Duncan, would you do an old man a favour and answer a question?" The abbot's knees creaked, like worn floorboards in a forgotten home, as he stood, liver-spotted hands clasped before his belly as though they held it in from slipping free.

"It would be the least I can do for a man who has let two vagrants into his home without hesitation."

He smiled briefly, wide eyes full of an emotion I could not quite name. "Are you a believer? In the Creator, in Altar, it does not matter to me which."

I paused, feeling the faint tremble of the ground as the memory of Altar's temple falling down around me filled my mind and left a bad taste in my mouth.

"Yes," I answered, surprised at how easy it was. "At least I think so. I've learned a lot in a short period of time and witnessed even more. What I've seen makes it hard to turn my back on the potential of higher beings."

"I am glad to hear it," the abbot confirmed, head bowing. "There may come a time when everyone's faith, no matter in whom it is held, will become necessary. I fear something brews, something terrible and close. Having *someone* to fight for is as important as knowing whom you fight beside."

I found Duncan within a grand room in the heart of the church. Relief chilled the blush of warmth that my anxiety spread across my skin. He'd not left after all, which showed that he was not as stupid as I was beginning to believe.

The room was both elegant and rich, with colour, stone

and decoration that the rest of the church lacked. It reminded me of Altar's temple, instead crafted from wooden pews and marble columned pillars that stood guard down the sides of the room. Vines and greenery had not claimed this place of worship. Instead, stone walls were covered by draping banners, each depicting scenes of stories that I could not recall.

At the front of the room was an altar, covered in a cream sheet with the sign of the Creator sewn proudly across its hem. A chalice waited upon it, the remnants of red wine drying across its rim. White candles still burned across the altar, dripping wax. The small, amber flames danced in the breezeless room, shifting freely for an unseen audience.

The Creator's symbol, a four-spoked wheel with the arrow pointing northwards, could be seen all around the room. Even the flooring, tiles of black and grey arranged into the shape of the sign, spread out beneath my feet.

A creeping of thick incense crawled into my nose and clung on with desperate claws. I could taste the spice in the clouds of smoke that melted from the hanging golden burners which moved from side to side, pushed by an unseen hand.

I entered the room on gentle feet, concerned I'd shatter the ambience of blissful silence that held the room.

Duncan didn't show any sign that he sensed my presence, but there was no doubt he was aware. He stayed were he sat, in the middle of a pew facing the altar as though it entrapped his attention completely. Daylight streamed in from the large, stained-glass window that hung proudly at our backs, casting a glow of brilliance across everything. The colours seemed to sway across the floor, interrupted only by the winter clouds that drifted lazily before the sun. Imprinted on the glass was an image of a woman with white wings and billowing hair, clutching a hammer crafted from yellow glass that gave it the impression of being gold.

Were these the angels Nathanial spoke of? Did he drink too much of his blessed mind and lose himself to the ideals of this faith?

"Do you mind if I join you?" I asked, voice echoing against the rafters. Even the flames upon the many candles stilled, listening contentedly for Duncan's answer.

Duncan still had not washed. Hair soaked with blood, and dark clothing coated in grime. If anyone else entered this room they would have seen him and thought that the dead had risen. Instead, it was only me and him, plus the promise of the Creator who felt as real as the ground I walked on after the abbot's comments.

The Hunter didn't take his eyes off the altar as he replied. "I suppose it would be rude to refuse."

It was not exactly the yes or no I expected, but not pushing my luck, I moved down the middle aisle and stopped at the edge of the pew he sat upon.

"For a second there I'd convinced myself that you'd left me here," I admitted, scooting down the pew until I was beside him. Duncan's hand was splayed out upon the seat beside him, fingers claiming the space for his own. Before I took my seat, he removed his claim and put his hand upon his knees in offering. Without question, I sat beside him.

This relationship was only going to work if we made it amicable. I had to try, for the sake of my end goal.

"And yet here I am still, contemplating why I'm even here in the first place." His jaw feathered, eyes narrowing in on a spot at the front of the room. I kept looking at the chiselled lines of his dirt-covered face, recognising the gleam of grease that clung to his dark hair.

"You told me to come here. Believe me, if there was a reason not to drag you for miles at my side then I'd have preferred it."

Duncan was as stiff as a spike of steel at my side. "I wasn't exactly in my right mind after you almost killed me."

"Almost," I echoed. "You know, you never did say thank you. It wouldn't hurt you to try. Or does providing recognition to the very beings you have sworn your life to hunt not happen often?"

"You'll get over it." His reply was cold. It was the type of sharp tone that revealed the speaker did not wish to be spoken to.

Shame. I'm not going anywhere.

"Even in the presence of a god you are a rude bastard, Duncan Rackley."

"Is he going to smite me for my disrespect? Come here, right now, and punish me for my lack of belief?" Duncan didn't sound as angry as his words suggested, but the tension in his face, his twisting scar, gave the expression of someone in pain. "The answer is no. No, he will not, Robin."

"I sense I've hit a nerve." I flinched as Duncan leaned forward, gripping the edge of the pew until his knuckles were as pale as bone.

"*Severed* a nerve more like," Duncan confirmed.

I felt the urge to place a hand upon his back. The comforting thought caught me off guard. I soon realised he'd hate it and instead I kept them upon my own lap, useless and unwanted.

"You harbour a lot of hate for this place," I said quietly. "Care to explain what it has done to you to make you feel such a way? Because from what I've seen, Nathanial loves you – don't worry, I'm surprised by that too."

Duncan's nose scrunched as he shot me a side-eyed glare. "It's not this place that I despise, but what it stands for. Praising a god that allows children to be left without parents. Do you not see how unfair that is? What god would see his own creations go without the love of a parent? What made me and the other children left at this doorstep any more undeserving than those who dwelled in the homes throughout this village and others?"

Duncan looked at me then. Truly looked at me. Stubble scratched across his jaw, deep, forest-green eyes shining with sadness all without the need for tears. His eyes flickered across my face as though searching for something hidden, lips parted in the promise of a secret that he did not share.

"If you do not believe in a god, then why join the Hunters?" The question haunted the silence between us. "Call me ignorant, but I see no sense in your choice."

Duncan leaned back, blinking heavily, as my question settled over him. "The Creator promised peace, Duwar promised revenge. I picked what I felt was most just, as any young boy tormented by his parents' death would. Sound familiar to you, Robin?"

I reared back, his words punching me in the gut.

Duncan took my moment of surprised silence to continue. It was his turn to strike a nerve. "We share something in common. I admit when you first demanded your audience with the Hand, I couldn't help but notice how similar we are. I've never had the time to see your kind as more than just the means for the type of peace I required. Until you."

I wanted to tell him that we were different, list the reasons which made him the monster, and not me. But I came up short, with not a single reason to give.

"Silence speaks louder than the guilty proclaiming their innocence." Duncan's voice was warm, despite what he was saying.

"I never preached my innocence," I replied, looking down at my hands, fingers fidgeting on my lap.

"And I get the impression you are far from innocent." Duncan stood abruptly.

"So I do scare you?" I asked, standing up beside him to block the way out. "Running away from conversation seems to be a speciality of yours."

"I said intrigue, not fear." Duncan smiled slowly, large hands finding themselves upon the belt around his hips. "I better go wash myself down, *Duwar* knows I need it. Then we are going to carry on this conversation later. No one is running this time. Not yet at least."

Duncan stepped towards me, hands grasping my shoulders as he swivelled me out of the way. His grip was gentle, yet firm, a knowing touch with the confidence of control over another body. His toes touched mine as he shuffled past, looking down his nose at me as I glared up at him.

For a single moment, I couldn't catch a breath.

Once Duncan had passed me and his touch was no more than a faint whisper across my arms, he spoke. "I always found this place boring. Days long and nights endless. Do me a favour, if you are up to it. Behind the altar, through the wooden door, is a room filled with wine. Nathanial was always a magpie for the stuff and will have bottles, so many he will not notice if any are missing."

Duncan had a talent, one of distraction. Perhaps that was what set me at ease even after the tense conversation. It was impressive to recognise how Duncan could remove himself from his emotions and mask it. I wished I could do that, instead I was ruled by them, guided to make decisions that risked everything.

Perhaps I should've refused, demanded that he sat back down so I could understand him and, in turn, allow him to understand me better. That would have been important if we were meant to use one another to get to Lockinge. But what else was important was a distraction, and it had been far too long since I'd one of those last.

"You want me to steal holy wine from beneath the nose of a man who has shown us nothing but welcoming kindness?" I grinned as I spoke, chest warming as though I was a kid enthralled in mischievousness.

"I do indeed." He turned on his heel, walking towards the door with a confidence that demanded attention.

Before his grubby hand reached for the doorknob, I called out a final question. "I know that the older the wine, the more potent it is. Any preference on the age or are you happy with anything?"

"Surprise me," Duncan confirmed. "You seem to be good at doing that."

CHAPTER 23

I never intended to get drunk, but as the wine continued to fill me, my concerns dampened to a barely audible simmer in the back of my mind. Duncan clearly was the same. We drank until time became nothing more than an inconvenience, and the meaning of fey and Hunter faded into nothingness. We tipped bottles back as though feather-light, replacing them with another and another. There wasn't a need for gentle-stemmed glasses or tankards. Candles burned around us, covering the darkened space in a halo of amber and warmth. Not that we were cold with the alcohol roaring like a fire in our bellies.

The burning liquid hazed my mind and made my body sluggish. However, it did little to drown out the chanting of the church far below us. Floors beneath us, evening mass had begun some time ago, ensuring Abbot Nathanial was occupied. Just the thought of him finding the missing bottles had small laughs passing my lips alongside rushed hiccups.

Duncan sat upon the bed, leaning on his knees as he swung the half-finished bottle of dark wine before him. His fingers clasped the bottle's neck as though it was a lover, grip as gentle and firm as one would desire. He had washed what felt like hours ago, his chest still shirtless. Duncan had only bothered to pull on trousers, which I was thankful for at the time. But now, with the rush of alcohol present in every vessel of my being, I cared little for where I looked.

And look I did.

When Duncan laughed the muscles across his stomach would ripple like water disturbed by a stone. Hair coated his broad chest, spreading down and thinning as it reached the extremely prominent V-shaped carving at his hips. His hair was still damp, even now. It was at a length that could easily be swept behind ears, all but the two pesky strands that hung at both sides of his face.

Skin cleaned of blood, and half-dressed in the clothes of a common man, Duncan didn't like someone who had it in him to kill. He was my enemy yes, but somehow the more we drank, the less that title mattered.

"Ridiculous," Duncan bellowed, jabbing the bottle at me with one eye squinted. "You are expecting me to believe that your father was a Hunter?"

My tongue lapped the dribble of wine off my lips. "Are you suggesting I'm a liar?"

Duncan had shown keen interest in my parentage, firing questions at me whilst we drank, preventing what could've been an awkward silence. But what he did was incredibly smart, hardly allowing me any time to question him.

And I had a lot of questions.

Duncan bit down on his lower lip, head shaking slightly in disbelief. "With everything you say, I uncover more about you. You're like a puzzle, which is all well and good, until I find a missing piece. Then that'll piss me off again."

"You have patience for a puzzle? I don't believe that for a second."

"I too am full of surprises, Robin." Duncan took a long swig from his bottle, prominent lump in his throat bobbing with each gulp. The silence was utterly controlled by him. And he knew it. Eyes never leaving me as he drank, he lowered the bottle and then spoke again. "By the time we reach Lockinge it would not shock me if we've revealed too much about one another."

My thumb rubbed around the rim of the bottle, staining my skin red. "Have you not met the Hand before?"

The question came out of nowhere, whilst being one of the most pressing issues in my mind.

"A low life like me?" Duncan laughed. "No, never. The Hand is an elusive character. My orders come from higher stationed Hunters, whose orders come from those above even them. The Hand is occupied doing what one does when in commune with a god. We merely dance to his tune, and he dances to Duwar's beat."

My skin bristled at his flippant comment. "And if you don't know the Hand personally, how did you expect to grant me my audience?"

"At last, he asks the question that I would've thought was most important above others." Duncan sat back, stomach flexing and arms bulging. "The Hand will want to see you, even I know that. Son of one of the four fey Courts, your presence will be most interesting to him. Of all the fey he collects, it's the royal bloodlines he likes the most. The Hand likely knows of you even now, expecting your arrival, which we will be terribly late for."

"This sounds more like a hunch than fact."

He winked, the dark pupils of his eyes taking up most of their colour. "A strong one I must add."

It was my time to drink, doing as he had and not taking my stare off him. I took my time, enjoying the gentle burn as the liquid raced down into my belly, warming me from the inside out.

"Reading between the lines it would seem that I don't need you," I said, watching as his brows furrowed ever so slightly. "If you believe the Hand is expecting me, then surely I could leave you here and still make it to my destination without issue. Am I right in thinking that?"

"Indeed, you are," Duncan replied, scar deepening as he smiled. "It still doesn't mean I'm not going to be by your side as we reach Lockinge."

"And why is that?"

"Because *I* need you."

I scoffed, almost choking. "Need me?"

"That's right. I need you very badly, Robin Icethorn." Duncan winked, turning my uncomfortable shivers to a tender quiver, like cool breath over my skin.

"You spend a lot of time mocking me for a man who needs me more than I need him. I could freeze your skin, harden your bones until they were no different to shards of fragile glass. Leave you within this attic all without much effort at all. So, tell me, Duncan Rackley, why should I bring *you* with me?"

A cloud passed over Duncan's expression, narrowing his eyes and pursing his lips into a line so straight they paled. If my hearing was stronger, I might've heard the wheels in his mind turning as he conjured his answer – or as he decided whether to make his response truthful or not.

I waited, watching as Duncan finished the dregs of his bottle. Once it was emptied he discarded it on the floor and reached for the next. Lifting the new bottle to his mouth, he pinched teeth around the cork and pulled, the pop shattering the quiet between us.

"I require an audience with the Hand as well."

"Excuse me?" I said, unsure if I'd heard him correctly.

"Have I not expressed that we share similarities?" Duncan said, his grin faltering. "I also need to speak with the Hand personally. One on one. Delivering him a fey royal will grant me that."

"And here I had been left to wonder why you became so involved with helping me. Even freeing Althea to stop Briar. Standing against Erix when he came for me. You need me, far more than I need you."

"Well, if you say it like that, then yes. Tell me, Robin, what are you going to do with this information? The power is quite literally in your hands. The choice is all yours."

I sat up straight, uncrossing my legs in the chair and rooting them back on the floor of the attic. It was impossible to discern if the room spun because of what I had uncovered, or if it was the bottle of wine I had downed. "Is the Hand truly mysterious, so much so that a general of his Hunters cannot even request his time?"

Duncan shrugged, clicking his tongue across teeth. "You say it as though I've not already thought about or tried that approach too many times to count."

"You know my reasoning. Is it not fair that I know yours, since you've been plotting to use me this entire time?"

"Oh, Robin." Duncan pouted, gaze trailing me from head to toe. "Has my deceit hurt you? Did the wine make you forget who I am, and what you are? Do not grow comfortable because enemies break bread and drink from the same cup. They both do so with poison painted across their lips."

"Stop doing that," I groaned.

"What?"

"Changing the subject when it doesn't proceed down a path you are comfortable with." I stood from the chair, bottle tight in my hand and legs swaying as though the church was built upon wild seas. "Just answer the question, Duncan."

If I was honest with myself, I never believed he'd tell me. In the short time I'd come to know him I was prepared for the subject to change, or him to choose silence other truth.

Then he did the opposite and spoke the truth. I believed that's what it was the second the words left his mouth. I read the honesty in every crease across Duncan's forehead, and the heavy emotion that darkened his eyes. Most of all, Duncan looked nowhere else but at me. And his truth cut deep like a silver-forged blade.

"Names. Names only the Hand has access to. Dangled over my head from the moment I left Abbot Nathanial until now. A promise of the names of those who stole the lives of my parents. Names I would do anything to get," Duncan revealed, voice gritty with tempered emotion. "That's why I need you."

Perhaps it was the wine that made me take steps towards him, forcing me to cross the candle-lit room with nothing but the desire to provide Duncan with some form of ease. He shivered with the feeling that haunted him, not sadness or anger, but something guttural and wild. Desperation. A scorching desire that would have made him do anything to appease it. A feeling I knew all too well.

Duncan watched me with large, wide eyes. He didn't even flinch as my hand reached the side of his face. The tips of my fingers met his skin first, melting upon him until his cheek rested in my palm. His skin was warm. The scent of him freshly washed was as beautiful as a breath of fresh, winter air.

"What are you doing?" he asked, allowing me to step between his legs which he parted with a shuffle of his feet.

I peered down at him, feeling a lump form in my throat as I replied. "You're right, we do have many similarities. I wish it was different circumstances for the both of us, but here we are, products of the world around us. How can I look at you any different for what you desire when I wish the same for another?"

In a single moment, the tension between us shifted, guided by my unseen hand.

Duncan discarded the bottle, careless of the wine that spilt across his sheets. With straight, strong arms, he pushed himself upwards, face coming to meet mine with nothing but a sliver of distance between us.

I didn't move back, but the momentum caused my hand to fall from the side of his face like the tears he fought so hard to keep from spilling.

"After everything I've done to you, to your friends, to the fey, what do you see when you look at me?"

"I see a man who'd do anything for his family," I replied, voice no more than a whisper. "And I see a boy with scars, some visible but most unseen, looking for a remedy to ease their discomfort. I see you, Duncan Rackley."

His expression softened, the creases around his eyes dissolving into nothingness. For a moment I obtained a peek at the boy he would have been before, free from haunting torment and twisted desire for vengeance.

Duncan's face grew closer until the tips of our noses tickled one another. Spiced grape washed over me as he exhaled through slightly parted lips. "Do you care to know what I see when I look at you, Robin?"

I was fearful to know his answer but nodded anyway.

"Mercy. A chance for my mercy at least."

Somewhere, far beneath the room, Abbot Nathanial preached the teachings of his faith, telling those who cared to listen stories of the Creator through word and song, all without knowing that, within the attic, something strange occurred. A Hunter ran gentle, knowing hands up the arms of his enemy – at least that was what his enemy should have looked like; pointed ears and powers unknown to humans.

Duncan's eyes asked permission, flicking between my lips and my wide, unblinking stare. And before I could contemplate it, his permission was granted. I lifted onto toes, drew myself towards his face and stopped only when our lips met in a joining of flesh and desire.

CHAPTER 24

Thoughts were useless as our lips crashed together, senses exploding.

Duncan held me to him, hands grasping upon my arms as though I'd disappear if he let go. My own hands wove up his chest, fingers catching the bristly hairs as I combed through them, up to his neck.

Everything about him was hard, like warmed stone against the coldness of my touch. I felt him tense beneath me, our bodies pressed together with no want or need for distance.

I needed this, desperately. The touch, the tension, the distraction.

Duncan kissed like a starved man with coins finally weighing his pockets. Desperate and hungry. He moved with that desperation yet still demanded full control in the way his lips pressed atop mine. Noses clashed as our faces turned, shifting to allow for fluidity. I tasted him, sharp as wine. The kiss deepened quickly, his tongue joining the dance and parting my lips with ease, coaxing my own until they both twisted like snakes encouraged by their charmer.

I was lost to the dark of my closed eyes, allowing Duncan to guide me. He was the captain, I merely followed his physical command.

He urged me down upon the bed, leaning backwards, and tugging me atop him. The bed creaked as my weight was added, aged wood screaming in resistance. But we ignored it, along with many other things.

I clambered upon his lap, legs overlapping his until I was kneeling above him. Duncan's head rested upon the wall of the attic, hands now grasping the sides of my face as he refused to break his lips from mine. He moved with confidence gained only from experience. The thought alone made my cheeks bloom red and my insides warm with excitement.

It was Duncan who pulled away first, holding me at arm's reach. His breathing was laboured, as was mine. Without his kiss, I was aware of everything. How his legs felt firm beneath me, and the subtle movement of his hips as though we stood on a ship rocking above calm seas.

"Are we…" His words tapered off, lips red and glistening wet. Fingers now gripped my lower back, squeezing into my skin where he held me. "Doing this? Do you… want to do this?"

"I want to," I assured him, "if that's what you're asking."

He didn't smile, at least not with his mouth. Duncan's eyes lit up from within, brows raising as he exhaled a long, toughened sigh. "Say it to me. Tell me what I can have."

"All of it." I tensed, nails shifting down the hardened lumps of his stomach until goosebumps were left in their wake. "Take me, Duncan. Distract me–"

My hands fell limp as the image of Erix flooded my mind. *Distract me.* That was how it had started in the destroyed home in Berrow, sharing a bed as winter ripped at the outer walls with desperation to enter and watch us.

"Robin?" Duncan said, fingers reaching to my chin. I snapped back to the room, attention shifting from the haunting memory and the bad taste it left in my mouth. "This can stop before it starts. Blame this simply on a moment of drunken boredom and never discuss it again. I'll do as you wish."

I pondered his offer, forcing a smile as I blinked away unwanted thoughts.

"I know what I want, Duncan, and it's this," I murmured, eyes racing over him with honest wanting. "Let's make a mistake."

"I like the sound of that."

Duncan gasped softly as my hand wove down beneath my arse and gripped the hard cock that pressed into me. Even beneath his leathers, I could feel its thick, warm and pulsing desire.

A growl built in Duncan's throat. He grinned now, flashing teeth and tongue. "Some words of warning. I don't doubt your experience or lack thereof, but I must tell you this. You would have never been with someone like me."

No shit. My stomach jolted, but not from fear.

"Care to expand on that?" I asked.

He shook his head, dark hair shifting as though a breeze infiltrated the room. "No. I'd rather show you."

I gulped. It was all I could do as Duncan looked upon me like prey.

"Remove your shirt," he commanded.

I did as he wanted, tugging the clothing from my back with clumsy, nervous hands. Discarding my shirt upon the floor, I felt somewhat self-conscious, a feeling I wasn't familiar with. Duncan was built like a man, thick and strong in every sense of the words. Etchings of muscles covered my body, but I was slimmer and shorter.

He didn't seem to mind.

Duncan took his time, eyes drifting over my hardened nipples and taut stomach. Wherever his eyes dusted across, I felt them like a whisper of an unseen touch. He lifted a finger, running the coarse tip of it across the scar upon my chest. Twisted skin, left from the burn of Althea's touch as she had cauterised the stab wound Tarron had given me. I waited for him to say something, ask what had caused it. Then again, I didn't question his scars.

Shivers ran across my arms, the silence taut as I waited for his next command.

"If only I could taste you," Duncan groaned, touch becoming rough as he gripped the sides of my waist. "Delicious, irrefusable, Robin."

"You can." My voice was small as I replied. I began rolling my hips, not caring for the ache in my knees or the moaning of the bed beneath us. All I cared for was the lump of flesh that I rode atop and the way it widened Duncan's eyes and quickened his breathing.

"Careful, Robin," he warned.

"Of what?" I asked, gasping as his hands tightened and he looked down to my hips with burning hunger. Mouth parted, he watched in a strange trance as I rocked upon his cock, enjoying the feeling of it pressed beneath me, a reminder of the power I held.

Duncan snapped his stare to mine, low lip caught between his teeth. Then he spoke, replied with a single word that set my skin ablaze. "Me."

I was feather-light in his hold, ripped from my seat upon him and twisted with ease until my back was laid out across the bed. Duncan leaned over me, arms pinning me down at either side. There was no time to gasp before his mouth was back upon mine. Urgency fuelled the kiss.

My legs wrapped around his hips, and I pulled him down upon me. Nipping, biting, sucking at his lips and tongue to prove my own hunger for him. I was frantic, hands rushing up his bare, hard back. I got to his hair, grasping a handful and pulling. He was mine for the night – a few hours of pretending.

Duncan removed a hand, balancing on his other, as he fumbled with the belt upon his trousers. Silently I encouraged him, internally cheering as the belt smacked the ground and the thump of his trousers followed. By the time he broke away, bruised lips a faint blue, he was left with nothing but his cock standing proud between his legs. He was large, in every sense that mattered. In the glow of orange flame, shadows were cast across his scarred body. Muscles etched proudly, like mountains upon his skin. Dark hairs messy from the urgent spreading of my hands. And his cock. It looked at me as I looked at it. I wanted to reach for it, wrap my fingers around its warmth and pull him back to me. Instead, I studied him like a painter studied a landscape, memorising the curves, shapes and hardness of his body.

"Impressive," I said, eyeing every inch of him – and I meant *every* inch.

My mouth filled with moisture, cheeks prickling, hands damp; my mind raced to decide what I was going to do first.

"Time we get the rest of your clothes off, I think."

"You do it," I commanded this time, taking control. "Undress me."

Duncan did as I asked. He undressed me, hands tugging off my trousers, his knuckles brushing the bare skin of my thighs as he worked them down to my ankles.

As skin touched skin it felt like lightning.

Then he spoke, commanding the room as his own like the general he had worked so hard to become. "Suck me, Robin," he demanded, hand grasping the base of his cock where he shook it with a tight fist. "Let me feel what the mouth of a king is like whilst I fill it entirely."

One look down at his cock and I knew there was no way I'd have fit it all in. But I was going to try – I liked a challenge.

Duncan stood there as I pushed up from the bed and lowered myself down onto my knees before him.

"Have you ever had a king kneel for you?" I asked, brushing my hands up his ankles towards the warmth of his inner thighs.

"Ask me when the sun rises, and I will answer with honesty."

Duncan's hand worked in circles, up and down his shaft, never once taking his eyes off me. As I had with him, he studied me like a sculpture, searching for imperfections to smooth. I couldn't help but wonder what Duncan thought, watching me as he did.

I could've listed the parts of myself I hated. The parts I wished to keep hidden. The way the bones of my hips pushed out through skin, or the fact my chest seemed to never have the ability to grow hair like others my age.

I pushed myself towards him, reaching forward with needy hands. "May I begin, or are you going to just glower down on me until you make yourself come?"

"Wait a moment," Duncan said quickly, pulling his cock from my reach. "Until I give you the command. Be the good boy I know you can be."

A nervous laugh bubbled out of me. With Erix I had always felt in control, but now... This was different, thrilling and unnerving in equal measure. Like standing on the precipice of a cliff and jumping off.

Duncan finally tore his gaze from me, looked downwards, and pursed lips as he spat upon himself. The line of spit dribbled until it graced the pink curve of his cock's end. With a thumb he caught it from dripping to the floor, rubbing it around the tip until it glistened in the candlelight.

He then reached forward, took my jaw in his hand and pulled me until my mouth was full.

"Hands to yourself," Duncan commanded as he begun to move, in and out, slow and gentle. "I want your mouth only."

Despite my desire to, I really couldn't get the entire length inside. Duncan revelled in that fact. Tears streamed my cheeks, the deeper he thrust. Duncan cleared them with his thumb, but more spilled every time his cock brushed the back of my throat.

He moaned like an animal, head knocked back as I worked at him. The sounds he made encouraged me, the hand at the back of my head guiding the rhythm of my sucking.

Before the ache in my jaw turned from song to scream, Duncan pulled me from him, picked me up beneath my armpits until I practically dangled from the floor. Duncan didn't care for the spittle around my mouth, coating my chin and cheeks, as our mouths crashed back together. I lost myself to him, allowing myself to be moved around as though I did not control my own limbs.

Soon enough the world was tilted, and I was laid back down on my back.

"You never fail to surprise me with your talents," Duncan murmured, fingers leaving red lines in the skin of my legs as he dragged them upwards. "Do you know what restraint it has taken for me not to finish within your delightful mouth? Do you?"

I shook my head, gasping as his fingers tickled beneath my thighs. We held each other's gaze as he trailed his touch all the way to the sensitive part of my arse. "I told you that you had no patience."

"Wicked, Robin. Teasing me for my lack of control. I'll punish it out of you," he groaned, pressing the tip of his finger in ever so slightly, enough to make my body quiver. "I'm going to fuck you now, okay?"

I reached for his hand, desperation taking over. "Do it, please, do it."

"Where were my manners?" Duncan smiled in response to my begging. "May I fuck you, King?"

King. Such a funny title. I hardly felt like a king, especially now. On my back for a man who had sworn his life to hunt others like me. Oh, how the tables had turned. No, the tables had been completely flipped over, smashing into lots of tiny pieces.

With one hand, Duncan ran circles around the sensitive heart of my arse. With the other, he drew his tongue up his fingers, spitting upon them until they dripped.

"Yes," I breathed. "You may."

I closed my eyes as bliss overcame me. Duncan rubbed his wet fingers upon my sensitive entrance, the tip of his finger slipping inside of me as a promise for what was to come.

My back arched, forced down by his hand on my abdomen.

"I will give you a throne worthy of sitting upon," Duncan said.

Euphoria exploded behind my closed eyes like stars dying in the night. "And I'll ride within you like a steed worthy of royalty."

I opened my eyes, fixing them on Duncan, wondering why he'd not entered me yet. I was so completely focused on Duncan that the shadows around us swallowed the room entirely. There was something serious about his expression, a moment of pause that came with worry.

"Are you sure you want me, Robin?" Duncan asked.

"I do," I moaned as his finger slipped further into me. "Fuck me, Duncan. Take me for yours and do as you will."

He released a long, laboured breath. "Oh, Robin, you'll come to wish you never gave me permission. It's men like me who will ruin your life."

"Then shatter it," I replied, peeling back every layer or wall that I had built up around him. "Destroy it. Duncan. Ruin me… entirely."

And so, he did, without pain or discomfort. Duncan took my body and claimed it.

Duncan eased his length into me, a look of pure focus peppered across his brow. He watched himself slowly enter me, paying mind not to cause me pain, each breath allowing him to work further into me, shaft wet with his own excitement and spit.

Soon enough he built into a rhythm, each stroke sending bursts of pleasure up my spine. I closed my eyes, witnessing the explosions of colour that filled my mind. And my power… It crept out from me, cooling the sweat that laced my skin, without going too far. It held some restraint from breaking completely free and turning the world to ice.

This was divinity. Losing myself to a man who, in return, lost himself to me.

We were at it for an age. Fucking, bodies dancing.

Duncan surprised me most when he lifted my foot to his mouth, tongue twisting around my toes, sucking and nipping. At first the feeling stunned me, but soon I melted into it, enjoying every flick of his tongue and every graze of his teeth.

I never wanted it to end. But all good things stop eventually.

Duncan came to his end suddenly, moans building into a crescendo. I'd finished moments before, my spare hand assisting my climax. His fingers gripped into my leg as he cried out, lost in his relief. I watched him with pride, knowing I'd done that. With all the power I held, everything I could do, this… *this* was what gave me a sense of satisfaction with myself.

His thrusting slowed, breaths panting and chest heaving. When he opened his eyes to look at me, ringed with tiredness and hair sticky with sweat, he grinned. "You're magnificent, Robin."

I gulped as he withdrew his cock from me, the phantom feeling of it still lingering within, even moments after he'd turned his broad back to me. I thought I'd become an afterthought as Duncan began cleaning himself down with the discarded tunic I had taken off.

Then he turned back to me and took his time clearing the cum from my stomach.

"The feeling is mutual," I replied, rolling onto my side and curling into myself. All I had done was lay myself down, presenting my body like food upon a platter of gold for Duncan to feast on, yet still I felt deeply exhausted. "That was not how I envisioned the evening going."

It was sobering. My mind was crystal clear as though I'd not touched a drop of alcohol at all.

"I do hope that is not regret I hear in your voice, Robin?"

I looked up, concern pinching Duncan's brow into a scowl. "Not at all, merely surprised. At you, at myself."

Duncan stepped towards the bed, cock still hard between his legs. "May I join you before my legs give out? Exerting so much energy after my head injury has left me feeling like I'm standing on a boat."

I patted the bed, chest warming at the idea of sharing such a small space with him.

We both lay naked facing each other. My back was pressed to the wall, the bed mostly taken up by Duncan's large, demanding build. He ran his fingers up and down my bare arm, tickling over the bumps that had spread across my skin.

"When the wine wears off, and we wake tomorrow, you may think differently of what has happened tonight."

"Maybe, but I think you're going to be wrong," I told him, head as clear as summer skies, not an ounce of wine left to haunt me. Perhaps Duncan had fucked the drunkenness out of me. "But you will. When realisation of what I am, what you are, catches up to you. By morning you'll remember."

Until then, I will continue to pretend – continue to use Duncan as a means to forget the world outside this attic room.

Duncan pressed a kiss to my lips, gentle as snowflakes falling upon skin. He pulled back, eyes blinking. "It would seem it is *my* turn to tell you that you are wrong, Robin. Tomorrow we will wake, still here, inside the church which has been defiled by our actions."

That spurred a small chuckle from me. "The sex part?"

"Yes, the fucking in a church part, Robin. Sex isn't a sin, but I'm sure even a god would draw the line at 'time and place'. Let us hope the Creator, Duwar *and* Altar have taken the night off and won't judge us."

No longer did I hear the congregation of chanting beneath us. I only hoped that Abbot Nathanial had retired, and that his ears didn't work well. I could hardly remember if we'd made a ruckus whilst we fucked – the idea of the old man hearing us turned my stomach in knots.

"What happens next?" I asked Duncan as his soft breath eased against my damp skin.

The question dangled between us on a fine string, ready to snap at any given moment.

"I can't answer that, Robin," Duncan replied, allowing me to tuck a strand of dark hair away from his eyes. The scar across his face flickered as his jaw feathered with tension. "Not yet. But I promise, if you are willing, we will face what tomorrow brings together."

Together. A Hunter and a fey. A general and a king.

A killer and a killer.

CHAPTER 25

We grew complacent in the days which passed. Time moved in a blur of laughter, sex and connection. Duncan and I made a world for ourselves, hidden away from our responsibilities within the church's walls. The attic became our haven. In that room we were nothing but two men, no past or future, only now.

There was no talk about what was to come after we left these walls. Or *when* that time would be. Our stay should've been only a few days, but that stretched on to close to a week. I didn't bring it up, nor did he. In truth, during the time when Nathanial left us to his duties, we would clamber upon one another, limbs twisted and lips wet.

A flurry of snow had settled upon Ayvbury overnight, turning roofs white and hiding the roads beneath. We had watched from the window as fewer occupants joined for morning mass. With my hand pressed to the thin glass, I could sense just how cold it was outside. It had even invaded the room, affecting Duncan more than it did me. The chill felt like welcoming arms, wrapping around me and holding tight. Duncan didn't feel the same, instead swearing through chattering teeth, the tip of his nose as red as his cheeks.

He used my body to warm himself up.

Abbot Nathanial had called for our help later that morning, promising that some good, honest labour would help warm Duncan from the inside out. Not that I needed it, but I was happy to help the old man.

237

Our task was simple. We moved through the church, collecting religious tomes and tidying the many items left from the morning service. For people who respected the Creator, they certainly didn't respect his place of worship.

Duncan no longer seemed uncomfortable being here. In such a short time, something had changed within him. His patience no longer waned, as if he'd finally found the skill and clung to it. Even now he was captured in quiet conversation with Nathanial, helping the man as they discussed memories of his childhood. The tension that'd been strung out between them no longer lingered, cut clean by time and old wounds healed.

"Strange happenings indeed," Nathanial chortled back to something Duncan said, patting him upon the shoulder as he passed with tomes piled in his hands. "One will have to send word for soldiers to find the thief of all that wine!"

"It could be the mice," Duncan replied. "Thirsty little beasts. And I hear they've a liking for old, over-stewed wine. A cat would be more effective than a soldier for that matter."

"Hmm. Mice you say? How odd. Those same mice must have been alongside you all those years ago, and have seemed to return to my door the very same day you did. Do you play the pipe, Duncan Rackley? For they follow you, I am sure of it."

My cheeks warmed as Duncan winked across the pews at me. "What a mystery. I do hope you get to the bottom of it. Thieves or mice, the disappearing wine is a serious matter. Before long you will be without bottles."

All it would take was for Nathanial to saunter up into the attic to see the pile of green, brown and deep maroon empty bottles. But he didn't need to see them to know that we took them. Nor did he mind. It even seemed the old man enjoyed the banter, or perhaps it was just the smile across Duncan's lips that made the Abbot content.

"What do you say about the matter, Robin? Your silence is deafening."

I looked up, my own hands full of loose, torn scrolls that outlined the morning's service. "If it's mice, I'm sure they're more than thankful. Nothing warms a belly better than wine."

Nathanial looked between Duncan and me, smile beaming. "Then we shall let them enjoy themselves until their tastes move on to stronger spirits, or better places."

That was Nathanial's way of saying that he knew we'd leave sooner rather than later. I hoped it was the latter.

The abbot slipped into the back room of the church, clinking among stacks of books and cases of disappearing wine, his chortle still audible as he went about his business.

Duncan prowled over to me, arms straining against the dark leather jacket the abbot had obtained from the market the day prior. "You know, if you feel tired, I can tell the old man to finish the task alone. There's a bed waiting for you upstairs which I am certain requires warming."

I rolled my eyes, fighting the grin by looking to the books in my hands. "I would be careful of how loud your mind is, Duncan. I wouldn't want the Creator punishing you for the dark thoughts you harbour."

"My thoughts won't be the reason he smites me down." Duncan leaned down, pressing a kiss to my cheek that lingered for a moment longer than it should have. As he pulled back, he whispered, breath tickling my ear. "Are you going to make me wait? We could do it here. Quickly, before Nathanial hobbles back out."

I thumped the books into his arms, driving the wind from him. "You're a demon, Duncan. Have you ever been told that?"

"Many times," he replied, face twisted in both a scowl and a grin.

A shadow passed over Duncan's face. He looked up, focusing upon the large, stained-glass window behind me.

"That's one big bird," he said, brows furrowed. "Did you see it?"

I hadn't, until it happened again. Another shadow, fast and large, cutting through the sky beyond the church.

Then another, and another.

That's when the screaming began, high-pitched cries that clawed at my skin. I blinked, flashes of sharp teeth and blood-stained talons filling my mind.

"Duncan!" Abbot Nathanial shouted, bursting through the doors back into the room. "Get to the basement, we're under attack."

Books clattered to the ground, spreading across the tiles in a pile of broken spines and bent pages. Duncan had dropped them, hand instinctively reaching for a sword that did not wait at his hip.

"No," Duncan said. "I want both of you to stay here and wait for me. Don't leave until I come back."

I didn't need Duncan to investigate or want him to leave me. I knew these clawing screams as well as I knew my own name. My hand shot out, gripping Duncan by the jacket with a fistful of leather.

"Gryvern," I said, breathless from horror.

Confusion deepened the scar down Duncan's face as he grimaced. But it lasted only a moment. "Doran's sent them for you."

I swallowed, magic curling in my stomach. "It's the likely answer."

I'd told him the story of my parents' death during one of our long nights. How Doran had plotted to end the line of the Icethorn Court to encourage war against the humans for the abduction of his wife and child, using twisted creatures to slay them and putting the blame on the humans.

Duncan had explained in all his years within the ranks of Hunters he'd never heard of nor seen a gryvern before. It just went to show how easily the fey were manipulated with false propaganda.

The humans had never been to blame for the monsters, of course I knew that now.

Duncan took a hold of me by my arms, fingers holding on tight. "You are not going anywhere. Not with the gryvern, nor whoever is sent next to retrieve you. We should have left days ago and been ahead of them. Fuck! This is my fault."

"Stop it," I spluttered, reaching for his face with a gentle touch. "Calm yourself down and focus. I've dealt with the creatures before and will not let them best me. Abbot." I turned my attention to the old man where he stood. There was something strong about his stance, legs apart and arms in fists at his side. I could imagine that he had faced horrors before just from the expression of readiness. "We need weapons."

"A man of God is never unprepared to face his foe," he replied, feet thundering as he moved with haste from the room.

The screams beyond the church no longer belonged solely to the creatures. Humans cried, in horror or pain I couldn't see from our haven. A horde of the beasts flew beyond the window, shapes no more than dark outlines that blotted out the light as they passed beyond. Glass shattered and wood snapped. But from all the sounds that scratched at my soul, it was those curdling screams of the humans that set fire to the anger within me.

"This needs to end," I said, flinching as something heavy crashed into the church wall. "Doran will never stop coming for me. His obsession with my line has gone too far."

I was furious, sick to death of being chased by a man who had already taken so much. There was nothing else for him to hurt me with, nothing more for him to take.

"Then we end it. Together," Duncan replied as Abbot Nathanial burst back into the room.

Held in his shaking hands was a sheathed sword, bound in brown hide and a cream strip of material. Much like the weapon Duncan had left in the ruins of our party, it was broad and long, one that would require two hands to wield it.

"It's been many a year since this blade last saw light." Duncan took it from Nathanial, testing the weight of it in his hands. "But a blade is a blade, do with it what you must–"

The window shattered, glass cutting skin as it rained down upon us. I whipped my head to the side, throwing a hand up to save myself from the slicing agony. It happened quickly, too fast to act. Wind pulled at my hair, drifts of snow falling within the broken wall of the church. And blocking the chaos outside was a gryvern.

Shards of coloured glass embedded into its pale, grotesque skin. A stench so vile, pungent like rotting flesh, wafted through the church with each beat of the creature's leathery wings. But it wasn't the gryvern that made the bile burn up my throat, but what it held within the clasp of its talons.

"Nathanial," Duncan bellowed the name just as my soul screamed it.

Abbot Nathanial hung within the gryvern's grasp, feet kicking at open air. His mouth was split open in a scream, but no noise came out beside a raspy breath, tears streaming down his terrified face. Scarlet blood dripped from the wounds upon his arms, the gryvern's talons cutting deep, through flesh and muscle. I was certain I had heard a bone snap.

Duncan was screaming beside me, aged and blunt sword free from its sheath.

His cries were useless.

We watched, helpless, as the gryvern tore Nathanial's limbs apart with ease. The sound of flesh ripping had this morning's food spilling out across the books and glass strewn over the ground. The wet smack of his body against tiles echoed, torn, bloodied arms following as the gryvern discarded them.

He was dead before his skull cracked against the ground, eyes wide, skin ashen.

All I saw was red, blood and anger joining as one. My ears thundered with the pounding of emotion as I studied the broken, ripped and shattered body of the abbot.

Duncan rushed forward, sword raised and shouting. The gryvern lunged to greet him. Steel passed through skin until black gore rained down upon Duncan who slid beneath the attacking beast. Head severed, the gryvern crashed into the altar, cracking its warped bones against the marble. Candles fell, flames catching within an instant against the dry walls of the church. In moments the fire demanded control. This was their place of worship, scorching fingers crawling as it spread itself hungrily across the skin of the gryvern and the building around it.

"We need to go!" I shouted over the chaos, another gryvern circling through the air in response to my cry. I could see them past the shattered window, maws bloodied and talons full of human meat.

Duncan was hunched over the abbot's body, as still as a guarding statue. When he looked to me, skin sticky with gryvern blood, his eyes burned red. He looked as much the monster as the creature he had slaughtered.

"I'll kill every fucking one of them," he seethed, spit flying through his mouth, expression softening only when he looked back to the body of the abbot at his feet. "No mercy. They all die."

"Together," I repeated the sentiment he had shared before hell was unleashed upon us. I could not look at Abbot Nathanial. I did everything in my power to look away; ignoring his broken, bloodied body was the only thing keeping me safe from the guilt.

Another death because of me.

Wasted life.

Duncan took the hand I offered, his fingers slicked with dark gore from the gryvern. I had to urge him to his feet, coaxing him with a song of his name to look at me.

"I didn't get a chance to tell him I was sorry," Duncan said, voice a muted whisper.

"He knew," I said, still fighting the urge to look at the body as the fire continued to devour the church.

"I should have said it to him. I had the fucking chance!"

Duncan pulled back against my hand, but I held firm as a cracking filled my chest.

"We will avenge him," I said. "That is your apology. But for that, we need to survive this."

My words snapped some sense into Duncan who no longer pulled against me. He stood straight, face contorting with sadness.

We left the burning church as one – magic readied and sword raised. There wasn't a moment to look back as we ran out, not as the flames licked up the walls, ready to devour the haven we'd claimed.

A stabbing pain shot through my chest as I realised that I'd been wrong earlier. I had more to lose to Doran, something to fight for. Looking to Duncan, winds blowing his dark hair from his face as he roared like a warrior of old legends, sword raised to the sky in warning to the gryvern, I knew what I was ready to fight for.

And this time, Doran would understand what failure felt like.

CHAPTER 26

The streets of Ayvbury were stained scarlet. Dark blood splashed across the snow-covered ground as though the skies had bled over us. Gryvern circled the air, dropping human body parts as they finished gnawing on bones and flesh. The wet smack of flesh erupting against stone turned my stomach.

We left the church, unleashing a battle cry across the village, which did little to drown out the screaming of the humans still alive.

"Get into your homes!" Duncan bellowed, blade raised proudly, gryvern blood running down across the hilt, covering his hands in a glove of black.

Red, red, red.

Even as I blinked it was all I saw.

Humans scattered like ants, bodies running into the shadowed doorways of buildings. Taking advantage of the gryvern's distraction, they didn't waste a moment in following Duncan's command.

I stood, frigid winds whipping around me as magic pooled from my consciousness. Glancing up, I saw every pair of black, beady eyes pinned to me as though I shone like gold in a world of endless night.

Then, as one, they shot towards me.

Duncan's cry disappeared, buried beneath the lashings of wild, frozen air that I conjured. It exploded outwards, a wall of unpassable force that raced up to greet the demons. It tore at the ground like unseen claws, catching debris, stone and snow. I felt them as the monsters collided with the barrier of wind and ice, no more than whispers of contact, like bugs crashing into glass as they tried to get to the sweet fruit on the other side.

I *was* the fruit and they wanted me. And all I could think about was getting them as far away from the humans as possible.

Duncan was beside me, eyes wide with wonder, dark hair tousled and swept back from his face, revealing every inch of his handsome splendour. And like the gryvern, his entire attention was on me, pale lips slack with shock. He looked at me as though I was his god, blinking heavily to see if the image of me and my power would dissipate.

I revelled in his reaction. It alone urged the winds to push stronger, keeping the gryvern at bay.

"I need to get the gryvern out of Ayvbury," I said. "They want me, and they will follow me out. You need to check on those who are hurt. Kill any gryvern who straggle behind."

"No." Duncan's face pulled into sharp lines of disagreement. "We stick together. You can't take them alone."

I found my lips pinching upwards in a pout, brows raising as my eyes flicked between the wall of silver winds and the crackling of ice that turned my fingers blue. "I no longer underestimate myself. Don't underestimate me, Duncan."

"Stay alive. Remember, I need you." His expression was hardened steel. I waited for him to refuse, but instead he held his blade firm and nodded. "I will follow after you."

I felt like his need had differed from before, as mine had, but I'd question him on it if we survived.

"Are you ready?" I asked.

He looked back towards my barrier, eyes narrowed as he readied his stance. "Just come back to me, Robin."

I smirked, chest warming even as winter tore around us. "It will take more than this to keep us apart. I need you too, remember that, Hunter. How else do I get my audience with the Hand?"

Duncan smirked and with that I pushed out with my power, sending my winter force racing outwards.

We both moved, Duncan into the village, and me towards the path that led outwards.

My legs rushed forward, boots smacking across the ground, arms pumping at my sides, my entire focus on the stretch of ground beyond the village's outer homes. Inhuman screeches followed me, the flapping of wings, the monstrous howls as they shadowed me. There was no opportunity to look back, but I only hoped that they all followed.

The gryvern caught up with me quickly, bodies slick as they cut through the sky, wings more forceful than my mundane limbs. I turned, throwing my hands up to touch the creature that reached me first. My goal wasn't to remove myself from its line of attack, but to greet it. Power pooled around my hands, crackling and frozen. As soon as my fingers gripped the mangled, bone-thin limbs of the creature's arm the pale skin hardened to ice. All it took was a touch – a thought.

I threw myself sideways, watching the blue-tinged glint of my ice as it completely devoured the flying creature. By the time it hit the ground there wasn't an ounce of soft flesh left. The gryvern cracked on impact, body exploding in splinters of frozen blood, flesh and bone.

There wasn't a moment to marvel at the destruction I'd caused before the next gryvern was on me. But at the back of my mind, I felt satisfied knowing I had taken one down alone, killed yet another one of Doran's puppets, all without releasing the full storm within me.

I ran onwards, putting as much distance as I could between Ayvbury and me.

I got a few steps before more reaching talons clawed at my back. Skidding to a stop, I turned to face the horde. Gryvern clambered over one another as they flew towards me, fighting each other as though they were starved, desperate for the last piece of meat to fill their bellies.

I greeted them with a smile, breath coming out in misty clouds. "Come and get me."

It was easier controlling my power with a physical movement, like a horse being controlled by reins, I held onto my control with a firm grip, casting hands upwards so the force of winter followed.

Blades of jagged, mountainous ice speared up from the frozen ground. The earth split as the knife-edged talons reached for the gryvern that flew above. They had no time to act, not as I impaled them like pigs over a fire, others crashing into the ice without a chance to move out of the way. Many died in that split second, blood hissing as it dribbled down the spikes of ice. Others were trying to break free to no avail, wings torn apart by my ice-made blades.

The sky broke with the keening screams of monsters.

So, you feel pain. The thought was dark and terrible. *Suffer.*

The horde was more than halved now, the remaining beasts forced to change course to careen around the death between us.

I didn't want to look away from the scene. It was glorious to watch. Each gryvern flew with the face of Doran, as twisted and hideous as the fey king's soul. And seeing them captured in death was a beautiful thing. If only Doran was here to witness it. I wouldn't let a single one return to him. Their absence would tell Doran what I needed him to know.

He failed, *again*.

I picked the gryvern off one by one, toying with them as I ran only to stop and unleash more frozen horror. It was a game of chase, one where the prize was survival. And I would win. A trail of bodies was left in my wake, providing me a clear path back to the village without the need for a map or compass.

Each one I killed, I killed for Abbot Nathanial. For the humans who I didn't know, the ones the gryvern had slaughtered in search for me. This was for them – all of them.

And more than anything, it was for *me*.

There was no requirement for a weapon made of metal, not when I was one created from flesh, bone and fury. I released the full extent of my magic, sharpening flakes of snow to tear at leathered skin and turning any gryvern foolish enough to reach for me to glass. I fought so hard, delirious with power, that I hardly noticed when their advances stopped.

Blinking, I looked before me to see nothing but empty skies. Unlike Ayvbury's red stained streets, the ground here was stained black, the smell of death pungent in the winds that coiled around me. Gryvern littered the ground, limbs not even twitching as a fresh layering of snow fell upon their stiffening limbs like a blanket.

I called the magic back, willing its return into every corner of my being. The world seemed to calm before me, whereas the thumping of tension in my head persisted, the feeling melting from one of pleasure to discomfort after using so much magic.

Blinking, I saw the devastation before me from a different view, one no longer fuelled by power and fury. I looked to my hands, clean of blood and evidence of the horror I had caused; then I looked back to the bodies which caused a clawing of dread to slice through me.

I caught movement out of the corner of my eye, a gryvern splayed out across the ground, body covered in cuts and gashes that spilled black gore in a pool beneath it. One of its wings was ripped from its back, lying at an angle to its side. Its chest heaved with rasping breaths, blood splashing from the creature's mouth. I stepped up to it, the tips of my boots an inch away. Those wide, endless eyes flicked towards me as the creature weakly snapped its jaws in my direction.

Despite the many I'd battled against, there'd never been the opportunity to study one up close. What I noticed astounded me. It was its ears. Much like my own they ended in pointed tips, not the round, human-like curves I'd seen on the others. My mind raced, flicking through memories for some hint that I had noticed such a thing before. No memory rose to aid me.

Doran had convinced the world that the gryvern were human-made. Whereas they shared the features of the fey.

I left the dying gryvern, moving between the bodies as I searched for a reason to believe myself crazy. But my exploration only caused the dread to tighten in my gut. Many of the dead gryvern had the pointed ear tips, much like myself and the fey King who had sent them, but others had the curved edges of a human. I knew little of the pack-driven creatures beside their want for fey blood and the truth of Doran's control over them.

But I'd believed their origins to be linked to the humans in some way.

I was wrong.

A darkness hung over Ayvbury, the cloud of smoke and ash blotting out what little sun there was.

With the back of my blood-stained hand, I cleared clumps of ash as they clung hatefully to my eyelashes. At first it had disgusted me, knowing that each flake of ash was caused by the burning of flesh as a great fire devoured the bodies of the gryvern beyond the village. But the thought alone was not as horrific as the smell. It clawed at the back of my throat, stung my eyes and twisted my gut into knots.

Ayvbury was silent for the most part, all but the sudden wails of humans as they uncovered their loved ones beneath the mounds of snow and ash. It set me on edge.

"There is nothing more to be done here," Duncan said, voice dull of emotion as he studied the hell before us. "It's been made clear that our help is no longer required. We should leave before their grief sharpens and turns its focus on us."

Duncan was right. I'd felt the human's disdain towards us the moment I had run back to find him; hateful, burning looks were shot my way. And I couldn't blame them. My presence had brought this horror to their homes. There was nothing I could've done or said to return life to the bodies that they mourned over. Children, husbands and wives. Homes destroyed. Streets littered with dark stains of blood.

"How far is Lockinge from here?" I asked.

"By horse," Duncan replied quietly, fussing over the bloodied blade he still clung to, "two days. By foot, close to a week. We could steal a horse from the village's stables, I think it would go unnoticed–"

"I'll not give them another reason to hate me. Stealing their livestock is not an option, Duncan. We go by foot if that's the case."

I couldn't do it, couldn't take something from these people that didn't belong to me, after I had been the cause of so much loss already. Part of me wanted to beg for them to understand, to sympathise with what I had lost, turn their hate towards the enemy beyond the Wychwood border, to Doran. But this was not the time.

"This is not your doing, Robin. These people may not see it now, but one day they will."

"Such wise words are wasted on me," I said, feeling hollow in my core, knowing what was to come. "We should have left days ago when we had the chance. Instead, I chose to give in to this stupid little… whatever this is between us. It's done nothing but distract me from my goal."

Duncan inhaled sharply, breathing through his clenched teeth as though my words had stabbed him in the chest. I would've felt the pang of guilt for my harsh words, but I was already drowning in it. Duncan was quiet for a moment, watching the humans intently who regarded us with just as much fear as the gryvern who had attacked them.

When he finally spoke, it was with a tone I'd not heard from him in days; short and sharp, like any useful knife, he replied, "There is a long journey ahead, Robin, far too long to wallow in self-pity."

"Then let's go." I made to move, but Duncan grasped my wrist.

"Are you sure you want to do this," Duncan said, eyes wide, brows creased. "If... if you say you've changed your mind on meeting with the Hand, I will release you – let you go."

"What about those names you need me to collect?" I asked.

Duncan refused to look anywhere else but me when he replied. "They don't matter."

"What does then?"

He released my wrist, letting my hands fall back. "You."

One single word pierced me deeper than any arrow could hope to do. This was my chance to turn back. To walk away. But then I remembered all those innocent fey hidden in a prison that no one knew about.

I had to do this for them. For answers – for their freedom.

"My mind hasn't changed on the matter," I said.

"Okay." With that Duncan turned on his heel, pacing back towards the church.

I bit down on my lip, holding back the urge to call his name. But then I looked back at the scene of destruction and lost all ability to worry about Duncan and his feelings. I punished myself by glancing at every human I could see, studying their faces, remembering them. To imprint them each in my mind so when the time came to kill Doran it was for them as much as me. It was the least I could do.

But first I still needed an army, just not the one I originally set out for.

CHAPTER 27

Days seemed longer when they were consumed with silence.

Duncan worked hard to keep a gruelling pace as we travelled through Durmain's landscape. I couldn't speak on behalf of his body, but my feet were numb, my limbs aching to the point of feeling as though they'd given up on me. Not once did Duncan slow. Even if I picked up my pace, gritting my teeth against the discomfort, he always stayed ahead.

Nights were the worst. We were curled into balls with nothing but the jackets upon our backs for warmth. Still Duncan didn't speak. I wanted to say something to him, to spark a conversation just for the chance to hear his voice; the thought of it was all-consuming. But as time went on, it became more difficult to know what to say.

Duncan was stubborn, which only pulled the string of tension between us tauter. I could recognise that we also shared that in common. Father had once referred to me as a mule; thinking back on it I had the urge to smile. His nickname at the time was a way of mocking my childish, stubborn tendencies; now the memory warmed my chest. *Stubborn as a mule*, he would say through fits of laughter. I wished I laughed alongside him. I would've given anything to hear him say it again.

So far, the weather stayed mild with clear skies, but the chill of winter was persistent nonetheless. It didn't bother me, but I could see it effecting Duncan, chipping away at him slowly.

We had stayed clear of any villages or towns we had come close to. With the threat of more gryvern, it was best we didn't bring them to the doors of humans who were unknowing and undeserving. Which meant food was limited to the little that Duncan had brought with him in the pack draped across his back. And no more alcohol. It was a reckless mistake, one of many.

I wouldn't make them again.

Even when he offered me something to eat or drink, it had been without words, just an extended hand, held out long enough for me to silently take his offering. In hindsight they were perfect opportunities for me to say something to him.

To thank him at least.

I kept quiet and so did he.

The third day had been particularly full of persistent walking. Most of the terrain had been through woodland, rarely opening up to a rolling hillside that looked over Lockinge miles away. The previous two nights of short, broken sleep had at least been under the comfort of trees which gave some protection from the weather.

As night fell upon us it was clear our luck had run out. I'd been kept awake, from both the howling winds that tore over the exposed landscape and the rasping breaths that came from Duncan who was buried beneath his jacket in hopes of some protection. I felt his physical discomfort to the exposed elements as my own internal uneasiness that'd haunted me through the long days.

I crawled across the frost-claimed grassland and placed myself neatly behind Duncan. He was far taller than me, but I nestled my crotch into his behind and wrapped my arms around his side. Even through his leather jacket and thick tunic I could feel the violent shivers that overcame him.

As I had in the attic of Nathanial's church on the first night we arrived, I used my magic to draw out the cold from his bones. Duncan stirred. It was a wonder how he even slept in such conditions without magic flowing through his body.

His deep voice broke the night and shattered me into countless pieces. "Finally."

I held onto him tighter, fingers gripping into his chest as I clung to him as though the winds would simply tear him away from me. "You're so cold."

"I have never f–felt better," Duncan rasped, teeth chattering. His hands, frozen like ice, laced within my fingers and held me close. "Don't you dare l–let me go, Robin."

Pressing my face into his back, my smile tugged at his leather jacket, relief warming my insides.

"Tell me you don't see me with the same hate those in Ayvbury did," I pleaded, having convinced myself that was why Duncan had not spoken to me for this long. "I need to know."

Duncan groaned, pulling himself free of my hold as he rolled over to face me. Even in the dark I could see his features. Deep, forest-green eyes. Scarred, handsome face. I laid my arm over him as he snuggled so close to me that his nose was inches from mine.

"Is that what this has all been about? Your distance. Your attempts at pushing me away?"

"Says the man who hasn't uttered a word to me," I replied.

Duncan released a tempered breath, a misted cloud forming beyond pale lips. "Something you need to learn about me, Robin, and fast, is that only I can decide what lingers in my mind. And hate for you is not a possibility. Not anymore."

It was at that moment I realised that Duncan believed I had been ignoring him. Instead of facing the tension, we had let it consume our minds and fill them with negative thoughts about one another.

"Then what?" I asked.

"I worry for you, day and night."

Duncan didn't need to say it, but I knew the origin of his concern. Because the closer we got to Lockinge, the more dangerous it was going to become. "If what you said about me being a royal, and the Hand's interest, is true, I should be safe."

"It doesn't work like that," Duncan said.

"What about the Below? Surely if the fey are all still alive there, they are somewhat safe?"

I hadn't questioned the Below in a long while, not wanting Duncan to know the new reason I was using him. It hurt to even admit that was what I was doing.

"Death would be kinder than a lifetime beneath Lockinge castle, in a prison where you are treated like cattle."

Shock creased my face, noticed by Duncan, who trailed fingers down my cheek. "You have me. No matter what happens, I will find a way to get you out."

"You *should* hate me. You *have* hated me. I represent the very people who took everything from you, just as I was the cause of destruction in Ayvbury. Why look at me any differently now?"

Our noses touched as he leaned into me, sleep narrowing his eyes into slits. "I see you, darling. Not how you see yourself in the reflection of those who don't know you. You are gentle. You are concerned. In all my years I've never come across a person able to shift my mind and beliefs, but here I lie in the arms of a fey. Your arms. Robin, you're no monster. I've seen monsters, I've faced them. But when I look at you, I see the vulnerability of humanity. That's it."

I lowered my gaze, shocked by the fingers that found my chin to hold it in place as I tried to break eye contact.

"Don't look away from me, Robin. See the truth in my eyes. Go on, I dare you to look beyond what you think people see and learn what they actually see. What *I* see."

My entire soul quivered beneath his touch. A touch I had fought hard to stop thinking about these past few days. "I don't think I'm brave enough to pretend."

"Try. Do that for me," Duncan said, holding my chin in place. "Tell me what bothers you? What fills that mind and punishes you? Let us face your inner demons together. You may be scared of them, so allow me to be fearless for you."

I paused, the intake of breath shuddering as I readied myself to reveal my truth. And slowly I let it out, one terrifying word at a time; it didn't hurt as much as I believed it would.

"When I am with you, I feel close to them," I said, voice buried beneath the winter winds that raced across us.

"Who?"

"My father and mother." It hit me, the reality of their story intermingling with ours. Maybe that was why I drew so close to Duncan, like a moth to a flame, ready to burn in his fire. Because it was my grief making history replay itself. "There's so much of their story I don't know nor will have the chance to ever understand. But my father, like you, fell for someone they had been taught to hunt and hate. You both changed your way of thinking. Being with you makes me feel as though I understand them more than I would have if my father had the chance to explain it to me more. I have to believe, that if my father can change, you can change – the humans can to."

"You think I have fallen for you?" Duncan asked, making my cheeks burn red. His forefinger and thumb still gripped my chin, touch gentle and caressing.

"By the sounds of it I don't think I want to know your answer to that question," I replied, wanting nothing more than to change the subject for fear of hearing how wrong I was.

I was in the midst of punishing myself internally when Duncan leaned in. He pressed a kiss upon my lips, and I melted instantly. They were dry and chapped, but the connection was nothing less than pleasurable. I closed my eyes, enjoying every second of his touch. His fingers let go of my chin and instead cupped my cheek as he held me close.

When he finally pulled back, I could've cried out in frustration.

"If I admit that I'm falling for you, then I almost accept that the ground I'm to meet will be terrible and unforgiving. But yes, Robin Icethorn, I have fallen. For you. All of you, despite the inner voice that screams in protest. I know better now and ignore it for you are far superior to anyone I could've ever imagined. Which is why I don't want to do this – why I want you to change your mind and turn back."

My stomach jolted at his revelation. "But that will never happen."

Duncan's gaze darted across my face, eyes searching my reaction with keen interest. "Vengeance isn't all it's cracked up to be, Robin."

He still believed I did this for Doran. In a sense, I did, but not to the extent Duncan first believed.

"Do you hear yourself, Duncan? It seems like a lesson you should heed."

"It is."

Silence, once again, clashed between us, threatening to draw us further apart like a vicious tide receding. But this time Duncan refused the distance. He was the one to speak first, shattering the quiet with loud, demanding words.

"Don't hide from me anymore. Say something, Robin," he begged, fingers tracing my cold cheek. "No more silence between us."

I couldn't fight the smile that tugged at my cheeks, or how my chest warmed as his words still spun through my mind like an unrelenting hurricane. "And what is it you want for me to say?"

"Well." Duncan traced his thumb down my face until his touch ran across my lip. "If there was any time to tell me how *you* felt then there'd be no better opportunity. Or are you afraid to bare yourself to me, Robin? There's no one listening. Just me and you. Not even the stars will judge you."

I looked skyward, taking in the glowing balls of light speckled amongst the night sky. "Are you too ignorant to see what happens to those I care for? Think harder and you will understand why I keep my thoughts to myself. I don't wish to see another person I care for used as a weapon against me."

Erix had been on my mind a lot over the past days, haunting me with happy memories, burying the monster he'd been forced to become.

Duncan lay there, fingers still upon my face as I spoke, brows raised above his dark, all-seeing gaze; he hardly blinked for fear of missing the way my face changed during my confession. "So, you *do* care for me?"

"Nothing gets past you, does it?" I said softly.

"Not a single detail. Robin, stop fearing what could be, and enjoy what is. Doran, Erix, those are names which you can forget in time. I'm not as expendable as you may be used to. I will never allow myself to be used to cause you harm or pain."

"You say that now." Erix hadn't wanted to be used by Doran, he had no choice in the matter. I certainly never saw it as a possibility, until his hands took the life of my father, controlled by the bidding of a crazed man. "Time will tell what'll become of you and me. We are both equally foolish to keep pretending that our... whatever this is, will carry on when we reach Lockinge. Even Father had the chance to tell me how terrible it is for a Hunter and a fey to fall for one another. He gave up his life, his physical appearance and who he was, just for the chance of being with my mother. And look where they both ended up."

Six feet under.

I shivered, and not from the cold; from the honest and scary fact that our feelings were nothing but trouble. This would never last.

It was Duncan's turn to be lost for words. He let go of my face, hands falling beside him. I lay still as he turned onto his back, staring up at the dark skies. I was ready to hear him agree with me, to tell me that I was right and this stupid, childish relationship we'd found ourselves entangled in would have to stop before it ended in death.

But he didn't.

Instead, Duncan did what he did best and surprised me. "I never had anything to lose before you. No family. No friends beyond the ones I used to get the position I'm in today. Then in a matter of days, all that changed. I cannot speak for how you feel or how you wish to guard yourself from the world. But I know, with such burning and irrefusable fact, that I'd do anything not to risk losing the one thing of importance to me." Duncan turned his head, dark hair falling across his cheeks but not enough to obscure the glimmer of tears in his eyes. "If you tell me you want this to end, then it ends. Here and now. No matter how it will hurt, I will do it for you. But if you are brave and wish to face the risk ahead by my side, then I will do it too."

I couldn't deny him, nor myself; even if my mind told me to refuse him, my heart demanded the opposite. "Do we have a plan then?" I asked, voice meek.

Duncan exhaled through a smile, tongue tampering with his lower lip as he rolled back over to face me. "We?"

I nodded slightly, wanting nothing more than to take him right here, right now, with the winter frost sprinkling over us. "A wise man once told me that having someone to fight beside is as great as having something to fight for. You are that someone. So, about that plan?"

"I have ideas." But those never came as Duncan's lips crashed into mine, his cold touch frantic and desperate. He rolled me onto my back, strong arm holding himself up above me. Drawing away from my mouth, he replied. "We have time for plans. For now, I want you."

I giggled, hardly caring for how exposed we were, or the clear discomfort the cold had put upon Duncan. "Now? Here?"

"Let the stars watch. I will give them a show, one they have never seen before."

He dipped back down, body brushing my own as he kissed me deeply, my mouth spread open by his tongue, his hands rubbing up my sides, tugging my jacket upwards.

I found my own hands moving without command, gripping long, dark strands of hair, fingers buried through them. My legs wrapped around his waist as he bore down on me, pressing me into the damp earth we rested upon. Breaking away, I gasped for breath with tender and wet lips.

Duncan pressed his forehead to mine, equally flustered and breathless. "Roll onto your front for me."

Duncan's voice was full of command; he could have controlled the stars themselves.

I did as he asked, welcoming the return of his monstrous power which I'd craved since our last encounter back at the church. His expression was smooth as he watched me turn over. When our gaze finally broke apart, I felt a fiery thrill course through me. With my cheek pressed to the crisp grassland beneath me I could not see him, only *feel* him.

"Is this what you do? Pour your heart out and then fuck?" I asked, voice muffled by the ground.

Duncan's greedy hands ran up my legs, gripping into my skin through my trousers as he reached my arse. "I fucked those who meant nothing to me. You deserve far more than that. I will worship you with every inch of me. Devour you entirely. But first you must tell me, Robin... do you want me?"

I raised my arse upwards, pressing it into his crotch, his hard cock greeting me instantly upon contact.

"I will take that as your answer," Duncan muttered, hands grasping the length of my body.

I writhed beneath him, rubbing myself across the hard length restrained within his trousers. It dragged a tempered groan from him, one that gave me nothing but pleasure. There was an enjoyment to be had, knowing the reaction I could conjure in him.

Duncan took me with nothing but the night for cover. Tearing my trousers off, his cold fingers shocked my bare skin as they brushed across it. His actions spoke of his hunger for me, the way one hand pressed down on the back of my head, whilst the other hand wet the sensitive part of me with spit laced across his fingers.

"Speak to me," Duncan moaned as the tip of his finger pressed deep within me. "I want to hear your voice."

I opened my mouth and my own groan of pleasure spilled into the quiet night, the prolonged sound joining the winds that danced around us. "Wha – what is it you want to hear me say?"

At once his finger pushed deeper. He leaned into me, teeth grazing my ear as he replied, "There would be no fun in telling you what I wish to hear. Figure it out yourself."

Another finger joined the first, slick with his spit. There was the unmistakeable pop of buttons as Duncan worked his cock free. He was excited, rushed and quick-handed as though he did not want the moment to end before it truly begun.

"Duncan." I used his name with the power it deserved. "I – I want to feel you, entirely."

A warmth spread up my spine as the wet, soft head of his cock replaced his fingers all within a sudden moment. He held himself, with wonderous restraint, hard cock on the verge of entering me. "I love when you speak my name. Do it more. Louder, so the stars and the realms beyond hear."

"Duncan," I moaned, pushing my arse back upon him with desperation. "Fuck me."

"Do you lack manners, Robin?" His hand gripped my shoulder and squeezed, the feeling of his hold a thrill of lightning through my body.

"Please," I exhaled, needing him with a burning desire that overwhelmed me.

"Beg me."

And beg I did. My mouth dripped with lust and desire, cheeks prickling with excitement at the thought of pleasing him; for when Duncan became this version of himself, I wished nothing but to please him. "Give me all of you, Duncan." The stars were a witness to my shouts. There was nothing but empty rolling hills and endless landscape around us. I took full advantage of our lack of surroundings and opened myself up to the primal desire that made me want to scream to the heavens for the man who mounted me.

Duncan entered me with a slow, gentle stroke of his cock. The sound he made as he pushed every inch of himself inside could have torn the ground in two. "Robin," he groaned, pushing my lower back downwards. "You're divinity. Pure, honest bliss."

It was the last thing he spoke to me, for we let our bodies converse without use of words.

Duncan made love to me, thrusting with surprising, sudden changes of his movements. For the most part I simply lost myself to the feeling, until I felt him wane with energy and I took over, throwing myself back upon his length until my arse clapped into the leathers of his folded down breeches.

It was a miracle the entirety of Durmain's realm didn't hear us.

"I never want for this to end," Duncan called, hands gripping my hips as he worked within me – faster, *harder*.

The pitch of his deep voice told me he was close to his end. And the power it made me feel had me working harder for him. I'd not once felt the need to pleasure myself as he took me. It hadn't even crossed my mind, I was too occupied with riding the storm of pleasure and indulgence his sex gave me.

"Come for me, Duncan," I bellowed as his cock pounded against the sensitive place deep inside of me.

His reply came as a guttural grunt, but then his movements slowed as his panting reached new heights. Duncan finished just as I knew he would, climaxing with gripping hands and laboured breaths. The moment was so sudden. He rode within me, his pace slowing as his rasping cry of pleasure filled the night sky. When he was done, I could've sworn I felt his legs shake.

I slumped to the ground, my own brow drenched with beads of sweat, no matter the frozen chill of the world around us. Here, in his place, we'd carved out our own world, and I was not ready to leave it.

It seemed that's what we achieved with one another. No matter the place, attic or rolling landscape, we claimed it as our own.

Duncan fell beside me, eyes closed and hands blindly fumbling to pull his trousers over the throbbing shaft lying across his lower stomach. He finally tucked it away, the imprint still more than a memory in my mind.

"Better?" I asked, rolling on my side.

Duncan's tired eyes studied the indent the grass left upon the side of my face. He nodded – twice – mouth agape as he still gasped for breath. "Better doesn't even cut it. I do not believe there is a word available to describe how I feel right now."

Duncan raised an arm, welcoming me to snuggle into the crook of him. I too lifted my trousers, hardly caring for the dampness that still coated my skin from his sex.

Effortlessly, he ran his fingers up and down my arm all without opening his eyes. "Forgive me, Robin, but I must do what a terrible shag does best and give into this tiredness. You've exhausted me, my darling."

I laughed, the sound so terribly loud, even compared to the ruckus we had both just created. "It is a well-deserved rest and far from a terrible shag."

"I feel as though my work isn't done. A real man should never sleep until he saw his partner satisfied."

"Duncan," I breathed, nestling into his body and inhaling deeply. "With you beside me there is no need to discuss satisfaction. Just hold me tonight and don't let me go. That is enough."

He turned his face, pressing a kiss into my hairline. Duncan pulled back slightly, whispering for only me to hear, his words far too precious for the star-filled night to witness. "My love, you are my weakness. I could not possibly ever let you go. I am many things, but a fool is not one of them. Not when it comes to you."

Everything about what he told me was a melody to my ears. But the one word that stood out amongst the rest could have shattered my reality entirely. It was frightening, giving in to the giddy and wonderous feeling that overcame me in that moment, yet there was no stopping the current as it swept me from my feet.

Love.

CHAPTER 28

I'd never seen so many Hunters in one place. There was a sea of them, a stain of leather-clad bodies passing across Durmain's landscape. They snaked in an organised path, one smudge of darkness which paraded along the ground towards the glint of a city in the distance.

The ledge upon which we'd made camp jutted over the landscape, giving a perfect view for miles upon miles. Duncan had promised we were close to Lockinge as we had stopped here the night prior. In the belly of darkness, it was impossible to see anything for proof.

Now, in the fringes of dawn when the sky was blushed with pinks and deep orange tones, I could see it, a faint jutting of grey among the notoriously flat landscape. Lockinge. Capital of Durmain. A place I'd never been allowed to venture even remotely close to as per my father's warnings. Of course, back then, I'd not understood why he'd wished to keep me from this place. Now, knowing what I did, it made perfect sense. Lockinge wasn't a safe place, not with the Hand's grip upon it, not for the likes of me.

I couldn't stop thinking about the prison of fey. It occupied my thoughts constantly, making my hands tremble. If only I could speak with Althea, determine how she got on with preparing numbers to come and aid me. So far there'd been no hint that a fey army followed – if they did the entire realm would be alive with whispers. But I knew she'd never leave me, I just had to play the long game and keep focused.

Shrouded in thinning woodland, Duncan had felt it was the perfect place to sleep, until the heavy thumping sounded, waking us up to the horror of the army that moved in the distance. And that was what they were, an army of countless bodies marching across the ground below with only the heavy pounding of their feet to warn us that they were close.

It was impossible to shake the exhaustion that had made a home in my bones from the days of travel and lack of food. I had not seen my reflection in days, but if Duncan's shadowed eyes and heavy features were anything to go by, I looked as terrible as I felt.

"Is this normal?" I asked, cautious to whisper even though we were leagues from any Hunter to hear us.

"No." Duncan pursed his lips, eyes scanning the snaking shadow of Hunters as he too tried to make sense of what we were seeing. "The Hunters are in an abundance around Lockinge, but never have so many been seen close to the capital at the same time. It's as though they have been called back. Previous commands from those above me have been to ensure my legion is spread. The further we are from one another the higher the chance of taking the bounty we need. But this... I can't explain."

His words set me at unease, seeing so many who would wish me harm. And throughout the crowd of my enemies, I saw countless cages. I couldn't count on both hands how many I saw; each was stuffed full of figures. *Fey*. Being carted towards their final destination. They didn't scream, nor fight, because there was no need. Those locked within the cages had given up; even from our distance I could feel it.

Where these Althea's soldiers, those sent to help me? I hoped not, but still the idea made me sick to my stomach.

"And you still think you can get what you need from them?" I asked.

We had drafted a plan, one that required thievery. I was truly confident it would've worked, but seeing the numbers below had stabbed doubt within me.

"Regardless, it's our only option. If we are to enter Lockinge together, it is with you at the end of an iron chain. Without it you will be cut down before stepping foot through the city's outer suburbs. Birkhill is known for being the Hunter's final checkpoint. The busier the town is, the less I'll be noticed."

The idea of Duncan separating from me was not my first choice, but it certainly was the only option. We'd planned for him to visit Birkhill, a town shadowed beneath the city. He would retrieve an iron cuff and return, alongside a horse if he could take one. It would give us entry to Lockinge without stirring much interest, and the iron cuff would certainly play into the story we had put together as to what had happened after the attack on our party all those days ago.

"There must be another way," I pleaded, already knowing the answer as well as the lines upon my palms.

Duncan raised a finger and pointed to the dark shapes that flew over the army. "Those hawks mean that Trackers are among the numbers. If you are seen by those before we get a cuff back around your neck, you will draw the attention of that entire army. I know their kind. Kayne, someone I'm as close to trusting as any other, is one. They grow complacent that fey will not be roaming free this close to Lockinge, but one wrong step will ruin everything. Capturing their attention unprepared will not be wise."

Kayne, the name rang a bell. He was the red-haired man I'd seen back in Finstock speaking to Duncan. I remembered the hawk, perched across his broad shoulder, and now put everything together about the creature's purpose.

"Could Kayne be down there now?" I asked. "Maybe he will help you."

"I would hope so. If something goes wrong tonight, then he would assist, I believe it. I don't doubt his loyalty to me as a brother, more than a fellow Hunter. But even he cannot know about you – about us. Even brothers turn on each other when they go against a shared belief. I'm not ready to test our friendship, not under these circumstances. If I'm recognised, I am merely a lucky fucker who survived the attack on the party." He gestured to his unkempt appearance. "I certainly look the part."

"In and out," I echoed something he had said to me the night prior.

"Indeed," he replied, the sultry smile returning to his face. "And am I not an expert of that already? Trust in me, Robin. I go at dusk and will be back before the sun reveals itself tomorrow."

"And if not?" I asked, the words no more than a whisper.

Duncan placed his hand upon my cheek, letting me melt into his touch. We cared little for the dirt and grime that had caked our bodies from the lack of washing. "If I don't return, then I forbid you to come looking for me. Turn back. Return home. I cannot guarantee your safety if you come for me. Nor would I wish for you to risk going to Lockinge alone."

"So, I'm expected to sit here and wait for you like a good little pup? I still think you are a fool to not let me come and help. I have the skill–"

"Skills that will have you killed before you can use them." Duncan laid a hand on my shoulder and squeezed. "If you walk into a town full of Hunters, they won't see you as a king, but as a blood bag ready for draining. No, you stay here. Put your trust in me. And if I'm the one to fail, then you turn away. Understand?"

It took a moment to reply, and I couldn't do it with words. Instead, I nodded, hating how difficult it was to lie to him.

"No more talk of this, okay?" Duncan said, placing a kiss between my brows. "We should rest whilst we can. We can't afford to expend any unnecessary energy whilst being this close to Lockinge."

Duncan was right. We did need to rest. But I wanted nothing more than to rain down my power across the army beneath us. Watching those cages being carted towards the city did not sit right with me. It turned my stomach into knots, discomfort repeatedly stabbing into my chest.

For all we had planned, nothing prepared me for when we'd finally enter Lockinge. Duncan would return to his act of general and me as a captured fey. Then what? We relied on his title, and mine, to get us through the doors. Duncan was still confident my presence as king of a fey court would be enough to get the Hand's attention.

That did little to keep my anxieties at bay.

I missed Althea and Gyah. More times than I cared to count I would lose myself to what-ifs and maybes. What if I'd returned to Wychwood with them? Then I remembered what waited for me beyond the border.

Nothing.

An empty, abandoned Court. No family. No Erix. Doran Oakstorm and his endless petition against me. Just cold, endless, nothingness.

At least here, with Duncan, there was warmth. His body close to mine, his promise ringing loud and true in my head. But there was also the promise of saving the fey the Hand had captured. That was my focus. I wouldn't leave without them.

Since leaving Finstock, this was by far the quickest day to pass. All we could do was watch as the seemingly endless army finally moved on until it was nothing but a dot on the horizon. We did so in silence. No matter how I willed the day to slow, for Duncan's hold on me to carry on without any need to stop, dusk finally came and with it his departure.

"Remember, wait for me until dawn. If I don't make it back, then you forget me and return home."

Home. What a strange concept. It was a word I felt had no meaning to me anymore.

I gripped his cold, calloused hands and squeezed. "Duncan, don't leave me until you promise you will come back. If we are bargaining promises, that's what I need to hear from you."

His hand cupped the side of my face, gently but shaking slightly. "I will do my best. But I also need to hear you say it – tell me you will not come after me."

I couldn't lie to him again. Instead, I looked up at him through my dark lashes, blinking slowly at him, fighting back tears. "I can't help but feel as though this is a goodbye."

Duncan leaned forward, pressing his brow to mine. "It is merely a see you soon, darling."

My hands felt strange as he let go of them. They seemed to hover in the space they'd been as he turned away, straightening his jacket as he faced the dark path still visible through the tree line before us.

I waited, wrapped in the chill from the dropping evening temperature as Duncan took his first steps away from me. Just as he was to be engulfed in shadows Duncan paused, looking back at me with verdant eyes glinting and lips upturned. "I haven't even left and already long to return to you, Robin Icethorn."

I exhaled all the tension that had built within my chest. Smiling back at him, I clung to the hope that this plan would work, stealing his confidence. "Then get on with it and hurry back to me. Who knows, perhaps my bed will not be cold tonight after all."

CHAPTER 29

I woke to the thud of feet upon the ground. The sound tore me from my light slumber, unnerving me. Sitting up, mind heavy and body grasped in panic, I combed the dark woods for what could have caused it. That was when I felt intense eyes upon me, a trail of discomforting prickles spreading across my face.

A figure peeled itself away from the dark outline of trees ahead of me. I scorned myself for falling asleep in the first place.

"Duncan?" I called, ice already spreading beneath my palms across the moss-covered floor.

"In such a short period of time you already have another man's name filling your mouth," the shadow-figure replied, voice gruff as though he spoke through blunt knives embedded within his throat. "What has he got that I cannot give you, little bird?"

It wasn't Duncan who spoke.

Before the man stepped into the faded, silver moonlight, I threw my hands forward, commanding the ice to follow. It crackled, a wave of deep, ominous blue as it tore across the ground towards him.

Towards Erix.

He did the impossible, pouncing into the air as though he weighed no more than a feather. Two strange-shaped limbs exploded from either side of him, keeping him afloat for a moment, before gently falling back to the ground on light toes.

"Can we not just talk?"

My magic retracted as my mind made sense of what I saw. Perhaps this was a bad dream, the impossible blend of reality and fiction. "You died."

"No," Erix replied. "I did not – unfortunately."

I couldn't believe it. This had to be a nightmare, except one haunting the waking hours. Relief and fear blended into one within me, so seamlessly that I couldn't discern one from the other.

"Step into the light," I commanded, slowly pushing myself to standing for a better view. "Let me see you."

"It is best I stay here," he snapped, voice sounding as though three people spoke at once. Erix took a breath, those strange limbs flexing back down to his sides as they folded in on him. "I want to know something first, before you see me."

"You're in no position to be asking questions."

"Please, little bird–"

"Don't call me that."

I studied to the outline of Erix's hands as he flexed them at his sides. His fingers seemed longer – sharper. I blinked, wishing the vision was wrong.

"Do you remember when you told me what you fear the most? How is it you can stay alone, in the dark, with your Hunter so far away? There would have been a time when you could not have slept without a candle being lit by your side. Now look at you."

A chill wind danced between my hands, tugging my dark hair away from my face and wrapping around me protectively; magic spilled from my skin. "I've learned that monsters are not unique to dark places, but *all* places. Why would I fear the dark when what is revealed in the light is far more frightening?"

"Is that so?" Erix said, voice rough as stone against stone.

"Step into the light and let me prove it." I had to see him, to know what caused his body's outline to be different, his voice to sharpen and mutate. Whatever stood in the shadows before me was not Erix, at least not the one I had known.

"I am in need of something from you."

"Then you're sorely mistaken," I shouted. "Your needs are not important anymore. Everything you do is for Doran. I will be the first to remind you of that."

"Listen to me, *little bird*," he snapped, a guttural growl of frustration building within him. "Please."

"My name is Robin!" I stormed across the ground, closing the space between us as my cold wind spread its freezing embrace around me. A prickle of tears stung my eyes, from both sadness and desperation. "Even that name shouldn't dare cross your lips after what you have done to me."

His response stopped me dead in my tracks. "I know."

I gained closer. Erix stepped back, his pleading becoming frantic. He raised his hands before him, as if that could keep me away. "*Please*, just wait."

I was steps away from seeing the truth that hid in the shadows. This close I could see torn bits of material flapping as my cold winds reached him. Whatever Erix wore was ripped, hanging off his frame in tatters.

"Who do I speak with?" I asked, breathing laboured.

"Me. I'm… fighting it – fighting him."

His words didn't make sense.

"Doran, go on, Erix, tell me what he wants you to do with me."

"I feel nothing but agony," Erix replied, voice tortured with sadness. "Yes, I can sense my father, but his voice is quieter than it has been before. A whisper that is easier to ignore at most times. These moments don't last long, so please, I beg that you hear me out before you do what it is you require."

I shouldn't have believed him. Now was the time to act and deal with Erix as I first believed I had. But that small kindling of hope that the person before me was in fact the Erix I had known made me hesitate.

"You are expecting me to believe that he does not command you now?" I asked, nails cutting half-moons into my palms. "I find it hard to see the benefit in letting you roam freely."

Erix's outline shifted. He raised a contorted hand and pressed it to the side of his face. "I'm changing. I *have* changed."

"Step forward, Erix. I won't ask again."

This time Erix did, slowly moving from the shadows of the forest until he was bathed in the silvered light of the moon.

My breathing faltered. Gasping, I tried to claw back some air which the horror before me had stolen.

Erix had indeed changed. His limbs were longer, fingers ending in sharp, bloodied points. His skin no longer held the colour of life but was washed out and grey like a corpse. Wings hung limp at his sides, one larger than the other by a noticeable amount. As his outline had suggested, his clothes hung from him in tatters, as though the impossible growth had overwhelmed him in such quick and surprising power. But it was his face that shocked me most, hardly a whisper of what it had been before. Cheekbones stood out, pushing through skin to the point of breaking. His mouth was full of jagged teeth, overlapping lips I had known as well as my own.

And his eyes, once as silver as the blade he carried proudly, far brighter than any jewel those with coin could afford, were no more. Pits of pure darkness surrounded by some softness, as though there was some humanity left amongst his monstrous appearance.

As I studied him something clicked within my mind. A truth of what stood before me.

Not Erix. Not a berserker.

"Gryvern," I spluttered, voice faint beneath the rushing winter winds. Seeing the truth before me pieced together the horrifying puzzle that had presented itself days ago.

"Yes, Robin. Gryvern."

"That's what happens to Doran's children, isn't it? Why he can control the creatures to do as he wishes? Because they are simply his children doing anything to please their sire."

Erix bowed his head in confirmation, wings twitching irritably. "Metamorphosis, from one monster to another. The Berserker was a name given to the creatures by Doran's court. The name *he* gave them was gryvern."

It made sense, more than anything else in that moment. The gryvern I'd killed outside of Ayvbury, some had the small points of half-human ears and others the points of the full-bloodied fey. They were Doran's creations, what happened when a berserker followed the silent control of their sire and mutated.

"I can't believe this," I muttered, taking steps back.

Couldn't believe that he was alive, that he was really the monster he'd once protected me from.

"My father is a man with greedy tastes. And look where it led him. Now you can understand why Tarron was so precious to him. The perfect boy – not afflicted by this disease that Doran passed to the rest of his offspring because of his mother. Elinor Oakstorm... healed him. That was her power. The rest of Doran's offspring were not so fortunate, but why would he stop? The more his seed spread, the further his control would. Humans, fey, it does not matter to him."

"Why are you telling me this?" My chest ached as I looked upon him; all hope for the Erix I had wished to return was gone. Although his mind, right now, seemed his own, his body was not. Erix stood on the precipice, looking into the abyss at the pending monster he was going to become.

"So you know all you need to finish him," he said.

The winds picked up as I willed them, air thick with frozen ice that made each breath hard and full of prickling discomfort.

Erix lifted hands, pointed nails clawing at the air between us as if he longed to reach for me. "I understand I am not in the best of positions of putting forward requests to you. Not after wha – what I have done. But there is something I feel you deserve as much as what I need."

I stood, unblinking, as I waited for Erix to reveal what caused him such torment. "Nothing you can do or say would relieve the pain you have already caused me."

Erix looked up at me with those dark eyes filled with desperation. I searched them for some spark of silver, something to tell me that it truly was him, free from Doran's control, speaking with me.

"I want you to kill me, to finish the job you started." Erix shattered my reality with his request. "Save me from being used by him. These moments of peace, moments of reprieve from Doran's control will not last long, and even now I can sense him trying to claw back into my mind. I don't want more blood on my hands, blood I am not aware I am spilling."

Erix begged, talon-like fingers clasping one another in a signal of prayer. I could sense his legs quivering as though he was moments from falling to his knees. And I shared in that moment of weakness, my own body numbing as his request settled over me.

"Don't ask that of me, Erix." Hot tears stung my eyes; my magic retreating like a scorned dog. "How dare you come here and say such things. Do you think you're in any position to ask me even the simplest request, let alone that?"

Erix took a single step forward, and I retreated two. I could see the discomfort my repulsion caused him. "Little bird…"

"Stay away from me, Erix," I shouted, cringing as my voice echoed between us.

"You are disgusted by me. Yet I remember not long ago when you would look at me how you do the Hunter. You have no problem doing as he desires when he asks."

I scowled, forehead pinching into countless lines. "You've been watching us."

It was not a question, but a statement, one he didn't deny.

"Not by choice."

A sour taste filled my mouth. I hardly cared to know what Erix had seen and what he had not because the idea of him watching no matter the action churned my stomach. "Regardless of who controls you, I look into your eyes and see the man who took my... my father from me."

"Hate me then," he replied, voice low. "In fact, punish me. *Kill* me. I deserve it, you know I do. Robin, you have to."

He tried to trick me into a corner, force me to feel anger for him to ensure that his command for me would be complete.

But I couldn't do it.

"Gone are the days I'm manipulated by puppets of tormented men. No matter what you become, no matter what you do, what you are, I will not be made to take a life. Especially not yours. That, Erix Oakstorm, is your punishment."

He staggered back as the slamming of his full true name crashed over him.

Erix dropped to his knees, hands pawing at the ground as he wailed. "I would never have done it by choice. You do not understand what it is like having the mind of Doran within your own. I watch, from a dark room, as he manipulates my body to cause you pain. I would never have done that out of choice. You must believe me."

His wings jolted at his sides, moonlight washing out the little colour of life he had from his greying skin.

"I do believe you, but my answer stays the same." I choked back a sob, trying to control my emotions was harder than my magic. "You left me that night. If you hadn't, then perhaps we wouldn't be in this place discussing such matters. I hate you for what you have been made to do, but you are right. I can't kill you – I won't."

"But you must." Erix bellowed. "If you leave me, I will become a gryvern. That fate is worse than anything."

"I will save you," I said, chest aching. "I'm going to save everyone from Doran's poison."

I longed for nothing more than to flee, turn my back on the creature before me and forget him forever. In truth, I felt the memory of Erix slipping as this new version of himself stood before me.

"If you do not end this then Doran will gain his eternal control and you know what will become of me. I will be used to hunt you down until you are forced to take my life. Save yourself the time. Please, do it. For yourself if not for me."

"Get up!" The cry tore out of me. If my hands were not shaking so violently, I would have gripped my chest as a twisting agony filled it. "Turn your back and leave me."

"I promised I would never leave you." His reply was as urgent as my own words.

"You broke that promise many days ago and there is nothing that will fix it again. Go. Don't come back searching for death because you will not find it from me."

A deep growl rumbled from the pits of Erix's mutated body. He threw his head back, wings spreading wide when an inhuman scream of pure brokenness tore from his throat. His boiling desperation devoured the night; the sound was so haunting, it ripped at my skin, making the very night shiver in response as though it recoiled from him.

I'd never forget it.

I stood there, body trembling and rooted to the spot as I listened to his endless cry. I spoke only when Erix finally caved in on himself, forehead pressed to the ground, silent and exhausted. "I'm sorry I cannot offer you the relief you desire. I'm sorry this ended the way it did. And more than anything, I'm sorry I gave up on you."

My teeth ground together in response to the tearing sound of clawed hands scratching through the dirt. Erix's back heaved, as though his laboured breaths did nothing to satisfy his body.

"Then this is where it ends for us," he finally spoke, voice rough as jagged stone. When he looked up, dark, muddy tears coursed down his gaunt cheeks. They dripped to the frost-tainted ground and hissed. He winced as though his entire being was gripped in physical agony. "You are right, little bird, I do not deserve your aid. Not after what I have done to you. But know, from this day forward, my actions are not mine and will never be. As I leave you, I need you to know that the person you have known is no more. Never forget how sorry I am. Because even when this monster takes over, I will not allow myself to forget. I could never forget you, but I do wish for you to forget me."

I couldn't stop the tears from falling. No matter with how much pity and discomfort I looked upon Erix, I cried with grief, feeling as though yet another person had been taken from me. Killed. By Doran all the same; even if Erix's heart still beat as he left me, it was no longer to the tune of his own soul.

"Do not remember me as the man who tore your life in two, but the person who would have given his life to see you thrive."

Words failed me as my chest was racked with deep sobs. I could hardly catch a breath as I watched Erix stand, his dark tears drying upon his ashen skin. He held my gaze, blinked, and for a moment I saw the warmth of his golden eyes as though they shone through the shadows of Doran's hate.

"Thank you," I called as he turned from me. He paused, face still to the side for me to see the stretched points of his ears flicker in recognition of my voice. "Thank you for holding my hand whilst I discovered myself."

It was the least I could say to him.

Erix smiled, serrated teeth flashing in his brief grin. It was disturbing and beautiful.

I waited for him to reply, but instead Erix turned his back on me again, and walked away. His stretched leather wings dragging across the ground behind him. And with each step he took, I knew that I would never see even a flicker of the Erix I'd known again.

Standing alone in the clearing of the forest, night bathing the world in shadows, I remembered why I had travelled such a way from Wychwood. All concern or doubt about my end goal evaporated.

Killing Doran was a necessity, one I desired more than anything after learning several ugly truths. He'd die slowly for what he'd done. It was time to make him pay for his latest sin.

For the destruction of the man I cared so much for, for using the best part of my new life as a weapon against me.

For Erix.

CHAPTER 30

Erix's visit was a distant memory when dawn arrived without Duncan's return. I paced the forest, mind whirling with what to do. His warning not to follow him was no more than a whisper, and one I knew I'd no choice but to ignore.

As if I was ever going to listen.

It was a crisp and cloudless day. The winds had retreated, giving room for the tension of his absence to roar around me in its stead. Even with my usual comfort during the colder weather, a shiver was present across my skin.

Each moment dragged into an eternity. I found myself scanning the distance begging for him to return, holding out hope that he'd only be minutes away from finding his way back to me. *Perhaps he was lost*. That was the first thought I had, which soon perished with the realisation that Duncan was a man who knew himself as well as his surroundings. Losing himself on a path back to me wouldn't have been an option. The wave of what-ifs that followed grew darker and more horrific with every hour that Duncan did not return.

Soon the sky was bright blue, not a single smudge of pink dawn tones across it. The sun was reaching its apex above me, rays no more than cold beams across the landscape.

The view of Lockinge was clearer than yesterday, the outline of the castle upon the hill nothing more than a dark mark against the flattened land before me. A city sprawled beneath, clustered in its shadow. From such a distance I could not make out any important details of it, but I could understand its size without uncertainty.

I chewed on my nails as I watched Lockinge helplessly. My eyes followed the city downward, snaking across the grey stone path that cut across the landscape, the very one the Hunters had paraded upon. And there, no more than a faint marking of buildings, was their final checkpoint.

Duncan.

He had to be there. And regardless, I had to pass through there to get to the city's only main entrance. Duncan had explained the toll for entering Lockinge, a single payment for travellers to make in tax towards the kingdom. Coin, preferably, unless you bore the mark of the Hand, then entry was free.

I left our makeshift camp, focusing on putting one foot in front of the other before I changed my mind. The only way into Lockinge was with Duncan. Regardless, something was wrong. He wouldn't have left me for longer than he had planned. It was for that reason I swallowed my anxiety and began my journey to Lockinge's outskirts.

I thought of nothing but finding him. The small hope that we would simply bump into one another upon the road to Lockinge dwindled within me. The closer I grew the more I let that thought slip through my fingers.

The place where hope had lived soon hollowed and filled with rage. The feeling was hideous and overwhelming. It caused my teeth to grind together, and my hands to clench into hardened fists at my sides.

At first, I walked alone, cutting down the middle of the dirt path with not even a bird to witness my journey. Then I recognised the closeness of humans, hardly caring or noticing as they passed me on wagons or by foot. I kept my head down, my hood drawn up to cover my ears hoping to stay as unnoticed as I could.

Then I heard the squawks of birds – *hawks*.

Large, winged creatures circled above me and cried out in warning to whoever listened. They were brave little fuckers who dived as though to peck the hair from my head. *Tracker's companions.*

The Hunters were close.

I didn't need to wave the birds off, a single thought brought on the frozen chill of winter as I finally set loose my power. I watched the birds with a sense of pride as they flew back towards the looming outskirts of the final checkpoint. My eyes tracked their flight until my attention landed upon a wooden wall, spiked and towering, which came into focus ahead of me.

People stood upon the wooden barracks as I walked towards them. Hunters. I knew it for certain as the hawks landed upon outstretched arms. Those without a bird to greet them held up crossbows, sun catching the sharpened points of the bolts readied and loaded across them.

They were expecting me – that much was clear.

I could've stopped them, thrown forward the storm that twisted within my bones, my blood. There was no doubt in the power within me. Although still new to me, I trusted in the ability to become a force to be reckoned with.

Instead, I kept up pace, each footstep leaving a scar of ice across the dirt path, as I closed in on the checkpoint. I'd left my ability to think clearly at the camp, perhaps even further behind on my journey. Now was only action. Only anger and power.

Only madness, a whisper confirmed.

"Halt!" someone unseen shouted from the barracks. I didn't care who. More Hunters raced out through the open gates, each wielding an unsheathed blade or a different weapon of choice, each one raised in honour of my arrival.

I lowered my hood, there was no point in hiding anymore.

Power crackled in the palm of my hands, the sound as melodic as a mother's lullaby. It echoed the frantic beat of my heart, thundering faster as I grew closer to the Hunters.

"I demand the release of Duncan Rackley," I called, voice filling the space before me. "Return what you took from me."

Silence replied. Not a single one denied me, nor responded in confusion. It was unspoken what they had taken from me, and their hush told me my deepest worries were real.

A red-haired man stood forward from the line, hawk perched upon his broad shoulder and hands free of a weapon. His expression was placid and void of emotion, all beside the slight crease of skin around the sides of his eyes.

It was Kayne, Duncan's friend and supposed ally.

"There is no need for the fanning feathers to prove your magic. Even with your power there is one of you and many of us. I recommend you listen, before someone *else* gets hurt."

"Kayne," I muttered, rejoicing as he winced, hating that I knew his name. "Where is he?"

"Paying penance for his sins," he replied, teeth gritted in turmoil. "He was a fool to return and even more a fool for not destroying you when he had the chance."

"And what sins are those you speak of?" I questioned, toying with the idea of conjuring powerful, ice-kissed winds to freeze each and every one of these twisted fuckers.

"I hardly imagine you would like me to repeat his crimes for all to hear."

The laugh that tore out of me was ugly and sharp. The beastly hawk upon Kayne's shoulder flared its wings, releasing a shrill cry through its snapping beak.

"Don't mock me," I called out. "I'm not leaving this place without Duncan, so let the choice be yours. You either return him to me willingly, or you will see what a king will do for those he cares for."

"Your threats are wasted, fey. King or not, Duwar protects us. Before you raise your power against us you will find a bolt in your chest followed by a noose around the neck of the man you've bewitched. Tread carefully."

I silently refused to lose another person. Duncan was mine, I'd claimed him. "Give. Him. To. *Me*."

There was an emotion across Kayne's face that I could almost place. He chewed subtly on his lower lip, eyes heavy as he studied me at our distance. My breath caught as he closed his eyes, his forehead creased in whatever silent torment overwhelmed him, and he turned away from me.

"Now," I demanded, letting the frozen air amplify my voice.

"Bring Duncan out for the fey to see that our threats are not empty like his," Kayne shouted, raising a fist in the air beside him. "If the *fey* wants to see what has become of those requiring repentance, then we shall show him."

I followed the commotion behind Kayne, eyes scanning the line that shifted to make room for a huddle of three people to be clearly seen. *Duncan*. His name screamed throughout my very being. He was shirtless, the expanse of skin peppered in silver whispers of past scars was now mostly hidden behind the bleeding gashes that covered them, countless lines of dried and angry welts. His head hung, chin to his bare chest, dark curtains of hair hanging limp and greasy before him.

Duncan limped ahead, urged on by the sharp points of swords held at his back. If he faltered the tips would catch his skin and tear new cuts. I blinked, wishing to rub my eyes and rid myself of the scene before me.

"His fate will be far different from yours," Kayne called, voice breaking slightly as he did everything in his power to not look at Duncan. "Duwar doesn't look favourably upon sinners. They must pay for their immoralities with blood. Only when the poison leaves them will Duwar decide to bless them with renewed purpose. And as you now understand, Duncan has had many chances before."

Numb and lost to the roaring in my mind, I took a step forward. Only one. The air screamed in warning, a screeching whistle as a bolt shot towards me. It missed on purpose, the dirt beside my foot ripped up in a cloud of dust as the projectile stabbed into the ground.

"The next one will not be as kind."

Perhaps it was Kayne who spoke. I didn't care for anyone else now as Duncan finally raised his head, veins of struggle protruding from his neck, and looked at me. His eyes were narrowed with haunting determination. Even now he bled, ruby droplets crashing into the ground and pooling beneath him for all to see.

I had no choice but to comply. If I attacked, as my mind desired to do, it would only solidify me as a monster – proving their warped thoughts. I had to use sense. Duncan's life was at risk, evident from the sword held to his throat.

The magic I clung to disappeared in a moment, retreating into the pits of my soul as Duncan's weakened voice broke over the crowd. "I – I told you to lea – leave me." It took everything in Duncan's power to speak through his agonising pain, spitting as he forced the words out. His lip was bust, his eye blackened by bruises.

I shook my head, focusing solely on him. "You should have known I was a liar."

Duncan let loose a raspy breath. He looked to Kayne who stood rigid and stiff. I caught the prickling of discomfort across the tracker who Duncan had called a friend. Not once had he looked Duncan's way, his gaze kept upon me. Was it out of carelessness or fear for what Kayne would see if he looked upon the wounded, bleeding Duncan?

Hunters started prowling towards me with caution.

"No matter my disgust, I'm not in a position to judge your fate," Kayne said. "Duncan will be tried before Duwar as his judge, but you... You have turned many eyes upon you. The Hand has waited for you to arrive and wishes to discuss matters with you directly. On your knees, fey. If you care about Duncan, you will not resist."

Kayne knew he'd won. I did as he asked, dropping to my knees. My hands slammed into the ground and no matter how I wished to push my power across it, the magic would not aid me.

"If you hurt him, I'll coat all of Durmain in a storm," I warned, watching as Duncan slumped forward only to be stopped by a blade at his throat. I sobbed as I watched fresh blood spill down his torso, staining the dark material of his ruined trousers. "There is a power inside of me, one that you'll face the full wrath of."

"I'm a man of my word, fey," Kayne spat.

"You're supposed to be his friend. Duncan trusts you. A man of his word means nothing if he cannot protect the ones he cares about."

"Duncan has only hurt himself with his own actions. Going against his faith, his purpose. That was his doing."

"*You*," I growled as Hunters reached me, hands gripping my arms and twisting them behind my back. I didn't fight them off, for Duncan's sake. "He trusted you."

Kayne rocked back an inch, enough for me to know my words caused him discomfort. He then turned away from me, calling his command for those who would listen. "Take them both. We leave for Lockinge immediately." And with the uncaring swish of his cloak and a cry of the hawk upon his shoulder, Kayne turned his back on me and walked through the line of Hunters all without glancing towards Duncan.

Iron clasped around my wrists, nullifying a power inside of me. Another cold kiss of it strangled my throat, pinching my skin and squeezing tight.

I was hoisted from the ground by chains. They were connected between my neck and wrists and held in the grasp of a boulder-like man as though I was a dog at the end of a leash. All the while I studied Duncan, begging for him to look at me, praying to whatever god would listen to keep him alive long enough for me to petition for his safety. If there was one voice strong enough to end his suffering, it was the Hand.

And I now had my invitation to meet with him.

But at what cost?

CHAPTER 31

The streets of Lockinge city were crammed with humans. They watched, leering and spitting, as I was dragged like cattle before them; tugged, kicked and pushed by my captor. There was nothing I could do to shield myself from the hateful shouts of humans, or the stones and other unseen objects that were thrown at me. From the moment I'd passed into the city I felt nothing but hate around me. It was demoralising.

Even though my legs burned, and my feet felt broken, I wasn't allowed to stop. If I did it awarded me another jarring push. I focused on putting one foot in front of the other whilst keeping my head held high.

Something smacked into my face, cutting the skin beneath my eye. It happened so fast I didn't see what had been thrown, but it hurt. Badly. I took the pain, gathered it up and fuelled my focus. I tasted the sharp tang of blood as it dribbled into my mouth; it coated my teeth, splattering onto the cobbled street as I spat it out. With the iron cuff strangling my neck there was no healing ability that would help me.

Lockinge was built upon a natural incline of land. It felt like every street we walked leaned upwards, each leading towards the haunting castle that waited ahead of us. The dark grey stone towered above the city like a crown atop a king's head. It was harsh and ugly against the cloudless sky, it blocked out the winter sun and bathed a chill across me that prickled at my skin.

I focused on the castle, drowning out the screams from the humans as they spat their detestation at me. It was all I could do. Chin held high I tried everything in my limited power to not let their words hurt me.

Fey scum. False king. Demon. Freak.

There was something deadly about words. I feared them more than a blade or arrow. Words spat with hate may not spill blood, but they left deeper scars that were harder to heal. And in this moment, I felt as though my soul had no room left for pain. It was already riddled with it.

Duncan was somewhere in the crowd behind me. I heard the humans scream at him too.

Traitor. Sinner. Unclean.

That hurt me deeper than anything they could've done or said to me. Because I'd been the cause of those names, I'd done this to him.

I wondered if the Hand watched, peering out of one of the castle's dark and lightless windows as I walked through the city to greet him. It was clear his poison had spread like wildfire. Buildings I passed held his banner, the white hand symbol stitched onto an array of materials. I couldn't see any marker of the Creator and his faith, only the Hand, as though he was a god and not the strange promise of Duwar.

What has happened here? What had allowed such twisted hate to spread through the people of this city and leak into the world of Durmain beyond? I'd been so lucky and untouched in Grove for most of my life, and it was clear why Father had kept me there, far away from Lockinge's poison.

The incline to the castle worsened the closer we got, yet the crowds of humans thinned, which gave me some reprieve. Lockinge was not a city surrounded by walls, but the castle was, as though whoever dwelled within it was granted protection but those who lived in its shadows did not. As we entered beneath its gates, I recognised the glint of sun against metal. Guards watched from positions within the walls and upon turrets. They weren't garbed in the markings of the Hand but held billowing cloaks of deep scarlet and pointed helmets that could have been used as weapons. Kingsmen, a rarity, weapons jewelled and decorative, a perfect symbol for what they were now. They were nothing but decoration. No longer required as the true army of soldiers now entered the castle's grounds – this was the Hunters' playground now.

My legs shook violently as we came to a stop. The Hunters fanned out across the courtyard we had entered, a wave of bodies that stomped feet and called out to one another with excitement. There was a buzz here. I could sense it.

I caught a blur of red hair and spotted Kayne at the front of the crowds. He spoke with the Kingsmen, then he pointed towards me. I felt every eye upon me until the soldiers moved towards the main doors of the building before us and disappeared within.

Kayne cut across the courtyard towards me, his gaze on mine as he muttered something to the hawk that still perched across his shoulder. He finished sharing whatever secrets to the bird before he reached me, and it threw open its wings and flew off.

"I'll take him," Kayne said to the large Hunter who still held my chained leash. "Join your fellow brothers and prepare for the evening's celebrations."

Unlike Duncan, Kayne didn't have a natural command about his tone. It almost felt forced. From the hesitation of the Hunter behind me handing over the chains, I could recognise that he felt it too. But alas, the chains were handed over and I had a new owner.

"You don't understand what you've done," Kayne muttered out the corner of his mouth. He watched the crowd around us, as though he didn't want a single one of them to hear him. "Duncan does not deserve this. He's suffered enough. But you wouldn't care about any of that, would you?"

"Why are you telling me this?" I said, shoulders crying in agony as my hands had been held clasped behind my back for such a long time.

"If he dies because of you, I will personally make sure you suffer the same fate. No matter if your life is protected by the command of the Hand, I *will* kill you."

It wasn't a threat, but a promise.

"If you care for his wellbeing then do something," I seethed, not caring who heard me. "Help him, Kayne."

Kayne panicked and tugged on the chains, hissing through the side of his mouth. "Watch your words. They'll personally seal Duncan's fate before he has had the chance to survive the night. I have spent years trying to help him so don't speak on something you don't understand. Even I know when he is beyond saving, no matter how painful that is."

Kayne suddenly straightened his posture in response to the three new figures who exited the castle and walked towards us. It ceased the little conversation we had between us. One was the silver-clad Kingsman, who didn't wear a single hint of the Hand's symbol. Beside him, garbed in gowns that practically dripped with wealth, were two women.

Fey women.

Their long hair was pulled free from their shoulders, piled upon their heads in woven curls. From a distance it looked like crowns. The noticeable similarity between them both was the iron collar around each of their necks – similar to the one I wore – except theirs presented more like elaborate necklaces than a shackle to drain power.

Fey, walking free and without leashes.

I felt the crowd of Hunters stiffen. Some sneered and others spat at the ground at their feet. But the women didn't flinch. Their unblinking, vacant stares were kept forward without showing much realisation that anything happened around them.

"The Hand welcomes you, Robin Icethorn."

The blood drained from my face, every muscle in my body hardening into stone as I listened to them both speak in unison. It was up close that I could see the blue stains of bruises that hid beneath the necklaces and the dark purple shadows that hung beneath their wide eyes.

I looked to Kayne who showed no sign that the scene before me was not an illusion of some kind.

"You must be hungry. Please, follow and we will take you to your rooms. Food awaits you. A wash if you desire."

Even if I wanted to follow, I couldn't. My feet were rooted to the cobbled stone ground.

One of the fey women held out a hand for Kayne who welcomingly handed over my leash. She didn't tear her eyes from me, not even when the chain was placed within her grip.

"Wait," I spluttered, straining as I turned back to Kayne who started to walk off.

He paused, spared me a glance that reached straight into my soul; his eyes burned with such disgust, it had me swallowing my next plea. Kayne disappeared into the crowd of Hunters with the swish of his cloak, leaving me in the hands of strangers.

"It is best we go inside, Robin Icethorn," the women spoke as one again, not a speck of emotion in their voice. "The castle will soon be full of Hunters, and it is best *we* are kept out of their way."

I couldn't resist as they began to walk back to the door, pulling gently on the chain, guiding me towards the castle.

"What's going to happen?" I said, skipping a step to catch up, all the while searching through the crowds of Hunters for a sign of Duncan. He was nowhere to be seen.

"You will rest, eat and bathe."

My skin shivered as they spoke again, not a syllable or word out of sync.

"I wish to speak with the Hand," I said, hands grabbing the chain and adding resistance. "I need to see him urgently."

"And you shall," they replied together. "The Resurgence is shortly upon us. The Hand will see you soon. But first, there is much to prepare for tonight's festivities. Until then, you are in no fit state to be speaking with him."

Resurgence? There was something of importance behind the word; it caused the Hunters close to us to react with a childish excitement.

"I don't understand," I replied, neck aching from being pulled along. Desperation burned within me, in the same place my power would have been if the iron was not wrapped around my neck.

"In time you will. We *all* will."

Something was terribly wrong with the fey who escorted me into the castle's door, that much was clear. There was hardly time to make sense of what was happening as they finally tugged me into the cold, barren corridor of Lockinge castle. As we left the muted light of day behind us and entered the shadows of the castle's innards, I was certain I'd spotted something on the fey's arms. A dark mark, right in the exposed crook where their forearms met their elbows. Like their necks, it was covered in bruising, a perfect circle around a small puncture wound that was so fresh it had hardly scabbed over.

Before I could catch a glimpse again, we were in complete darkness. There was nothing but my heavy breathing and rushed footsteps that echoed around the strange walkway. The floor dropped out into steps, and we began our steep and terrifying descent bathed in shadows.

I felt as though we walked into the deepest pits of the underworld. And I knew where we were going the moment we descended beneath Lockinge castle. The fey were taking me to the Below.

The stairs we navigated were endless. For a long while, I

had no sense of direction as they guided me through the dark, except that we went only downwards. But soon enough the narrow, steep corridor glowed with burning torches held in metal frames across the damp walls.

I felt as though I held my breath, unsure what to expect when the Below was finally revealed to me.

One of the fey women plucked a torch free then waved it before her as we trudged on. Whereas the other held a firm grip on my chain as though her life truly depended on it.

I wanted to ask after Duncan, to demand to be told where he was and what was happening to him. All I could think about was his slashed and bloodied body. Did he bleed now? Had he given in to the pain his fellow Hunters caused him? I should never have let him leave. If I'd refused him then perhaps his skin would have been unmarked by new scars.

Kayne was right, he'd suffered enough before. Then I came along and ruined him.

I focused on my surroundings for a reprieve from my mind. There was nothing I could do for Duncan, no matter how that fact pained me. I only hoped time was in my favour.

"Where are you taking me?" I asked, even though I knew the answer. I needed to hear it from them myself. The walls around me had gone from smooth layered brick to rough edges of rock; moss covered most. Dark splashes of water wet the carved steps beneath our feet, making each step risky, the threat of falling inevitable.

All I knew was that we had entered the castle, but wherever we walked now was far from it.

Far *beneath* it.

"It is not permitted for the fey to walk freely above ground. Too many risks. The Hand's influence is strong, but not infinite. Not yet."

They spoke about themselves as though they did not have points at the ends of their ears.

"I asked you a question," I spat. "Answer it."

The fey shot each other a look that spoke of a silent conversation. Then one of them answered, already confirming my suspicions. "The Below. It is a place in which the Fey can be kept safe."

"A prison." I pulled back, gripping the damp wall for security.

They didn't tell me I was wrong – there was no point in lying this far beneath the ground.

"But the Hand allows you both to move freely," I said, voice echoing over rough stone walls. "What grants you such special treatment?"

"We have our reasonings," one of them said.

"Our purpose, in his eyes," the other added.

My skin itched as though fire crawled across it, the discomfort caused by the synchronisation both women spoke with. This was all wrong. The Hand petitioned for the death of fey. I had seen it with my very eyes. But that was only for those fey without magic. The Hand needed those with power in their veins, and I knew it had everything to do with the human who displayed magic in Farrador.

"This is where he keeps them all then," I said, feeling the realisation overcome me. "The fey with power, magic in their blood. That is what he needs, isn't it? Keeping them like livestock for whatever he needs to create his powered humans."

"Come, you will see. Everything you have come to know about the Hand may not be true. A short walk to go and your questions will be answered. You will hear them from the Hand himself."

I didn't stop again; the urgency of seeing what waited at our destination fuelled me onwards. I'd come all this way to see the Below. Knowing I was close renewed my sense of confidence. But what I saw, as the pathway opened up to a balcony of rock that overlooked the scene in the open cave chamber, was nothing that I could've ever imagined.

CHAPTER 32

There were hundreds of fey and not a single one imprisoned, not in the sense I would've first expected. They walked freely among the monstrous cavern, speaking with each other and doing as they pleased. Some sat upon worn wooden stools, drinking from tankards and laughing with one another. Others were laid across cots along the far wall that had been lined up, side by side. Like ants in their hill, they scurried amongst each other, dressed in rags and mismatched clothing that made them look more like vagrants than fey.

It was a city beneath a city – a hidden place, a cavern of secrets.

"The Below is safe for the likes of us – for you, Robin. You will dwell here until called to stand before the Hand. Until that request comes, you must take advantage of your time here. Eat, wash and find something less… offensive to wear."

My escorts gestured towards steps that jutted out of the cave wall, leading down to the lower ground. That was when I saw the guards, dressed in the same silver the Kingsmen had been garbed in above ground. There were no Hunters here.

The Kingsmen stood before an iron gate that had been welded into the stone wall as though it had always been there. From what I could see, it was clearly the only way into the cavern and the only way out as well. Yet not a single fey below me bothered to break free. No one stood before it nor did they plead with the Kingsmen for freedom as I imagined prisoners would've done. For beings who had been forcibly taken from their Courts, they seemed... comfortable.

Unless they'd given up – how long had they been here for? Weeks, months... years?

"Here," the fey woman said and the one holding my chain offered it to me. It was a strange exchange, the passing of my chains from my captor to me. "When you go down, those guards will take the chain before you enter. There is no requirement for you to keep it on. Only the iron will remain, to keep you in line with our needs. Our suggestion, if you would listen... Do not fight against this fate. It is easier for you if you comply."

I looked back down, hands weakly gripping the draining metal in my hands. "And if I resist?"

"Think of the Hunter you call Duncan." They laughed, and for the first time, they did so out of their strange synchronisation. "Goodbye for now, Robin Icethorn. We will see each other soon."

I watched them leave, all without knowing their names. Not that it mattered. They were puppets, their voices no longer their own. I didn't know how the Hand controlled them, but I believed, without need for question, that he was their puppet master.

The Kingsmen at the bottom of the steps did as the women said they would. With a worn key, they disconnected the chain from the collar around my neck. With silent command, they urged me through the gate they had opened with a terrible screech, before locking it back behind me.

I stood, looking out at the underground city of my people, and lost myself to the horrifying realisation.

This was more than an army – but they were no good if they didn't want to fight. From what I could see, they'd long given up. And I didn't blame them. No one had come to save them, they'd grown complacent with their new lives here.

Fey moved before me, like water parting around stone. I stood among them. Not a single one looked towards me. And why would they? I was nothing special. No different to them, besides dirtier and clearly out of place: not a single one paid me mind.

I walked through the crowd blindly, having no idea what to do and where to go. As I passed through the cavern it became clearer that these fey, no matter if I believed them to be, were not prisoners. They were happy, speaking in loud, booming voices as they laughed and shared food.

"Lost?"

To my side sat a girl, leaning back on a chair with her legs up on another stool. Dark midnight hair tumbled over her shoulder – only one shoulder, for the other side of her head was shaved down to the scalp. There was nothing pretty about her face, sharp and pointed, her chin and cheekbones protruding through milky skin. But she was striking nonetheless, a face that would catch an eye, even in a crowd, like the glittering of a jewel.

"Unfortunately, no. I'm not," I replied, stopping and studying her as she studied me.

"Don't worry, it gets easier in a couple of days," she said. "The fresh ones always take a few days to settle into their new life."

"And are you the welcome party?" I replied.

"In a sense. Although, I usually only spare the time for the new ones who look like frightened little boys. And you've hardly blinked since walking over this way. That and the fact I saw you being carted in by the Hand's faithful servants. The Twins are nasty bitches, they're the true welcome party, the one that no one asked for."

I glanced back, spying the balcony that waited far above us. I half expected to see both the women again, but they had left swiftly; the balcony was empty.

The girl leaned forward, the cuff around her neck worn from time. Resting an elbow on her knees, she reached out a hand. "Welcome to hell. But you'll know it as the Below. Where the price for staying is blood and your tenancy never comes to an end." She thrust out a hand between us. "The names Jesibel, but you can call me Jesi."

It felt wrong to ignore her hand, so I took it, noticing just how strong her grip was.

"Robin," I replied.

She barked, her laugh catching the attention of those around her. "Pretty name. We like pretty things down here, they are far and few between."

I tried to snatch my hand away, but she held firm. Her eyes narrowed as she pushed up my sleeve and surveyed my skin with keen interest. "They have not taken from you yet then?"

"Excuse me?"

She dropped my hand without care. With an unimpressive huff Jesibel rolled her own sleeve up, flashing her moon-kissed skin. In the crook of her arm was a fresh, angry wound surrounded by a halo of red-stained skin. "Now, what makes you so special? Even the newbies are drained before entry. It is payment for this wonderfully comfortable accommodation we are provided with. Yet here you are, skin unmarked."

"I'm sorry, Jesibel–"

"Please, Jesi is fine."

"Jesi." I forced a smile, unable to ignore how I annoyed her. "I saw that same mark on my escorts. The women had it on their arms as well."

Just the memory of the welts made me want to reach out and scratch my own arm.

"Good to know that the Twins aren't above paying with their blood like the rest of us then. It has been almost two weeks since I last paid my tithe. And far longer since this fucking iron has been free from my neck. Healing is slower as you will understand, but there is something about the leeches they use that hold off the skin's regeneration, I'm sure of it. I think they soak in a bowl of iron-infused water or something. Hunch, but a strong one."

So that *was* where the Hunters took the blood from. Leeches. My skin crawled at the thought. I believed the extraction to be far deadlier; images of necks sliced and skin flayed had not been impossible to imagine. But it made sense. Keeping the fey with power alive, taking blood and waiting, giving them time to refill until the next time they were bled for the Hand's gain.

"Do you know what he does with it?" I asked, knowing that answers came easily from Jesi. I needed as many as I could get before I met him. "Your blood, that is."

Jesi shrugged. "No. Not that it matters. Stuck here until we are bone dry, so what good is thinking about the above world anymore? My advice for you, Robin, is you should put the thoughts of the world you knew behind you. It's what the world has done to us. The sooner you give up on it, the easier your future will become. Trust me."

Pain. It started in my heart, before spreading down every limb and filling every vein. Jesi was but one of the products created when an entire realm forgot about her. The fey had been here all along, and we – the fey courts – had done nothing to help them.

It was on the tip of my tongue to tell her just how wrong she was now. But I didn't have the heart to tell her of what my appearance meant. Not yet. If I was to inspire a revolt, it had to be at the right moment.

"Listen," I said, the urgency that festered in my chest becoming hard to contain. "I need to get out of here."

"Ha. Don't we all. Don't worry, that feeling will pass when you realise that leaving is not an option," Jesi replied, a smirk across her lips but hardly reaching her eyes.

"You don't understand…"

Jesi scrunched her nose, pulling a face of pure disgust as I got close to her. "You smell like shit warmed up, Robin. How about you have a wash before you put me off tonight's dinner of gruel and bread. Wouldn't want my hunger being ruined. If you follow the cavern to the far end, you will come across an area of fresh springs. Beside the springs is an area where you can be given clothes. There will be something in there that will fit you, no doubt."

I looked where she pointed, noticing how the cavern we were in seemed to spread out further than imagined. This place was a system of interconnecting caves, a honeycomb of rock and stone filled with the bodies of fey stolen from their lands.

Jesi gave me a push as she leapt out of her chair. Even with the iron around her neck, she was still naturally strong. "What are you standing around for? Go and clean yourself."

"But if I go, how will they find me again?"

"Who?"

"Those fey women, The Twins, they told me they'd come for me. You need to understand I have to be ready."

"The Twins said that to you?" She tilted her head, intrigued.

I nodded, wanting nothing more than to return to the gate and demand the Kingsmen to take me to the Hand immediately. All I could think about was Duncan and what had happened to him, and what else was in store for him. The thought threatened me with a terrible sickness. It gripped my stomach and would have likely made me vomit if it had been full of food.

"I've been promised an audience with the Hand." I felt the need to say it quietly. "And you need to understand that I cannot just wait here for them to get me at their own leisure. I don't have the time to wait."

"And the Twins told you this?" she repeated, as though saying it again would make it easier to believe. Her sharp brow rose, clearly proving she didn't believe a word that came out of my mouth.

"Yes," I snapped, annoyance itching at my skin. "They said they would come back. You don't believe me?"

"Actually, I do." Jesi gripped my upper arm, squeezing with a strength I couldn't fathom. Her face was pinched, brows furrowed; there was a scar across one, slicing the dark lines in half. "The Twins do not lie. But I'm now wondering why you are so special to get a sit-down session with the Hand. Seems odd, doesn't it?"

I gritted my teeth, aware of her nails digging into skin. "Let go of me, Jesi."

She ignored my plea. "The Twins do not lie because they *cannot* lie. No one in the Below has ever seen the Hand. Except one. And if what you are saying is true... I think you need to come with me."

She began pulling me towards a pocket of shadows within the rocks that snaked off into another system of caves. "Jesi, get off of me."

We came to a stop, face to face. There was something distrusting about her stare. It was as black as her hair, seemingly blue when the strands caught the flames of the burning lanterns hammered into the walls. "Why would the Hand desire an audience with you, Robin?"

I swallowed, heartbeat thundering in my ears. Whatever I had said had caused such a visceral reaction from Jesi, triggering my anxiety to spark and spread like wildfire.

Others listened in now, watching our interaction as though they paid coin for a front row view of the show. I was not prepared to reveal everything about myself. With the reaction I had from the fey in Wychwood, I understood first hand that a good number of them had wished to see me dead. What was to say she wasn't the same? That determined how long she, and those around me, had been captive. They could've shared in the same feeling.

My mind raced with possibilities. What if their reaction caused the scene I desired? A big enough one would draw the Kingsmen's attention. Surely they'd remove me sooner if that was the case. That thought started as a spark in my mind, but soon exploded into an inferno of possibility.

So, I told Jesi the truth.

I spat my secret out, alongside my title as though it was the easiest thing to say aloud. "I'm Robin Icethorn, King of the Icethorn Court, and if you lay your fucking hands on me again you will find yourself without them."

I kept my chin raised, my voice void of discomfort at what I said. I could only hope that they believed me. And the way Jesi reacted, eyes widening, and lips pulled tight into a white line, I knew she believed my false confidence. My breathing was laboured. I did everything to focus on the girl's surprise, then darted my gaze around and registered the shock of the many who now watched.

Just when I thought Jesi would throw her head back and laugh, she surprised me again. She bowed, bending her knees, and lowering her back until I could see the top of her head. "My Court lives." Jesi's voice shook as she spoke. When she looked up at me, her dark eyes glistened with thick tears. And that was when I noticed our greatest familiarities. Her hair, her eyes, black as night and skin the colour of fresh-fallen snow.

I had no doubt, and required no confirmation, that Jesibel was an Icethorn fey. Like Eroan, the kind-hearted tailor, she was from my family's Court. She looked as if she'd seen a ghost, which suggested she'd been captured by the Hunters before my existence became known to the fey.

"I can't believe it..." she muttered, shaking her head as though the tears that clung to her dark eyes annoyed her. I watched, trying to hold onto my confidence but wanting nothing more than to break down and overload her with questions about the Court I'd claimed, but had not yet allowed myself to dwell within.

"It is true," I said, calm voiced although my mind was a storm of anxiety.

"How – how did they take you from–" Jesi stopped herself, physically shivering as she reined in her shock. "No. My questions can wait. There is somebody best suited to discuss matters with you, Robin Icethorn. Please, follow me."

This time Jesi didn't need to take me by gripping my arm. I followed her willingly through the throngs of equally astonished fey towards the unknown destination.

"It makes sense now," she muttered, looking sidelong at me as I caught up to her. "Our magic is not as potent as those from a royal bloodline. The Hand no doubt wants to be the one to see you in person. I cannot speak of what the Hand is like, but there is one person who will answer your questions with a clarity I cannot – someone who has sat with the Hand on a number of occasions."

"Another like me?" I asked, tearing through the possibilities of people in my mind.

I could feel her desire to question me just as I wished to question her. It was evident in the way her mouth would open, pause and close again, as though she thought it would be best not to speak what was on her mind.

"She will not believe you are here, in more ways than you could imagine."

We reached a narrow pathway of jagged rock with a low ceiling. Unlike the rest of the cavern, this place was covered in crystals that glowed in deep blues and gentle lilacs. Large, devouring stalactite formations seemed as though they dripped from the ceiling, solidifying into frozen points above us.

It was a wondrous place, for a prison at least. In any other circumstance, I might have stopped to ponder at the beauty of the place, admiring its natural design and formation. But time was not a luxury I possessed.

The narrow pathway ahead was empty of other fey. It darkened at a point, bathed in shadows as we moved further away from the light of the main cavern's atrium and into this new chamber. Then the crystal formations began to glow, not reflecting light but creating it as a result of some incomprehensible natural magic. A glint of the bluish glow caught across iron bars. The first I'd seen since entering through the main gate of the cave. Before us, in a small chamber of stone that gave hardly enough room to navigate freely, was a cell. It seemed that the cave had slowly begun to devour the iron bars, swallowing them into their surface.

If it wasn't for the crystals that gave off their subtle light, I wouldn't have noticed the hunched figure who sat upon the dusty floor of the cell. It was a haunting vision. Bowed and bent, the back of the person was curved in as though the weight of their thin shoulders was far too much to bear.

"Has my time to bleed come again so soon?" the fey called, their words a symphony of light, dulcet and defeated tones. It was that of a woman's voice but one that had roughened around the edges.

"No, my lady," Jesi spoke up, voice cracking with nerves I couldn't imagine she held usually. "Forgive my intrusion but there is someone I believe you'd like to meet."

"Jesi, darling. Is that you?"

"Yes, my lady," Jesi said, bowing her head.

There was a shuffling and the hunched figure pushed herself from the ground, bones clicking like crickets in summer fields. Stepping into the light, wobbling slightly on numb feet, the woman gripped the iron bars to steady herself.

She was beautiful, it was the first thing I could think of. Old enough that grey hairs mixed with her chestnut curls, but not so ancient that her skin was marked with lines and creases; it was smooth. Her skin was pale from lack of sunlight; I could imagine it once shone with warmth and vivacity, but now it looked drained and delicate to the touch.

I stepped closer to her, encouraged by a silent siren call as I drank in the woman behind the bars. The closer I got, the more a spark of familiarity burned within me. It was the eyes that gave away the truth eventually. At first, I thought the piercing blue was simply a reflection from the crystal lights; two pools of deep-ocean azure watched me as I closed in on her.

I saw another face as I blinked, one that spurred a fear within me.

The same wild, curly hair and stunning gaze. It was the face of Tarron Oakstorm, but that was impossible because he was dead.

My mind whispered to me the name of the person before me, the impossibility of it – but then again, after everything that had happened up until this point, nothing was truly impossible.

"Elinor?" I said, stepping closer to the bars, drawn forward like a moth to an open flame. "Elinor Oakstorm?"

She blinked – fluttered those bright-sky eyes and said, "Yes, and who might you be?"

CHAPTER 33

I stared deeply into the eyes of Elinor Oakstorm, watching as my name sank into her psyche. Up until now, I'd believed her dead, but the woman before me couldn't be more alive, nor anyone else but an Oakstorm. I saw Tarron in every feature, small and imposing. Then again, Elinor reacted to my name in the exact same way. Shock, horror, disbelief and… hope.

"It cannot be." Elinor's voice shook as she spoke; disbelief creased her features. It was as though she clawed the very words from my mind and spoke them aloud.

I stood there, unable to formulate a response that would make sense.

"It's true, my lady. Robin, he told me himself. I believe him," Jesi began, until the sharp retort of the woman cut her off entirely.

"I know who he is. I do not require a name to see the truth in his face." Frail, bony hands reached out of the iron bars towards me. "And never did I think I would look upon the face of an Icethorn again. But here you are, and my, don't you look like your mother. Like the reflection of a mirror – beautiful, cold and an Icethorn without question."

I kept my hands at my sides, trying to hide the violent shaking as I gripped them into fists. It was impossible not to notice the hurt that pinched her brows into a frown. Slowly and with an air of regret, the woman pulled her offending hands back into her cell. Turning my back on the caged woman, I looked at Jesi with a plea in my eyes. "This is a mistake."

Jesi ignored me, her body almost blocking the pathway back towards the main atrium of the cavern. I had to get away. I would rather have perished than be looked at by those same eyes for a moment longer. *Tarron's eyes.*

"If I have said something to offend you, I apologise. But you must understand, I have not looked upon your family for many years. I am shocked, that is all."

Looking back to the woman, I forced all guilt from my expression. Guilt for knowing what had become of her son. Her family. Guilt for knowing the very reason I was before her in the first place was because of my plot to side with the Hand to ensure her husband's death.

"They are dead," I said, matter-of-factly. "My family – because of–"

Do you know that they died because of you? Fuelled by Doran's jealousy that you had not been given the freedom my mother had? Those were the questions I silently screamed as I studied the shell of the woman before me.

The woman didn't so much as flinch, instead held my stare indefinitely. "I know why they perished, dearest Robin. And I am so, so sorry for what my husband did. But the Court lives on in you," she added, breaking the prolonged moment of silence. "Word of the Icethorn heir came only weeks ago with the recent batch of captured Fey. We all believed it to be false. Fake. Made-up stories. Yet now, with you standing before me, I do not doubt your lineage for a moment."

I held my chin high, searching for a reason to hate the woman from first impressions; thus far I was empty-handed. "Elinor," I said. "You have been here, in the Below, all this time?"

"I have."

"I was told that you were taken by Hunters alongside my mother. She made it home. You... you didn't. Wychwood believes you died years ago."

"In a sense, I did. Yet I was stolen by the enemy and still live. Julianna's fate was no better than my own."

My entire body trembled.

"Jesi," Elinor said, turning to her. "Thank you for bringing him to me but the matters we have to discuss are not for your ears."

"Noted." Jesi bowed her head for a final time, midnight hair falling before part of her face. "Robin – my king – find me if you need."

I couldn't reply, not as her sparkling, tear-filled eyes regarded me. Then Jesi turned and left, leaving me alone with a ghost of flesh and bone.

"Robin," Elinor said when Jesi's footsteps quietened as she departed. "I remember when your mother told me that her next child would be named as such. Never did I believe it would have been the name given to the secret child of her human lover."

"You must be sickened then," I replied. "Your stomach turning sour as you look upon me."

A heavy sadness passed behind her dull, tired eyes. "No matter what I think of the scum who dwell in the castle above us, your father was different to them. And your mother loved him. Even I could see that. I look upon you and see nothing but a memory of happiness for me. I see Julianna."

I felt the heavy, burning truth of her words. Part of me wanted to lift a hand to my cheek, remembering the fleeting memory of my mother in my dreams, dark hair and melodic voice. Many had told me of our resemblance, but there was something about hearing it from Elinor that made it more believable.

I swallowed hard, trying to clear the guilt that had lumped within my throat. "I would have thought you hated her for leaving you."

"Leaving me?" She looked confused, almost taken aback by my comment. "Julianna would never have left me if I hadn't demanded she did so."

"I don't understand."

"Sit." Elinor gestured to the dirt ground as though there was a chair of comfort for me to rest upon. "There is much to discuss, and it has been many years since another arrival has merited enough interest in me to speak with."

I did as she asked, lowering myself to the ground on quivering knees. "Why would you have told my mother to leave you?"

The question danced between us, flirting with the silence as Elinor prepared her answer. "My home had become unsafe. Your mother wished to help me, during a time when help was hard to come by. I was running. Your mother and I had an ironclad plan, or so we had believed. Escape the Oakstorm court and find a new life. But the Hunters found us not more than a day's ride away from the Wychwood border. That is where this story begins."

"What were you running from?" I asked quietly, yet another question I felt as though I knew the answer to.

And I was right.

"Not what, but who. I had to leave Oakstorm, Wychwood – hell, I needed to be clear of this entire realm to protect my child. It was never for me, but for him. I would have traversed the entire world, discovered and unknown, to keep him safe."

My breathing hitched. "Tarron had a brother…" I remembered the story. It wasn't only Elinor who was taken by Hunters, but Doran's other child. His name was just out of reach, no matter how hard I tried to reach for it, it slipped away. Perhaps everything that had happened thus far had made me forget about the details, but I understood without looking further that Elinor was alone in this cell.

Elinor, with the help of gripping to the iron bars, eased herself down onto the floor and sat opposite me. She didn't moan, but her face winced as though she hurt from the simple action. "You may wonder why I could not judge your mother for her infidelity to her first husband. I know what it is like to fall in love with someone whilst being eternally tied to another. Just like Julianna, I too had a child outside of wedlock. I loved him, but he was not safe in Oakstorm."

I pieced together the picture Elinor laid out before me, the missing fragments forming an untold story.

"Lovis,"– Elinor choked on the name as though it was the hardest thing she had ever spoken – "was a dear, sweet boy."

Was.

"I don't mean to be insensitive–" I stopped myself.

"Ask the question, Robin."

I swallowed hard. "What happened to him… to Lovis?"

Had he become like Erix and the gryvern? Or had he survived that curse because Elinor was his mother, and her magic was to heal even the darkest of fates?

It may have been an insensitive question, but I harboured far harsher ones in my mind.

"He died many years ago. Killed by the treatment of the Hand and his acolytes. I failed my Lovis. I wasn't able to provide him with the safety he should have been promised. That is my failure as a mother."

I looked to the dust-covered rock ground, feeling my eyes sting as though needles pricked into them. "I'm so sorry."

It hurt to hear of the loss of Elinor's son, knowing that Tarron also no longer lived. But did she know?

"I am too. I often wonder, if I had not made the choices I did in my life, would I ever have needed to leave Cedarfall? Your mother would not have needed to help which ultimately led to her demise. I should never have had my Lovis. So many lives would have been spared if I had only curbed my longing."

I understood now why Elinor looked as though she carried the weight of the world across her hunched shoulders. Guilt was a heavy burden to carry, and she bore it all, no matter how misplaced that guilt was.

"Whoever you were running from must have been awful enough to separate you from the family you left behind." I found myself saying it before I even had the chance to truly think. "It was Doran, wasn't it?"

Elinor nodded, her sadness morphing to the pinched expression of angry. "Tarron was the spitting image of his *father* in mannerism and darkness only. All I gifted that boy was his looks and power. The rest, his soul especially, was the perfect mirror of Doran. Tarron did not need me. Doran, on the other hand, required me for what I could bear him: perfect, unmarred children. Yet imagine what he would have done when he found out that Lovis was not of his flesh and blood – death was fated for my youngest child no matter if I stayed or left."

For a moment my body chilled so deeply that I was certain I was free from the iron cuff at my neck and my power had returned. A shiver sliced across my skin, my mouth drying as Elinor's truth settled over me.

"Doran was not Lovis' father?"

Elinor tipped her head, but didn't once release my gaze. There was something proud about her expression. It hardened the features of her face, eradicating any whisper of sadness that had only a moment before aged her.

"There was nothing Lovis shared with Doran. Lovis was kind. Innocent. Perfect. I had once thought the same about Tarron, but as the years passed by, I knew I had lost him to his father's warped soul. Unlike Doran's other children, Tarron was physically perfect. But inside he was just as tormented as his sire. Lovis was different. Entirely, completely and undeniably opposite. It was only a matter of time before Doran noticed. I left believing that I was doing the right thing by Lovis and by me. I have learned that no matter the choices we make in life, there are always countless outcomes. Ones that we do not even consider when making our decisions. This…" Elinor gestured around her. "This is simply one outcome I had never contemplated. Now I am left here to bleed for a man who speaks to demons, without my son, without my future."

There was a long pause between us. Elinor allowed me a moment to decipher all she had revealed. Questions upon questions layered upon one another and I almost forgot about the urgency of getting out of here. I could have sat there for an eternity speaking to a woman I had believed dead.

"You know my story now. Tell me, Robin, what has happened in your life to end up here, with me, imprisoned by a madman?"

I took a deep, shuddering breath, and chose to tell my truth clearly, just as she had shared hers. "I came for an audience with the Hand. To barter with him for his army and power. Then I heard about the Below, and those desires shifted. Although my being here, in the pits of the castle with you, is not how I imagined my welcome, I'm no more deterred from what I desire from the Hand, but the army I want is here."

"So you've come to save us?"

I swallowed hard. "I have come to try."

"And what brings you to ask for help from your enemy right at his doorstep?"

I looked at her with a storm in my eyes. "To kill Doran Oakstorm."

Elinor rocked back, a small fluttering gasp escaping from her. She brushed the loose waves of brown curls from her face, not wanting a single strand to obscure her view of me. "And what has *he* done to you to bring about such a desire?"

My jaw hardened; teeth gritted together as I replied. "He took everything from me. And I vow to do the same in return."

I told Elinor almost everything. How Doran had plotted and succeeded in the murder of the Icethorn Court. How he pointed the blame on the humans to cause a war, doing so because of his jealously that my mother returned but Elinor never did. I told her of my father and the lengths he took to keep me from the realm of the fey and how it ultimately ended in his death at the hands of Doran Oakstorm.

The only thing I held back, finding myself swallowing the admission at the last moment, was what had become of Tarron – what Erix did to him, because of me.

So much death left in my wake, in such little time.

And all because of Doran's infatuation with a woman who never loved him as he had led me to believe she had. It was clear, from everything I'd heard and learned, that Doran never knew of Elinor's infidelity. He believed Lovis to be his son just as Tarron was. Elinor was his prized love after all, the only one who gave him children whose blood was not infected with the berserker lineage.

If Doran had known, would he have gone to the lengths he had? Would my family still be alive?

I blinked and saw a storm of gryvern. I saw Erix and his mutated and tormented appearance. So many lives devastated because of a secret. Secrets were destructive – secrets were the world's greatest evil.

"I understand," Elinor finally said, a hint of reminiscence in her gaze. "We have all been forced to make choices and I can understand now how you have ended up before me. But I feel as though I should ask you something. Something I wish someone had asked me."

"Please," I replied softly. "Ask me anything."

"Will it be worth it? In the end, when Doran and his presence has been removed from this world, will it bring you whatever it is you seek?"

My mouth opened, lips parting for my initial confirmation to come out. But silence responded. I couldn't answer. I wanted to, but I couldn't. Because I didn't know what it was I longed for. My family? Revenge? It wouldn't bring them back, I knew that. They were gone no matter what happened tomorrow, or the day after, or the day after that.

"You do not need to answer me yet," Elinor said softly, although her voice still hummed with the air of command, which had not vanished during the many years in this dark cell. "I am not going anywhere, and time is very much a luxury we have in the Below."

"I'm here now," I said. "I have no choice but to keep moving forward. It is too late to give up, but my focus is on saving you, Elinor. Saving everyone in the Below. Doran must die, but even I know that my desire is not as potent as those around me who want their freedom."

"Freedom, what a funny and long-forgotten concept. And what will you do to accomplish that?"

I shook my head, not knowing the answer. "Anything, no matter what it takes. I will set you all free."

"And what of Doran, the reason you first embarked on this journey?"

I opened my mouth to reply, but closed it again like a fish out of water.

"It is never too late to change one's mind, Robin," Elinor added. "Simply alter your desires and join a cause worth fighting for."

"And what would that be?"

Elinor frowned, her entire face pulling downwards in displeasure. "When you meet the Hand, you will understand the pure size of the evil that is coming to this realm. Doran's will be nothing in comparison. There will be a time in which his misfortune will be brought to his door, and I would argue that now is not it."

I stood quickly. Part of me wished to stay with Elinor and question her about my mother, but the burden her words put upon me had singlehandedly shaken my world. Bowing as one would to a queen, I bade her farewell. "Thank you for your time."

Elinor stood abruptly too, reaching a hand beyond her cage. "Wait, Robin."

I couldn't look at her as she pleaded for me to stay.

"May I be selfish and indulge myself with a final question?"

I hesitated, facing towards the path I had walked down. "How could I refuse a queen?"

She sighed, a hitch in her breath. "Tell me of my firstborn. Tarron. Do you know if he is well? How he has fared to the years of being left in his father's care?"

It felt as though a sharp and boiling hot needle was pierced through my chest. A part of me whispered that I should just walk away, leaving her with some hope that Tarron was in fact alive, but I couldn't lie to her.

"He died," I said quietly, wishing for the cave to swallow me entirely.

There was no need to tell Elinor of the details, nor did she ask.

Instead, her small, broken voice changed into one of strength and relief as she replied, "Then he has found peace, and my Lovis is no longer alone on the other side."

CHAPTER 34

I found Jesibel at the end of the pathway which led away from Elinor's personal cage. She had waited for me, silently beckoning for me to follow her all without pressing questions of my conversation with the captured queen. I could see from the flickering of her gaze that she was interested in what we spoke of, but not once did she ask.

The pathway to Elinor wasn't the only one within this cavern. Jesi guided me down another until it opened up into a barren space that sang with dripping echoes. The walls of the cave were slick with water which dribbled and steadily flowed from unseen holes within the cave wall. Bundles of green moss spread like stains across the rocks. I even noticed the odd, small white flower that thrived in the darkness.

"Scrub yourself down, it will make you feel better." Jesibel turned her back on me. "I'll keep watch."

"Thank you," I replied, finding the words being all I could manage. After my conversation with Elinor, my mind was lost and frantic.

I didn't waste another moment with tearing the clothes from my back and standing beneath the spring of water. It was so cold; it felt like a slap to the face, making my mind alert and my body sodden. It was displeasing for only a moment. After a while I simply stood there, letting the freezing stream envelop me like a welcoming hug.

I almost forgot about Jesi's presence until she cleared her throat in an I-am-still-waiting kind of way.

Against my wishes, I stepped free of the spring and changed, body numb and limbs almost refusing to cooperate. My dirtied clothing had been discarded at some point, leaving me to dress in a set of mismatching clothes, a tunic and trousers that did nothing but hang off my body. Although I was thankful not to smell. Lifting my arm to my nose, I was greeted with the faint musk of age, and not dirt and blood.

After I changed, I shadowed Jesi, moving through the Below like a ghost. Deep in thought, I lost myself to the conversation I had with Elinor, my body acting of its own accord and carrying me every step of the way. Jesi allowed me the silence. It was clear she wished to break it, but I was thankful she didn't.

"I should be thankful for something to eat, but this is disgusting," I said, perched upon a stool beside Jesi. She had brought wooden bowls filled to the rim with a dark grey slosh of what could only be described as edible mud. I couldn't even brave a spoonful, not as the waft of something terrible offended my nostrils when I brought the spoon to my mouth.

Jesi replied with a mouthful. "It does the job. We're not exactly overwhelmed with choice in the Below. Trust me, in a matter of weeks you'll salivate at the thought of this gruel."

I could hardly watch as she stuffed another spoon into her mouth, teeth dragging the food from the utensil like a wolf ripping the skin off a lamb. Defeated, I dropped the spoon back into the bowl.

"Well," she said, swallowing hard with furrowed brows of displeasure. "If you're going to let it go to waste, then give it to me."

I thrust the bowl into her hand and she snatched it greedily. As her sleeve shifted, I saw the puncture upon her arm again.

"Do you know why they're taking fey blood?"

Jesi's expression pinched, as though the memory was as painful as the mark on her arm looked. "There is a price to pay for staying here, no matter if it is out of our control or not. Blood. They take us, without warning, drain us until we are too weak to stand. Then we are brought back here. Sometimes the letting of blood can feel as though it is without gaps. Other times they leave you here until you start to believe they have forgotten about you. Then your name is called once again, and the cycle begins."

"The Hand, he uses the blood to change his followers," I said, remembering the human who had wandered into Farrador. He had displayed power that didn't belong to him. I had yet to understand how the Hand could create such a thing but understood clearly that it came from fey blood. "I've seen it with my own eyes. But I expected more of them – more humans with access to magic."

Which suggested whatever the Hand was doing didn't work. Or that was what I hoped.

"Honestly, I don't care." Jesi's response surprised me. "He could bleed me dry, and I would still find it impossible to locate a fuck to give him."

"Why?" I looked to her, studying the way her brow twitched and she nibbled at the skin of her lower lip.

"I have nothing left to care for." She shrugged, discarding the bowl by her feet, and sitting back until her head rested against the wall of the cave. "You will soon come to learn that no one is coming for us here. The ones who do only end up locked up behind the same bars. Just like you. It has been years since I was captured, shortly after Queen Julianna…" She trailed off, wincing slightly. "After your mother died and our Court was left unprotected. We had to flee, all of us. The Icethorn magic was left uncontrolled. It was destroying everything, ruining homes and tearing families apart. We thought it was safer to make for the other Courts, but some of use ventured too far South. Durmain was not welcoming. It made us easy pickings for the Hunters who seemed to wait patiently for us to step out of our protection. No one has come since. Not the Cedarfall Court, our closest allies. I don't see them funding a rescue. *We* are forgotten. So why should I care for the Hand's plans, when those his sights are focused on do not care for me?"

For a moment I wanted to disagree, but I soon realised Jesi was right. Not once had I heard of plans to save the fey taken by the Hunters, only the plans to avenge them. Perhaps it was because no one in Wychwood believed that they would still be living. Hell, even I had not thought of such a thing.

"They do care," I replied weakly. "I know people who would raze every realm to find you if they believed there was a chance you still lived."

I had seen Althea herself, Princess of the Cedarfall Court, lead parties of soldiers to infiltrate Hunter camps. First hand I had witnessed her fight for them.

"Then where are our saviours? I have lost count of the number of years I have been kept here. Some, like Elinor, have dwelled within this prison far longer. No one is coming, Robin. You may think they care, but they don't. Every now and then a new bunch of prisoners will be brought here. They bring news of the outside world and with it, the lack of desire to rejoin it again. It would seem that we are safer in the Below than out in a world where the realms are on the cusp of war."

I looked up towards the raised podium, wishing that the Twins had returned for me as they had promised. Watching and waiting stretched out time, but as it went on, I began to believe they would never return for me. I was stuck, like Jesi and Elinor and the hundreds of other fey.

"Jesi, believe me or not, I promise to get you out of here."

Jesi laughed. It was a painful, horrible sound that did not reflect happiness or joy, but disbelief and irritation. "Many have said and promised the same. And if you look around you, I could point them out even now. They may have forgotten, but I haven't. I won't. Because the day I forget is the day I wish to perish entirely."

I felt a sense of responsibility for Jesi, knowing her life was displaced due to the chaos that followed my mother's death. When the Icethorn Court fell, so did the lives and homes of many people. Jesi, in that moment, represented them all.

There was a strange atmosphere that had followed my meeting with Elinor. I had noticed the shift in attention as soon as we had returned from the springs. From when I arrived, no more visible than a phantom, now it seemed that everyone within this cave saw me. Jesi didn't show signs of noticing or caring, but I felt the tension as crowds of fey huddled together in whispers.

It all came to a head when a group broke apart and walked over towards where we sat. I first thought they would simply join in with our conversation until the lead fey, a bulky man with a wild beard and an equally eager gaze, clamped his hand down upon my shoulder.

Jesi was standing up in second, towering in comparison to the man, both bowls she had held protectively now spilled across the dirty ground. "What the fuck are you playing at?"

The man gestured towards me with a fist, seething from gapped teeth, "Word around is this one calls himself our king."

I was also standing then, sensing his anger as though the emotion itself had barrelled into me. "Is there a problem?"

"Yes, actually, there is," he replied, knocking his fist into my chest so suddenly that it had me jolting back two steps.

Jesi was between me and the man, not a sense of care for the rock-hard fist that was now held before her face. "Return to whatever it was you were doing. Now is not the night for trouble, big boy."

I felt myself redden as the entire cavern seemed to silence, listening in with tense and quiet interest. Looking towards the glinting of silver I noticed even the guards beneath the gates watched intently.

"You're standing up for *him*? Have you forgotten what happened to our homes when his family failed us? And now he wants to call himself a king whilst he has done nothing but fail us again." He looked at me dead in the eyes. "I see no kings here."

These men, like Jesi, were Icethorn fey. Unlike Jesibel they did not share the same midnight toned hair and moon-pale skin as I, but there was no doubt that they had come from my Court long before it was ever truly mine.

"Turn. Back," Jesi warned, her stance preparing for more than a conversation. "It would be an awful shame if I was to embarrass you before all of your pathetic friends."

The man chuckled, cracking his fist in his hand as though every bone sang with desire to connect with me. "Move out of our way, little girl, or you will–"

Jesi sprung forward, hand slashing out towards the lead assailant's neck. It happened too fast to make sense of the blur of limbs. The fey man doubled over, eyes bulging as his hands instinctively grasped at his throat. Gasping, he then cocked his head back as a sickening crack sounded. Jesi attacked, not once but twice, all without allowing him to finish what he had to say. His neck was red from her first hit, but it was his nose which gushed with blood. It poured between his fingers, deep and scarlet, as he wailed like a cat whose tail had been stamped upon.

She moved like water around stone, dancing between the next two that jumped into the fight. It was over before it truly begun. Before I had a chance to react, three writhing bodies lay at my feet.

"Anyone else?" Jesibel cried, face red with fury. "Go on, give me a reason to break bones, you cowards."

No one else stepped forward. Even the three who had greeted us with such aggression were now scuffling away, the lead man leaving a trail of his blood across the ground as he retreated.

I placed a hand upon Jesibel's quivering shoulder. "Jesi, it's over."

She gave the crowd a final look, one full of warning, before she shrugged off my hand and took her seat once again. "They all forget their place. The podium of your status to ours may be levelled, but you are still an Icethorn. You are due respect, regardless of what they think."

"Respect is earned," I replied, still on edge by the attempted attack. "I appreciate you standing up for me, but I also understand why they see me the way they do. I'm nothing but a reminder of what was left behind and I'm here, not in the capacity they would've wished."

Jesi rubbed her reddened knuckles, still physically seething from the reaction. "You are a reminder of home. Sometimes reminders are painful for some, and not for others. Your presence will have effect on those here in varying ways."

"And how does my presence make you feel?" I questioned, catching her black eyes as though they reflected my own.

"It reminds me of–" Jesi's voice ebbed back into silence, her stare being lost to an unimportant place on the floor between us.

I swallowed audibly, picking at the frayed material of the trousers I wore. "Of what?"

When she looked up, it was with bright eyes brimming with tears. "It reminds me of what was taken from me, and what I would do to get it back."

The Twins returned as they promised they would, looking down upon the crowd of prisoners from their podium with blank and empty expressions. Their presence snatched the breath from my lungs.

"Robin Icethorn," they called, silencing the crowd until I could've heard a pin drop upon the floor. "Step towards the gate and await your collection."

Jesibel startled from her slumber. She'd fallen asleep a long while ago, but I didn't have the heart to wake her. She gave me a look, one brimming with concern. We'd yet to discuss the matter of what occurred to the fey when they were collected for their payment of blood. I hadn't asked because it wouldn't happen to me. I was here for an audience with the Hand, confirmed by the Twins themselves. He would not require my blood. At least that was the lie I told myself over and over.

"Whatever you do, don't fight back." Jesi took my hand and squeezed. She was cold to the touch, a whisper of the Court she would have once lived among. There was so much I didn't know about her but in the short time I'd spent with her, what I had gleaned was that I could trust her. She oozed conviction which made me warm up to her with ease. "The process of bloodletting is uncomfortable, but not utterly painful. It will be over before you know it."

I forced a smile, hoping to keep my thoughts from creasing my expression. I hadn't the heart to admit aloud that I wasn't planning on returning here – not yet. I would speak with the Hand, petition for my release and the safety of Duncan. Then I would come, with support behind me, and free Jesi and all the fey around me.

At what price?

"Thank you for everything, Jesibel."

"Sounds an awful lot like a goodbye," she replied, winking with tired eyes. "Go quickly and good luck. I *will* see you soon."

Luck. I needed more than that.

Jesi released me, crossing her arms before her, and watched me leave as though she was my guardian on my first day of freedom. Her entire being oozed with apprehension. As I left her, I buried a promise into my soul. If I was to succeed, I'd do everything to release the fey kept captive here. Jesibel, Elinor. All of them.

I walked towards the gates, chin raised high. The Kingsmen finally took keen notice of me from where they waited beyond the bars. The Twins watched too, not once taking their attention off me, their gaze prickling my skin. I looked up at them, holding their stare in competition.

It was a rehearsed process, I understood that as the imprisoned fey watched me as I passed, the ones closest to the exit of the prison rushed to put distance between it and them. I understood why when the gate screeched open, and the guards rushed in with unsheathed and sharp blades.

"Steady and slow," the Kingsmen warned, urging me into a circle of them. Only when I had passed back out of the prison's gate, and it closed securely behind us, were the swords put away.

It was all happening so quickly. Rough, gloved hands grasped my arms and moved me around as though I couldn't do it for myself. I caught the flash of the metal leash that'd been removed from me upon my arrival, listening to the snap of the clasp as they promptly connected it back to the collar at my throat.

"I will not resist you," I sneered, skin aching from their pinching and tugging. "There is no need to be–"

A cloth was held above my mouth and nose, silencing my appeal. The scent that followed stung at my nose, itching at my eyes. I tried to reach up and pull the hand away, but my arms didn't seem to move. My mind grew heavy. Blinking, my vision doubled. The sounds around me seemed to stretch out as though I was disappearing further and further away from them. But in truth, I'd not moved an inch. Sluggishly, my eyes looked up towards the two figures of the Twins who still watched from their perch. Darkness crept in the corners of my vision. Still, they stood and watched.

The last thing I remembered were hands that caught me as my body gave up.

Then there was nothing but emptiness.

CHAPTER 35

I came out of the darkness slowly. It was a sluggish, painful dragging of my consciousness as it fought back from the brink. My hearing was the first of my senses that returned to me. I recognised the sound of dripping, gentle splatters as though a bowl caught droplets of slow-falling rain. The *drip, drip, drip,* quickly became torturous as it was without rhythm or pacing; even if there were other sounds, it was impossible to know as I fixated on the dripping.

Soon enough I could smell again. I half expected the stinging scent that'd coated the cloth to still cling within my nose, but it was the sharp tang of copper that greeted me. Pungent and undeniable, I wanted to hold my breath to rid myself of the disgusting smell that soon became a taste at the back of my mouth as that sense returned.

Then I could see again. Desperation had me crying out as I opened my eyes. That cry soon spluttered as the shock of light had me gasping and clamping my eyes shut again for relief from the brightness.

"Do not worry, Robin Icethorn, it will be over soon." The person who spoke was close enough that they only needed to whisper for me to hear.

My body stiffened in response. I could feel that I sat in a chair with armrests that held my arms up at my sides at an odd angle. Only when I tried to pull away did I realise I couldn't move – not because my body refused, but thanks to the strappings that kept my arms and my legs pinned in place.

I squinted, straining against the light to see who it was that spoke. Before me sat a man – a fey; the twin points of his ears revealed as much. A helmet of silver hair, wild and untamed, haloed his aged face. A messy beard covered his jaw. His eyes were hooded by heavy loose skin that did well to hide their dull green. A film of smoke seemed to cover them, catching the orange-flame light strangely. He too was sitting on a chair, an arm's length away.

"Struggling will not set you free," he said, voice gruff and expression bordering on annoyance. "It is best you keep yourself calm. Every drop spilled beyond the container is classed as a waste which will only prolong the letting of your blood. Let the creatures fill their bellies, and then it will be over."

Creatures?

I looked down to my forearm, mouth dry and still filled with the taste of copper. Dark leeches clung to my skin, plump bodies wriggling as they sucked at my blood. Droplets trickled down my arm, falling over my fingers like water over rocks, where it splashed onto the ground beneath me. The sound torturous to my ear. There were a few other wounds upon my arm, small but angry. No doubt more leeches had been drinking their fill, and it wasn't long until I found them, writhing in a ceramic bowl next to my boots.

Disgust rolled like an incoming storm within me.

"Are they... so desperate they must do this whilst I am incoherent?" I said through gritted teeth. "Is this how it always happens?"

The fey man looked down, shirt rolled up to his elbow to reveal the wounds that we shared; his arm was covered in the brown splotches that usually peppered an older person's skin. Like me, fat leeches slithered against his skin, full to bursting. If someone didn't come in and remove them soon, they would pop. "Depends on the person. Bloodletting can be a discomforting process. The more one does it, the less it is bothersome. But the little buggers love it. For the leeches, it's a grand feast."

Turning as much as the chair and my restraints allowed, I made sense of the large room we were kept within. A towering ceiling, walls carved from a white stone with veins of darker stone throughout, lit mainly by the burning fire that leaked warmth and the countless pillar candles that stood erect on metal holders along each of the four walls.

The two chairs we sat upon seemed completely out of place. There was not much furniture to compare them to, but what few dressers and cupboards I could see were crafted from a white-stained wood. My chair, and the one *he* sat upon, were darker and older, with worn, scuffed red material that pulled apart in clumps across the armrests, likely a result of nails that scratched away at it. I could see the marks beneath my hands, gouges torn from the wood from other fey who had likely sat upon the chair over the many years of their captivity.

"Looking for someone?" the old man asked.

"I expected to be speaking with the Hand, not strapped to a chair and bleeding," I replied, lightheaded from the blood loss. The bowl was nowhere near full, but I could see that I'd been bleeding for a while.

He sighed, clenching his fist over and over as though attempting to locate feeling in the tips of his fingers. "It is payment. Even I have given blood for many years. Be grateful for the company, it is not usual to share this room during the process of giving up one's blood."

I winced, starting to register the cold discomfort of pain in my arm. Even my own hands were becoming numb at their tips. "Then I suppose it would be rude of me not to ask your name whilst we sit through this."

Conversation would at least take my mind off the discomforting lap of the leeches sucking my blood.

"Aldrick," he replied, eyes bloodshot and tired.

I waited for him to ask mine in return, but he didn't. Remembering Father's teachings of respecting elders, I swallowed the disconcerting feeling that revealed itself and decided to ask another question. "Do they only tie down the new arrivals?"

I'd noticed that his arms were free from the constraints I had. Perhaps he had been captured a long while ago and had grown complacent, allowing them to take his blood without any resistance.

"Yes. Since you're new blood, how you react is unknown and frankly a waste of time. It is less painful for all if the blood is taken without resistance. In time you will grow used to it."

I wondered if he noticed my recoiling at his response. It was defensive and harsh, reminding me of how my old teachers spoke to me when reprimanding me for something I had done.

Aldrick stood up. The sudden movement caught me off guard. From his back pocket he pulled forth a cloth and held it above his wound to staunch the bleeding, then tore the leech from his arm and deposited it in the bowl beside him. "All this way and these are the questions you have for me. When are you going to get to the more pressing matters, Robin?"

"I–" My heart filled my mouth, silencing me. I watched the fey man walk with confidence that did not belong to a prisoner. It was the second time he'd used it, only now my mind latched onto that fact. "I didn't tell you my name."

"You did not need to."

I gripped the armrests, body tensing as I watched Aldrick stand behind his chair. I had not noticed it before, but a jacket was draped across it. He plucked it off, and with a dramatic sweep, threaded himself into it one arm at a time.

"Who are you?"

His lips didn't lift from their hard, straight line, but his glazed eyes seemed to smile from within. Aldrick was entertained by my surprise, that much was clear. "Have a guess."

I shook the chair, legs clattering as I kicked upwards. "I'm not playing games with you. You are one of the Hand's acolytes. Like the Twins. Where is he? I demand to speak with him."

That was when I noticed one great difference between us both. His neck. An iron cuff was absent, unlike mine which seemed to strangle and pinch at my skin.

He raised both hands as though he welcomed my shouts – enjoyed them. "I can assure you this is *very* serious. Do you truly hold such shock and disbelief that you cannot see that it is I whom you speak with? Yes, you have known of me by one name, but you may refer to me as Aldrick... unless you prefer the Hand as a title."

"Liar," I hissed, not caring for the blood that spilt across the floor as I struggled to break free from the leather straps.

"Oh, do come on, Robin." Aldrick almost sagged in on himself. His old, tired body struggled to stay upright. "I know your story. You have seen many things that you would never have believed possible. Yet you look at me and cannot imagine it a reality that I am the very man you have sought?"

My eyes narrowed in burning incredulity. "But you are fey. You can't be the Hand."

The man who inspired hate *against* the fey.

"And why can't I?" he retorted, tilting his head to the side as he scrutinised me. "How is it you have come to believe you know so much about me? Remind me, have we met before? No." Aldrick straightened, as much as his aged figure allowed. "Your first lesson, Robin, is never to assume anything. Assuming leads to stupidity. And you have not struck me as one who suffers from idiocy, up until this moment at least."

I couldn't believe it, that or I didn't want to. The Hand was fey, which was the last truth I would have ever believed. Even from his mouth, I still couldn't trust he was telling the truth.

"Then tell me," I sneered, tugging forward at my restraints. "Help me understand why you would condemn your own kind. What has driven you to do what you have?"

"Condemn my kind," he repeated, contemplating the question as he ran fingers through his beard. "Have you not traversed this realm for my help in killing a man? Is he not the same as you?"

Doran Oakstorm. Aldrick didn't mention him by name, but I knew exactly who he spoke about. "I have my reasoning."

"As do I."

I couldn't catch a breath. My chest heaved, cheeks reddening as I replied, "Then *tell* me."

Fury thrummed through me. If I was without the iron band around my throat, I would've exhaled such force across the room it would have broken through stone and flesh. From the look of teetering pleasure, Aldrick knew it too.

"I, like you, do not solely belong to one realm. It is that truth that has led me here, and you to me," Aldrick began, clearing his throat as though it was cluttered with cobwebs. "We are merely products of the world around us. It causes us to act in certain ways. Some may call it desperate and deranged, where others would see us simply changing ourselves to find a place to fit in."

"That is an awfully long way of telling me you are half human and fey," I said, lip curling in disgust.

How could a man so old and frail inspire such demanding hate in a group of people? *Duwar*. The answer was at the tip of my tongue before I finished thinking. "Which of those halves causes you to inspire such bloodthirst? That is why you are doing this, isn't it? Blood."

Aldrick limped slightly, edging his way back around the chair until he could lower himself into it. Seeing his fragile nature stole all fear I had for him. Instead, I felt only pity. That was until a voice echoed through my mind. *His* voice.

"There was a time when fey would construct walls within their minds. I see those teachings have been forgotten with my absence."

I shook my head, feeling as though I bathed in filth with his presence in my mind. "How are you doing that?"

"It was a gift which was passed through blood from my father," he replied. *"Imagine the fey's distaste when a half-breed displayed such powers. How jealous they became. What they did because of that very jealousy."*

"Stop it!" I cried out, skin shivering as the voice tore through me. When Aldrick spoke, his voice reflected his age. Feeble and pathetic. Yet the inner voice was brimming with strength and vitality; it was loud and demanding, echoing slightly with each word.

"You wanted to know, did you not?"

Gritting my teeth I did my best to keep a hold of his glassy gaze, feeling how soaked my head was becoming with sweat. "So, they treated you like shit. You have harboured such hate for so many years and I can see how it has changed you."

"Assumptions," Aldrick spoke aloud. "Did you not heed my warning? It matters not why I do as I do, but you should be asking how. That is a question which I would perhaps answer. Tell me what it is you want of me, Robin." Again, his voice shifted to the pits of my skull. *"You wish for me to help you kill a king."*

I winced, his voice slicing like a knife across my mind.

"I sense that you feel as though you have made a mistake."

"Get out of my head."

"It could be done." Aldrick continued, ignoring my growling demand. *"Doran Oakstorm is, as the fey are, the epitome of delusion and selfishness. If his head is what you desire, then so be it. But there is a cost that comes with seeking revenge. Would you be willing to pay it?"*

"I changed my mind," I cried, feeling the mental pain of his claw-like presence. "Please, stop."

Aldrick retreated his presence from within me like a serrated blade being withdrawn from a fresh wound. "All this way for you to change your mind. Surely there is something you desire from me?"

Perhaps it was my exhaustion, or deliria from his horrific power that had me spluttering my deep, burning want. "Duncan, I want Duncan to be spared."

"General Rackley," Aldrick spoke, drawing out his name as though he thumbed through a list in his mind, trying to locate Duncan upon it. "Ah yes, the man accused of sinning. Forgetting his mission for our God and defiling himself, well, with *you*."

"Yes," I said, jaw tense and hands clutching the chair. "That's what I desire."

It was only half a lie.

"Do you truly care for him more than killing the man who stole not one, but both of your parents? That is an interesting priority. Not one I personally can understand."

"Too many lives have been taken in your authority. It would be wrong for me to add another to your list."

That amused Aldrick. He barked a laugh which soon turned to a barrage of hacking coughs. He clutched his chest, eyes bulging and bloodshot. I could do nothing but watch as he struggled to catch his breath, fighting for some control as if his aged and tired body was at war.

I spotted small flecks of blood around the corners of his mouth, staining his grey beard in places. He had coughed it up, noticeable by the splattering across his fist which he lowered quickly to his side.

"You're dying," I said, knowing it wholeheartedly.

"We all die. Doran will die whether you hold the knife or not. You will die. Duncan, the man you hold so terribly dear to your heart, will die."

I scowled, not caring for his distraction. "That is not what I asked."

"You did not ask, you assumed. Which will promptly end this conversation you have so desperately requested if it happens again." Aldrick's face was flushed red, from anger or his previous coughing, I could not tell. Speaking with him was no different than being scorned by a parent; it irked me.

"Spare Duncan," I said again, choosing to leave the man's pending death for another conversation. I cared little. Hell, he could have keeled over now and stopped breathing, and I would not have cared. "Surely your *god* will not care if one is forgiven. I hear you make all the decisions on Duwar's behalf."

"Duwar makes its own decisions," Aldrick said, rolling the letters down his tongue as though the name was not from his language, or any other I had heard before. "Duncan will require payment for his forgiveness. Are you willing to pay the tithe on his behalf?"

"I am." Anything.

"*As I thought so.*" Aldrick rolled his eyes, pushing himself back to standing with a chorus of bones clicking and creaking. "Do you wish to know the price before throwing yourself before Duwar's judgement?"

"From my understanding, Duwar is imprisoned and kept away. I do not fear the demon, only crazed fools who idolise false gods. You lead your Hunters blindly, with the promise of this Duwar. But what is it going to do? Long gone are the days of gods; you should realise that better than anyone."

"Sharp tongue for someone powerless and imprisoned in my care." Aldrick turned his back on me, taking careful steps towards a chest of drawers across the room. As he spoke, his voice echoed, amplified by the towering, barren chamber. "The world will soon remember Duwar. I cannot blame you for your insolence for you are not alone within it. I pity you, but do not blame you."

Aldrick withdrew a cloak from the drawer. It was midnight black, plain and hooded. I watched as he struggled to put it on, tying it around his waist with a grey cord and lifting the hood across his head to cover his distinguishing features. Suddenly he was simply an old man, crooked and unimportant.

"Tonight, you will make your payment for Duncan Rackley's pardon. Even I understand that if I desire you to work with me, not against me, I must earn your trust."

Aldrick was preparing to leave me; I knew it from his lack of attention as he shrouded himself in the cloak. Before he reached the door he paused, age-spotted hand hovering above the handle as though he had suddenly remembered somehing. That was when he looked back to me, his face completely concealed. From within the folds of heavy material he spoke. "I almost forgot the most important thing."

He limped towards me. I gripped onto the chair, kicking down at the ground to try and break free as his inner presence crept up my mind like a snake cornering a mouse. There was nothing I could say to him. No words that would affect him. Aldrick was so detached from this world, lost to his age and delusion, that I knew no words would reach him. He had likely heard them all before.

So, instead, I spat, a gob of thick saliva that splattered by his feet.

"With the years that have passed I have been in the company of many kings and many queens. I have shared an equal distaste for them all and yet I admit not one has ever been like you. Worthless, spitting like an animal without grace and decorum. Admittedly I had put you on a pedestal, understanding our similarities. Meeting you, Robin Icethorn, has been one of my life's greatest disappointments".

I gasped as though his words slapped me physically. If my hands were not strapped to the chair I would have scratched at my head, tearing through skin and bone to rip his presence out.

"Fuck..." My mind filled with images for a moment. The room fell away and in the shadows that replaced it were flashing views of lands riddled with fire. Skies awash with lightning and pregnant clouds. Sunless, dark and horrific. *Red*. Droplets of scarlet fell from the heavens and covered the ground. *Blood*. It was everywhere.

"A time of reckoning is upon us." My vision returned and with it came the roaring of screams that filled my ears. It was me – my throat aching as I unleashed the keening cry inside of me.

"What did you do? Get out of my head!"

"I showed you the future. Not tomorrow, nor the day after and the weeks after that. But soon. A time that is not far off from this very moment." Aldrick lowered himself with a symphony of audible groans, picked up the bowl of my blood from beside me, and held it before him. He was careful with it, while I struggled and thrashed as much as the strappings allowed. Not a drop of blood was wasted.

"You are nothing but an old, forgotten *madman*," I shouted, spit flicking onto my chin as I watched Aldrick turn back towards the door.

He didn't flinch or show signs that he could hear me as he opened the door with a yawning creak.

"Do you hear me, you bastard?" The chair almost toppled back in the chaos of my thrashing limbs. "Heed me. I *will* stop you. I will. I *will*!"

Aldrick closed me in the room without another word spoken aloud. The sounds that tore out of me no longer made sense. My throat grew hoarse, my chest feeling as though it burned with each breathless cry. Then that dreaded, scratching presence returned as strong as it had been when Aldrick had stood before me.

"It would seem, Robin Icethorn, that you are the mad one now."

CHAPTER 36

The human king and queen of Durmain sat rigid in twin thrones as they looked warily upon the grand room before them. At first, I'd believed they were made from stone, regal statues of wealth and power. Not a single muscle moved, even turning their heads seemed impossible. Their lips didn't even twitch as the chamber I was seated within filled with Hunters. The black wave of leather came at once, making the air sticky with body heat and the noise unbearable.

I noticed something flickering in the king's and queen's eyes – it was *panic* –unblinking and frantic as they darted around the room; it was almost as if they screamed through them, trapped inside a body they couldn't control. They were imprisoned to their flesh, bones now iron bars keeping them within a cage, a feeling I shared.

"Silence – watch – comply."

Aldrick's command had echoed through my mind from the moment the Twins had come to collect me from the chamber I was left tied down in. At first his words were nothing but empty commands, until I discovered my body refused to follow my rebellious thoughts. I knew he was controlling me in some manner.

I couldn't put up a fight as the Twins dragged me here. Imposing and dark, the room was overwhelming, arched ceilings so high that the top was shrouded in shadows. The walls were old, each worn brick filled with stories of this castle's history; some stones were so large that it must've taken giants to carry them.

They sat me upon a lavishly decorated podium alongside the human royals. It was carved from polished slabs of marble; dark veins cut through the white stone as though they wished to devour the light. I soon learned that the podium, once a place to hold royals at a higher esteem than those who came to see them, now felt like a stage. We were the puppets; Aldrick was the hidden figure at the end of the strings.

I was aware of the bodies who walked ominously behind us. Was it Aldrick? I suspected not. I was helpless, like a butterfly pinned to paper and kept from flying.

Aldrick's control meant I no longer required physical bonds to keep me still. I sat rigid in the chair, every bone in my spine pressed uncomfortably against the velvet cushion that was stitched into the chair's back. His control, however, didn't stop my mind from wreaking havoc; nor did it keep the anxiety from burning beneath my skin, making it feel as though it would melt away if I sat here a moment longer.

It was soon clear that we weren't the only ones enthralled by the Hand's immense power. As the Hunters who filled the room distracted each other with chaos and excited shouts, no one cared to witness Elinor Oakstorm being escorted towards a seat beside me. She walked, chin held high, and arms pinned to her sides. As she took her seat, silver chain connecting her collar to the personal guard who had brought her, she paid me no mind. But her eyes mirrored those of the king and queen. If I could've seen my reflection, I too would've looked as deranged as she did.

Aldrick, although nowhere to be seen, kept all of us complicit. Controlled. Puppets on a string of iron, moving only when he desired.

It was evident that his power didn't need to control the crowd. They were rampant and wild, shouting and chattering over one another as they filled every inch of possible space on the cobbled floor beneath the podium, like fish rotting and stuffed into barrels.

They flooded into the room until not a speck of floor could be seen. They *wanted* to be here. Their excitement soured the air. It entrapped me with horror and all I could do was watch, my neck frozen so I could only face the crowd and no one else.

Something was happening tonight, and my skin shivered with unwanted anticipation, dreading whatever was coming. The Resurgence, as Kayne had called it. But what that entailed was still a mystery.

At the far end of the room were two doors opened up to a courtyard full of bodies. More Hunters. Their grumbling displeasure mixed with the excited chatter, irritated that there wasn't enough room to accommodate them all inside.

I focused on the Hunters, trying to remember details to stifle my panic. Many looked upon me with the disgust I'd grown accustomed to. *Imagine if you knew whom it was you followed blindly.* If I could've smiled, I would have, but the echoing voice that bounced across my mind kept me from doing anything but watching silently.

"Silence – watch – comply."

There was a part of me – a hopeful yet foolish part of me – that scoured through the crowd in search of Duncan. Although I knew he wouldn't have been among them, I still yearned to see him. Aldrick was many things, but I hoped he kept promises for Duncan's sake.

It took a while, observing the many faces, before I spotted Kayne. He'd been looking at me the entire time, expression stoic and unreadable. Unlike those who pressed in around him, laughing and shouting, talking and stamping with excitement, Kayne was as still as me, but not for the same reason.

The entire room silenced within a moment. From terrible noise, to dead quiet, I watched almost every pair of eyes shift to the left side of the room. I strained my own vision to see what it was that kept them quiet, but the movement was just out of sight.

Then the chanting began.

"Duwar, Duwar, Duwar."

It was low at first, then the stomping began, and the room seemed to shift and shake as though the stone beneath us all would crack.

I could see Elinor from the corner of my eye as I strained to witness what caused the commotion. Although statuesque, there was something calm about her posture, as though she physically sat in the same room, but her consciousness was elsewhere.

"Duwar, Duwar, Duwar."

The human king and queen didn't look towards the chaos, instead their eyes strained to look at one another. I could almost sense their desire to reach out and touch – but Aldrick's control was stopping them. Fear spilled out from their gazes, framed by exhaustion and shadowed skin.

"Look at them all." My eyes snapped forward and looked to the crowd, but not out of choice. Aldrick filled my mind again, voice loud and demanding attention. *"All this time they have longed to see me. Unlike you kings and queens, they follow my dictation all without the need for heavy metals atop my head and a title that is given to you but never earned."*

Aldrick spoke to every single one of us upon the podium. I sensed it as though his voice was stretched across us, growing louder and quieter as he spoke, as if he walked from either side of the podium.

"All these Hunters have come for me. See how they hunger for what I can promise them. Possibilities beyond anything you can provide them."

There was no denying that the Hand was in control here, the human royals no more than his playthings. It explained everything. How the law had turned its back on the brutality that filled the lands in the name of the Hand and Duwar. How the faith of the Creator had dwindled, like a candle beneath a storm, on the edge of being extinguished, snuffed out in the name of Duwar.

The chanting ceased, stomping feet fading until silence bathed the room once again. And everyone watched as the limping cloaked figure of the Hand entered and paced slowly across the podium as though it was his birthright.

"My ferocious, dedicated Hunters, welcome." Aldrick spoke from beneath the shadows of his hooded cloak. His voice was strained with age. It cracked as he shouted, breaking with the great effort it took for his frail body to pretend it was strong. "My, how many there are of you! It warms my soul to see that you have all received my invite for this evening's festivities. Unfortunately, not all those who have been invited have come, but what more can we expect from the cowards lingering across the Wychwood border?"

Aldrick turned his crooked posture towards Elinor and me. From beneath his hood, I caught a glint of those glazed, narrowed green eyes.

"But alas, the show must go on. That is what you are all here for, is it not?"

The crowd released a shout of agreement in unison.

Aldrick turned his back on the sea of his adoring followers, looked towards the human royals and bowed. It was strained. Anyone with vision could see it caused him discomfort. It was all part of his act. Aldrick's head tipped slightly, but enough to notice the respectful gesture. "As always, we thank you for your warm hospitality. Duwar will favour you both for turning your back on the old god of lies."

Both of their eyes flew wider, yet not a sound came from them. He commanded such, I was certain, filling their heads with his overwhelming presence so that they reacted just the way he wanted.

"I can sense your hunger." Aldrick's voice rose, speaking back to the hundreds of Hunters who'd come to see him. They were enthralled by his presence, waiting with bated breath for his every word and movement. They looked towards the cloaked man as though he was a god himself, keeping silent for fear they'd miss a word he said.

"All of you have travelled from near and far for the Resurgence," Aldrick continued with the sweep of his age-spotted hand. "A spectacle I have not shared with you until now. Do you wish to see why your bounties have been so important to Duwar's cause? To see what it is I do to aid its promised release? Tell me, Hunters. Let Duwar hear your enthusiasm from the realm it's trapped within. Do you wish to see?"

The noise nearly knocked me back out of my chair. It filled the room, likely spreading across the entire realm for all to hear. I could only imagine how terrifying it would have been for those living within Lockinge who knew little of what occurred this night.

Aldrick spoke to someone out of view, my eyes could not see who it was no matter how hard I strained. "Bring in my chosen one."

There was a thud of heavy dragging feet. The clattering of chains sent a shiver up my spine. Then I saw *him,* and my mind screamed a name which caused Aldrick's pleased chuckle to fill my head.

Duncan.

His chest was bare, scars both new and old on display for all to see. A glistening sheen coated his head and caused the strands of dark hair to link in damp chains down his neck. Duncan scowled, paying no mind to the crowd who sneered at him. Among the broken chatter, I could hear slurs being hurled towards him.

Not once did he flinch.

At least until he looked at me.

My heart panged for him. I wished nothing more than to clutch my chest, hoping a hand over my heart would stop it shattering through my ribs. But Aldrick's control didn't allow such a thing. I was forced to watch from my seat, unable to do anything but allow my horror to burn from my eyes, windows to the turmoil that devoured me internally.

Duncan's dark brows furrowed, pale lips pulling into a tight, harsh line which tugged at the prominent scar that I'd memorised so perfectly. I wondered if Aldrick filled his mind. It would seem so because Duncan walked freely and without refusal. There was something utterly rehearsed about his movements.

"Some of you may recognise General Duncan Rackley as he stands before you," Aldrick spoke. "A Hunter held in high esteem, who, like you all, had pledged his life to better the world in Duwar's name. He has personally delivered countless fey into my hands. Because of him, and you all, we are even closer to seeing through Duwar's greatest request. General Rackley is the perfect candidate for the Resurgence. To show you all what I have been doing with your bounty and how your belief will alter the unfair balance that we all recognise in the world."

Resurgence, a word that had been used enough times to grip sharp talons into my consciousness.

"It will soon make sense," Aldrick's voice echoed across my skull, as if reading my mind.

That thought alone had me trying to clear my head. His reverberating laugh only proved that my fears were correct.

The crowd were tense and silent, as though they stood on the precipice of a sky-piercing cliff, waiting for the clouds to part to see what lurked below. I understood what was going to happen. Unlike the crowd before me, they clearly did not know what occurred with the fey blood. How it changed humans and gave them access to power that did not – *should* not – belong to them.

"You have seen my failed creation. This one will be different – I hope."

The vision of the thin, weak-looking human who had infiltrated the Cedarfall Court filled my mind, conjured by Aldrick's will as though to tease me.

"This will be different because I have the missing piece to my puzzle. Many of my chosen have lived long enough to spread a message, but not to thrive as Duwar so wished. This – Duncan – will succeed."

As his horrific voice filled my head, Aldrick retrieved something from the folds of his cloak. A dagger. Duncan didn't seem to notice, nor did the crowd as they were transfixed on Aldrick as he carried on speaking about Duwar's promise and what the entity wished to gift its followers.

But I noticed. And couldn't do anything to warn Duncan. I studied the blade as though my life depended on it, noticing the swollen handle made of glass that sloshed with dark liquid. Aldrick held the flat side of the blade to Duncan's back. Surely Duncan sensed it? Yet he didn't react.

"… how unfair it is that some are born with power and others not. It was why the Creator failed. Unlike the fey's god Altar, the Creator was selfish with his power, keeping it for himself when he moulded you in his image. It was his greatest downfall. Duwar sees this and forgives you for following a god who never truly cared for you. Not like Duwar will. Duwar sees us all as those before it in equal measures of deserving – no matter whom we are created in the image of. Duwar adopts us all. And in thanks for following Duwar's promise, I have been instructed to carry out their wishes as you all know. In Duwar's name I will give you all a chance to become warriors in its making. Our campaign will soon spread like wildfire. When those who still cling to their old Gods see what Duwar can promise, they will run to us with open hearts just for a taste of what Duwar can provide. Witness. See for yourselves. And then decide… are you willing to meet your end to better your future?"

Aldrick hoisted the dagger high into the air. The action snatched the breath from the crowd collectively. I managed my own shuddering inhale through tight lips.

Duncan stood stock still. He didn't move as the dagger arced downwards, sharp tip aimed for his chest. Then the blade met

its mark with a sickening thud. It passed through his flesh with
ease, stopping only when the hilt slammed skin-deep. Time
slowed to a horrifying stop. Aldrick held Duncan to him with
a vice-like grip, keeping him from falling to his knees. All the
while the dagger was left impaled through his ribs, reaching all
the way into his heart.

I pinched my eyes closed. If I couldn't see what was
happening, it wasn't real. Someone shouted Duncan's name
from the crowd. Kayne. I recognised his voice. Then his
struggling grunts as he fought his way towards the podium.

*"Open your eyes and watch the Resurgence, Robin. Do not be
afraid."*

I fought to ignore Aldrick's command but failed. My eyes
flew up in time to watch Duncan stagger back. He was far
taller than Aldrick, who was beginning to struggle holding
him up.

"Blood is the key. It always has been. I can take power from
the undeserving and give it to those who would do better with
it in their possession. As there is a cost of everything in life,
so is there for the Resurgence. But those with burning, strong
faith will make it through. Watch! All of you witness what
your belief can do. See what you can become."

Duncan did nothing but look forward, the dagger in this
chest changing with every passing moment. Blood. That was
what had splashed within the glass handle. Now it drained
slowly, down through an unseen hollow compartment in the
dagger and into the heart that the blade had pierced.

Only when the vial-like handle was empty did Aldrick tear it
free and discard it across the podium where it skipped to a stop
at my feet. My entire world shattered as Duncan finally made
a sound. He cried out, suddenly breaking out of the prison of
silence Aldrick had locked him in.

"General Rackley's faith will see him through the change."
Aldrick stood back, still a hooded and crooked figure, as he
gestured towards the staggering man. "The stronger your

faith, the more blessed you shall become." Aldrick was frantic, shouting, throwing his arms around as though he battered an unseen swarm of monsters that flew around him.

No matter how he delivered his desperate speech, not a single set of eyes was taken off of Duncan, not as he struggled against death itself.

"Ro–Robin!" Duncan screamed, voice trembling. He swallowed back his shout then shattered the world with my name – as clear as day – as it tore out of his throat for a second time. "Robin!"

Blood filled my mouth as I bit down on my tongue. I'd never wished so hard for anything other than to speak. To tell him I was here. To make him understand that he wasn't alone. Duncan faced his death like any other would, fearful like a child looking into the dark unknown, crying out with harsh, sharp breaths. Then it all stopped. Not because Aldrick commanded so, but because there was no more pain to scream about.

I watched everything unfold, my heartbeat thundering like the hooves of a stampeding horde in my ears.

Duncan uncurled, panting heavily. He stood tall, chin raised as he faced the crowd. The room let out a collective gasp at something I couldn't see. From beneath the shadows of Aldrick's hood he released a bubbling, manic laugh that itched at my soul. The air seemed to shift, thickening as it crackled with a wave of unseen energy. I looked down to the tickle across my arms, watching the hairs standing on end.

"It has worked!" Aldrick cried, voice almost muffled by the dense and crackling air. "See how the balance can shift. And in Duwar's name we will cleanse the land and prepare it for the arrival of a better future. Together."

Duncan turned slowly to look at me. A glow of stark blue light emanated from him. His eyes were overcome by the bright radiance that also spread across his arms and hands, which he held before him as though he feared their proximity, lines of sharp, splitting light which fizzed and popped. *Lightning*. As though he was a goliath, reaching into thunder clouds and tearing the power from the sky himself. Duncan's skin was covered in jagged, snaking lines that moved with such speed they didn't stay in one place for long. His chest showed no sign of a wound, only the blood that dried before my eyes.

I longed to speak. To say something to Duncan as I recognised the fear that creased his handsome, glowing face. He looked from me, to his hands, and back again as though he could not make sense of the power that radiated from him.

A single tear dripped down my cheek. I felt my skin shiver, my body shaking with the tension that built within me. Still, Aldrick didn't release me from my imprisonment.

The crowd's awe held them in silence. I could've heard a pin drop upon the floor with ease. All I could do was focus on the heavy breathing of Duncan as he stood there bathed in power that should *never* have belonged to him.

Then Duncan turned away from me, face hardening, eyes narrowing, as he focused all his attention on Aldrick. My heart leapt in my chest, stomach jolting as though I rode upon the back of Gyah in her Eldrae form.

"Settle down, General Rackley," Aldrick spoke sternly. "The rush of power will pass. Give your body, soul and mind a moment to adjust–"

Duncan faltered, expression pinching as though he fought something internally. Then he continued, taking a shaking step forward. Aldrick backed away, cloak shuffling around his awkward feet. The crowd began to shout, and all I could do was *think* my encouragement.

Kill him, Duncan. Do it. I hoped that Aldrick was still in my head, listening to my dark thoughts as I willed Duncan to act.

"Guards," Aldrick cried, and the clink of metal replied, as armoured men and women ran towards Aldrick. I could see they held an iron cuff identical to the one strangling my throat.

They hesitated as they drew closer to Duncan. His crackling power intensified and spread, singeing the ground where it touched; smoke hissed like reaching snakes around his feet.

"Tell me their names," Duncan growled as he closed in on the Hand.

"Stand down."

"Give me their fucking names!"

Despite Duncan's request being somewhat vague, I knew he asked after his parents' murderers, and I wondered if Aldrick's hesitation was a sign that he knew that too.

The crowd was riled up, some pushing past the lines of Kingsmen as they tried to clamber onto the stage and provide aid to the Hand.

The air split with a thundering clap, blending with Duncan's demanding shout. "Tell me!"

I began to feel movement in my limbs, a prickling of needles as the feeling returned from my feet upwards, spreading out across my spine into every part of me. Aldrick's presence retreated slowly from my mind as he fought to get Duncan under his control. Elinor gasped at my side, sucking in a breath as though she had held it this entire time. She too was released.

Then the human king cried, voice croaky as though it hadn't been used for years. "Sei–seize him!"

It was hard to tell if he spoke of Duncan, but the shaking finger he attempted to raise pointed straight towards Aldrick. But the king was ignored in the chaos, his voice no longer important to those who filled the room. Not that he had any power here anymore. The Hunters were here for the Hand and the promise of Duwar, not the king and queen who were merely brought before them for show.

Everything happened so quickly. It was almost a shock when I heard the distant, scratching scream from beyond the chamber room. I put it down to someone fighting in the chamber below the podium until I heard it again.

"Duncan…" I whispered, my voice finally my own again.

"What is that?" Elinor spoke over me, leaning forward with a grimace as she looked to the dark sky beyond the open doors and stained-glass windows. "Do you see it? There – outside – in the sky…"

I tore my eyes from Duncan and Aldrick as another screech reached me, this time louder than before. Beyond the chamber room and filling the sky were large, winged beasts.

Gryvern.

The skies were filled with Doran Oakstorm's gryvern.

Well, this is going to get interesting.

CHAPTER 37

Windows exploded as slick grey bodies shattered through them. The shards of glass fell upon the crowd like rain as they froze, gripped with terror. It was impossible to know who screamed louder, the petrified humans or the monstrous gryvern.

There was no time to think, only act.

In the panic, Aldrick had withdrawn completely from my mind. Duncan's distraction had been the beginning, but the gryvern flooding the great hall had been the knife that separated his cord. My body was mine again, and so was my voice.

"Duncan!" I shouted over the chaos. "Leave him."

Aldrick was being surrounded by the silver-plated guards. His aged, drawn voice was muffled by the thundering of feet, screams and horror that clasped the room.

For a brief moment, I'd never been so thankful to see the sickening creations of King Doran's curse.

I pleaded for Duncan to join me. This moment of distraction was what we needed to get away from Aldrick.

"Stay with me, okay?" I said to Elinor, who faced the horror with an expression of stern power. I gripped her wrist and held it as though she was the most precious thing in the world. "We are getting out of here. Now. Duncan, come!"

I could do little but watch as the gryvern picked humans up without care, ripping limbs apart with a sickening wet noise that turned my stomach inside out. The death transfixed me, as well as Elinor, who muttered her husband's name quietly as though she *knew* what these creatures were to him.

By the time I looked back towards Duncan, Aldrick was no longer in sight, removed from the room with haste. Meanwhile, the human king and queen were left for the feasting creatures, holding onto each other upon the floor. No one went to help them. They were not even an afterthought.

"I will help them," Elinor shouted as though reading my mind. She tore her arm from my grip and positioned her body towards the human royals. "Go and calm *your* Hunter before my husband's monsters reach us. If this is our chance to get out of Lockinge we will not have long before the window closes."

I nodded, feeling the warmth from my body drain. My throat tightened at the prospect of escaping. Perhaps I should've demanded we left the human royals and thought of ourselves. But the steely look in Elinor's diamond-bright eyes told me she would've refused.

The humans who circled Duncan had either fled with Aldrick or raced towards the beasts with forced confidence. Hunters swung short swords and fists, both as pathetic as the other against the clawed and sharp-toothed monsters. Many flooded out beyond the open doors, beneath the dripping of flesh and blood, only to be greeted by a sky filled with the flying demons.

I reached Duncan with ease. He stood before me, shoulders rising and falling dramatically. I reached instinctively for him and was met with a sharp, sudden pain that had my fingers rearing back.

"What's happening to me?" His voice popped and crackled, charged from within as the bolts of stark light still raced across his skin. Duncan held his hands before him, looking down at the snakes of power that circled his fingers and set the hairs across his strong arms aloft.

"We can figure it out," I replied, breathless from urgency. "But only when we are far away from this place. You're alive, that's what matters."

Duncan's glowing gaze widened. It was the only warning that something was wrong before his hands pushed hard into my chest. The world faded into darkness as the air was driven out of my lungs. Nothing made sense for a long, painful moment until I caught my breath, noticing smoke curling from the burned handprints on my tunic. I was at a distance, my body aching as though every bone had shattered, mended and broke again.

Duncan was no longer standing where he had been. Instead, he dangled in the air, kept from the ground by the gryvern whose taloned claws pierced his arms. I couldn't conjure enough breath to shout as the prickling of Duncan's new power still coursed through my body. I watched, splayed across the floor, as Duncan reached up, wrapped a hand around the gryvern's long, bent leg and forced the blue twisting light into it. The gryvern burned from the inside; the wet pop that followed was beautiful.

Duncan fell hard to the ground as the creature exploded, chunks of gore, bone and skin splattering everywhere. I was stunned, awed by the power that crackled beyond Duncan's skin. He looked to me, horror and concern creasing his brows.

That was when I saw the Twins. "Be–behind you!"

Duncan had not a moment to spare before they attacked. Each wielded a blade, equally deadly and beautiful with its sharp steel and bejewelled handle. Their lack of trepidation to the power emanating from Duncan only confirmed that their actions were not their own. Duncan threw out his hands before him, a bolt of crackling light following, missing the Twins but colliding against a wall; stone split and exploded, leaving a charred crater in its wake.

My arms shook as I pushed myself from the ground. I could recognise Elinor fussing over the hysterical king and queen, whilst shouting my name to see if I was alright. Her pleas didn't matter.

I had to help Duncan.

Despite the unknown power crackling around him, Duncan was fluid and precise as he danced around the two fey women, years of training put on display. The Twins did everything to stay away from his fists and reaching hands, but they too had enough training to keep out of harm's way.

Beside me there was a human body, lifeless and still, clothing drenched in his own blood. His dead fingers gripped a sword that had done little to keep him alive. My body screamed as though it was lit by fire from within. Gritting teeth together against the agony from Duncan's touch, I clawed myself across the floor, tore the sword free and claimed it as my own.

I raced towards Duncan and the Twins; sword held high. I did so without uttering a sound, knowing the element of surprise would be the only thing to give Duncan a fighting chance. There was no hesitation. Neither paid me mind as they spun and twisted, swords flashing towards Duncan's exposed skin. As I cut my blade downwards, it was met with steel instead of flesh.

Kayne. He looked over the edge of his blade, eyes narrowed. With a great push he forced me to take steps back, his strength unparalleled.

"They will kill him!" I said, knuckles white as I stared the tracker down. Kayne's disdain for me was palpable, and his tall body acted as a barrier, preventing me from saving Duncan.

Kayne hesitated, the lines creased across his forehead softening for a moment. My breathing became shallow as I watched his mind turn behind his narrowed eyes. He was captured in his own internal war; then he replied, jaw tightening as he spoke through gritted teeth, "I'm going to fucking regret this."

Kayne spun, grunting as he brought the hilt of his sword down on the back of one of the Twins' heads. The crack could have been heard over any level of noise. She dropped, and her narrow body crumpled in on itself. Her counterpart screamed, her entire focus on her sister, who lay in a heap upon the floor, ignoring everything else around her.

Duncan took his chance and joined my side. "Brother," Duncan panted, facing Kayne who still held the sword determinedly in his fist. "Glad to see you've found some sense."

"What has he done to you?" Kayne whispered, sweeping his sweaty, ginger curls out of his eyes. "Give me a good enough reason not to put you down right now."

"You won't do that because it is *me*," Duncan replied. "I can't tell you what has happened because I don't know."

"It's not right, Duncan. None of this is right."

"Then help us," I interrupted, aware that the crowd was thinning and the gryvern would soon be focused on us. "If we don't get out of here, all of us will die."

I could see the hesitation in Kayne's gaze as he looked between Duncan and me, then to the blood-soaked room.

"By helping you I go against the Hand and Duwar. We have been warned about your kind's trickery. Duncan has been too weak to see it but–"

Sparks of light reached for Kayne as Duncan's sudden anger exploded around him. "It has all been lies. Kayne, see it for what it is."

"We really don't have time for this." I wanted to tug on Duncan's hand and draw him away from here, but his power frightened me, and it was still crackling in the air around his body. Even now I felt the lingering pain from his touch; the burns in my shirt were enough warning as to what would happen if his charged touch met mine again.

Elinor cried out, capturing our attention. She pulled back on the arm of the queen who was being dragged by the claws of a gryvern. Her cry was one that would inspire war. Powerful and determined, Elinor did everything in her strength to hold on without the help of the cowering king at her feet.

Kayne sprung to action before we had the chance to help. He raced forward, sword held with two hands above his head.

With a great leap he swung it downwards, aiming for the
gryvern's claws. But he was too late. Elinor let go, tumbling
from the momentum until the back of her head hit the slabbed
floor. The human queen was ripped into the air, thrown into
the claws of another gryvern who treated her more like a toy.
Kayne's sword slapped into the ground, sparks emanating from
the collision. With the strength of his strike, I was surprised the
floor didn't split in two.

I raced to Elinor's side, helping her up. "We need to leave."

She grunted her response, reaching for the back of her
matted curls with a wince. "I tried to help her."

"I know, you did all you could," I replied, witnessing as
Kayne consoled the human king. "But now is our chance to
run. Do you think you can manage it?"

Elinor nodded, stern and resolute. "I would rather die by the
hands of my husband's children than visit the prisons again.
We leave, or I die happily."

Husband's children. In that one comment she confirmed what
I'd learned after seeing Erix's transformation.

"There is far too much that is required from you in
Wychwood," I told her, gritting my jaw as I pulled her to her
feet. "Dying is not on the cards today. Not for any of us."

"Fine," Kayne shouted. "We leave together. Now. Before I
change my mind. Those doors will take us out into the belly of
Lockinge. I need to find Lucari and she will scout the skies for
the safest time to leave."

Lucari, as Duncan had explained, was the hawk I'd seen
nestled upon Kayne's shoulder.

There was no time for further discussion. Kayne took the
human king, arm draped over his shoulder, and I helped Elinor
as we left the room together. The gryvern were growing restless.
They'd successfully picked through the crowds, toying with
the dead flesh of the humans with growing distaste. Without
living humans to feast upon, it was likely they remembered
why they had come all this way. For me.

Duncan led the way, an illuminated torch of power. He kicked open the door, boot leaving a scorched mark across the wood. Into the dark corridor beyond we ran, Kayne forced to close it behind him.

Something heavy thumped into the other side as Kayne lowered the slat across the door, locking it in place. Then another. And another. Gryvern flew into the door, straining the wood until it groaned and snapped beneath their weight. Even the aged wall around it shuddered, fluttering dust upon us like snow.

All we could do was run.

"Don't let go of me," I said to Elinor.

"Never," she replied, breathless. "I did with your mother and vowed I never would again."

Her words kept me going, each step less of a struggle as the memory of my mother raced through my mind. Even with the heavy, draining echo that the iron collar left upon me, I felt close to her, with the hand of her friend enclosed within mine.

Duncan led us blindly through the castle. Every now and then Kayne would shout a direction. It was clear the Tracker had been within these walls before. It was a maze of darkness and stone for the rest of us. Putting my trust in him to guide us to safety wasn't my first choice, but I was out of others.

The sky beyond was dark, Lockinge alight with terror as gryvern wreaked havoc. I had caused every pain and death beyond the castle's walls. It should've made me feel guilt. If the humans within the city didn't already hate the fey enough they would despise us even more now. Just like the humans in Ayvbury had when they had been senselessly attacked by the fey king's creatures. The horror from this evening would snap the little hope of tolerance between both realms, a wound that might never heal.

Pushing all of those thoughts aside, I focused on the burning need thrumming through my blood. The need to survive. It made thinking about anything else impossible. One foot in

front of the other, breathing harsh yet focused, I kept my
attention on putting as much distance between myself and this
place as I could.

"Robin Icethorn, where do you think you are going?"

Aldrick's presence crept back into my mind like a vicious
snake, constricting and hungry. I opened my mouth to cry out
in warning until his command kept me quiet.

"Silent. Until I tell you to speak, you will listen."

My body kept moving despite my wish for it to stop. I looked
to Duncan's back, wishing nothing more than to call out and
tell him what was happening. Aldrick kept me compliant, his
controlling, unseen strings tied tight around my body and
mind once again.

*"Did you truly believe I would simply let my two most valuable
assets leave my castle so easily?"*

I screamed back, voice filling my head. *"It is too late."*

*"It is not. Now, you are going to do what it is I tell you to do.
Understand?"*

"No."

Aldrick's laugh bounced across my skull. *"Like a fly within a
spider's web, you have flown too close. I will not let my treasure slip so
easily through my fingers. Come to me. All of you."*

I blinked as directions filled my head. Without being able to
stop myself I called out, voice mimicking what Aldrick spoke
within me, "If we leave now, we will only be picked off by the
gryvern. Follow me."

"Robin," Duncan shouted as I turned, pulling Elinor with
me. "What are you playing at? If we go back, we will only lose
ourselves within Lockinge. We need to get outside to make
sense of our direction."

"Trust me," Aldrick made me reply. Elinor was more trusting
than Duncan, but even she noticed a shift in my behaviour.

I pleaded for her to comment about it. To say something,
anything for me to reply and tell her what was happening
within my mind.

"*Why me?*" I asked as my hurried footsteps lead us back into the heart of Lockinge, right towards Aldrick.

"*Because your mind is wide open, and your will is weak. If you did not wish to be such an easy catch, then you should put up more of a fight like Duncan did. My, how he impressed me.*"

There was nothing I could do or say to stop the inevitable from happening. That spark of hope that I'd clung to dissipated as I led Elinor, Duncan and Kayne, who still carried the king, towards Aldrick.

We were all flies, and this castle was an elaborate web that not even the king could have crawled out of. This was Aldrick's domain now, we simply dwelled within it.

CHAPTER 38

There was nothing I could do to stop our group from being ambushed. As I pushed the door open, I knew what waited within. Aldrick told me so, showed me flashes of images; Duncan in chains; Elinor kneeling upon the ground, arms shaking as she fought to hold her bleeding body up.

Duncan had felt unsettled as I urged them towards the specific room. I screamed with my mind, my eyes, for him to listen to his gut and not me. But alas, he did as I said. His blind trust in me would be his end.

Like lambs to the slaughter, I led them all into a dark room where Aldrick waited with a body of Kingsmen. The silver-plated men and women rushed forward and Aldrick's control on my mind did not waver; I couldn't even cry out in warning or shock.

"Run!" Duncan screamed to the rest of our party as an iron cuff was snapped around his bulging neck. Like rain upon a fire, the crackling light across his skin fizzled out, the iron severing his new abilities.

Kayne handed the king to Elinor when Duncan cried his warning. Now she was struggling beneath his weight, throwing her off balance and dragging her to the ground. It was clear he feared Aldrick greatly; just his presence alone had him on his knees.

Kayne was backing away when a figure detached from the shadows of the hallway we had left and stopped him. The sole remaining Twin held one knife to Kayne's throat and the other pressed above his spine; one wrong move and he'd suffer greatly.

"Well, well." Aldrick limped towards me, wrapped a hand around my shoulder and placed a rough kiss upon my cheek. His touch made me sick. I couldn't even move my hand to wipe the trail of spit from my cheek.

"If only it was that easy to simply leave through a back door and never return. What did you think would happen to you all? The streets beyond Lockinge castle are full of my Hunters. I would have given you hours before you were returned to me," Aldrick boasted.

His control over my body and mind didn't take away my choice to cry. Tears spilled from my wide eyes as I looked over the line of my companions. Duncan's expression was as hard as stone, but the scar upon his face was not as deep as it usually was when he was livid; that small feathering of softness told me that he understood. My actions were not in fact mine.

"You will not succeed," Duncan growled, trying to pull free from the three soldiers who held him down. They struggled as he fought, but he still could not break free; it didn't deter him from shouting his thundering threats. "One moment of weakness and I will end you. That is all it takes."

"I sense there should be a warning to follow," Aldrick replied, old fingers tightening on my shoulder until it hurt. "After the power I have gifted you, you turn upon me immediately, General Rackley. Have your years of faith been turned to ash with a mere matter of days with this fey boy?"

Elinor's lips were pulled into a tight, sharp line. She looked at Aldrick with pure hatred; if her stare was a weapon he would have been covered in deep and agonising wounds.

Aldrick was still hooded, speaking from the shadows he hid within. Were Elinor and I the only ones to know of his true identity?

"It is our little secret," Aldrick confirmed, his youthful voice echoing across the cavern of my mind. *"Not for long. When my task is complete the people of this realm and the next will not see me as a fey. They will see me as the Hand. Bringer of Duwar. Ruling at the god's side. A new era."*

"If I had known you were nothing but an old man cursed with the cancer of delusion, I would have never followed your false promises," Duncan spat as he replied, teeth bared, and arms taut with muscle.

"Ah, but you did not join my army as the others did. Did you, Duncan?"

I watched in horror as Duncan's eyes rolled back into his head and he pinched his eyes closed. Duncan struggled, not physically but mentally, throwing his head from side to side.

"Get out of my fucking head!"

It was becoming harder for the guards to hold him down. Others had to join, gripping his sweat-slicked skin, and keeping him from breaking free.

"Names," Aldrick said, drawing out the word as though it was the first time he'd ever spoken it. "Your friend Kayne joined because of the promise for a new world. He heard the words I spoke and, like many others, wished to help bring forth this new realm in the name of the punished and forgotten Duwar. You… You simply wanted names. A selfish want."

"Get. Out," Duncan pleaded, eyes scrunched in pain.

"Please…" I said breathlessly. "Leave him. This has nothing to do with him."

"Not as strong-willed as you first thought," Aldrick said, speaking solely to Duncan, swatting my pleading away with the wave of a hand.

Duncan's eyes snapped wide, and he panted, lips and chin wet. He looked deranged; a wild animal caught within a trap. He didn't plead for Aldrick to withdraw from his mind anymore, instead he stared at a spot on the floor as his dark-forest eyes filled with stubborn tears.

"Does it change anything for you?" Aldrick asked, releasing me and stepping forward. "All these years and you have wished for something that is pointless and useless. Names are not as powerful as you have been led to believe. What will you do with the information you have sought?"

I couldn't catch a breath as I watched Duncan retreat from this room and this world before our very eyes. No longer did he struggle. The guards did not relax their holds, but I could see that he had given up fighting now. Whatever Aldrick had revealed within Duncan's mind had broken him.

"Talk to me, Duncan," Kayne shouted, breaking his silence as he looked worriedly towards his friend. "Come on, boy. Say something to me."

Duncan ignored Kayne. Perhaps he didn't hear him through the roaring of whatever information he had gleaned from Aldrick.

Kayne turned his attention towards Aldrick. Still, he was the only one who didn't look upon the old man with horror. There was still a gleam of admiration for the Hand, even if the wince across his face told me that he struggled with it after what he had witnessed.

"What of the Hunters?" Kayne said. "Those creatures likely hunt them through our streets. Should we not be fighting them? Helping the innocents who wait within their homes for the beasts to pick them off one by one?"

Aldrick shook his head. "It would seem a disgruntled fey king waits outside our walls. And I wonder who led him here." Aldrick's hollow eyes flickered to me. "Those creatures are known as gryvern and only Doran Oakstorm can control them. Twisted and evil creations of the very king who sent them. War is upon us, but I will not waste my precious Hunters in fighting beasts. This war is not for them. They are here for something and when they retrieve it… they will leave."

At this Duncan looked to me. So did Elinor, whose stern expression cracked and revealed concern for me. A name whispered across her lips. *Doran.*

"Do not worry." Aldrick leaned into my ear and whispered, his lips uncomfortably close. I could not pull away as his strong will still gripped me firmly. "I will not give you up that easily. As a show of my good faith, and my desire to work with you and not against you, we will kill Doran Oakstorm together. That is what you wished for, was it not? My help in defeating him? You came all this way for an army, an army I can give you. With your help we will create one. Look at Duncan Rackley. Do you see what your blood can do now?"

"Monster," Elinor snarled. "I have faced men like you before and believe me, it will never end in your favour."

"And you would know one wouldn't you, Elinor Oakstorm? Robin came all this way because of your dear husband. As did you. Both for different reasons, but it is poetic that you share such a similarity, is it not?"

"From the arms of one, to the prisoner of another. Yes," she spat, "I do know a monster and you are the greatest of them all."

Aldrick laughed, deep and rumbling, like the warning of thunder through dark-stained skies. The remaining Twin echoed his chuckle as she paced behind the line of my companions, each of them on their knees, the human king still sobbing into the stone slabs at his feet. Not a single guard had to hold him down; he was no threat.

Dark lines sliced down the Twin's grief-crazed face. Her hair was a tangle of wild and messy strands. Her clothes stained with the blood of her sister.

"Please," Kayne said, flinching as the Twin came too close. "The more time we waste the more people will die at the hands of those… the gryvern."

"And their lives will not be wasted," Aldrick snapped, displeased with Kayne's sudden interruption. "Have you not seen what I can do for those who die? Look at your trusted companion. Stabbed in the heart, yet still he lives. Ask yourself why that is."

"Blood," Elinor said quickly. "He steals it from our bodies and puts it into the vessels of his followers. Just like my *dear husband*," she mocked. "Your Hand is no different. He creates beings that should not exist under Altar's or the Creator's rule."

"Right and wrong," Aldrick replied. "The result of my work does not belong to me, Altar or the Creator. These are the children of Duwar. Beings who do not belong. Beings who are not claimed by either the fey's god or the human's beloved Creator. Just as Duwar did not belong among its siblings, Duncan and the rest of my Hunters do not have a rightful place among the realms. That will all change soon enough. We will become a world of beings crafted of pure power and chaos."

"Do you wish to say anything?"

Suddenly, my voice was mine again. Aldrick's claws pulled free from the flesh of my mind, allowing my control to return.

"Burn. In. *Hell*," I hissed, spittle flying past my lips.

"That judgement does not belong to you, Robin Icethorn. I think it is time that you all see for yourselves the promise of a future that is coming."

Aldrick looked towards the Twin. *"Seraphine*, it is time we show them."

The Twin, Seraphine, nodded, sheathing her blades at her waist. It was strange to understand that she had a name; she was a nameless puppet in my eyes.

"Go to him," Aldrick said to me, hand urging me to move. "Be with your love and witness this together. Perhaps you will both understand what it is I work towards. Now go."

"Fuck you," I managed as my feet began to step forward and I walked, without my own doing, towards Duncan. As I joined his side the guards took a hold of me, dragging me to my knees. I bit back a gasp as my bones smacked into the stone ground. With the echo of a haunting laugh, Aldrick finally retracted from my mind.

"I didn't mean to–"

Duncan stiffened beside me. "I know."

I longed to reach for him, but the guards held me firm. Elinor looked down the line at me, eyes brimming with worry. I could see the question within her stare, and I nodded subtly to answer. *I'm fine.*

There was a screech of wheels, an awkward, unrhythmical squeaking as Seraphine struggled to pull a large object covered in a deep red velvet cloth. Aldrick stood still, hands clasped before him, as Seraphine guided the object behind him. From my view point it looked as though it was a large frame, and Aldrick was the painting trapped within it.

"The humans have followed the Creator for centuries, all without seeing Him, hearing His command or feeling His presence. The fey believe stories of Altar and how He created the four Courts from His blood and gave His children access to magic that placed them above anyone else. Stories. That is all it has been to each and every one of you. I cannot blame you for thinking me a fool, a cruel old man preaching the promise of a god that has been erased from the realm's stories."

Seraphine moved towards Aldrick and reached for his cloak. With bated breath, I watched, knowing what was coming. Slowly she lowered it, exposing the face of the man beneath, and the two points of his ears.

Kayne released a sound that was both a gasp and a growl. I was silent as Aldrick finally revealed his truth before us all. Even the guards who held me relaxed their hold as they too shared their shock at what they witnessed.

Aldrick had revealed himself as the very being that he had commanded his Hunters to hunt. He was fey and that truth snatched the sound from the room entirely.

He smiled, flashing stained teeth as he surveyed each of our reactions.

"I don't understand." Kayne broke the silence. "You cannot be…"

"Fey? Was the possibility far from your mind, Kayne? Was it truly that hard to imagine that one of their own could sign the seal of command that demanded the fey to be rounded up like cattle and brought here? I am part of both realms, Wychwood and Durmain, just like Robin here. It is why Duwar chose me to herald the new world, to create an army strong enough to fight for them. *Free* them."

"You tricked us," Kayne shouted, finally fighting back against those who held him. "Why?"

"It is time you see why I've done all of this." Aldrick tipped a head towards Seraphine, who grinned. She reached for the velveteen sheet across the large object and gripped a fistful.

I studied the hard, sharp profile of Duncan, who did not take his eyes off Aldrick for a moment. His lip was curled, his scarred face pinched deep in disgust at the man he saw.

"History will remember the names of those who witnessed Duwar before freedom was granted to them. And each of you will help in shattering their bindings and bringing the possibility of a new realm, one combined in Duwar's name. There is still much work to do, but the wheels are turning."

Seraphine yanked the cloth and it fell from the object, gently fluttering across the floor. It was a mirror, golden frame carved with intricate designs of stars woven among vines and flowers. The golden-painted surface had become worn in areas, revealing an uglier truth of ancient wood beneath it. The mirror held within the frame was equally as aged. In the corners were webs of small cracks spread across like greedy fingers wishing to claim the entire surface of the mirror.

Someone sucked in a sharp breath. I didn't look around to see who it had been as a strange movement caught my attention. Something was moving. I looked harder, narrowing in on Aldrick's back which was reflected in the mirror, then to the hand that reached out and wrapped around Aldrick's shoulder. There was nothing in the room to explain what it was we saw.

This was no ordinary mirror. It was a window, revealing a realm that was not ours. The figure stepped forward from the darkness slowly. At first it was only the hulking outline that I could see. I blinked, unable to believe that what I saw was not one of Aldrick's mind tricks. But it was as real as the floor beneath my knees. As real as the hands of the guards who still held me down.

Then I found myself muttering a name I had never believed I would call out for. "Altar, help us."

CHAPTER 39

Demon.

It stood within the mirror's reflection not an inch behind Aldrick's back.

Duwar.

It was inhuman with a towering body crafted from molten rock. It seemed the layer of its hardened skin cracked in places. Beneath glowed a body of deep, burning red that shifted tones from angry scarlet to warm orange.

I felt the creature's piercing red stare cut straight through me. The presence stole every possible sound from the room so that even the king of Durmain ceased his heavy sobbing. Duwar stood deathly still, only the shifting of its eyes drifting across the room as they drank us in.

"Do you see it now?" Aldrick asked, visibly affected by the unseen, clawed hand the creature rested upon his shoulder. Only in the reflection could Duwar be seen, but its touch was as real as the glass of the mirror itself. "Until now only I have been blessed with the vision of Duwar. Never has another seen what I have seen. Witness what has kept my feet stepping forward in this direction. You see now, don't you? You see Duwar."

"It's a trick," I muttered, unable to form another reason for what I saw. The creature looked back at me and tilted its head like a curious dog – but no dog had horns that burst through its exposed skull, or cracked lips of scorched earth. "Just another vision you have filled our heads with – an illusion."

Aldrick looked displeased with my outburst, fighting the urge to look behind him with a face of astonishment. "Is your lack of faith so pungent that even with a god presented before you, you are unable to grasp truth from trick? Robin, what you see is very much real. A glimpse to Duwar in its prison. But not for long… soon you will be free."

It was disconcerting how Aldrick shifted his conversation from me to the creature that waited behind him.

"This proves nothing," Duncan hissed, straining against the hands of the guards once more.

Aldrick shot his attention back to the man at my side. His expression pinched, eyes storming with curiosity. "You dare question after all you have seen?"

I slowly reached my hand out sideways until I touched Duncan's sweaty skin. Aldrick was too occupied to notice, as well as the guards at our backs who were just as shocked as we all were with the scene before us.

Duncan stilled under my touch, then leaned into it. My heart swelled. The moment between us felt as though it could be the last.

"You said you wish to free Duwar," Elinor spoke up, snatching Aldrick's attention from the disgraced Hunter general. "But if Duwar is real then what is stopping it from breaking free itself? It has enough power to ensnare you, but is kept locked beneath a thin pane of glass?"

"So much history of Duwar, Altar and the Creator has been left untouched that you all do not know the stories. It is a crime, one worthy of the greatest punishments. But I am merely the Hand, voice of Duwar and speaker of the truth which has been kept from the fey and the humans for too many years." Aldrick stepped forward, shoulder raising as Duwar released its hold. The creature, silent and burning, watched as the old man stalked towards us. Aldrick reached Elinor and put a single finger beneath her chin. Without much effort he lifted her face upwards, smiling down upon her like she was a child preparing to listen to a bedtime tale. "Duwar has promised a new realm, one undivided by its siblings' laws and differences, a world with space for those who did not fit in. A home."

"I can take him," Duncan whispered beneath Aldrick's speech. The Hand was too enthralled as he unleashed his story as though he had held it in for many years, desperate to tell a soul.

I looked at Duncan's profile, keeping my movements muted and my voice equally as quiet as his. "It won't work."

Duncan's scowl deepened, eyes unmoving from the reflection of the burning, molten creature that watched from the face of the mirror. He looked at it as though he waited for proof that it was an illusion.

"I would rather die trying than perish not knowing," Duncan finally replied, the muscles across his exposed chest tensing.

"… keys." I looked back to Aldrick, trying to make sense of what he'd just said. "It was my task to locate them. The first key was easiest and most obvious to find. Faith. Destroying the belief bestowed on the egotistical god the humans call the Creator. Complacent that His rule would last forever, the Creator put His forged key in faith itself. The more who worshiped Him, the stronger His lock was kept upon Duwar. The weaker the devotion became… well, do you see now? The barrier between our realm and the hell Duwar has been kept within is thin as a result."

In another world, during another time, I may have believed Aldrick's story to be nothing but fiction a parent told a child at night to keep them behaving in the following days, a way of manipulating the naïve to behave with threats of demonic monsters that would come for you in the darkest of times. But then I looked back to the mirror and saw the very creature he preached about, still shrouded in shadows, its skin glowing as though fire burned beneath it, visible only through the cracks across his rock-hard skin. Eyes slitted like a cat's, forged from flame and blood, redder than the freshest of blood, glowing brighter than the proudest of fires.

"Indeed," Aldrick murmured, releasing Elinor's chin and stalking back up the line. Kayne stiffened, eyes glancing towards Duncan as though he waited for something. The king's sobbing returned again, this time more frantic and pathetic than before. Aldrick paid him no mind as he continued with his story.

"It is the final keys that were harder to uncover, scattered among the fey courts. They would not have been simple to locate and destroy. More physical than the Creator's faith, but more elusive. It would require an army to aid me, one I had to create myself."

"One chance," Duncan muttered, lips thin and jaw tight. "Together."

The terrorising screams of gryvern sounded beyond the room, the noise of them increasingly louder than they had been before. Still they searched for me, but Aldrick showed no sign of caring. Was my capture by Doran's creatures a better fate than the one that waited for me here?

"I can't." My whispered reply was laced with defeat. We were trapped in both outcomes. By an old man with a demon at his back, or a bloodthirsty king who would traverse the realm to see me dead.

Elinor spoke up again, shouting towards Aldrick with a sense of misplaced urgency. "Why would Duwar entrust you? Of all people, Duwar has chosen an old man to encourage its return. I cannot make sense of it."

Aldrick stopped just before he reached Duncan. He turned on his heel, crooked body bent inward at his shoulders as though he held the weight of the future upon his back. "It matters not how Duwar believed me worthy. Ask yourself, why did Altar choose the families of those who rule Courts in Wychwood? Why did the Creator make soldiers of his own, only to discard them out of trepidation that they would, like he had with Duwar, overthrow him?"

That was something I had never heard of before. Abbott

Nathanial had mentioned angels before, but I'd put that down to his aged mind. Was he right all along? There was no room to question Aldrick on his mention of the Creator's soldiers as he continued.

"Perhaps it was my willingness, or lack of selflessness and pride, that captured the attention of Duwar. Whatever it may have been I am merely thankful that it was I who was chosen. When the final keys are destroyed and Duwar is free to take their rule across the realms, you will have the privilege to ask the question again."

"I would rather die," Elinor replied, causing a cold shiver to race up my spine.

"Unfortunately, that is not a privilege you have. Ensuring you live is highly important. I need you for Duwar's sake."

"To poison more like me?" Duncan said, spit falling down his chin.

"Precisely."

The screams of the gryvern intensified, finally causing a reaction in Aldrick. He frowned, tired eyes glancing towards the door. "Seraphine, I think they have seen enough."

She didn't respond.

In fact, one look around and I could see that Seraphine was nowhere to be seen.

"Robin," Duncan pleaded. "Please, it is now or never."

Aldrick turned his back on our line and walked towards the mirror, searching the shadows of the room behind it as though his puppet waited within. "Seraph–"

He never got to finish his word. The mirror toppled, falling upon Aldrick, and there was nothing the old man could have done to stop it; Duwar's form shifted, shrinking from view before the glass crashed down.

Aldrick was lost beneath shattered glass.

Standing behind the mirror, chest heaving and arms outstretched, was Seraphine, her face as white as snow. "Get them out of here!"

Kingsmen, in the panic, released us and sprang forward to help. At least that was what I believed until they turned on one another. Swords pierced through backs, perfectly placed between chinks of armour. When the blades were pulled free, they were covered in the dark sheen of blood.

Duncan was up on his feet, throwing a fist towards the back of an unexpecting guard's head. It connected with a crack, bone upon bone. The guard fell. I caught the glimpse of broken skin across Duncan's knuckles for a brief moment before he threw yet another fist at a new target.

"Stay with me," Elinor said, gripping my arms and pulling me back. Kayne was beside Duncan then, joining in the fight. They fought, side by side, creating the perfect barrier between the chaos and us.

"What the fuck is happening?" I spat, eyes scanning the room.

"I don't know," Elinor replied.

Soon enough the fighting stopped. It started and ended so quickly. Human guards lay at the feet of our allies, boots crunching over shattered glass and puddles of blood.

Seraphine stood among the crowd, an unwavering calm amongst a tidal wave of chaos. "We do not have long."

Duncan stepped forward, fists covered in his and other's blood that were still held firmly before him. "You just killed the Hand."

"Aldrick is not dead. He is demon-touched," Seraphine replied sharply. "It would take far more than that to kill him. Now, if you do not come with us, then there will be nothing to stop him when he takes control over all of our minds again."

"Why would you do it?" I shouted, tugging free from Elinor whose nails scratched into the skin of my arms as she held on with such ferocity. It was clear that the guards who were left standing were allied with Seraphine. They stood before her, a barricade of flesh and steel.

"Because a rather handsome price has been put upon your head and I wish to claim it. It would be easier to take you willingly, so I suggest you cease your questioning and we leave."

"No," Duncan said as Seraphine took a brave step forward. "No one leaves this fucking room until you tell us what is going on."

Seraphine shared a look with me that suggested I already knew what she was doing. And in a strange sense, I did. I had seen that look before, many weeks ago, upon the face of a girl who had been promised money for my head. Instead, Seraphine's expression was not as twisted and malicious, but still captured the same hunger that had glinted in the eyes of Briar.

"We are all Children of the Asp," Seraphine confirmed my thoughts. Assassins. Hired mercenaries. "Usually, we work alone, but the price for Robin's return is too delicious to ignore. Enough to share."

Duncan had seen Briar himself and understood the danger associated with that title, how skilled the assassins were.

"Doran," Elinor said, voice shaking with a fear that was all too real.

Seraphine hardly spared her a glance.

"Who sent you?"

"Sent?" Seraphine laughed. "We have always been here. We are everywhere. Hidden amongst crowds, placed among the realm for when we are required to act. Aldrick just didn't suspect anything because of the *Mariflora* we've been ingesting for how ever long. It doesn't stop him entering our head, but it keeps us in control. We just played along."

"Answer his fucking question," Duncan growled. Even with the iron cuff strangling his throat, I could sense the power that dwelled within him.

Seraphine looked directly at me, a glint of pleading in her stare, perhaps created from the trunk of coins she saw when she looked at me, but I hoped for something more genuine.

Then she replied with words that sliced through the tense room. "A friend sent us. Not Doran Oakstorm, but someone who wishes to see you alive by dawn."

CHAPTER 40

We ran, feet pounding through corridors and endless connected rooms each as barren and lifeless as the next. Mixed with the sound of our heavy footfalls were clattering steel and the occasional screech of gryvern that still tore through the castle in search of us.

There was no room for trust as we moved with haste, surrounded by the party of armed assassins. This fate would've been far better than being left to the Hand's plans or the desperation of Doran and his twisted creatures that filled the skies beyond the castle.

A small part of me felt guilty that we had left the human king behind, crying on the floor. Elinor had tried to take him with us, but he refused, pushing her and demanding to be left behind. It seemed my boon did not cover the human king's survival as Seraphine and her fellow companions did not waste any time retreating, not with the threat of Aldrick awakening and regaining control of our freewill. He had the power, infused with his undeniable connection with the demon God, to overwhelm all our minds and take over.

Run. I screamed at myself, filling my head with that single word as we navigated through the castle.

Duncan held my hand from the moment we left. His grip was certain, full of unwavering strength. He didn't let me go – *wouldn't* let me go. Duncan's legs were longer than mine, far more powerful and faster; he had to slow himself down a few times to stop from pulling me over.

Seraphine knew where she was going. All we could do was follow instinctively as we raced towards her promise of a *friend*. I wondered about her twin sister. Had she been part of the Children of the Asp too? Perhaps her life was the price Seraphine had to pay to see me delivered to the highest bidder.

Our party came to a sudden stop when the breeze of nightly air cut through the stuffy, stone walls of the castle. We'd flown down a narrow corridor that ended in an open doorway. Two, maybe three figures stood waiting for us, shapes outlined against the night behind them. If it was not for Seraphine's continuous running, I would've believed them to be enemies, yet another barrier stopping our escape. We rushed towards the open door, only slowing our run as we reached the figures.

"They wait for you at the shore, Seraphine," one said the moment we reached them. They spoke to her only, caring little for our party. Duncan stood before me, hiding me from view behind his back. "You told us you would have one. Not four."

"Plans change," Seraphine replied, voice light and full of twisted pleasure. "We accommodate."

"But the bounty doesn't cover–"

"Send a report only when you hear that the Hand has crawled his way out of the predicament I've left him in," Seraphine interrupted. "Monitor his movements and keep me informed. Be wary. He will be furious as a result of our betrayal and will likely see all those around him as traitors. Keep your distance. Continue ingesting your stores of Mariflora. Strike for information only when the time is right."

They nodded in agreement, their silence telling me all I needed to know about the hierarchy of the group.

I noticed as other beings peeled from the balcony of sorts that we had come to. Duncan did too as his hand tightened in mine.

Wind ripped around the towering walls and the heavy scent of salt itched my nose; as I breathed in, I could taste it, thick and undeniable. The swollen moon's reflection rippled across the expanse of darkness below us; even the winds could not hide the lullaby of water rushing over rock and stone.

"The path down to the coastline is old and worn, tread carefully but move quickly." Seraphine's command was meant for all of us. "If we don't get you far from Lockinge now, there will not be another chance again. Go. With haste."

We continued running, feet clattering down the steep set of steps that seemed to have been carved into the castle's outer wall. Light was sparse which made it feel as though each footstep down was another closer to our final fall. Seraphine led the way, each of us following behind, wind ripping at our faces.

I felt pure relief when the world seemed to settle, and our feet touched down on solid, flat ground. Cold sprays of water splashed across our skin. Our feet crunched over stones, slick and wet from the swell of the dark ocean before us.

When I spoke, my voice felt shattered, as though I spoke through shards of glass embedded in my throat. "I'm frightened."

Duncan wrapped his arm around me, body damp from the ocean's spray. "Rightly so, but I'm not leaving your side this time. I won't let you out of my sight ever again."

I pressed my forehead into the mounds of his chest, feeling his hard muscle push back against my face. "If I could have done this all again, I would never have come. I put you in danger and I'll never forgive myself."

"My actions are my own," Duncan replied, large hand taking the back of my head and rubbing it in calming circles. "I wished to meet the Hand as much as you, yet it would seem that hope was all in vain."

Seraphine busied herself, shouting towards our crew as she waded into the body of rocking dark water. A boat, small and weak, clattered into the pebble shore. I was certain the rough sea could have broken it into pieces of useless wood if the weather was any wilder. It was incredible to believe that this small vessel was our only hope of leaving this city.

"He told you their names," I whispered, lips pressed to his skin. Duncan tasted of salt and copper. "Tell me that it was worth it at least. Give me a reason to cling onto some feeling that this was worth something."

Duncan stilled, his hand ceasing its circles as it paused upon my head. My face moved, rippling as he took a hulking breath inward. "I don't believe I'm ready to face the truth the Hand has revealed to me. Not yet."

I pulled back, glaring up through the darkness at Duncan's stern, glassy-eyed expression. "When you are ready, I will be here to help piece it together with you."

He looked down, forcing a smile as the world around us drained away. "Repeat that promise to me when we make it far from Lockinge, okay?"

I had no plans of leaving Lockinge, not yet. I had a promise to those fey beneath the castle to see through. However, I couldn't admit it yet.

Reaching up onto my toes, body aching from tiredness and deliria, I pressed a feather-light kiss upon Duncan's lips. I felt his own quiver in response, pressing out to greet mine for a small, brief moment. There was a tension between us, taut and harsh; I only hoped we had the space and time to deal with it soon.

"There will be plenty of time for that." Seraphine pulled us apart, hands harsh and nails unforgiving. "Get in the boat, both of you."

Her urgency and unruly panic had us both moving towards the shoreline. Kayne already waited within the small vessel, standing with legs wide as he steadied himself against the rocking. Seraphine's fellow assassins held the boat as steady as possible like an anchor, some chest-deep.

"Come quickly," Elinor spluttered, hand outstretched as her chestnut curls flew wildly around her face. For a moment, it was like seeing the vision of my mother that had haunted me all these years. Face obscured by floating hair, lullaby voice soft and gentle, even beneath the bellowing of winds that tore around us.

Seraphine waited for us to move. She took up the rear, looking back up towards the castle as though Aldrick would fly out from the windows in search of us at any given moment.

I reached for Elinor, taking her hand, and she led me ankle-deep into the water. We were only a few steps in when the dark night exploded with unwanted light. I clamped my eyes shut, almost losing my footing as the sudden light shocked me with its blinding brilliance.

"This ends tonight as it should have many years ago," a voice called out over the crashing waves.

I stopped dead in my tracks, water lashing up my legs. Elinor's grip on my hand weakened and fell, and I felt entirely alone and helpless as I turned to face the speaker.

King Doran Oakstorm stood upon the shore, outline glowing as though a star burned beneath his skin. His power stained the rocky shore and the castle far beyond him as he lit the scene like a beacon. The rippling of the portal he had stepped through faded behind him. At first it was hard to see his features until his glowing skin died down to a smattering of embers. Bloated belly, sunken, grotesque skin, short, awkward frame. For a man with such tremendous power, he looked as though it did not belong to him.

"Get in the boat!" Seraphine said, voice deep as the ocean that waited behind us.

"Quiet, *Asp*," Doran spat, displeased. "I have come for the boy. This time I will not leave without seeing him dead."

Fury erupted within me. All the pent-up emotions, all the regret and hesitation evaporating on the wind the moment I laid eyes upon him.

"You have come all this way for me?" I asked, wading back through the water towards Doran.

This was what I wanted. Army or not, I didn't need them to take him down.

Even with my power cut off by the iron cuff, and the lack of weapons in my hands, I felt the urge to run at him, to destroy him with my bare hands. Seeing him conjured the faces of all those who had died. Mother. Father. The memory of Erix. All the innocent lives, human and fey, lost in the crossfire of his hate. And the gryvern, his children, warped and twisted into creatures. They didn't choose to be born. Doran condemned them from the moment he spread his careless seed. For them all, I would kill him.

I had a hunger in that moment, one that was only quenched by death. Seeing Doran reminded me of my father and the way the light dulled from his eyes. How I carried his broken and lifeless body to his eternal resting place within the Icethorn Court. Seeing Doran reminded me of it all, the storm of feelings smashing into me all at once. Even with my power severed, the hate that fuelled me made me feel like the most powerful being in the world.

"And who is this?" Doran mused as Duncan stood between us. His frame was wide and strong, hands balled into fists of stone at his sides. "Ah yes, Erix told me of you. The human Hunter whose heart has been touch by his enemy. Poetic how your parents' story has followed you like a cursed shadow. It would be a pleasure killing you, Hunter, to see Robin suffer and to know your kind could never do as you have to my family again–"

"Dearest husband, is that you?" Elinor called out, passing me with grace and ease. Her voice was a song, soft and welcoming. It was as though the water parted as she walked through the shallows with an ease that belonged only to those who demanded respect. Even nature bowed to Elinor.

Duncan took the moment of distraction to his advantage. Wrapping his arm around my chest, he turned his back on Doran and spoke. "This is no longer your fight, darling."

Perhaps my hearing was damaged, or the reality of what was happening finally came through the pure undeniable wish to cause Doran pain. But it took me a long moment to grasp what Duncan said and what he meant by it.

Doran's light faltered as his long-lost wife stepped free of the dark water. Her torn dress clung to her emaciated frame. The longest strands of her hair hung in clumps from where they had dragged through the water.

"It cannot be," Doran said, voice breaking with each word. "A trick. A ghost."

We all watched as the fey king trembled where he stood. Doran's heavy body thudded to the ground, knees slamming into stone without him showing an inch of care. In a heartbeat the burning power of his light dwindled to nothing, and he was simply a broken man, watching the phantom of his beloved wife walk towards him.

The far-off screams of gryvern built in the distance. They grew ever closer. But the night-washed sky made it harder to make out their shapes, or how close they were.

"Time to go," Seraphine spoke, appearing suddenly from the shadows. "I've got coin to collect, and for that all I care about is seeing you out of this place. Enough time has been wasted to distraction." She snatched my arm and began pulling me towards the boat. Duncan did not hesitate to follow nor refuse to leave without Elinor.

"I can't leave her," I said, watching as Elinor reached up for the full cheek of her husband. Greedy, stout hands reached for hers with frantic urgency and I heard his small, broken voice speak with a furious desperation.

"My love," Doran cried, his heartache amplified across the night sky. "I have found you."

"Indeed," Elinor replied, standing above Doran, back straight and unwavering. "All these years and I thought I would never see you again."

"I – I searched for you," Doran said, spluttering like a pathetic fool. "Given time I would have ripped this entire realm apart in your memory. Everything I have done since you were taken has been for you. Everything, my love."

"That I do not doubt." Her reply was cold and void of any love.

Something hard smacked into my back and I realised I was now waist-deep in water. Seraphine shouted something at Duncan who promptly followed by hoisting me up. Kayne reluctantly aided me into the boat. All this happened without taking my focus off Elinor and Doran.

"The Court has been poisoned since you were taken," Doran said, ignorant to Elinor's change in demeanour. "But your return will make it a home again."

Behind them the air split, untethering in two lines of pure golden light that created a portal.

Elinor stepped back. "I can't come with you."

"Pardon?" Doran replied, breathless as he forced his body from the ground as he stood. Elinor towered above him, in height and grace.

"I was never taken from you, Doran. All these years and the deaths that have followed have been nothing but wasted life. They would have never brought me back to you, then or now. And I would rather face a lifetime imprisoned within this realm than ever stand proudly beside you. How could I rule willingly beside a monster?"

Doran stumbled, swallowing his words thickly. We were in the boat now, feeling it rise and fall over the waves as the other assassins guided us out towards the endless, dark expanse.

"Wait," I said, gripping the boat's edge as I continued looking out towards Elinor and Doran. "Wait."

From a distance it would have seemed that two lovers embraced after a prolonged time apart, but I knew different. Having shared our truths, I knew how Elinor loathed Doran – even more than I did.

Elinor's hand drifted into her dress and quickly pulled free, as though she never had moved. Even from far away, with the splashing dark water between us, I could catch the glint of metal in her hand.

"But I love you," Doran cried out, fingers glowing as he raised them before him. "Everything I have done has been out of my love…"

His voice faltered when Elinor drew her arm backwards until it bent at her elbow, then thrust it forward with strength only one scorned could hold. She stabbed the Oakstorm king, over and over, the beating of the dagger's hilt against his chest melding with the beat of my frantic heart. Elinor held the king within her arms, thrusting and jabbing, until a ragged cry tore from her throat and filled the night sky. Even the winds died down as her anguish spilled into it.

Duncan held me, arms wrapped around my chest as he stopped me from falling out of the boat; only then did I register that I cried her name out across the water, throat ripping to shreds as I equalled Elinor's cry.

King Doran Oakstorm fell onto the shore, not a speck of light left within his body, the portal gone. Elinor dropped her arms to her side, dagger falling into the waters that rushed up and claimed it. Then she turned her back on the body and waded out towards us.

"Hold," Seraphine shouted. I could hardly care that Kayne and Seraphine had begun rowing, each slicing an oar through the water. The boat calmed, rocking only because of the waves beneath it now.

And we waited – waited patiently for Elinor Oakstorm. She swam towards us, face held above the water. I imagined Doran's blood being cleaned from her hands, her clothes, as the ocean drank it away. By the time she reached us, Duncan practically threw himself into the water to help her up. She fell upon her back in the boat, hands clasped over her chest as she looked up into the night.

"It is truly over," I said, looking down at her. There was an empty, light feeling of relief that filled my chest. It shared the space with another feeling, a darker one of jealously that it was not I who had the chance to pierce the blade into his chest. "For good."

Elinor blinked, tired eyes flicking over the stars as though she wished to remember every single one she saw. "I did it for Lovis. For your mother, Julianna. And for you. Doran will never hurt you again – never hurt anyone. His tirade of pain and suffering is over."

I leaned down, pressing my forehead to hers, tears spilling freely. Duncan placed a hand upon my shoulder, his touch a welcome anchor as I lost myself to my emotions.

"You," I added, voice no more than the flutter of a bird's broken wing, weak and tired. "He will never hurt *you* again either."

CHAPTER 41

"Elinor," I said softly, unable to stand the torturous silence a moment longer. I'd clambered across the narrow boat and took a seat by her side. There was nothing comfortable about the journey, not with the pool of saltwater in the belly of the boat, soaking through our clothes and injecting the cold deep into our skin. My stomach thrashed with the continuous rocking, and it took all my restraint not to lean overboard and vomit.

"I'm here if you need to speak about what has happened. If not, we can sit here in silence if that helps," I murmured to Elinor. "Whatever makes you comfortable."

The sky was stained with blush pinks and oranges. Our boat raced towards dawn, Duncan and Kayne pumping the oars through the ocean's surface with a furious desperation to put as much distance as possible between Lockinge and us.

No one had uttered much of a word since Elinor was pulled into the boat all those hours ago, other than Seraphine who had answered Duncan's question about our destination with a short, "Anywhere but here."

Elinor looked away from the expanse of blue, where the brightening sky touched the ocean's edge at such a distance it was unclear where one started and the other ended. She was pale, azure eyes heavy, framed with shadows and skin pulled taut. In the blush hues of dawn, it was impossible to ignore the look of pure, draining exhaustion that aged her tremendously.

"It had to be done. Doran's death has played over in my mind for many years and if it had not happened then you would not have gotten away from him," Elinor muttered, lips cracked and sore. "But the feeling that is left within me is not one I expected. The relief I thought I would feel has not yet reached me. I keep waiting for it, but that place within me is still as empty as it was before I did it."

"I should have been the one to do it," I replied, guilt curling within me. "You have suffered enough."

"There is little point in dwelling on what could have been. I have learned that lesson the hard way."

Elinor had spent years punishing herself with the ideas of what if. What if she had never left the Oakstorm Court? What if it had been later? By a day, a week. Would she not have ended up in Aldrick's ownership if she had just delayed her action?

"What does it mean for the Oakstorm Court?" I asked. Tarron was dead, Doran following swiftly to whatever hellscape claimed their kind.

"Oakstorm is still my home. By marriage, it belongs to me, unless others wish to petition against it, I am its queen by law."

"And do you want it?" I asked. "To be the Queen of a Court you longed to run from?"

She smiled, a small fluttering tug of her lips. "I believe I do. Oakstorm is mine, even though it was poisoned when Doran claimed me for his own. I never believed a time would come that his presence was no longer a threat in my life. My actions pain me, but knowing he cannot harm another is the promise I have given to the world. Doran hurt far too many people. One life for the rest is justified, I believe that."

Her hand grasped mine where it lay upon my knee. Elinor's fingers were strong, no more than bones and rough skin, but they were not weak, not as she squeezed and held on tight.

"You are finally free," I said, tongue catching the taste of dried salt across my lips. "From Lockinge – from Doran. The path ahead of you is yours to take, to decide which direction you wish to go in."

"But not from Aldrick," Duncan's deep voice sounded from behind us. "This is merely the beginning of something terrible, I know it."

Seraphine cleared her throat, lowering her feet from the edge of the boat. Unlike Kayne and Duncan, she had done little but study the far-off shoreline that we rowed beside. "You are not wrong, Hunter."

"Please," Duncan gasped as though a bolt struck his chest. "Don't call me that."

Elinor nodded simply in agreement.

Kayne's voice rose from the side of the boat, his gaze fixed on the Asp at the helm "How long have you infiltrated the Hand's ranks? You must have seen what was coming. And yet you did not stab a knife through his back and stop this all from happening when you had the chance."

"There has been many a chance for me to kill Aldrick, but never has a price been put upon his head. The Children of the Asp have a code," Seraphine explained. "A conduct we follow that stops us from taking life into our hands and snuffing it out when we want to or not. Until a bounty is put out, we do not act. We watch. We wait. We learn."

"None of this needed to happen if you broke your fucking rules and killed the old fool long ago," Duncan said, spitting each word.

Seraphine huffed, part laugh and part refusal to truly take in Duncan's anger. "Up until recently, the Hand has not been much of a threat. Yes, I have heard him whisper of Duwar, as we all have. But seeing the creature within the reflection tonight is the first time I truly believed what he has been saying is real."

"And what of the fey that have been captured? All those innocents being kept and bled like cattle?" I said, jaw tense from gritting my teeth. "Did you not believe that was wrong enough to intervene? I have met your kind before and am aware of the conscience you lack. Knowing that you have simply watched–"

"I am the wrong person to question," Seraphine sneered, cheeks flushing with colour. "My sister and I have not simply stood by and watched. Aldrick is a powerful fey as you each have witnessed. He can enter minds, read them and bend the person to his will. *We* had to comply, poisoning ourselves with Mariflora to keep our minds our own. If Aldrick had even caught the scent of mine and my sister's origin, then we would not have gleaned the information we have. You would not be here, with me, sailing far from the very man we speak of. And my sister..." She choked on her words for a moment, clearly struggling with keeping her voice level. "My sister is dead because of our cause. Do not think for a moment you are the only ones who have lost something this night."

I blinked and saw the lifeless body of Seraphine's sister.

"What you know, what you have seen, would be imperative to bringing Aldrick down before that thing is released into the world." All eyes snapped to Elinor as she spoke. "I know of your guild and understand that you act if the price is high enough. Is that what you have been waiting for? The right bid for the information you've obtained?"

Seraphine leaned forward, two elbows resting upon her knees as her hands held her face up. "For half a coin I would spill my soul if it meant stopping what Aldrick has planned to achieve. Before, our involvement was business, now it is personal."

Just a glance at Kayne and I could still see that he wrestled with the truth he'd uncovered tonight. Like Duncan, Kayne had given his life to the promise of Duwar. For him to learn that his god was in fact a demon that had been locked away for a reason must have been tearing him to pieces.

"What next then?" I asked. The question was not for any sole person, and each in our small, strange company would likely have answered it differently.

While I waited for someone to speak up, I thought about what I wanted to come next. There was nothing more in this world that I wished for than to crawl into Duncan's arms and feel his body against mine, to let my mind release my worries and think only of him. His touch. His distraction.

"We could keep rowing," Kayne spoke finally, eyes lost to something unimportant on the floor of the boat. "Stop when this realm and the responsibilities within it are long forgotten."

Seraphine replied, knocking the tracker's knee with her fist. "Trust me, there are realms beyond this that are far more terrifying than the darkest corners of your deepest secrets. My sponsor has requested Robin's return, alive and well. After I complete this task of returning you then we can contemplate what comes next."

"Sleep," Elinor added, forcing a smile. "In a feather-stuffed bed so large that I could not reach the edges if I wished."

"And a hard drink," Kayne listed quickly, looking to Duncan who patted him upon his shoulder in a form of silent communication between them.

"Peace and time," I added, speaking the first things that came to me. *And a plan, to free the fey in the Below.* I wouldn't give up on them like the realms had.

"Two things, Robin? How greedy," Seraphine said, brow peaked in jest. "And what about you, Hunter? Do you wish to be normal again? Because I am afraid that I have seen others who Aldrick had changed and there is no coming back."

Her comment brought down the mood instantly. Duncan raised a finger to the iron cuff around his neck and tugged down on it.

"No," Duncan said finally. "What comes next is revenge. Only when Aldrick is killed will I sleep soundly, or even enjoy a drink and live in a state of peace. Until the threat has been dealt with, those luxuries will be yours to claim."

Duncan was right, there was work to do. Every moment of every day counted towards stopping Aldrick, and wasting time allowed him to create his army of powered humans.

I'd glimpsed a god, something I would've believed impossible before that fateful night when I was sold off to Hunters. Before now the Gods were nothing than names in stories. Now, I had come to quickly realise they were real, and that was frightening.

"Pick up your oars," Seraphine said suddenly, standing up and looking out towards the stretch of sands that we had drifted closer to. She had seen something. We all looked, following her stare, to the patch of flat landscape and the smudge of dark outlines standing upon it.

People, standing in the distance, waiting for us.

My heart sank into the pit of my stomach.

"About time," Seraphine said, jumping into action. "Come on, both of you. Row. It is time we get out of these waters. I have always hated it out here."

Kayne sprang into action, but Duncan held back. I could see his distrust. "If you want my help reaching the land then you will tell us who is expecting us. Or I push you overboard and leave you to the creatures that dwell in the dark beneath us."

Seraphine scowled, both hands resting upon her hips as she broadened out her stance. "Put emotion into your threats and it might make it more believable next time."

I ignored their argument, no matter how relevant it was. Raising a hand to my brow, it was easier to see. There was a handful of people, four, maybe five, standing among sand dunes, watching us as we watched them.

"We haven't got time for this, *Hunter*."

"Duncan," he snapped. "That's my name, use it, give it a try. Although Robin will tell you, it's a mouth full."

One of the figures broke from the group in the distance. I watched as they ran towards the shoreline, arms waving above their head.

"Give me your fucking oar," Seraphine snarled, throwing herself across the boat at Duncan. "I will do it myself."

"Stop this," Elinor scolded, her tone motherly and harsh. "Enough, all of you, before–"

I didn't hear the rest, not as the breeze carried a sound towards me. At first, I thought it was just the whistle of the wind as it skipped across the choppy waters. Then it grew clearer.

"Robin."

"Quiet," I said.

I heard it again, although barely, beneath the arguing in the boat. *"Robin."*

"Shut up," I snapped, this time louder.

"Robin!"

The boat and its occupants silenced. Seraphine and Duncan had stopped their argument, and I could see them both in my peripheral vision as they looked towards me. But I paid them no mind, not as the figure in the distance stopped waving arms and instead unleashed an explosion of bright ruby flames into the sky from her hands. Tongues of fire turned to clouds of dark-grey smoke that billowed far into the cloudless expanse.

Tears of relief filled my eyes. As sure as I knew my own self, I knew who waited for us upon the shore. Seraphine's sponsor. The person who had placed the bounty for my return with the Children of the Asp.

Althea Cedarfall.

Keep reading for an exclusive
bonus chapter for
A Kingdom of Lies,
told from Duncan's point of view...

BONUS CHAPTER

They'd hung me by my wrists, each taking turns to carve lines into my flesh.

With every nick of a blade, I thought of Robin. I pictured him in full colour, resting upon the earth, curled on his side as he waited for my return. If I focused hard enough, I could feel the brush of his midnight hair tickling my chest, his light fingers resting upon my navel.

I was unable to smell the blood that covered me, despite its sheer amount. My nose was filled with Robin's scent of juniper berry, fresh breeze and crisp winter. Instead of hearing the wet shuck of iron to flesh, I imagined Robin calling for me, shouting my name, demanding to know where I had gone.

Every one of my senses was captured by him, saving me what likely were my last moments.

If only I could tell him what waited for him here. If only I could ensure he would not come looking for me. But I knew, deep down, that this hope was futile.

He would come, because he was Robin: stubborn, determined, focused and, more than anything, selfless. And although my brothers and sisters – the Hunters who'd punished me over and over for the past how ever many hours – didn't know Robin like I did, they also knew he'd come for me eventually.

And so we waited. By waited, I mean I could do nothing but endure the retribution of my greatest sin. Loving a fey. I had no choice, as the cuffs dug into the skin of my wrists and the bruises formed beneath my eyes and across my torso, painting my body in a patchwork of blue, black and green. If they weren't cutting my sins into my skin, they were hammering them in with fists to my face and gut.

These Hunters had found me en route to the makeshift town just outside of Lockinge. It was once a small toll passing, but in recent years it had become a hub of activity for Hunters. Now it was known as a place of exchange where the fey were brought, prepared and carted into the city.

My original plan was simple, but like all plans, it had not been without its risks. Come here, retrieve an iron-cuff undercover and then return to Robin. Of course, I had been worried about it, but it was our only option. Or so I thought, because my concerns intensified when Hunters rode out to meet me, all hopes of success fading as those I once called my brothers drew their swords and pointed them at me.

It was not the welcome I'd expected. They'd arrested me before I could even state my name. Not that it was required, they knew who I was.

They called me a traitor. Fey-fucker. Obviously, word from what happened in Ayvbury had reached the Hand's followers: a Hunter and an unchained fey working together. How we'd been hidden within Abbott Nathaniel's church – alone. Surviving together. Escaping together. That was all they needed to know. In their eyes, I was guilty. If I was given the choice to speak my piece, maybe I would've lied and told them they were wrong. My silence was incriminating, I knew that. But I found keeping silent was easier than opening my mouth; I didn't want to risk saying something that would jeopardise Robin.

They believed the pain they imposed on me would make me speak, but they were wrong. Pain was my only constant, my only comfort and I relished in it. If anything, the more they cut my skin, the more they smashed batons into me and cracked fists into my gut or face, the more I retreated into my silence.

Then they sent someone into this dark room I was imprisoned in, someone who could cause me more agony than any weapon could.

"*He* will be found eventually, Duncan."

I could barely lift my head up to see who spoke, not that I needed to. The man's voice was as easy to recognise as my own was.

"Brother," I mumbled, wondering if it was blood or vomit that crusted the side of my mouth, almost forging my lips together. "Good to see you, finally. I was wondering when you'd be brave enough to show your face."

I fought against my weakness enough to lift my gaze. Kayne stood at the precipice to the dank room, staring at me like I was some sort of monster. His taut frame was haloed by daylight. It surprised me to see the light because I'd convinced myself days had passed, but perhaps it had only been hours of this torment. Either way, it was never-ending.

"Are you… waiting for an invitation?" I slurred. "Or did you come to marvel at your fellow Hunter's handiwork?"

"You speak on our kind as if you are no longer one of them." Kayne finally stepped inside and drew the door closed behind him, sealing us away from the nasty world beyond.

"What would it matter what I think, when my opinion will not save me?"

Kayne scoffed, his skin slightly pale as though he'd be sick without a moment's notice. "You should answer their questions, if you know what's good for you."

"I know what's good for me, brother. That's why I keep my mouth shut."

"Because that fey has enthralled you, Duncan." Kayne braved another step, coming closer, nose wrinkling against the smell of my blood, sick and shit. "I can't bear to see you like this."

"Then do something about it."

Kayne dropped his head, but his eyes never left mine. "I can't until you talk."

There was no point lying to him. I hadn't before, and I wasn't going to start now. "I'm under no thrall, Kayne."

We used each other's name like a weapon, waiting to see whose cut deeper.

"So all these whispers of you laying with a fey, working with one, fighting beside one are nothing but made-up stories? Because trust me, I'm holding out the hope that this is all some grand misunderstanding."

The chains above my head rattled as I tried to reposition myself. Kayne winced as he noticed the deep gashes around my wrists, hesitating as though he wanted to run to me, coddle me in his arms and save me from this torture.

I found it easy to ignore him. He wanted a certain answer, and it wasn't one I was going to give. Instead, I took the conversation and changed it. "Are you here to help me, because if not, there is a table of pointy weapons over there and I've got a few areas of skin that are still unmarked. Come, bleed me for Duwar, if that makes you feel better."

Kayne's exhale whooshed through the room, heavy as his sagging shoulders and unwavering attention. "I don't want to hurt you, Duncan. In fact, I want to help you."

A deranged laugh escaped my ruined lips. "How so?"

Kayne looked behind me as if someone was watching. We were alone, or so I thought. Just his stray glance told me that others waited outside, ready to catch my admission of guilt, desperate to hear where Robin was hiding so they could find him.

Betrayal carved through me, cutting deeper than any blade could ever.

"Where is he, Duncan?" Kayne asked, his monotone voice making the hairs on my bare body stand. "Where *is* the Icethorn king?"

I let my chin fall back to my chest. My eyes closed, blocking out the truth laid out before me. Kayne, once my brother, my closest friend, had come in here to use my devotion to Robin against me and sell me out.

Feet shuffled across the straw-coated floor. Boots squelched in blood and mud, every sound heightened as Kayne closed in.

"Please, all I want to do is get you out of this mess. But I can't do that if you don't cooperate." A cold hand pressed upon my shoulder, soft as a bird. And yet the fact it was Kayne touching me made his hand feel more like talons, ready to sink into my flesh.

If I could have pulled away, I would have. But the chains kept me in place, and my body no longer belonged to me, but to the pain I had endured for the past hours.

"Keep your hands *off* me," I growled, snapping my teeth in his direction.

Kayne stumbled back, shocked. That shock quickly hardened into resolve and focus, the mask of a Hunter who was trained to deal with anyone or anything that stood before them.

"Every Tracker has sent their birds out to search Durmain for him. Sooner or later, Robin will be located, and he will face the judgement that the Hand has requested."

That had me opening my eyes. "Punishment?"

"Isn't that what every fey has experienced in the Below? Or did you think it would be different? That you could petition for the Hand to let this one go free? That isn't how this works, and you know it. Whatever has gotten into you is foolish and stupid. You – Duncan – you're not the same person that left Finstock. What happened?"

"Robin," I hissed, his name so sweet in my mouth. "*He* happened."

"Finally, the truth." Kayne traced his sad, haunted eyes up and down my body, teeth gnawing at his lower lip. "Although I could already see the effect he has had on you. To be honest, I don't even know who I'm looking at anymore."

"A feeling we both share, *brother*."

We found ourselves in a stare-off, both of us refusing to look away first. But it was Kayne who broke. He turned on his heel and made for the door. "If this changes anything for you, maybe you'd like to know that the Hunters we've sent out to look for him have been found mutilated beyond recognition. Even some of the hawks have been found with their wings ripped from their bodies, necks torn apart by what we believe is teeth. *Sharp* teeth. Whether that is Robin, or someone else – we believe it the missing Hunters, the deaths are tied to him."

Bodies? Mutilation? Those two words together made me laugh again.

"Is that really funny, Duncan?" Kayne sneered. "Finding joy in the demise of those you once led, the brave men and woman that fight for the balance of this world?"

"Robin is many things, but he wouldn't do that." It wasn't his style.

"Then someone else is looking out for him in your absence."

The blood – the little my body had left – drained from my face, casting me in a bout of cold shivers. "You're baiting me."

"I'm simply keeping you up to date. Maybe I'm wrong, and whatever is out there attacking our Hunters will eventually find Robin before we do. What outcome is better? A life alongside his own people, giving up blood to better their world. Or a life where he dies, at the hands of a monster in pursuit, someone you will be helpless to save him from."

It couldn't be. Could it? Erix had died – Robin had made sure of that. Maybe it was King Doran Oakstorm's gryvern, but then again, the entire camp would've known about them if that were the case.

Either way, Kayne was trying to make me talk and now – for the first time – I almost gave the answers that he and those listening outside the room wanted.

Before the words could rupture from my soul, I sunk my teeth into my torn lips until the copper tang of my blood washed away the last scrap of Robin's sweet taste. Kayne watched, refusing to blink as I caused myself pain. Then the door behind him opened, and three, four, maybe five Hunters rushed in. Kayne slipped out. But wherever he'd gotten to, I'd make sure he couldn't run from the suffering of seeing me in pain.

It was one thing witnessing it, but hearing it was another.

So, as the blades began to cut back into my skin, as if they could draw Robin's location out with my blood, I bellowed. I didn't keep quiet. I screamed, not from agony, but from desperation. I did so until my lungs were empty and my head light. I didn't stop, not until fresh blood cooled my boiling skin and wet the knives held in the Hunter's hands.

If I could've held onto my strength and continued, I would have. But quickly, the creeping darkness of peace danced at the corners of my eyes. One by one, my senses failed me until my eyes drew heavy and I stopped refusing them.

Somehow, I knew that when I closed my eyes and gave into the darkness, I'd see Robin again. And I was almost right. Because it was when I opened my eyes again, no longer in the punishment room but outside beneath the glare of daylight, that I saw him.

My Robin had come to find me, alive. But he was walking into the mouth of a monster. And there was nothing – *nothing* – I could do to save him.

ACKNOWLEDGEMENTS

Reader, thank you for taking the chance on another one of my books. I know A Kingdom of Lies has been a RIDE, and I am glad to see you made it to the end. Writing this book was such a therapeutic experience for me, playing with the concept of love, how deep it goes, and its limits. I can promise you that the concept of love only gets bigger and more dramatic as we go forwards with the series.

Once again, a massive thank you to the amazing Angry Robot Team. Eleanor, Desola, Caroline, Amy, Lauren and all the incredible professionals that have worked on this book. It has been such a thrilling journey, and we are only in the beginning. I can't wait for all the excitement that is no doubt to follow.

To my DBD girlies. Millie, Beth, Lola and Jasmine. Giving you a shout out because our little gaming session really get me through edits, so thank you. You're all McMazing.

We are Angry Robot, your favourite independent, genre-fluid publisher, bringing you the very best in sci-fi, fantasy, horror and everything in between!

Check out our website at
www.angryrobotbooks.com
to see our entire catalogue.

Follow us on social media:
Twitter @angryrobotbooks
Instagram @angryrobotbooks
TikTok @angryrobotbooks

Sign up to our mailing list now: